Also by Suzanne Brockmann
available from Random House Large Print

Flashpoint

HOT TARGET

SUZANNE BROCKMANN

HOT TARGET

A NOVEL

RANDOM HOUSE
LARGE PRINT

Copyright © 2005 by Suzanne Brockmann

All rights reserved under International and Pan-American Copyright Conventions. Published in the United States of America by Random House Large Print in association with Ballantine, New York, and simultaneously in Canada by Random House of Canada Limited, Toronto. Distributed by Random House, Inc., New York.

The Library of Congress has established a Cataloging-in-Publication record for this title.

ISBN 0-375-43394-5

www.randomlargeprint.com

FIRST LARGE PRINT EDITION

10 9 8 7 6 5 4 3 2 1

This Large Print edition published in accord with the standards of the N.A.V.H.

when you played the soundtrack to **Secret Garden** over and over again. I smiled. "It's just Jason being Jason."

At nine, you had a class project—write a letter to someone you admire. "Why Bette Midler?" I asked when you told me your choice. "She's my favorite actor in the world," you proclaimed after watching **Ruthless People** thirty times in a row. She wrote back, and you framed her signed picture, putting it in a place of honor on your dresser.

"Wow, that's interesting," I said to your dad, after we once again agreed that Jason was truly unique. "I wonder if he likes Cher, too?"

(You did! Along with Bernadette Peters and Debbie Reynolds and . . .)

At ten, you went to see a show that featured an actor friend you'd made while appearing as Winthrop Paroo in **The Music Man.** On the ride home, you asked me, "Did you know Charley Dude is gay?" "Yeah," I said. "Wasn't his performance excellent tonight?" You agreed, but were unusually quiet for the rest of the drive.

A few days later, we had friends over to watch a movie, and as Eric and Bill sat together on the couch, they started their usual banter. "Raising the homo-shield!" Bill announced, invoking the invisible force field that would supposedly allow him to sit so close to Eric without anyone making gay comments.

It was all supposed to be funny, but how, I wondered, would those jokes sound to someone who was gay?

That night, after everyone went home and you were

DEDICATION

To my fabulous son, Jason:

Even as a tiny child, your smile could outshine the sun, and your cheerful disposition and kind nature made you countless friends. Everyone who met you loved you!

At three, walking became too mundane for you. Instead, wherever you went, you danced. And occasionally you swished! One of the first times you did that, your dad looked at me. "Where did he learn that?" I shrugged. We didn't let you watch TV. "Got me. It's just . . . Jason being Jason," I said, and went off to play with you and your vast collection of cars and action figures.

At eight, you discovered musical theater. You wanted to sing and dance onstage, so you auditioned for a semipro production. You were just a little too young, but you charmed the director and became the tiniest pickpocket in an eight-week run of **Oliver!**

Your dad loved Stevie Wonder, and I, a former rock-and-roller, was in my country music phase. "What's with all the show tunes?" your grandmother asked me in bed, your dad and I discussed it, and we agreed. We gathered all of our friends together and announced that from this moment on, there would be no more gay jokes in our house. No more inadvertent gay bashing.

Because if you **were** gay—and I was pretty sure even then that this was, indeed, the way God made you—you were not going to grow up thinking there was anything wrong with you.

Years later, when you were fifteen, you still wanted me to tuck you in at night. So I'd stand by your bunk bed and we'd talk a bit about the day. I'd also gather up your dirty clothes. You were supposed to put them in a laundry basket, but sometimes your aim was off.

One night, you took a deep breath and said to me, "Mom, I think I'm gay."

"I know that," I told you, giving you a hug and a kiss. "I love you. I'll always love you. **Where** did you put your dirty socks?"

A day or two later we sat down and talked about safe sex and personal safety. I have to confess that it made my heart ache to have to tell you that there were people out there, people who didn't even know you but who hated you anyway—people who might try to hurt you because you were gay. Because you were simply being you. And it was your turn to give me a hug and say, "I know that. But, Mom, the world **is** changing."

Today, as I write this, you are eighteen. You are a grown man, and I am so proud of you.

Yes, the world is changing, but it's not happening

quickly enough for me. I was outraged when we went to the Gay Pride parade last June and you saw that hateful, ignorant sign that read, "God hates you."

I wish the person carrying that sign had seen you at three, at eight, at nine, at ten. If he had, then he would know that you are a true child of God. If he had, then he would know that by being gay, you are just being Jason.

God loves you, I love you, Dad loves you. Unconditionally. You know that.

And I know that you love and accept yourself. You are confident and strong. Just like when you were three years old, you allow Jason to be Jason.

Shine on, my son!

This story is for you.

ACKNOWLEDGMENTS

Thank you, first off, to my wonderful readers, especially those who clamored to see more of Jules Cassidy.

I love writing this ongoing series of books about SEAL Team Sixteen, Troubleshooters Incorporated, and Max Bhagat's FBI Counterterrorist Team. These characters have become my dear friends. It's beyond cool that so many readers feel the same way!

(FYI, I'm currently writing Max and Gina's story, **Breaking Point,** due out next summer. Watch my website, www.SuzanneBrockmann.com for details!)

A shout out to my early draft readers: Lee Brockmann (Hi, Mom!), Deede Bergeron, Patricia McMahon, and Scott Lutz. Thank you so much for your input!

Thanks, also, to the team at Ballantine: Linda Marrow, Gilly Hailparn, Arielle Zibrak . . . As for my editor, Shauna Summers . . . Thank you, THANK YOU, **thank you,** thank you!!!

A ton of appreciation goes to Those Who Help Keep Me Sane: Eric Ruben, Christina Trevaskis (aka

Tina Fabulous!), and my terrific agent, Steve Axelrod! Thanks also to fellow writers, Pat White and Alesia Holliday.

A special note to Donovan and Betsy Trevaskis: Thank you for sharing your wonderful daughter with me. I know how hard it must be for you, with her so far away. I promise she will visit you often!

Thank you to my own precious daughter and son, Melanie and Jason. I love you guys!

Thank you to Michael Holland for providing musical inspiration. As I wrote **Hot Target,** I listened repeatedly to "Everything in the Whole Wide World," "(It Came As) No Surprise," and "Firefly IX" from Michael's latest CD, **Beach Toys Won't Save You.** (Michael's CDs are available at www.CDBaby.com.)

A huge HOO-YAH to Capt. Josh Roots of the United States Marines for being my contact in Iraq, and for distributing dozens of care packages to the young men and women in his unit. Thank you, too, to the readers who contributed to those packages during my **Flashpoint** tour—especially those who helped us out by bringing the boxes to their local post offices!

Thank you to my relentlessly patient husband and best friend, Ed Gaffney. (Ed's first book, a legal thriller called **Premeditated Murder** will be published in June! I'm so proud!)

Last but not least, thank you to PFLAG—Parents, Families, and Friends of Lesbians and Gays—an organization dedicated to changing attitudes and creating an environment of understanding so that gay family members and friends can live with dignity and respect. For more information, go to www.pflag.org.

As always, any mistakes I've made or liberties I've taken are completely my own.

HOT TARGET

PROLOGUE

Every now and then, a SEAL Team was handed a silver bullet assignment.

Rescuing a dozen kidnapped supermodels.

Working extra security, blending with the crowd in the stands at the Olympics.

A training op in Honolulu during spring break.

But no matter how Chief Cosmo Richter looked at it, jamming his six-foot-four-inch body up the shaft of a thirty-five-year-old garbage chute in a terrorist-ridden country in the middle of the night was not on his top-ten list of dream assignments.

Nope, whoever labeled Special Operations as the most glamorous branch of the U.S. Military didn't have this in mind.

As Cosmo led his men farther up the chute and into the building that was an alleged orphanage, he could hear Tony Vlachic, SEAL Team Sixteen's newest and youngest member, working hard not to gag at the overpowering stench.

He could also hear the gunfire from the street, as a

second squad of SEALs—Mikey Muldoon and seven men—was led directly into an enemy ambush.

Of course, it wasn't really an ambush. Not anymore.

The SEAL leader of this op, Lieutenant Mike Muldoon, had guessed correctly that Ziya, their informant, had terrorist ties. It was true that Ziya **had** revealed that the civilian hostages were being held in this building—information that was verified by U.S. intelligence. And, for sure, the Big Z was all "Please allow me to help."

But he was never quite specific enough about exactly **how** he wanted to help.

Mikey had guessed correctly that helping the hostages escape to freedom wasn't what the Z-man had in mind. No, it was now clear that the informant's goal was to "help" the American forces get chopped to bits in a deadly ambush.

Ziya had been on some kind of alternate timetable as he'd led them here tonight. It wasn't all that obvious, but Mikey—a smart man and quality officer— had paid attention to the man's careful stalling. He'd noted Z's barely perceptible undercurrent of intense excitement.

Mike had glanced at Cosmo, who'd sent him back a microscopic nod.

Yes, sir, he'd picked up on it, too.

With just a little froggish imagination, it wasn't hard to theorize that Ziya was waiting for, oh, say, a terrorist cell or two to get into place, so that when the SEALs attempted the rescue of the three American civilians in that thar orphanage, they'd instead be hit by a carefully placed wall of bullets.

So while Mikey had played along, cheerfully following Z's "shortcut" that added nearly a half mile to their trip, Cosmo and his band of merries peeled off from the group. They moved much faster and slipped silently and invisibly past the ambushers, eager to begin—and therefore end—their exploration of this building's waste disposal system.

At the same time, a third group of SEALs who'd been following at some distance behind had taken on the task of ambush removal.

It was that group—a brawny SEAL officer known as Big Mac and his seven-man squad—who were now exchanging some purposely poorly aimed, nonlethal fire with Mikey's men. They were creating a nice little diversion out there in the dark of night as Mikey's squad worked their acting chops for Ziya's benefit, pretending to be compromised and calling for air support to get them out of Dodge.

The intention was to make Z-dog's terrorist friends here in this so-called orphanage believe that they were winning, that the Americans couldn't break past their perimeter defenses.

They'd relax and maybe even start celebrating their victory a little too early.

The last thing they'd anticipate was that Cosmo and his squad were already inside—having squeezed their way through that sphincterlike entrance to the building's garbage chute down in the back alley.

It helped to keep a sense of humor at times like this, and Cos smiled at the idea of his squad of SEALs as a giant laxative, inserting to flush the hostages free. Military Metamucil—able to get the job done as quickly, as easily, and as painlessly as possible.

It worked particularly well as an analogy since this chute smelled like rotting ass.

Cosmo took a deep breath of relatively fresher air as he wiggled his way out and onto the building's kitchen floor. It was quiet in there. The lights were off and no one was around—just the way he liked it when entering a facility where everyone inside wanted to kill him. He helped pull the rest of his team of enlisted men from the chute—Izzy, Gillman, Lopez, and Jenk.

And Petty Officer Third Class "Chickie" Vlachic, the new guy, who was looking at Cosmo as if he were insane because he was still grinning at that ass joke.

Go, he told Chick with a hand signal. **Careful.** Even though no one in Intel believed there were actually children in this "orphanage," the last thing any of them wanted was to hurt an innocent.

He didn't need to signal anything more to remind Vlachic that they had to work their way back down to the basement, where the three hostages were being held. They all knew what they had to do and they got right to it.

He and Izzy Zanella went first.

Silently down a stairwell, creeping through a dimly lit hallway . . .

And there they were.

The hostages. Three bedraggled-looking women huddled together in the corner of a prison cell.

It was a vital part of any "orphanage," don't you know—the old prison cell in the basement. This was typical slimeball terrorist tactics—using a hospital or school or Red Cross facility in a U.S.-friendly neighborhood as a cover for a bomb factory or hostage-holding area.

There appeared to be no guard, and Izzy stepped out of the shadows a tenth of a second too soon.

Because the key word was **appeared.** A guard was there, hidden behind a stack of crates. Cosmo saw him just as he turned and spotted Izzy. Surprise and alarm widened the man's eyes and he fumbled with his weapon, a modified AK-47.

Jerking off a few shots into the floor would have brought the rest of the guards down on top of them, but luckily their guy was more focused on pulling his weapon up into firing position.

And thus Cosmo reached him first.

One swift grab and sharp twist, and the weapon clattered on the concrete.

It was then, as he was lowering the guard's limp body to the floor, that he looked up directly into the horrified eyes of all three of the women who were locked in that cage.

Sister Mary Francis, Sister Bernadette, and Sister Mary Grace.

He'd just taken out a terrorist guard while three nuns watched.

Nuns, for christsake.

There was no time to do anything but keep going. Besides, what could he do? Stammer an apology?

Lopez—good man—stepped in front of both Cosmo and the guard's body, and was doing his best to reassure the women that they weren't being kidnapped by a rival terrorist organization.

"Good evening, ladies. We're U.S. Navy SEALs and we've come to take you home. I'm Corpsman Jay Lopez—I'm a field medic—and as soon as we get this door open—"

Vlachic was already starting to prep the C4 needed to blow the lock, but Jenk—always thinking—was ahead of him. He'd rifled the dead guard's pockets and come up with the key.

Much easier, much quieter. Although, truth be told, Chick wasn't the only one who looked a little disappointed.

"—I'm going to give you a quick check"—Lopez continued talking to the nuns as he went inside the cell—"see how much help you're going to need getting up to the roof. We're going to have to move fast, ladies . . ."

"Jenk," Cosmo said in a low voice, as Lopez kept talking, explaining to the women that a helicopter would be coming in to pull them off the roof. Lopez was telling them how, even though the tangos—terrorists—in this building would hear the thrumming of the helo's blades, they wouldn't worry too much about it. They'd think the rescue was intended for the SEALs caught in the "ambush" in the street.

Jenkins knew what Cosmo was going to ask, and he nodded. "Good idea, Chief."

Their original plan had Jenk and Izzy leading the way to the roof, with Lopez, Chickie, and Cosmo assisting the sisters—carrying them if need be. Gillman would guard their six—take up the rear.

But Cosmo—after breaking the biggest of the Big Ten—was pretty certain that none of these nuns would want to get anywhere near him. So he and Jenk would switch tasks.

"Ready, Chief," Lopez reported, with one last reassuring smile at the sisters.

And away they went.

"So that story I've heard about Chief Richter . . . Is it true?"

The question was asked right on schedule.

As he asked it, Tony Vlachic had just the right amount of feigned casual curiosity in his voice. Like, there wasn't a whole hell of a lot to talk about, so they might as well talk about this, yanno?

Sure.

The SEALs from Team Sixteen had been tossed into wait mode as their flight back to the States was yet again delayed. The euphoria of completing a successful covert rescue had worn down. The debriefings were finally over and most of the reports had been written and filed.

Most.

But not Cosmo Richter's.

He was sitting at Mikey Muldoon's desk, hiding

behind the workstation divider and staring at the cursor flashing on the laptop's screen, cursing the day he'd taken the chief's exam.

God damn, but he hated written reports.

"Is which story true?" Collins asked Vlachic, his voice carrying in quite clearly from the hall.

Cosmo stopped pretending to write and listened instead. Because, Christ, was there more than one story about him now?

"**The** story," Vlachic said, a hint of impatience in his voice. "I'm not an idiot, sir. The recruited-from-Rikers-Island rumor is just that—a stupid rumor."

Ah, of course. Collins had been thinking about the Rikers Island thing.

As far as rumors went, that one actually bothered Cosmo. It was a smudge on the honor of the Teams. It had the potential to make people—naive people, sure—believe that the SEALs were no better than hired killers or thugs.

"Civilians might believe it," the new guy continued, "but we both know an ex-con is never going to get into the SEAL Teams."

Vlachic had all the makings of an excellent spec ops warrior, despite the fact that he was proving to be dead-ass average when it came to asking about The Story.

Sooner or later, everyone asked. **Is that story about big, scary-looking Cosmo Richter really true?**

Most of them asked somewhere between one and forty-two hours after first going out on a real-world op with him.

And sure enough, twenty-four and a half hours ago they'd delivered the rescued hostages—Cosmo still thought of them as "My Three Nuns"—into the arms of the waiting doctors here at the air base.

But even though everyone asked about the story, no one had ever asked Cosmo directly. And most of them waited to ask at a time when they were certain he wouldn't overhear.

Although, granted, neither Vlachic nor Ensign Joel Collins would've expected to find Cosmo here, deep in Officer Country, hiding out in this little cubbyhole of a half an office that had been temporarily assigned to Lieutenant Muldoon.

"According to the official report, no, it's not true," Collins told Vlachic now. They'd stopped right outside this door. Unbelievable. "Chief Richter was barely mentioned."

"Yeah, well, with all due respect, sir, what's a report going to say?" Vlachic pointed out.

Cosmo tried not to listen as the team's two newest members argued about what would or would not be acceptable information for an official report. And whether or not there was another version—this one top secret—that included the exact details of what had gone down that day all those years ago. And whether Lieutenant Commander Lewis Koehl, the newly appointed CO of SEAL Team Sixteen, had seen a copy of that second report. Oh, and if such a report existed, did it contain Cosmo Richter's real first name, because no one seemed to know what that was.

He stared at his computer screen. Where the hell

was he? He reread the last thing he'd written in his report about the rescue of the nuns.

0507. Hostages found, IDed, and freed from barred cell. Sole guard removed before alarm raised.

0510. Headed for roof. Intel reports correct—zero children in this entire facility. Two guards encountered, resistance minimal, surprise 100 percent—ruse on street working well. Guards eliminated before alarm raised.

He was repeating himself. His college comp professor had always been on Cosmo's ass, chastising him for repeating himself.

God **damn,** he hated report writing.

"What **I** heard, sir," Vlachic said, and Cosmo used the excuse of checking out The Story's latest mutation to take a break from this seventh level of hell, "was that Chief Richter single-handedly wiped out over a hundred men."

Whoa.

The number was up to a hundred now.

If it kept growing at this rate, by the time Cosmo retired, the story would credit him with the destruction of an entire battalion.

Back when the number had reached a grand total of fifty, he'd thought it had overstretched the boundaries of believability. Yet it still continued to grow.

The wide-eyed new guys continued to believe him capable of damn near anything.

"I heard that he lost it," Vlachic continued, "and—"

"He didn't lose it, Chick," Collins interrupted, disdain in his voice. "He doesn't lose it. The man doesn't even blink. You were just out there with him. Am I wrong? While you were inside that orphanage, how many of those al-Qaeda fucks did Charlie squad take out of the picture?"

"Seven," the petty officer said.

"And how many did the chief personally send to their reward?"

"I don't know," Vlachic admitted. "At least four. Maybe five." His laughter was disparaging. "I was too busy wetting my pants to notice exactly. And you're right, sir—the chief was a robot."

Yeah, Cosmo wished. If he truly were a robot, the looks of horror on those nuns' faces wouldn't still be haunting him. Damn, but he was going to carry that with him for a long, long time.

0514. Additional four terrorists removed from orphanage roof. Before alarm raised.

With all due respect, fuck you, Professor Harris. This was hard enough to write without having to find new ways to explain over and over again that if the guards had been allowed to make noise, an entire platoon would've come down on their heads, and a whole lot more people would've died.

As it was, the body count must've seemed outrageously high to the hostages. Cos hadn't had time to do more than push the fallen guards aside. At least the sisters hadn't had to step over them.

Yeah, great. What a guy.

0518. Extraction via Seahawk helo from roof.

   0542. Out of hostile airspace.

And he was done. Christ. Writing this had taken longer than the actual op.

He saved and printed the report.

And then realized that if he left this office, he'd have to walk right past Vlachic and Collins, who were just getting into the details of The Story.

"So the chief walks through what used to be some kind of village square," Collins was saying, "and it's a bloodbath. Half the population of this town had been executed. Men, women . . . there were even dead babies, you know? Dozens of kids."

"Jesus," Vlachic breathed as Cosmo closed the laptop and put the report into Mikey's in-basket. "I hadn't heard that. It sounds like—"

"Bullshit exaggeration?" Collins asked. "Yes, it does, but detailed info about the casualties was in the written report, so . . . And Sam Starrett—you ever meet Lieutenant Starrett, Chick? Tall officer? From Texas? He's gone from the Teams now, but—"

"Yeah, I know who you're talking about," Vlachic

said. "I saw him a few times during BUD/S, out in the grinder, laughing at us."

"Starrett was there at the village," Collins said. "I heard he was, like, down on his hands and knees in the dust, retching. The carnage was that bad. And Chief Richter—although he wasn't a chief then, you know—he's just walking around, taking it all in. He doesn't look upset, doesn't look anything. You know Cosmo—he plays his cards close to the vest. He also never says much of anything unless he's giving a direct order, but he's standing there in that square, and he says kind of quietly—like, he's not talking to anyone. He was just standing there by himself. But he says, 'Whoever did this is going to fucking die.' "

Actually, what he'd said was "Whoever did this deserves to die." Somewhere along the way, as The Story had been told again and again, someone had added the infinitive-splitting profanity and done that little verb switcheroo. Cosmo couldn't blame them. It made for higher drama.

He himself was partially to blame, because he'd never bothered to correct it.

The op in question had happened years ago, early in his career. SEAL Team Sixteen had been sent to a terrorist hotbed of a country known as "the Pit." In the mountains up north, two warring factions had been duking it out, and someone in a remote little village had pissed off one of the warlords, who had wreaked that terrible havoc.

The SEALs' orders had been to escort negotiators

into the mountains, to help get talks started to end the bloodshed, and to keep other villagers in the area safe.

Several of the officers were given an order—to locate the warlord's encampment. A squad had left to do just that.

Cosmo, though, had helped handle the cleanup. Even though it was winter, something had to be done about the dozens of bodies lying in the village square.

He'd done some crap jobs in his life, but that one had been the worst. It made yesterday's garbage chute seem like a picnic in the park with Nicole Kidman.

And Renée Zellweger.

"The theory is that he discovered the location of the warlord's camp," Collins told Vlachic now.

By **he** he meant Cosmo, who now surrendered. He sat down in Mikey's office chair, put his head back and his feet up, and closed his eyes. This was going to take a while.

"No one remembers seeing him at the briefing," Collins continued, "but he could have been listening outside of the tent. During the night, it's said that he went into the mountains and paid that warlord a little visit. And instead of negotiating a meeting, the next morning those diplomats ended up helping load up a hundred more body bags. That warlord and most of his men were dead."

"And everyone's certain it was Chief Richter?" Vlachic questioned.

"No," Collins said. "But apparently he was unaccounted for that night—just short of UA. And—if he was doing something else, why doesn't he talk about it and end the speculation, huh?"

Because what he'd done one night, all those years ago, was no one's freaking business. Cosmo almost got up and said it aloud as he walked out into the hall. But he stayed seated. Vlachic was a good kid. It would embarrass him to be caught gossiping this way.

Collins, however, was one of those cocky young officers that the chiefs prayed would either move quickly into the civilian sector or grow up—preferably **before** he got someone killed.

"And," Collins continued, "get this: a SEAL name of Hoskins—he's no longer with the Teams, but he hangs out sometimes at the Ladybug Lounge, so you can ask him yourself—he says he spotted the chief around dawn, heading toward the river to get cleaned up because his uniform was covered with blood. And Bill Silverman—you've met him, right? He heard one of the village elders thanking Cos, like 'I can never repay you for what you have done.' "

"Shit," Vlachic said, the word filled with meaning.

"Yeah," Collins responded. "But seeing as how it brought peace to the region, at least until a new warlord moved in . . ."

Their voices faded as they finally moved off down the corridor.

"Do you think he did it?" Cosmo heard Vlachic ask. "Killed all those men?"

He couldn't hear Collins's reply.

He waited until he heard the door closing down at

the end of the hall. He reached for his sunglasses as he got to his feet. "Free at last." It was little more than an exhale, barely audible and certainly not meant to be overheard.

"Are you?" a voice asked. It was female and faintly Hispanic, and he recognized right away that it belonged to Sister Mary Grace, the youngest of his three nuns.

Despite that, it took everything he had to keep himself from jumping. How was it possible that he hadn't heard her approach?

The sky outside the window was overcast, but he put his sunglasses on before he turned to face her.

Fortunately, she didn't expect him to answer her question. "Lieutenant Muldoon thought I might find you here."

Cosmo waited, and sure enough, she kept going.

"I didn't get a chance to thank you," she told him. "So . . ." Her hands fluttered. She had long, graceful fingers, with short but well-kept nails. "Thank you."

"You're welcome, ma'am," he said with a nod that was meant to give her permission to exit. "I'm glad you and your friends are safe."

But she didn't leave. "Do you have a minute?" she asked. "Do you mind if we sit down?"

That's when he secured his spot in hell. He picked up that report he'd put in Muldoon's basket and lied to a nun. "I'm afraid I need to get this to the lieutenant right away."

She nodded solemnly, as if she believed him. "May I walk with you, then?"

Cosmo hesitated, and she didn't wait for him to answer. She led the way out the door.

There was nothing to do but follow.

She was pretty in a very nun kind of way, with short dark hair and glasses that didn't hide the luminousness of her eyes. Whatever she wanted, it wasn't going to be good. Best-case scenario was that she was intending to preach at him for using deadly force during the rescue.

Thank you for saving my life, but couldn't you have done it without hurting those poor terrorists . . . ?

He knew how to answer that. If she were someone he knew well and considered a friend, he might say, **You mean risk your safety and that of my teammates by doing anything other than permanently removing the "poor" terrorists who were responsible for three different bus bombings and 268 civilian deaths over the course of one week, who attacked the hotel where the delegates from your peacekeeping mission were billeted, who executed eleven members of your delegation, and who kidnapped you and your two friends with the intention of videotaping your impending torture and death as a warning to others who might defy them?**

But no. Instead, if she asked that question, he would merely respond with, **No, ma'am, I could not,** politely excuse himself, and walk away.

If this woman's recent experiences hadn't made an adjustment to her never-use-violence way of thinking, nothing he said was going to change her mind.

And she sure as hell wasn't going to change his.

But she didn't speak until they went down the stairs and out into the crisp, cold sunshine.

"I was wondering," she said then, "and forgive me if this is too personal, but . . . Are you married?"

What the fah . . . ? Cosmo couldn't help himself. He looked at her over the top of his sunglasses.

It wasn't often that someone managed to surprise him so completely. And Sister Mary Grace—who'd also sneaked up on him—was two for two.

"No," he said.

"Do you have a girlfriend?" she asked.

He broke eye contact. "No." Jesus, was she . . . ? Cosmo prayed—for the first time in years—that she hadn't sought him out to hit on him. That would be too ungodly weird.

But it would be just his luck when it came to women. He attracted the strange ones. Or the needy ones—needy in the sense of "I need to be tied up." Or even worse—"I need to be treated like crap, so if you're going to be nice to me, I'm leaving right now."

He had some kind of homing beacon that drew in the desperately dysfunctional—the women who thought he was dangerous and got off on that. If there was such a thing as a nympho nun, it made sense that she would seek him out.

Please, God, if You're out there, make this woman's desire be for nothing more than to sing a verse or two of "Climb Ev'ry Mountain."

"Any kind of significant other?" she persisted. "Someone that you can talk to?"

And just like that, he understood. She wasn't hoping

to jump his bones, thank you, dear sweet Jesus. She just wanted to make sure he had an outlet for his emotional and spiritual relief.

Sister Mary Grace didn't falter as he stopped walking, as he gazed silently down at her. He knew damn well that the combination of his mirrored shades and his poker face could make strong men shake in their boots and back away.

But she took a step closer. "I just wanted to let you know that I'm here if you ever need to talk," she told him.

She had beautiful eyes. They were so warm, so peaceful. So nonjudgmental.

"I'm all right," he said.

"I know." The way she said it, with that smile—it wasn't just a platitude. "But everyone needs someone to talk to. Don't you think?"

"The team has a shrink," he told her, mostly because she was standing there with those eyes, waiting for some kind of response. With anyone else, he would've excused himself and been long gone.

"That's good," she said with another warm smile.

It made him feel like a liar. "I don't go very often, or . . ." He corrected himself. "At all, actually. Except, you know, when I'm ordered to. . . ."

"But you can go if you ever need to," she said. "Right?"

"Yeah."

There was silence then, but she didn't try to fill it. She just stood there, smiling at him.

Collins and Vlachic were across the yard, talking to

Izzy Zanella, who was trying to get a softball game going. All three of them were watching Cosmo and the nun out of the corner of their eyes.

"I'll pray for you," Sister Mary Grace finally told him, and, Christ, what could he possibly say in response to that?

"Thank you, Sister."

Jenkins saved him—God bless him. He came running out of the administrative building. "Hey, Zanella, have you seen Cos?"

Izzy pointed, and Jenk jogged in his direction. "Excuse me, Chief," he called. "We just got a call from the States. Your mother—she's going to be all right—but she's had an accident. I guess she fell and . . . Sounds like she broke both of her wrists."

Oh, shit. "Excuse me," Cosmo told the nun.

As he ran for the admin office, he heard Ensign Collins say to Vlachic and Zanella, "Chief Richter has a **mother**?"

CHAPTER ONE

Cosmo's mother was driving him crazy.

Well, okay, to be fair, it wasn't his mom, but rather her choice of music that had pushed him out of her condo, into his truck, and back down the 5, here to San Diego.

He parked in the lot next to the squat, ugly building that held the offices of Troubleshooters Incorporated. The sun was warm on the back of his neck as he crossed to the door. As usual, it was locked—apparently Tommy Paoletti had had no luck yet finding a receptionist for his personal security company. But he **had** installed a system that would allow him to let people in without having to run all the way out to the door twenty times a day.

A surveillance camera hung overhead, and Cosmo looked up at it, making sure Tommy would be able to see his face as he hit the bell.

The lock clicked open as a buzzer sounded, and he went inside.

"Grab some coffee—I'll be right out," Tom shouted from one of the back offices. "How's your mom?"

"Much better, thanks," Cosmo called back.

And she was. Right after the accident, when Cosmo had first gone to see her, she'd been in a lot of pain. Her face had been almost gray, and she'd looked old and frail lying in that hospital bed.

But she'd been home a few days now and was feeling far more her old self.

Which was great.

But, dear sweet Jesus, if he had to listen to the soundtrack from **Jekyll & Hyde** one more time, he was going to scream.

"You just haven't had enough time to appreciate it," his mother had told him. "A few more listens and—"

Oh, no. No, no, Mom. I've heard it quite enough, thanks.

Cosmo poured himself some coffee from the setup in the Troubleshooters waiting room.

He'd actually liked **Urinetown.** He could handle repeated listens of **The Full Monty,** too. And **West Side Story,** if done properly, could bring tears to his usually super-cynical dry eyes.

But most of his mother's very favorite Broadway musicals were those which Uncle Riley had dubbed "screamers." They were filled with hyper-emotional ballads with crescendos that swelled to triple forte, delivered by sopranos or tenors who, as Riley had insisted, deserved immediate arrest by the "too-too" police.

Uncle Riley had gotten away with it, but God help him if Cosmo ever said anything like that aloud.

Not just to his mother, who would give him her best injured look, then subject him to several hours of lectures on true music appreciation.

But God help him also if he talked about such things to the other men in SEAL Team Sixteen.

They would look at him as if he were, well . . .

Gay.

Which he wasn't.

Not even close.

Not, of course, that there was anything wrong with it.

Shoot, with his mother, it would've been easier if he had been. He might've been born with some special genetic ability to actually enjoy **Jekyll & Hyde.** And **Phantom** and **Les Mis** and all the other screamers he'd gritted his teeth through, as he'd taken his mother to see them through the years.

Cos took his coffee and sank down into one of the new leather sofas in the Troubleshooters waiting room. Buttery soft and a light shade of honey brown, they replaced the former mismatched collection of over-stuffed chairs—thrift shop rejects—that had cluttered the area in front of the receptionist's desk.

Whoa, the walls had been repainted, too.

Magazine racks, potted plants, real lamps instead of overhead fluorescents . . .

Tom's wife, Kelly, had been threatening to redeco-rate for months, insisting that the image Tom was try-ing for with his new company probably wasn't "piss poor and tasteless to boot."

But huge leather sofas—as nice as they were—
weren't exactly Kelly's light and breezy New England
beach house style.

Someone else had done this.

Someone besides Tom—who was a great leader but
seriously fashion and design challenged.

"Are you here for the meeting?"

Cosmo looked up. The woman coming down the
hall toward him was a stranger. She was wearing a pin-
striped suit that had been tailored to accentuate her
feminine shape. Petite, with blond hair cut short and
delicate features in a launch-a-thousand-ships face,
she had blue eyes that were coolly polite. Professional.
Intelligent.

Ivy-league intelligent.

Her hands were ring-free. Both of them. Her fin-
gernails were short, bitten down almost to the quick—
a direct and intriguing contrast to the career-woman
persona.

She took a few steps closer and tried again. "May I
help you?"

"No, ma'am," he finally answered her, then mentally kicked himself. Talk, asshole. She most certainly
could help him. He would love for her to help him.
And at least be polite. "Thanks. I'm waiting for Commander Paoletti."

She finally smiled, and it transformed her
from merely breathtakingly beautiful to full-power-
defibrillator heart-stoppingly gorgeous. He wanted to
drop to his knees and beg her to bear his children.

"You must be one of his SEALs," she said.

"Yes, ma'am." Stand up, fool. But, Christ, don't spill the coffee . . . Too late. It splashed over the edge of the cup and onto his fingers. Gahhhhd, it was hot.

She pretended not to notice as he pretended that he hadn't just been scalded. She even held out her hand to shake. "I'm Sophia Ghaffari."

Sophia. It was a beautiful name, and by all rights violins should have started playing when she said it. She looked like a Sophia, she dressed like a Sophia, she even smelled like a Sophia.

He tried to wipe his fingers dry on his pants, but it was hopeless. "Cosmo Richter. Sorry, I'm . . ."

A freakin' idiot.

He crossed to the coffee setup, where he found some napkins, thank the Lord.

But Sophia didn't run out of the room screaming, "Save me from cretins!" as he wiped off his hand. "You must be here to help out with the Mercedes Chadwick job," she said instead.

"I'm not sure," he admitted. "Tommy said something about an easy op in L.A."

"That's the one." Now that his hands were clean, she had crossed her arms. "She's a movie producer— and I guess a screenwriter, too," she told him. "She's been getting death threats."

His chance to touch Sophia, to shake her hand, had apparently passed. What a crying shame.

"Hey, Cos." Tom Paoletti came out from the back, smiling his welcome. "Sorry to keep you waiting."

"No problem, sir."

"Before I forget, Kelly said to say she's on for lunch tomorrow."

"How is she?" Cosmo asked. Tommy's wife, Kelly, was pregnant with their first child.

"Other than pissed that she can't fly?" Tom asked. "She really wanted to go back to Massachusetts for a week on the beach before the baby was born, but her OB just grounded her. We had a four-hour discussion the other night on the definition of 'highly recommend.'" He rolled his eyes. "The happy ending was that one of our clients owns a house right on the beach in Malibu, and he's always telling me to use it. So we're going tomorrow. Actually, you can do me a big favor and drive Kelly up there after lunch." He looked at Sophia. "Soph, you better get moving, if you're intending to catch that flight."

"Yeah. It was nice meeting you," Sophia told Cosmo, then turned back to Tom. "Tell Decker I'm sorry I missed him."

"I'll do that," Tom told her. "He's stuck in traffic. It's bad—really, you better get going."

As she hurried down the hall, he led Cosmo back toward his office. "We've had a change of plans," he continued. "Originally Decker was going to meet us here, but the 15's a parking lot. I'm going to meet him tonight, at the client's. Any chance you can come along?"

"Sure." Cosmo couldn't help hesitating, turning to watch Sophia hustle out of her office and down the hall and out the door.

Tommy, of course, noticed. "Sophia's handling our paranoia accounts. You know, people who are panicked by the changing terrorist-threat levels. They want to make sure they have the best security system possible. She sets up a team to try to get past their system, see just how good it really is against professionals. She does the face-to-face work, initial meetings, report presentations, that sort of thing. She's very good at it."

"Sounds like fun," Cos said as casually as he could as he closed Tom's office door behind them. "Right up my alley. The breaking-in part, I mean. She need any help?"

Tommy laughed as he gestured for Cosmo to take a seat. Someone had gotten him new furniture for his office, too. A real desk instead of that rickety table he'd been using. "Her current assignment is out of state. I thought you wanted to stay close to your mom in . . . Where is she? Laguna Beach?"

"Maybe I could commute." There was actual artwork up on the walls. Watercolors. Scenes of a coastline that was definitely New England and quite probably Tom and Kelly's hometown on Boston's North Shore.

Tom lifted an eyebrow. "To Denver?"

If it had been Phoenix or Vegas, he would've tried it. But Denver . . .

Tom knew what he was thinking. "Nice try, Chief," he said. "But she's recently widowed—she's not looking to get involved with anyone right now. And I really need you in L.A.—Hollywood, actually."

"The movie producer who's getting death threats," Cosmo repeated what Sophia had told him. "Is Deck the team leader?" Decker was a former SEAL and a former Agency operative.

"Yep," Tom told him.

Cos nodded. If he couldn't work with Sophia, Decker would be his strong second choice. "Count me in." He backpedaled. "If, you know, he wants me."

Tom nodded. "I've already spoken to him. He wants you."

Lawrence Decker was a spec ops legend. He'd left the SEAL Teams shortly after the terrorist bombing of Khobar Towers, a U.S. military complex in Saudi Arabia. According to the grapevine, Chief Decker had been frustrated by the red tape that, at the time, kept the SEALs from actively hunting down the terrorist organization that had killed so many American servicemen. He'd left the Teams and joined the clandestine and nearly nameless organization known as the Agency, where he'd gotten his wish— going deep into countries known for harboring terrorists. Now he was one of many former SEALs and Delta Force, Marine, CIA, FBI, and Agency operatives who were working for Tommy Paoletti's civilian consultant group.

Yeah, Troubleshooters Incorporated's personnel list read like a Who's Who of the elite from the Special Operations world.

"You've got how many weeks of leave left?" Tommy asked Cos.

"Three weeks, two days, seventeen hours."

His former SEAL CO smiled. "Well, at least you're not counting the minutes."

Cosmo glanced at his watch. And fourteen minutes.

"And you're sure you don't want to use this time as a vacation?" Tom asked.

"I'm quite sure, sir." Like many SEALs in Team Sixteen, Cosmo wasn't good at taking vacations. After just a few days, he got bored. Restless. "I just want to be able to check in on my mother once or twice a day, even just by phone."

"You're an only child, aren't you?" Tom asked.

"Yeah. I'm it," Cos said. "That's why I took the full thirty days." He'd taken the extra time off even though his mom was adamant that Cosmo not be the one to provide her personal care. She'd put it in bottom-line terms by saying no way was she going to allow her grown son to accompany her into the bathroom. "She's doing really well, but I still want to be close by, you know? She seems to like both her day and night nurses—which is good, because with both wrists in a cast, she can't do much of anything without help."

"That must be frustrating for her," Tom said.

Understatement of the year. "She has her coping strategies," Cos told him. "She loves listening to music, so she's been doing a lot of that. The Card's also putting together a special computer keyboard for her, so she'll be able to go back online."

God bless WildCard Karmody, SEAL Team Sixteen's computer wizard.

"So tell me about this Hollywood producer." Cosmo got down to business. "Her name's . . . Mercedes? Like the car?"

"J. Mercedes Chadwick," Tom told him, then smiled at the look of disgust Cosmo shot in his direction.

"What'd she do," Cos asked, "to piss people off enough to make them want to kill her?"

"I don't need personal protection—a team of bodyguards? That's absolutely ridiculous!" Jane Chadwick told Patty, her new college intern.

Patty didn't seem convinced, so Jane turned to Robin, hoping for just a teensy bit of brotherly support.

But he wasn't paying attention. He was giving Patty one of his "hey there" smiles. The girl, naturally, was dazzled. Of course, she was impossibly young and didn't yet have the mileage that would enable her to see past Robin's gorgeous face to the inner low-life womanizing scum within.

"Yo," Jane said, clapping her hands sharply at her brother. Half brother. At times like this it helped to remind herself that they shared only a fraction of their genetic makeup. "Robin. Focus. Patty, go call the studio back and tell them no. Thank you, but no. I'm perfectly safe. Be firm."

Unlike that of many young movie-loving girls who made the pilgrimage to Hollywood, Patty's freckle-faced cuteness wasn't an act. She actually wore knee-socks and meant it. Jane didn't know her very well yet, but unfortunately being firm didn't seem to be high on her skill list.

But at least she was out of Jane's office, closing the door behind her, releasing Robin from her captivating spell.

"If you touch her," Jane told him, "I will kill you and I will make it hurt."

"What?" Robin said. Mr. Innocent. He made that sound that was half laugh, half indignation. "Come on. I was just smiling at her."

One thing was certain: Her too-handsome half brother was a brilliant actor. If they could get this movie made, and—most important—if they could get it distributed and seen, he was going to be a star.

"Besides," he added, "you of all people shouldn't be making idle death threats."

That was supposed to be funny. Jane didn't crack a smile.

"That wasn't a threat," she said. "It was a promise. Let me put this in terms you'll understand, Sleazoid. If you sleep with her, she'll think she's your girlfriend. And when she finds out that she was merely your Friday night distraction, she'll be badly hurt. Now. Maybe you don't give a rat's ass about Patty's feelings, but I do. And I also know what you do care about, so listen close. If you break her heart, she will quit. And if she quits, you will take her place and become my personal assistant, and you won't have a single minute to yourself from that moment until we are done making **American Hero.** Which means in Sleazoid-speak that it will be two months before you have sex again. Two. Months."

Her little brother laughed. "Relax, Janey. I'm not going to sleep with her."

Jane just looked at him. She liked Patty. A lot. The girl was smart, she was sweet, she was way overqualified for this glorified gofer position. The lack of backbone could be worked on—besides, Jane had plenty of that to go around.

Best of all, though, despite being paid only a stipend, Patty liked Jane. It was a win-win situation.

As long as Robin kept his own little win zipped up tight inside his pants and out of the equation.

Problem was, Patty had a serious crush on Robin. Which meant it was going to have to fall to him to keep his distance.

God help them all.

"You need to lighten up," her brother told her now. "What is it **Variety** calls you?" He reached for a copy of the trade magazine that was out and open on her desk and started to read the latest section that Patty had highlighted. " 'Never too serious, party girl producer and screenwriter J. Mercedes Chadwick heats things up at the Paradise.' " He looked at her over the top of the oversized page. "Who are you, you too-serious she-bitch, and what have you done with my real sister, the party girl producer?"

Jane gave him the evil eye that she'd perfected back when she was six and he was four.

It didn't scare him as much anymore. "Look," he said, "I know you're freaked out by these e-mails—"

"But I'm not," Jane interrupted. "I'm freaked out by the fact that the studio's freaked out. I don't need a bodyguard. Robbie, come on. It's just a few Internet crazies who—"

"Patty told me you got three hundred just today."

"No," she scoffed. "Well, yeah, but it's, like, three crazies each sending a hundred e-mails."

"You're certain of that?"

"Yes," she told him.

Robin was silent, obviously not believing her.

"Really," she insisted. "How could this possibly be real?"

More silence. "Who's paying?" Robin finally asked.

"For my lifetime of sin?" Jane responded. "I am, apparently."

He gave her a get serious look—which was vaguely oxymoronic. Robin—telling someone else to get serious. "For this added security that HeartBeat Studios wants to set up," he clarified.

"They are," Jane said. Her budget for this film was already stretched thin. She was using her personal credit cards to pay for craft services. No way could she afford round-the-clock guards.

"Then I don't see what the big deal is," Robin said.

"You don't understand," Jane said. And he didn't. Her brother, while not exactly simple, presented his true self to the world at all times. Well, except for lying to her about his intentions toward Patty . . .

Robin was a player and he didn't try to hide it. **Too many women, too little time**—he'd said as much in his first interview with **Entertainment Weekly.** Consummate actor that he was, he came across as charming. The reporter—a woman, natch—portrayed him as boyishly honest about his inability to resist temptation, rather than selfish and spoiled.

To be sure, his being spoiled was partly Jane's fault. As his older sister, she'd bent over backward to try to make life as easy as possible for him. Well, at least she had after she'd ended that phase where her every waking moment was devoted to tormenting her wimpy little freak of a half brother.

It had been difficult growing up with their parents. Between her and Robin, they'd had three households—Jane and her mom's, Robin and his mom's, and their father's, where they spent every other weekend with him and his wife du jour.

Which meant that most of those weekends it was just Jane and Robin and their father's housekeeper, who rarely spoke English and was replaced with an even greater frequency than the stepmom of the moment.

It was during one of those weekends that Jane first discovered that Robin's entire life reeked of neglect. His mother was referred to by her own mother as "that drunken bitch," so she probably shouldn't have been too surprised.

Somewhere down the line, just a few years before Robin's mother died and he moved in full-time with their father, Jane stopped being his chief tormentor and became his champion. His protector. His ally.

"What's not to understand?" he asked her now.

"HeartBeat wants to hire a couple of bodyguards for you. Use it. Spin it into something that'll get us two, maybe three stories in the trades. If you do it right, maybe AP'll pick it up."

"I don't want a bodyguard following me around day and night." Jane's public persona, "Party Girl Producer Mercedes Chadwick," was as much a fictional character as any she'd ever created for one of her screenplays—the real-life gang in **American Hero** not included.

For the first time in her career—a crazy, seven-year ride that had started with a freak hit when she was still in film school—Jane was making a movie based on fact.

And was getting death threats because of it.

"I don't want to have to be the 'Party Girl Producer' here in my own home," she told her brother. Her feet hurt just from the idea of wearing J. Mercedes Chadwick's dangerously high heels 24/7. Which she would have to do. Because her bodyguards would be watching her—that was the whole point of their being there, right?

And no way would she risk one of them giving an interview after the threat was over and done, saying, "Jane Chadwick? Yeah, the Mercedes thing is just BS. No one really calls her that. She's actually very normal. Plain Jane, you know? Nothing special to look at without the trashy clothes and makeup. She works eighteen-hour days—which is deadly dull and boring, if you want to know the truth. And all those guys she

allegedly dates? It's all for show. The Party Girl
Producer hasn't had a private party in her bedroom for
close to two years."

If HeartBeat Studios hired bodyguards, she'd have
to lock herself in her suite of rooms every night.

Patty knocked on the door, opening it a crack to
peek in. "I'm sorry," she reported. She started most of
her conversations with an apology. It was a habit Jane
intended to break her of long before **American Hero**
was in the can. "They've set up a meeting here for four
o'clock with the security firm they've hired—Troubleshooters Incorporated."

Jane closed her eyes at Patty's verb tense. Hired.
"No," she said. "Tell them no. Leave off the thank-you
this time and—"

"I'm sorry"—Patty looked as if she were going to
cry—"but the studio apparently called the FBI—"

"What?"

"—and the authorities are taking the threat seriously. They're involved now."

"The FBI?" Jane was on her feet.

Patty nodded. "Some important agent from D.C. is
going to be here at four, too. He's already on his way."

Jules Cassidy hated L.A.

He hated it for the usual reasons—the relentless
traffic jams, the unending sameness of the weather,
and the air of frantic, fear-driven competition that
ruled the city. It was as if all four million inhabitants
were holding their breath, terrified that if they were
on the top, they'd fall; if they were climbing, they

wouldn't make it; and if they were at the bottom, they'd never get their big break.

It was called the City of Angels, but the folks who gave it that name had neglected to mention that the particular angels who lived there didn't answer to the man upstairs.

Jules could almost hear one of those satanic types laughing as he gazed at his current number one reason why he hated L.A.

A kid, barely out of his teens, was pointing a handgun at Jules' chest. "Give me your wallet!"

There had been a sign saying, "Park at your own risk" posted at the entrance to this parking garage that was cut into the hillside beneath his West Hollywood hotel. But Jules had foolishly assumed any risk would occur at night, not during broad daylight. Of course, in here it was shadowy and dank. The small lot was only half-filled, and no other people were in sight.

The garage walls were concrete block, and the ceiling looked solid, too. A bullet would ricochet off rather than penetrate and injure someone on the other side. The open bay doors on his right, however, led directly to the street. It wasn't a major thoroughfare, but there was occasional traffic.

"You don't want to do this," Jules said, carefully keeping his hands where the kid could see them, even while he inched his way closer. He was glad his sidearm was in a locked suitcase in the trunk of the car, so he could hold his jacket open and take his wallet out of his pocket with two fingers without flashing his shoulder holster. "Just turn around and walk away—

and do yourself another favor while you're at it. Wipe the gun so your prints aren't on it and—"

"Shut up," the kid ordered him. He had primitive tattoos on his knuckles—despite his tender age he'd already done prison time. His hands were also shaking, another bad sign. He was obviously in dire need of a fix—the most desperate of all the desperate Los Angelenos.

He was in such bad shape, he'd forgotten to pull his ski mask down over his face. He was wearing it on top of his head, which didn't do much to conceal his identity.

Clear thinking wasn't part of the heroin withdrawal process, so Jules tried to eliminate any confusion on his end.

"I'm putting this on the ground"—Jules did just that—"and here's my watch and my ring, too." The ring—nothing fancy, just a simple silver band—was going to do the trick. The kid's hands were shaking too much to be able to pick it up without his looking down, and when he did . . . "I'm going to back away—"

"I said shut the fuck up, faggot!"

Well, all-righty then. Jules could just imagine the conversation shared over a needle. **Hey, if you ever need some fast cash, go on over to West Hollywood and rob a homo. They're all rich, and if you do it right, you can probably make 'em cry, which is good for a laugh. . . .**

"So this is a hate crime?" Jules asked in an attempt to distract because he just couldn't bring himself to cry.

But it was too late. The time for conversation was definitely over.

The kid realized that his mask was up.

Jules wasn't sure what changed, but he got a heavy whiff of **I can't go back to prison,** which wasn't a good emotion to combine with **I need a fix. Now.**

He couldn't wait for the kid to fumble with the ring.

Instead, Jules rushed him, taking care to knock his gun hand up and to the left, away from the open bay door, which proved to be unnecessary as the weapon went flying, unfired.

It skittered on the concrete as Jules sent the kid in the opposite direction.

He used the basic principles of Newton's second law to launch himself after that weapon, scooping it off the floor and holding it in a stance that was far less theatrical than the kid's had been, but also far more effective.

The kid rolled onto his ass, his face scraped and bleeding, and he looked at Jules with a mixture of disbelief and horror. "Who the fuck **are** you?"

"You didn't think a fag would fight back, huh?" Jules asked. Holding the gun steady with one hand, he took his cell phone from his pocket with his other and speed-dialed the LAPD number he'd programmed in—standard procedure for an out-of-town visit—on his flight from D.C. "Yeah," he said into the phone as the line was picked up. "This is Agent Jules Cassidy, with the FBI."

"Ah, shit," the kid said, too stupid to realize his mistake hadn't been that he'd mugged the wrong man, but rather that he'd left his home this morning intending to commit felony armed robbery instead of checking himself into a rehab program.

"I need immediate police assistance in the underground garage for the Stonewall Hotel in West Hollywood," Jules told the police dispatcher. He looked at the kid. "You, sweetiecakes, have the right to remain silent. . . ."

CHAPTER TWO

Producer J. Mercedes Chadwick's house in the Hollywood Hills was an elegant old monster built back in the silent film era. But when Lawrence Decker followed Cosmo Richter and Tom Paoletti into the front hall, he'd realized that **old** was the defining word. The building probably hadn't been renovated since the late 1940s.

From the gate, it had looked impressive. From inside, with a collection of buckets strategically positioned under obvious signs of water damage on the ceiling, it was clear that the place was a major fixer-upper.

"Someone else is paying the bill, right?" Cosmo had murmured to Tom as they stood in the foyer, waiting for the girl clutching the clipboard to fetch Ms. Chadwick from the back.

"HeartBeat Studios," Tom murmured back.

Decker was well aware that securing HeartBeat as a regular client would be quite an accomplishment for Troubleshooters Incorporated. The work would be easy—silver-bullet assignments—compared to most of the operations Deck had been on overseas. While providing security for a Hollywood studio wouldn't quite be paid R & R, it would be close.

Easy assignments, good money. That's why Tom himself was here today with Deck, and why he'd dragged Cosmo Richter along, too.

The SEAL chief was tall and muscular, with a lean face and pale blue eyes he usually kept hidden behind sunglasses. Yeah, he was impressively dangerous-looking—something no one had ever been able to say about Decker, even during his own years with the Navy.

Cosmo was here as a human exclamation mark, strategically in place for the client to gaze upon after Tom and Decker assured her that they would, indeed, be able to keep her safe.

Of course, the first thing they needed to do was install a security system. Currently, there was nothing here—aside from a fading sign on the creaky automated gate at the end of the driveway: "Beware of Dogs."

This place dated from the time when state-of-the-art security meant a stone wall with bits of glass in the concrete on top, a front gate, and a matched set of big, loud, and ugly, with lots of sharp teeth.

"We have a list of improvements a mile long that we're planning to make," Ms. Chadwick had told them breezily as she'd led the way to the suite of rooms she and her brother were using for their production company's main offices. Her impossibly high heels had clicked on the marble tile floor. "But we're wait-listed with the contractor. You know how hard it is to get work done these days. . . ."

According to the file Tom had given Deck, she'd produced her first movie—a low-budget horror flick called **Hell or High Water**—back when she was in film school. She sold her little student film to a distributor for a ton of money and put herself on the map as a mover and shaker.

Apparently, in Hollywood, youth was in. And J. Mercedes Chadwick was still young, barely twenty-six. She dressed younger, looking like Britney Spears' brunette twin, with long, dark hair cascading down her back and a significant gap between the below-the-hips waistband of her microskirt and the bottom edge of her shirt.

Which was . . . quite a shirt. It had one hell of a neckline.

J. Mercedes Chadwick was a very healthy young woman, no doubt about that.

Her long legs were bare and as golden tanned as her stomach, her toenails painted an exotic shade of dark pink.

She had what Decker thought of as Greek goddess eyes—bluish green and an unusual contrast with her dark hair and rich Mediterranean complexion. She was gorgeous—although not by Hollywood's standards, because she hadn't managed to starve herself boyishly thin.

And that was a choice that was quite intentional—

calculated, in fact. He'd realized it when they were introduced, as she'd held his hand just a little too long and gazed into his eyes just a little too meaningfully.

She knew what most of Hollywood had forgotten. That as fashionable as it was to be whip thin, most men still liked women with substantial curves.

But if his libido had kicked on from that soulfully probing look, it kicked off just as quickly when she gazed at Cosmo the exact same way.

Cos, bless him, didn't crack a smile. He just looked back at the woman with a total lack of expression, as if all that cleavage meant absolutely nothing to him.

Of course, maybe it didn't. Decker didn't know the younger man very well.

One thing he did know was that J. Mercedes Chadwick liked standing out. Hence the three-inch heels that pushed her well over six feet tall and made her tower over mere mortals such as Deck.

There was, he also realized, probably nothing that this woman ever did that was unintentional.

She couldn't have been more different in height and coloring, but she made him think of Sophia Ghaffari—whom he hadn't seen since that drink they'd shared in a bar in Kaiserslautern, Germany, over six months ago.

Sophia was working for Tom Paoletti now—as a matter of fact, for the past four months both she and Deck had worked out of the same office in San Diego. But Decker had spent most of that time OUT-

CONUS, on various assignments. The few occasions he'd been back in the States, she'd been out of town.

Which was probably a very good thing, considering.

They all sat now—Cosmo, Tom, Decker, Mercedes, and her brother Robin who was as fair as she was dark—on a series of sofas and easy chairs in a huge room with windows looking out over the wilderness that was the back garden.

"Isn't a high-tech security system going to be enough?" Mercedes was arguing with Tom. "I mean, great, if HeartBeat wants to pay to install a system, I'm not going to say no. But really, with the kind of technology that's available these days, isn't the idea of two guards—one inside and one outside the house, around the clock—just a little extravagant?"

Decker answered for Tom. "Considering the size of this house, Ms. Chadwick, no."

She was obviously not happy with the idea, but as she turned to look at him, he knew what it was about her that reminded him of Sophia. It was that smile and the eye contact as she asked, "But does it have to be day and night? I have . . . friends who can keep me safe at night."

Across the room, her brother covered a laugh with a cough.

Mercedes Chadwick didn't bring the question "Do you want to make it with me?" to the table. No, her attitude was "**When** do you want to make it with me?"

It was an approach to being a woman in the business world that was a direct 180 from the dress-and-act-like-a-man school. Instead of trying to de-sex, Mercedes Chadwick used her sexuality to try to gain control.

Just like blond and beautiful Sophia Ghaffari had done back in Kazbekistan, when she and Deck had first met.

As Mercedes smiled at him, Decker wondered if she would go as far as Sophia had to gain the upper hand.

Jesus, was he ever going to stop thinking about that?

"Your privacy won't be compromised," Tom told Mercedes, trying to reassure her.

She laughed. "Yes, it will. Look, can't we just pretend that you've got guards posted here around the clock? I don't mind having one of your men tag along when I go out. That actually might be kind of fun. And it's okay with me if someone hangs here, guarding the place while I'm gone, but . . ."

Deck exchanged a look with Tom. **Fun?**

"I know this may seem inconvenient—" Tom started.

"And I know you really want this gig," she cut him off. "So let's compromise."

"There is no compromise." Tom was absolute. "We're talking about your personal safety."

She rolled her eyes. "Yeah, I'm so sure some of those scary e-mailers are going to come out here and try to hit me with their computer keyboards. Or maybe they'll chain-mail me to death. 'If you don't forward this to ten people in the next two minutes, great misfortune will befall you . . .' "

Cosmo Richter, who'd seemed all this time to have his full attention focused on the garden, finally looked over at Mercedes and spoke. "Is there a reason, miss, why you feel the threats that have been made against your life are a joke?"

"Joke," she said, looking from Cosmo to Decker to Tom. "Yes, joke. That's a good word for this, thank you. It's a giant joke, gentlemen. It's probably a stunt that the studio's come up with to get publicity for this movie. You don't **really** think someone wants to kill me, do you?"

Her intercom buzzed, breaking in before Tom could respond.

"I'm sorry to interrupt." The voice of Mercedes' personal assistant came through a speaker. "But an FBI agent named Jules Cassidy is down by the gate, and"—she cleared her throat—"the opener's stuck again."

The brother—Robin—stood. "I'll go."

The FBI agent drove a rented Mercury Sable.

Robin wasn't sure exactly what he'd expected, but it sure as hell wasn't a four-door family sedan.

The FBI agent was also shorter and younger than he'd imagined, getting out of the car as Robin approached the gate. Compact, with a trim build, he had dark hair that he wore cut short and a face that could have appeared next to Robin's on the cover of **Tiger Beat** magazine.

He could just imagine this guy's meeting with his high school guidance counselor. "You could be a model or a TV star—you don't really need any acting skills for that—or . . . Oh, here's something just perfect! *NSYNC is looking for new blood—"

"Well, you see, Mrs. Smersh, I hate to disappoint you, but I really have my heart set on becoming an FBI agent. . . ."

"Sorry," Robin called as he came the last few feet down the drive. "It sticks sometimes."

The gate actually stuck most of the time, and they'd gotten into the habit of leaving it open. But Jane had wanted it closed today—probably to fool the private security team into thinking she was taking precautions with her safety.

It took him four tries to get the damn thing to work. His smile definitely felt strained around the edges by the time it finally opened.

Now that they were both on the same side of the fence, the agent flashed his badge as he held out his hand. "Jules Cassidy, FBI."

"Robin Chadwick, SAG." They shook hands. "I'm the brother."

"Nice to meet you. SAG?"

"Screen Actors Guild," Robin explained. "Sorry, I have this inability to not be an asshole, especially when I'm not provoked."

The double negatives didn't stop Jules for even a second, and he laughed, taking off his sunglasses and . . .

Hello. Big eye contact. The FBI guy not only was

shorter and younger, but he was also gayer than Robin had expected.

Ever since he'd gone blond to play Hal Lord in **American Hero,** he'd been hit on by gay men more times than he could count. It had been a little nerve-racking at first, but he'd learned to remove any potential mystery as quickly as possible.

"Not gay," Robin said now. He thought of sweet little Patty up in Jane's office, who'd given him that shy smile when he'd emerged from the meeting. He knew without a doubt that he'd be welcome should he come a-calling at her apartment later this evening. Yes, he knew he'd promised his sister that he'd be good, but Patty was **so** cute. . . . "Don't waste your energy."

Jules laughed again. He appeared to be genuinely amused. "You're making some pretty large assumptions, aren't you?"

"Assume everything," Robin told him cheerfully. "That's my motto. It keeps me out of trouble."

"I would think it might get you into it," Jules countered.

"And still you flirt with me, you devil. What part of 'Not gay,' did you not understand? Drive through, will you, so I can try to close this behind you."

Jules Cassidy, FBI, was still laughing—and he was pretty damn adorable when he laughed. Harve and Guillermo and Gary the Grip and even Ricco, who was in a long-term relationship, were going to swoon when they met him. He got back into the Sable and drove through the gate. He stopped just on the other side, though.

Robin gave up on the idea of closing the gate after his fifth try.

"I hate that motherfucking thing," he said, adding as he realized Jules had rolled his window down, "There, does that convince you? A very heterosexual use of the manly verb **to motherfuck,** positioned in my sentence as a salty adverb."

"Salty adjective," Jules corrected him. "If it were an adverb it would be motherfuckingly."

"Whatever. My sister's the writer in the family," Robin told him. "Which is why she's the one getting the death threats—which she's not taking at all seriously. Tell me the truth, Jules Cassidy, FBI. Do we really have something to worry about here?"

The FBI agent got real serious, real fast, morphing from happy, flirty gay boy into completely grown-up hard-ass with a nearly palpable sense of purpose and a determination that matched his set of giant steel balls. Holy macaroni, Mrs. Smersh. Wherever did you get the idea that Jules Cassidy couldn't act?

"Yes," Jules told him. "You do. Have you ever heard of the Freedom Network?"

It was very clear to Cosmo that J. Mercedes Chadwick couldn't believe what she was hearing.

"You're telling me," she repeated, making sure that she got it right, "that there are thousands of people—tens of thousands?—who consider Chester Lord—a little-known Alabama district court judge who's been dead since 1959—their personal hero?"

FBI agent Jules Cassidy nodded. "Yes, ma'am. They

call themselves the Freedom Network. Chester Lord wrote a number of books and—"

She was incredulous, her lip-glossed mouth hanging open. "And these are people who don't even live in Alabama . . . ?"

"The majority are in Idaho."

"This is a man who was überconservative even for his time," she pointed out. "There are rumors that Judge Lord looked the other way and allowed lynchings—"

"I believe they refer to him as honest and old-fashioned," Jules told her. "And his son Hal was a hero in the war—you surely know more about that part of it than I do. But I can tell you one thing—apparently these people are very protective of the memories of both father and son, and they're not at all happy at the idea of you outing Hal in your movie."

Mercedes' assistant Patty had put a copy of the **American Hero** script onto the table in front of them, along with the warning that they could not take it out of this building.

Like . . . what? They were going to sell it on eBay? Or give a copy of the most provocative scenes to a tabloid like the **National Voice**?

Cosmo flipped through it. It was the story of Jack Shelton and Harold "Hal" Lord, two young American soldiers who met in Paris in early 1945, toward the end of World War II.

Hal was already a highly decorated war hero, and because he spoke fluent German, he volunteered to be part of an Allied team determined to find out whether

Hitler's scientists had succeeded in creating an atomic bomb. The movie alleged that Hal Lord was gay, but in total denial. He was not just in the closet, but he was sitting so far in the back with his eyes shut, he couldn't even see the door.

Until Jack Shelton made the scene.

Jack was as openly, cheerfully gay as a young man could be back in 1945. He was a member of the Twenty-third Special Combat Group, and he was assisting a Hollywood costume designer who'd been brought in from London to create authentic-looking Nazi uniforms for Hal's Allied team to wear on their trek behind enemy lines.

It was apparently love at first sight, which terrified Hal. Bringing his gay lover home with him after the war was not an option for a man whose father wasn't exactly known as Judge Tolerance and who also just happened to be the leader of his local KKK.

In Hal's opinion, he had no other choice but to get himself killed in the war.

The screenplay also included the story of the more traditional romance between real-life Oscar-winning costumer designer Virginia Simone and Hal's team leader, Major Milton Monroe. From the looks of the gruffly spare dialogue and the physical description of the major with his Bronx accent, Mercedes had written the part of the major for Humphrey Bogart.

Or maybe Spencer Tracy. It was obvious she was a fan of Hollywood's golden era, which was a point in her favor.

"Hal's own granddaughter has given our movie her blessing," Mercedes pointed out. "If you're looking for the sex, the first gay love scene isn't until page seventy-two."

Cos looked up, directly into her eyes, which were a remarkably pretty color. She was talking to him. She thought he was flipping though, looking for . . .

"The hetero couple doesn't get it on until close to the end of the movie, either—page seventy-nine," she continued. "I think you'll find it's all tastefully done. We fade to black in both of the subplots. We've been very up-front about that, so I'm not sure why all those Internet crazies have their panties in a twist."

"I wasn't—" he started to say, but her attention was already back on Cassidy. Fine. Let her think whatever she wanted to think.

"The Freedom Network's not too happy with Hal's granddaughter right now, either," Jules reported. "She's gone overseas—she's going to keep a low profile for a while. I would recommend—"

"No." Mercedes cut him off, steel in her voice. "Not an option. I'm not going to hide. I have a movie to make, a schedule to meet."

"Jane—" her brother started to say, but she hushed him.

She did, however, soften her tone. She even managed a smile. "Can we back up a bit? You said earlier that these Freedom people—all mega-thousands of them—have these weekend get-togethers up in . . . in . . . Monkey-Fuck, Idaho, where they sit around a campfire . . . Doing what? Reciting eighty-seven-verse epic poems lauding the glory that was Chester 'Baby Lyncher' Lord?"

"Well, we're not exactly sure what they do during their retreats," Jules told her. He was trying to keep this serious, but Cosmo could tell that "Monkey-Fuck" had him biting the insides of his cheeks. "They're pretty adamant about not letting outsiders into their inner circle. Still, whatever they do up there, we think it probably has more to do with firearms than poetry."

"But whatever they're doing, they're doing it in Idaho, right?" she asked. "So I should be okay as long as I stay in California." She looked over at her assistant. "Patty, call Steve Spielberg with my regrets. I won't be able to attend his potato-picking party in Boise next week, gosh darn it."

Jules was hanging in. "Ms. Chadwick. With all due respect, yesterday this was a joke. But today the Freedom Network's involved. There have been several e-mails that have raised a red flag. I don't have the details yet, but my boss, Max Bhagat, is concerned. And believe me, when he becomes concerned, you should take it seriously."

Mercedes looked again at the computer documents Jules had given her—pages upon pages printed directly from the Freedom Network's website. They included a sheet that had a picture of her face in the center of a target's bull's-eye.

She laughed, but to Cosmo's ears it sounded a little

forced. "This is priceless, you know. I couldn't buy this kind of publicity."

Her brother spoke, his voice sharp. "I think we've all agreed this has gone too far, Jane."

Mercedes—or Jane, as her brother called her—looked from Jules to Decker to Tom and finally to Cosmo, as if she'd somehow decided that she trusted him above everyone else in the room. "Am I really in danger?" she asked.

He put down the script. Not from him. Nothing moved him less than a woman like J. Mercedes Chadwick. Yes, she was beautiful, with a perfect oval of a face that hinted at Middle Eastern ancestry. And her body . . . Cos let himself look at her, because the way she dressed, she obviously wanted him and everyone else in the universe to do just that. And why not—she had one hell of a body.

And okay, yeah, he was a freaking liar. She moved him. He'd have to be dead for at least a year for cleavage like the kind she packed not to make him sit up and take notice. But she moved him kind of the way catching a glimpse of one of Silverman's favorite porno flicks moved him. He was embarrassed and vaguely disgusted with his reaction. Because there was nothing real about it.

Sex with women like J. Mercedes Chadwick was just a step up from getting it on with an imaginary girlfriend.

And okay, yeah, it was a big freaking step. But it was just as impersonal—maybe even more so because it involved pretending that it wasn't. And that always left him feeling no less alone.

Cosmo was glad that this woman was a client—which would make her off-limits. Even if she threw herself at him, he'd have a solid reason to resist the temptation, thus avoiding all morning-after regrets.

But right now she and the rest of the people in the room were looking at him, waiting for him to speak.

He cleared his throat. "Lotta crazy people out there," he told her. She seemed to want more, so he kept going. "Seems like a no-brainer to me—letting us come in and provide security, with HeartBeat paying for it."

She looked down at that picture again, frowning slightly. And Cosmo suspected that it scared her more than she was willing to admit.

But she kept up her act. "They spelled my name wrong," she said.

"Yeah, but they got our address right," the brother pointed out.

There was silence then, as that bit of info sank in.

J. Mercedes finally sighed, swearing under her breath. Then she looked up, again directly at Cosmo. "How do we do this?" she asked him. "How, exactly, is this going to work?"

Badly.

That was how this bodyguard thing was going to work.

Until they installed a security system, someone was going to remain within earshot of Jane at all times.

Welcome, boys and girls, to her personal hell. Until this was over, or until she convinced HeartBeat that the threat wasn't real, she was going to have to stay in J. Mercedes Chadwick mode around the clock, just as she'd anticipated.

Right now she even had to stay in character here, in her upstairs private office, where she would have slipped into a pair of sweats as she attempted to write that blasted D-Day dream sequence she'd told the studio she'd consider adding to the movie. She hadn't even kicked off her shoes because her desk was the stupid kind with a modern, open design, and someone standing in her doorway would be able to see her bare feet.

Such weaknesses were for mere mortals. J. Mercedes Chadwick never slipped her feet out of her expensive and trendy shoes.

In about five minutes, someone was going to appear to tell her that most of her new security team from Troubleshooters Incorporated had gathered in her conference room and could she please come downstairs to meet them.

God, this was **so** going to suck.

Jane had to take Robin's advice and turn this fiasco into free publicity for **American Hero.** And since a picture was worth a thousand words, she had to make sure there were plenty of photo ops.

And there would be. When she arrived at the studio every morning, she'd have a hunky bodyguard on either side of her, hustling her from her car.

Jane could practically hear the sound of the camera shutters, feel the heat from the flashbulbs.

It was slightly less annoying to know that her movie would benefit from the inconvenience, but it didn't mean she'd be any less exhausted when it was over and done.

She'd had one moment of panic when Decker, the quietly nondescript team leader, had suggested they make use of her garage—have her get into her car with the garage door closed and open it only when they were ready to leave.

There'd be no chance for pictures if they did that, at least not on this end.

But then he'd opened the door that led into the three-bay monstrosity. The previous owners had collected such fascinating and useful items such as old newspapers and magazines and carefully cleaned-out sardine tins. They were stockpiled in the garage, along with fifty years of empty milk and orange juice containers and empty port wine bottles. The gallon size.

Apparently one could consume quite a bit of port wine in fifty years. So much so that there was no longer room in the garage for one car, let alone three.

Decker and Cosmo Richter, the Navy SEAL, had let her prattle on about how she'd bought this place "as is," and how she didn't have time to call for a Dumpster, which was, obviously, step one in the remodeling process.

Neither of them said anything, although she was certain they both knew it was lack of funds, not time, that kept her from cleaning up the mess. Of course she hadn't expected the SEAL to comment. He spoke in telegram—as if every word he used cost five bucks, and he only had a twenty in his wallet.

He sure was jacked, though. Hugely, gigantically, fabulously ripped.

Hard bodies were a dime a dozen in Hollywood, but somehow his was different. Maybe it was knowing that he was a SEAL and that his muscles weren't grown in the air-conditioned comfort of a gym. Or maybe it was the way he moved, as if completely unaware that he was so drool-worthy.

Most of the men Jane dealt with were hyper-self-aware. They couldn't walk past a building without checking out their own glorious reflection in the windows. They broadcast a continuous "look at me" message. It was, quite frankly, the Hollywood way.

But Cosmo Richter and his startlingly pale-colored eyes came from the planet Oblivious.

She hadn't decided yet if that was weird or refreshing.

"They're ready for you." Jane looked up to see that it was neither Cosmo nor Decker who knocked on her door. It was Patty. She could have taken off her shoes after all.

"Thanks." Jane saved her document, closed her laptop, and headed for the stairs.

Cosmo was waiting at the bottom, and he stepped back, politely letting her lead the way to the conference room.

Tom Paoletti had gone, leaving Decker in charge. FBI agent Jules Cassidy had left, too. In their place at the conference table with Deck were three men and a woman. Apparently there were two other team members, too, whom she'd meet over the next few days.

Jane stopped short in the doorway, the financial reality of this craziness sinking in.

Apparently protecting her was going to be a full-time job for more than a half a dozen people. That had to be costing the studio a crapload. God, she'd far rather have HeartBeat dumping this kind of money into the distribution of her movie. She'd take her chances with the lunatic fringe.

They all got to their feet as they saw her, so she pasted on her best smile, went in, and shook a bunch of hands.

Vinh Murphy, a former Marine, was even bigger than Cosmo. He was at least part African- and Asian-American, with a smile that lit his entire face. Jane would bet big bucks that he was plenty photogenic, but he wore a wedding ring and commented that he'd just gotten back from his honeymoon.

If she knew the tabloids, any picture they ran of her would include plenty of wink-wink, nudge-nudge innuendo. It was amazing, really, how much time was spent speculating about who she was currently shagging.

Particularly since the honest answer was "no one."

The really depressing thing was that the story about her death threats would stay in the news for only a very short time. But a story combining the potential danger with her love life could run for weeks.

Months, if she milked it.

No, it wouldn't take much to launch a convincing

story about J. Mercedes' hot and sweaty lustfest of an affair with her personal bodyguard. All she'd have to do was lean close, lay an impersonal hand on one muscular arm, and whisper into an ear as the photos were being taken.

And the papers would imply that she and the owner of that ear—possibly PJ Prescott, whose hand she'd just shaken—were doing the nasty five times a night and twice in the limo on the way to work.

PJ was a helicopter pilot and paramedic who'd served in the Air Force as part of the elite pararescue jumpers, or PJs, hence his nickname. Tall, lean, and good-looking, he suffered from what Jane thought of as "God's gift to women-itis." He was an open-mouthed, gum-snapping grinner who apparently had learned that it was okay to ogle women as long as he remained boyishly charming and sincerely appreciative of what he was looking at.

He would, no doubt, believe what he read in the tabloids. Jane made a mental note never to be photographed standing next to him. She didn't need that kind of trouble.

Which left only Cosmo Richter and James Nash, who was one of Decker's XOs.

"Executive officer," the woman standing beside Nash explained as Jane shook his hand. "Second in command. I'll be filling that role, too, when necessary. I'm Tess Bailey. It's nice to meet you, Mercedes."

Nash was tall, dark, and elegantly handsome, but it was extremely obvious that he belonged to Tess, who looked more like the president of the elementary school PTO than a trained security operative. Her grip was solid, though, and her smile managed to be friendly and pleasant even while holding a warning.

Even if Jane wanted to—which she most certainly didn't—it was clear that this was not a woman to mess with.

They all sat down to go through the procedures, to review what they knew about the Freedom Network, and to set up a preliminary schedule.

As Decker spoke, Jane couldn't help but watch Cosmo Richter, a man they often addressed as Cos or Chief. And all she could think was, **Congratulations, Chief. Get ready to be whispered to.**

"Your sister is an angel," Jack Shelton said as Robin sat down next to him in the viewing room.

"I bet you say that to all the boys," he said to the elderly man, his eyes on the movie screen. He both loved and hated watching the dailies—the film footage shot during the day. He'd done two different short scenes and—Oh, Christ, there he was. He had to watch his close-up through slitted eyes.

"She may have the habit of dressing like a three-dollar hooker when she goes out in public," Jack said loudly enough for Janey to overhear from out in the hall, where she'd gone to take a phone call. It was hard to know if Jack was deaf or if he just didn't care. "But do you know how many producers I've worked with who would've extended an open invitation both to the set and to the viewing of the dailies to an eighty-four-year-old opinionated queen?"

"One," Robin answered. This was not the first time they'd had this conversation.

"That's right," Jack said. "Jane."

"Considering this movie is about your life—"

"She treats everyone with respect," Jack said. "Star, best boy, caterer's assistant . . ."

"Here's our little angel now," Robin said as Jane crossed in front of them to sit on Jack's other side. Up on the movie screen his face was gigantic and— Shit, was there something nasty in his nose?

"HeartBeat wants a Normandy scene, Jack," she told him in true Janey fashion—point-blank. "I know you weren't part of the D-Day invasion, but Hal was, and I think I've come up with a compromise."

"A D-Day dream sequence," Jack said.

Jane glared at Robin across the old man. "Did you tell him?"

"Did you see my nose in that last shot?" he countered.

Jack spoke over him. "Your assistant did. It's a good idea. Make it a nightmare."

"I intend to." Janey ignored Robin. "I'll run it past you first, all right?"

"You don't have to," Jack said. "I trust you."

Janey kissed him. "Thank you. That is **so** nice. But I'll still run it past you first."

"You guys always talk through my scenes," Robin complained. "Always."

"Because you always do your scenes perfectly," his sister said. "Every take is usable. We know that, so we don't have to watch."

"Yeah, well, you missed a **perfect** unidentified object in my nose just then. Do not let that scene get into the movie," Robin told her. If it did make the edit, he just knew he'd end up nominated for an Oscar, and—just his luck—that would be the footage they'd show when his name was announced as a nominee. He'd have to sit in the Kodak Theatre on the big night with his hand over his eyes, unable to watch.

"We think we've finally found the actor to play young Jack," Janey told old Jack.

"Think?" he repeated. "Shouldn't we be past the **think** stage by now?"

Absolutely. They were well past the wire, having started filming. They'd better have found the right actor this time around. "His name's Hugo Pierce," Robin said.

"It's Pierce Hugo," Janey corrected him. "We have his screen test—it'll be up in a sec. But first, shhhh! Listen."

On the screen, old newsreel footage appeared, accompanied by a voice. Hey, that wasn't just **a** voice; it was Jack's voice.

"It was 1943. Looking back at the recent history of the gay rights movement, one might think, peering down through the murky tunnel of time, that 1943 was the dark ages for gay men in America. But the truth was, darlings, 1943 was a very good year to be queer."

"God," Jack said. "I sound old."

"Honey, you are old," Jane shot back, which made him laugh.

"Young men enlisted or were drafted into the armed forces," Jack's reedy, crackly, voice continued, "leaving their farms and small towns by the millions. We all crowded together in the big cities—Los Angeles and New York—as we prepared to go overseas to fight for America, for freedom.

"And, indeed, it was freedom we found, even as we prepared to fight and die. Those of us who knew that winning the Peoria Husband of the Year Award absolutely wasn't in our future discovered—some of us for the first time—that we were not alone. We found each other in those cities that teemed with uniformed young men, away from our homes and our parents—away from all small-town, middle-class expectations, and our impending, unavoidable failures.

"In December 1942, I was twenty-one and slightly ahead of the game, having come to New York the previous September to attend art school."

"When we finally cast our young Jack," Jane leaned closer to tell him, "we'll film scenes showing him at school and at the recruiters, and so on, beneath this voice-over."

"When the Japanese attacked Pearl Harbor, I raced to the recruiting office, as eager as any of my fellow Americans to defend my country.

"Within days I'd finished a battery of tests and had already been shipped off to boot camp, when suddenly I was pulled out of line and given new orders. I was being assigned to the Twenty-third Special Combat Group—to a unit that no one had ever heard of.

"After a full day and night of travel, I finally reached Pine Camp, back in good ol' New York. I was brought into a barracks that was almost completely filled with men, told absolutely nothing, and left there to wait.

"For what, no one seemed to know.

"Back then it wasn't called gaydar, of course, but whatever you label it, mine was clicking furiously. I was far from the only homosexual in that Quonset hut. In fact, darlings, I quickly realized that instead of the usual small handful, a large percentage of us were friends of Judy Garland. So to speak.

"What were the odds of that happening by coincidence?"

"That's the end of the voice-over segment," Janey said. "Now here's the first part of Pierce's screen test. Please, God, let him be good. It's the scene that immediately follows the voice-over, where Jack—"

"I remember," Jack said.

The camera's focus would be on the auditioning actor's face as the scene—a conversation among the other enlisted men in the army barracks—went on around him. The final version would be intercut with close-ups of classic gay code—eye contact, smiles, a red tie or two, jingling keys—all from young Jack's point of view.

But right now, on the screen, Pierce Hugo swung an army duffel onto an empty bottom bunk, as the actor playing relentlessly hetero Ducky McHenry said, "Special combat. What the fuck is special combat anyway?"

As young Jack turned, the camera began a slow zoom in on him.

"He's not as cute as I was," Jack pointed out.

Janey laughed. "No one is as cute as you were, Jack."

"Shut the hell up, McHenry," one of the actors said wearily as the camera moved to a full close-up of Pierce's face.

He was good-looking in an extremely superficial Abercrombie ad way. Robin tried to imagine kissing him and couldn't.

"Ah, Christ," another off-screen voice complained, "is he starting with that again?"

"No, no, guys," Ducky's voice said. "This shouldn't be so hard. I been thinking, and what we need to do is figure out what we have in common, right? Then we'll know what they'll be sending us out there to do."

Meanwhile, the camera stayed on Pierce's face.

"He's not **too** awful," the Jack sitting beside Robin said.

"Hey, new guy," Ducky said, and the camera pulled back to include him in the shot. He was speaking directly to Pierce. "What do **you** think?"

The audience was supposed to see a flurry of emotions cross young Jack's face as he wondered how to answer that question, because he knew damn well what so many of the men in this barracks had in common. Pierce Hugo managed only to look frightened.

Jane made a sound that was half pain, half disgust.

"Whaddya do before Uncle Sam got his hooks in ya?" Ducky asked.

Relief appeared on Pierce's face. It was a little too obvious, too "I'm acting!" and again Janey made that unhappy sound.

"I'm—I was—an art student."

"Aha!" Ducky exclaimed. "Another artist! That makes twenty-two artists, seventeen actors slash waiters, and three radio announcers—"

"It's obvious, friends," someone interrupted as the camera stayed focused on Pierce, who was about as interesting an actor as a wooden spoon. "We're going to put on a show for the Nazis."

"I'm serious here," Ducky shouted over the laughter. "New guy—were you pulled out of whatever unit you were supposed to serve with, all mysterious-like, no questions answered?"

Pierce nodded. "Yeah."

"See?" Ducky said, triumphant. "Same as the rest of us."

Jane stood up. Thank God. "Thank you, I've seen enough. Patty!"

The film sputtered to a stop and the lights came up.

"You didn't give him much of a chance," Jack chided gently. "What did he have, eight words of dialogue total?"

"Dialogue's easy," Jane shot back as Patty came down the aisle.

Robin smiled at her. Unlike kissing Hugo Pierce or Pierce Hugo or whoever he was, he **could** imagine kissing Patty.

She blushed and smiled shyly back at him.

"Jack's main role in this movie is that of observer,"

Janey continued. "The audience is going to get their cues about how to feel from Jack. And if he's feeling like a two-by-four—"

"Pierce wasn't that bad," Jack objected as Robin got lost in Patty's blue eyes. "Need I remind you, you've started filming. You need to cast this part."

"Schedule another session with the casting director ASAP," Jane ordered Patty. "The right Jack is out there, and I am going to find him, so help me God."

CHAPTER THREE

His mother would've loved this.

Cosmo sat quietly in the back row of the screening room as J. Mercedes Chadwick managed to be even more dramatic than the movie clips they'd all just watched.

Although, truth be told, Cosmo agreed with Mercedes' assessment. The kid they'd seen hadn't been up to speed. But apparently they didn't have a big enough budget to hire a well-known, experienced movie star.

As Cos watched, he wondered if she knew that her intern was only catching a third of what she said. The girl, Patty, was totally distracted by the brother, Robin.

Robin, however, was fully aware of Patty's crush and seemed to be mutually intrigued. Damn, and wasn't that a train wreck just waiting to happen?

Cosmo would have bet two months' pay that neither of them—not Patty and definitely not Robin— knew the least little thing about the other. Questions as basic as **What's your favorite color?** or **Who was your favorite rock band when you were twelve?**

had obviously been ignored. And if by chance either subject was touched on before the frantic removal of clothing, the responses would be short answers with no follow-ups along the lines of **Why Duran Duran?**

Of course, some people went out and got married without bothering to dig deeper and ask **why** questions.

As for Patty and Robin, sooner or later they were going to wake up in bed together, orgasmed out, and then, look out. As soon as they started using their mouths to talk, all those little bubbles of happy fantasy were going to start bursting. Patty would realize—the hard way—that the man she'd welcomed into her arms didn't exist, that the real Robin couldn't hold a candle to her idealized, imagined version.

Or maybe she'd never see her mistake and spend lots of time crying and wondering why her Prince Charming had suddenly "changed."

And Robin, well, he'd leap out of bed and hit the ground running. He was one of those super-insecure guys who hid all his self-doubt behind good looks, fast talk, and that hyper-confident attitude. He was one of those guys who rarely stopped moving, who never let anyone get too close, terrified of all that might come to light if he opened up and let someone in.

As for his sister . . .

Cosmo rose to his feet as Mercedes marched her red-hot bod up the aisle, the elderly man in tow.

Cos had had his share of close encounters with her type before. He knew without asking that her two favorite words were **me** and **now.** Although it **was** possible that she actually cared about this movie she was making, as well as this old man.

" . . . round-the-clock bodyguards," she was saying to Jack Shelton, "and Chief Richter here is the winner who pulled the first night shift."

"I'll be here only until 0200. Vinh Murphy'll be replacing me then," Cosmo reminded her. Tonight was something of an exception. Once they got the team set up, they'd alternate shorter and longer shifts, with irregular end times. The key was not to get into any repeated, regular patterns that could be anticipated by anyone watching the house.

"Vinh Murphy's a former Marine," Mercedes told Jack. "I'll also be spending lots of time with James Nash and Tess Bailey, former Agency, and Larry Decker, who's a former Navy SEAL like Chief Richter—you know, the commando types who got so much spin during the wars in Afghanistan and Iraq?"

"A chief in the Navy. Eureka." Jack's dark eyes twinkled, young in his wrinkled face, as he smiled at Cosmo. Slender and slight of build, he still stood arrow straight—time hadn't stooped his frame in the slightest. His suit was obviously new and hand-tailored. Cosmo didn't doubt for one second that, should he flip through the pages, he'd find similar styles in the most recent issue of **GQ.**

"Silly me," Jack continued, "here I was trying to figure out exactly how a Richter could've become a Native American tribal leader. Of course, I've lived long enough to know that anything's possible."

Cosmo shook the elderly man's hand. "It's an honor to meet you, sir. I'm familiar with your work."

Mercedes and brother Robin did a visible double take, both of them looking at him with varying degrees of surprise and shock. Cosmo could practically read the producer's mind. **Aha. So that's why the Wonderbra and bootilicious miniskirt haven't produced the requisite amount of drool.**

Cosmo almost laughed out loud. People were so quick to judge, so willing to leap upon the most obvious conclusion.

Most of them, anyway. Patty was oblivious, smiling dreamily at Robin.

"Now, isn't this intriguing," Jack murmured, still holding tight to Cosmo. "But note, children, that he didn't say he's a fan, like, **Ooh, Mr. Shelton, I've been such a fan for years.** My guess is he got this assignment, did his homework—looked me up on the Internet Movie Database—and realized I'd dressed the sets of some of his favorite pictures." He patted Cosmo's hand. "He's three hundred percent hetero, but the two-second fantasy that he might not be was lovely. Thank you, darling." He turned to Mercedes. "If you've got to have one of those terribly clichéd affairs with one of your bodyguards, this is the man for the job. Of course, I haven't met the others, but how can they even come close? He's delicious."

"Yeah," Mercedes said. "Thanks a million, Jack. Look, I need you to be really careful, okay? If you get the sense that anyone's following you, or if you get any weird phone calls or threatening e-mail—"

"I'll make sure I let both you and HeartBeat know," Jack said. "Although Scotty might not appreciate my sudden acquisition of a Navy SEAL bodyguard." He turned to Robin. "Walk me to my car, Harold; my driver is waiting."

"Nice meeting you, sir." Cosmo found himself grinning. He was finally on an op where he could divulge the details—well, some of them—to his mother, and she was going to love hearing about this.

As Patty followed Jack and Robin out the door, Mercedes went down to the front of the little theater to collect a legal pad upon which she'd scribbled some notes.

"Sorry about that," she said on her way back up the aisle, obviously not sorry at all. "Jack does love to stir things up."

The woman didn't walk. She paraded. Sashayed. Slunk. Or was it slinked? Whichever it was, she did it. On heels that were ridiculously high.

Cosmo went out the door ahead of her, checking the hall both ways. It was empty. And dimly lit. Most of the bulbs in the ornate ceiling fixtures were out.

"We have three days, tops, to find an actor to play young Jack," she told him as he followed her up the stairs to the first and then the second floor. "If we don't find him by then, we're going to have to settle for Pierce Hugo."

There were too many shadows. Every lightbulb in this place needed an increase in wattage. Cosmo made a mental note to tell Decker.

Mercedes was on her way into the suite that made

up both her bedroom and her private office, but he stopped her. He stepped in front of her, opened the door, flipped on the light switch, and quickly scanned the room. The desks were all open, more like tables, and impossible to hide behind.

There were framed movie posters on the walls, including that of **Hell or High Water,** the low-budget **Blair Witch** knockoff that had kicked her career from zero to sixty before she'd turned twenty.

Apparently one of the problems with being an overnight success was the difficulty in making lightning strike twice. There were two other movie posters on her wall that carried her name as producer, but Cosmo hadn't heard of either of them.

He went through her office to her bedroom beyond, and into the bathroom, too. She kept the place fairly neat, but both her dresser and bathroom counter were cluttered. Perfume, makeup, hair care products, lotions . . . Panty hose and bits of silky underwear hung on the towel racks.

No doubt about it, a woman lived here.

The big bathroom had no windows. This was the predesignated safe room in the house. If there was trouble—a code red situation—Jane would lock herself in here until reinforcements arrived.

"Oh, come on," she was scoffing as he came out of the bathroom. "If someone really wanted to kill me, they wouldn't break into my house and hide in here, waiting for me."

Probably not, but wouldn't they all feel foolish if they were wrong? Cos went to each of the bedroom windows, checking the locks. They were old, but still in good shape. He pulled the curtains closed.

"Do you not talk"—Mercedes' voice was sharper now—"because you're supposed to be blending into the background, or because you have nothing to say?"

He thought about that. "Both, I guess."

"News flash," she said, rearranging the piles on her desk, paper rustling, her movements broadcasting her frustration. "You don't blend in, Rambo, so you might as well stop trying."

"Name's Cosmo." He came back into her office.

"Yeah, see, that was a joke. What, do they remove your sense of humor when you—"

"It's an insult, in the Teams, to call someone Rambo."

She stared at him. "You're kidding."

"No, ma'am."

Mercedes laughed her disbelief. "Rambo's some kind of giant, ass-kicking hero and you think—"

"SEAL **team,**" he said. "It's called that for a reason. Guy like Rambo, goes off on his own . . ." He shook his head. "It's an insult. Don't call me that again."

She was wide-eyed. He'd purposely left out the **please** and he'd scared her. She swallowed before she spoke, and her tone was no longer flip. "I apologize. I didn't mean to—"

"Apology accepted." He nodded and moved back toward the door.

She pulled a smile out of her arsenal and picked up her telephone, pushing one button. "Hi, Patty, will you remind my brother that he's got a five a.m. call tomorrow? He needs to go to bed, soon." As she listened to whatever her intern had to say, she kept that smile in place, but it got decidedly strained. "Thanks," she said, and hung up.

"I'll be in the hall," he told her.

"Is that how it's going to work?" she asked, crossing her arms in front of her, obviously still rattled and choosing to express it as thinly veiled defiance. "You're just going to lurk outside my door?"

He stopped. Nodded. "Until we get the security system up and running, yeah."

"I work with my door closed," she informed him coolly.

"Just don't lock it."

"Sometimes I take my laptop into bed with me," she said. "If the purpose of all this is to make me feel more secure, I have to tell you that sleeping with my door unlocked isn't—"

"It is," he told her, as he realized suddenly what that phone call to Patty had been about. It was a message. To him. She was reminding him that her brother lived here, too, that she and Cosmo weren't alone in the house. She was actually afraid of him. "You can lock your door if you want," he added. "I'm sorry—I didn't mean to make you uncomfortable."

He could just blast right though that door with one well-aimed kick, if there was trouble.

"Thanks," she said, then rolled her eyes. "Thanks for giving me permission to lock my own door. God, I hate this."

"I'm here—we're all here—to keep you safe," Cosmo

said to reassure her, even though he didn't particularly like her. Because, Christ, she wasn't supposed to be afraid of him. "Your script . . . I read it. It's good. The movie's . . . It's going to be good."

Okay, and now she was looking at him as if he were a talking monkey in the zoo. What, didn't she think he could read? She didn't. She looked absolutely stunned that he'd actually read the script. Screw that shit. Disgusted with her, he headed for the door.

But she stopped him. "When's your next shift?" Mercedes flipped the page on her desk calendar to tomorrow's date.

"I'm not sure," he told her curtly. "Deck's making the schedule."

"I'm going to hold a press conference," she said, running a finger down a list of penciled-in appointments, "probably around four o'clock tomorrow. Any chance you can be there?" She looked up at him. "It's kind of a public thing, and, to be honest, I'm a little bit nervous about putting myself out there—at least for this first time like this. . . ."

To be honest, his ass. It was beyond obvious that she had some kind of ulterior motive for wanting him there.

"I'll bring it to Decker's attention," he told her.

She backed off, somehow knowing not to push. "Thanks. And . . . I'm glad you liked the script."

Right.

Patty hung around the office, watching the hands of the wall clock move closer to eleven.

She should have gone home hours ago, but Robin, who'd shouted, "Tell Jane I'll be back around nine-thirty," as he'd gotten into his sports car and followed Jack Shelton's limo out of the driveway, still hadn't returned.

This was crazy.

She knew it was crazy.

But all she could think about was when, when, when was she going to see Robin Chadwick again?

Jane had issued a warning about her younger brother during their very first interview. "His definition of long-term means he stays for breakfast," she'd told Patty. "Don't let him get too close."

But her very first day here, he'd picked up lunch, bringing her a selection of sandwiches and salads from the local deli. "I wasn't sure what you wanted," he told her with a smile that could only be described as sweet.

And Patty had found herself in a full swoon over a man who not only was gorgeous but who was going places fast. This was a man destined to be Hollywood's Next Big Thing, and maybe she had an overactive imagination, but it didn't take much to picture herself there, by his side, as he rocketed to fame.

She'd thought she'd see him again tonight if she stuck around, but it just kept getting later and later. She had to be on the set early in the morning—at five a.m. She'd read through tomorrow's pages seven times now, and she'd contacted all but three of the extras needed for the party scene.

She really had to go.

But Robin needed to be on set early, too. He had a

five o'clock makeup call. She shifted through the pages of schedules and . . . Yes. There was a car coming to pick him up at four-thirty.

He had to come home soon.

Patty's cell phone rang, and she lunged for it. Maybe Robin had gotten a flat tire and needed road-side assistance. "Hello?"

There was a pause, and then "I'm sorry," a male voice said. "Do I have the right number? Is this Patty Lashane? I was expecting an answering machine or voice mail . . ."

It wasn't Robin. Patty sighed. "This is she."

"I'm sorry to call so late. I just got home and got your message—I hope I didn't wake you."

"You didn't," she said. "You must be either Carl or Wayne or—"

"It's Wayne Ickes." He pronounced it "Ickies." Goodness, what a name.

She found his résumé and the form he'd filled out when he'd come for the extras casting. "Here you are. Are you available tomorrow at . . . Oh, we won't need you until noon."

"Noon's great. Absolutely. Thank you."

Patty told him the studio address and the check-in procedure. "You're all set," she said. "Thanks for calling—"

"Have you gotten used to the L.A. traffic yet?" he interrupted her to ask. "When we met at the casting call, you said you'd just arrived in town and that the crush on the freeways was blowing your mind."

"Oh," Patty said. "Yeah. No, I'm—"

"You said you didn't like driving in rush hour, even back in Tulsa," Wayne said.

"Oh. Yeah, that's—"

"And I said, my college roommate's sister lives in Tulsa and . . ." He laughed. "You don't remember our conversation at all, do you?"

She flipped over his résumé to look at his headshot. He was average looking, with brown hair, brown eyes, and a pleasant smile on an equally pleasant but otherwise unremarkable face.

He'd remembered she was from Tulsa, and she wouldn't have been able to pick him out of a police lineup if her life had depended upon it.

"I'm sorry," she apologized. "But I met over seven hundred actors that day."

"Don't worry about it," he said.

Beep.

That was the sound of Robin's car alarm being set, from out on the driveway. He was finally home.

"Hey, you know—" Wayne started, but she cut him off.

"I'm sorry, I've got to go." Sure enough, she heard voices in the foyer. Robin talking to what's-his-name, the scary-looking security man. "Tomorrow, noon," she reminded Wayne, and hung up.

Heart pounding, she went into the hall.

"I locked it," Robin said as the Navy SEAL—the one he thought of as the X-Man, because, like Cyclops, he normally kept his oddly pale-colored eyes hidden behind sunglasses—started down the curved center staircase.

"Yeah." The man came all the way down to the foyer anyway. "Thanks. I still need to check it."

"Be my guest."

Light gray. X-Dude's eyes were such a light shade of bluish gray that they appeared to be almost white. He looked a little like Neal McDonough's bigger, uglier brother.

As Robin watched, the SEAL checked the knob, but then threw the dead bolt—which he'd forgotten. "Oops," he said. "My bad."

"S'why I check," Cyclops told him, already starting back up the stairs.

"You ever think about getting into acting?" Robin asked.

He didn't break stride. "Nope." He gave Robin a nod. "Night."

Taciturn bastard—couldn't even take the time to say it properly.

Although it wasn't a good night. It was just another night that Robin had managed to get through without completely screwing things up.

All night long, he'd stayed far, far away from little Patty Temptation's apartment.

Instead he'd gone clubbing in West Hollywood with Harve and Ricco, two of his gay caballeros. He'd started hanging with Harve and company as part of his preliminary research for playing Hal Lord. He'd never played a gay character before—never gave too much thought to the entire alternative lifestyle thing.

So he'd watched a bunch of episodes of **Queer as Folk**—which had freaked him out a little—and had asked Harve, who'd done the special effects makeup on Janey's last movie, if there was even a modicum of truth in the Showtime TV series' portrayal of gay life.

Harve's response had been to take Robin clubbing.

And Robin had discovered that real gay bars weren't as "male only" as they seemed to be on cable TV. He'd also discovered that gay bars were a great place for a straight man to hang out. Because gay men had female friends who went clubbing with them. And most fag hags, contrary to what the name implied, were far from actual hags.

Tonight he'd danced with some young lovely named . . .

Crap, he'd already forgotten her name. She'd had a pierced tongue—that much he remembered. Which had made it hard to close his eyes and pretend he was with—

"Holy Jesus!" A shadowy shape was standing at the end of the hallway leading to the offices.

And okay, he'd thought he'd merely gotten his swerve on, but he must have miscalculated, because he was hallucinating now. Either that, or Patty really was standing there, backlit like an angel.

Either way, he was royally screwed.

"I'm sorry—" Yup, it was definitely her. "I didn't mean to scare you." She took a hesitant step toward him.

"No," Robin said. "That's okay, that's . . . What are you still doing here? You should've gone home hours ago."

"Oh." She was flustered. "I was working on . . . I'm sorry, I didn't realize it had gotten so late. . . ."

"You don't have to apologize." Robin was unable to keep from moving closer to her. "Just . . . don't let Janey take advantage of you."

"Oh," she said. "No. I wouldn't. I won't."

It was the freckles that did him in, he decided as he got into freckle-viewing range. Wide blue eyes, wispy blond hair, farm-girl complexion, willowy figure . . . Robin couldn't help himself—he touched her. Just one finger, along the baby smoothness of her cheek. "You are so lovely," he whispered.

She actually trembled, and he knew if he kissed her, she would willingly let him pull her back with him through the kitchen, through the swinging door into the darkness of the formal dining room that Janey never used and . . .

God, he wanted her. He discovered to his dismay that whatever relief he'd found with what's-her-name in the club parking lot had completely evaporated. He wanted **some**thing . . .

To his surprise, Patty took a step back so that his hand fell away from her. She met his gaze and said, "You've been drinking."

"True," he said. "I am aglow."

Her laughter was musical. "Robin! You've got an early call—"

"Have I missed a call yet?"

"No, but—"

"Do you know," he told her, "that when I'm Hal Lord, and I think about Edna Potter—you know, his high school sweetheart—I picture her looking just like you?"

Her eyes went soft. "You do?" she whispered.

Robin nodded. "Yeah," he said just as quietly, hypnotized by the softness of her mouth. She moistened her lips with the very tip of her tongue, and he nearly started to weep. She was so ready for this. He let his backpack slide down his arm so he could drop it onto the floor. "You know what would really help me?" He didn't wait for her to answer. "It would help if you kissed me, so I could have that to think about while I'm Hal and—"

Score.

She melted toward him and kissed him slowly, sweetly, a perfect first kiss. Not that he'd expected anything less from a twenty-year-old Hollywood movie intern with a head filled with classic big-screen romantic moments.

Her hands were on his shoulders, and he purposely didn't touch her, didn't pull her closer. He just let himself be kissed.

And kissed and kissed and kissed.

After weird and scary Cosmo Richter checked her room and went into the hall, Jane had gone into her bedroom and locked the door.

And finally kicked off her high heels.

God, but her feet hurt.

She'd peeled off her skirt, wriggled out of her too-tight bra top, and washed Mercedes' makeup off her face.

She'd taken a shower, then thrown on a T-shirt and boxers along with a pair of athletic socks to keep her feet warm.

As much as she had a sudden burning desire to surf the Internet for any information she could glean about Navy SEALs, she'd gone to work instead. Despite the fact that this no-Rambo thing fascinated her—and jeez, the comment about her script aside, could scary Cosmo be any more obvious about the fact that he so totally disliked her?—she had press releases to write, fax, and e-mail. If her feet had to hurt, if her entire life had to be turned upside down, then, damn it, her movie was going to benefit from this.

It was after ten before she got down to the work she was supposed to be doing—outlining that battlefield dream sequence she'd promised HeartBeat Studios.

At around eleven, she heard Robin come home. She heard Cosmo go downstairs, heard the two men talking, heard Cosmo come back up.

Robin had no doubt gone into the kitchen for a snack, except he didn't come upstairs. And he didn't come upstairs and he . . .

With a sudden sense of impending doom, Jane went to the window, peeked through the curtains and out onto the driveway . . .

Where Patty's car was still parked.

Damn it! Damn it!

She ran through her office, flung open the door, and came face-to-face with Cosmo Richter. He'd found a chair and set it out in the hall. He was on his feet instantly.

Shit!

She slammed the door shut in his face, ran back

into her bedroom. Cursing the entire time, she yanked open her lingerie drawer, grabbed the slinky night-gown on the top.

She shucked off her T-shirt and kicked off her box-ers even as she pulled the gown over her head. Hop-ping first on one foot and then the other as she took off her socks, she made her way to her closet, where her white silk robe hung—the one with the full 1930s-style train.

She slipped into it, tied the belt at her waist. She didn't have time for slippers—besides, she had less of a chance of killing herself if she went down the stairs with bare feet. She let her hair down, shaking it free and pocketing her ponytail holder as she ran through her office again.

This time when she opened the door, she flung her-self into the hallway.

He-who-was-never-to-be-called-Rambo was still on his feet.

"I need a snack," she said as she flew past him. He probably thought she was out of her mind, but she just couldn't bring herself to say, "I think my irresponsible brother is shagging my intern atop the conference table."

He followed her, of course, as she thundered down the stairs, rounded the end of the ornate banister and headed back toward the main offices, and . . .

Nearly knocked over Robin and Patty.

Who were standing there, talking. Saying good night.

With their clothes on.

"See you in the morning, then," she heard Robin say.

Patty had her big slouchy bag over her shoulder, her briefcase and car keys in her hand. "I'm sorry," she said to Jane, "did we wake you?"

Patty's cheeks were slightly flushed, and her eyes were sparkling. No doubt about it, the girl had been kissed. But now she was obviously on her way out the door.

Amazing.

"No, no . . ." Jane forced a bright, cheery smile. "Just getting a snack." She turned to look at her brother to admonish him for staying out so late, not to mention stinking of whiskey and beer, but she didn't need to.

Patty did it for her. Even more amazing. "Get to sleep," she said. "Really, Robin, it's going to be four-thirty before you know it. Everyone's counting on you to show up and be able to hit your mark. I know you don't have many lines tomorrow, but it's important that you're there and alert."

"Your wish is my command," Robin said, taking her hand and bowing deeply over it. "But I should walk you to your car."

Oh, no, no, no . . .

But before Jane could leap upon him and put him in a full nelson, Patty spoke.

"I'm perfectly safe," she said, "with what's-his-name—the other guard—out there."

"His name is PJ," Jane said. "Patty, good night. Robin, upstairs."

She took his arm and pulled him toward the stairs as Cosmo followed Patty to the door. The girl sent one last glowing look in Robin's direction before slipping out into the night. Jane heard the SEAL locking up behind her as she focused on helping Robin navigate the steps.

"Didn't we just have a conversation where you promised me you'd stay away from her?" she whispered from between clenched teeth.

"What?" Robin was all wounded innocence. "That means I can't even talk to her?"

"Talk, yes," Jane hissed. "Suck face, no. What is wrong with you? One girl. Stay away from just one girl. This one girl. That leaves, what? One million, two hundred thousand and fifteen twenty-year-old girls in the greater Los Angeles area? I ask you this one small favor and—"

"I'm sorry, I tried, but I can't do it," Robin admitted as they reached the second-floor landing. He held on to her with earnest intensity. "Janey, I swear, this one's different. She's special. I think I'm completely in love with her."

"Yeah, well, I think you're drunk," Jane told him. "Again."

"What if she's the one?" Robin asked.

She steeled herself against his baby brother eyes. "Then she'll still be the one when we wrap in two months." She pushed him toward his room. "Sleep it off. We'll talk tomorrow."

"I'm really sorry," he said before he closed his door.

Yeah, sorry, right.

Jane turned to see Cosmo waiting patiently at the bottom of the stairs—for her to come down and get her mother-loving snack.

God help her.

"I just lost my appetite," she said, heading instead for her room.

Somehow he made it up and over to her door just as she did. It was creepy how fast he could move when he wanted to.

He stopped her with a briefly placed hand on her elbow. "I need to go in first."

She stood there in front of the door to her room, wondering inanely if he would tackle her if she simply ignored him. Or if she made a run for it, screaming, "You'll never catch me, Rambo, Rambo, Rambo. . . ." Instead, she said, "You're kidding."

"No."

It was funny. He'd answered as if she were seriously asking. But she knew before the words left her lips that he wasn't kidding. He wasn't capable of kidding. Cosmo-the-humorless never kidded about anything.

"Why?" she asked, her frustration with Robin, with HeartBeat Studios, with the idea that the Freedom Network's crazy-ass, neo-Nazi beliefs could impact her life this way all pushing her extremely close to her personal edge. "We were only downstairs for a few minutes."

There was that maddening pause as Cosmo-never-Rambo either considered her words, perfected his upcoming predictably terse response, or mentally composed another verse of his latest love sonnet. Yeah, right. She actually laughed aloud at the idea of this man writing poetry. But really, God only knew what was going on inside that head.

"You need to let me do my job," he finally told her.

"No one's in any screaming hurry to check Robin's room," she pointed out.

"No one's threatened to kill Robin," he countered—for him, a lightning-swift repartee.

"Actually, I did," she quipped. "Just this morning, as a matter of fact."

No reaction. No laughter. No smile. He just stood there, gazing down at her. When she'd worn her high heels, he hadn't seemed that much taller than she was. But as she stood there in bare feet, she had to tip her head back to look him in the eye.

And jeez, his eyes were a weird color. Jane had always thought of herself as being pretty good at staring contests, but this time she caved and looked away first. It was just too odd, staring into those eyes and having absolutely no clue as to what he was thinking.

She shifted out of the way, silent in her capitulation, half afraid that if she spoke, she wouldn't be able to keep herself from calling him Rambo.

Chatterbox that he was, he somehow managed to keep from speaking, too.

Once again, he flipped the light switch.

Perfect. Glaring lights, and her with absolutely no makeup on.

But he didn't so much as glance at her again. He walked through her office, checked the windows, then headed toward her bedroom.

Then he did look back at her, but only to make sure she was following. Apparently he didn't want to leave her out in the hall alone.

Jane went to the doorway between her bedroom and office, where the light was less harsh, as he went through his whole search-the-room routine. The shower curtain screeched as he pulled it back. Yeah, this was going to get really old, really fast.

As if reading her mind, he spoke. "Won't have to do this every single time after the security system is in place."

Lawrence Decker had told her that the installation would be started tomorrow.

But finished when?

As Cosmo came back toward her, he stepped carefully over the T-shirt, boxers, and socks she'd left scattered on the floor, briefly meeting her eyes as he did so.

Great. He was silent, not stupid. In fact, Jane suspected that he was really, really, **really** not stupid.

She moved aside to let him pass, more than half expecting him to close her office door behind him with no more than a nod as an unspoken good night.

But he stopped and looked back at her, his hand on the doorknob. "If the costume change was for me, it's not necessary."

She was so surprised, she spoke without thinking, automatically playing dumb. "Costume change? I don't know what . . ."

He didn't even bother giving her an "oh, yeah, right" look. He knew she knew he'd seen the clothes on the floor. He was just patiently waiting for her to finish making noise. She trailed off, and they stood there in silence as he made sure she was done.

"Thing is," he told her, "you're better off in darker colors, nonreflective fabrics. Cotton. Gray's good."

Like the T-shirt she'd left on her bedroom floor.

"If we did have a situation," he continued, "at night, wearing something like that"—he motioned toward her white robe with his chin—"you'd be a clear target. You own a pair of sneakers?"

She blinked at his sudden swift change of subject. "Cross trainers. Yes. Of course."

His smile came and went so quickly, she was left wondering if she'd imagined it. "Cross trainers. Right. Good." He nodded. "Keep 'em by your bed. In case there's trouble and we need to move fast."

"I look stupid in sneakers, I never wear them outside of the gym, and I don't want to move fast." She gave voice to her frustration. "I don't want there to be trouble. I don't want a 'situation.' I don't want any of this!"

"No one ever does," Cosmo said, and with another nod, he closed the door behind him.

CHAPTER
FOUR

"She really is doing quite well," Kelly Paoletti said as Cosmo gave her a boost up and into the passenger seat of his truck. She waited, carefully fastening the seat belt across her rounded belly, as he climbed behind the steering wheel. Only when he was inside did she add, "You're right about Tanya. She's very good. Her concern for your mother is absolutely genuine, but you should know, I talked to her while you were helping your mom set up the new computer keyboard. Tanya's not a nurse—she's a home health aide. And there is a pretty significant difference between the two."

Cos glanced at her as he headed north. "Bottom-line it for me, Kel."

"Tanya is providing exactly the level of care your mother needs right now. Technically, she's not supposed to administer any medication, but considering your mom doesn't need help remembering when to take her pills, but rather getting them from the pillbox to her mouth, that shouldn't be a problem."

Despite the fact that she looked barely older than J. Mercedes Chadwick's college intern, especially with her hair pulled back into a ponytail, Tom Paoletti's wife Kelly was a doctor—a pediatrician who understood the complicated intricacies of the health care system. She'd graciously offered to come out to Laguna Beach on one of her rare vacation days to check up on both his mother and her nurse under the pretense of a lunchtime visit.

When Cosmo had picked Kelly up this morning, down in San Diego, he'd warned her that his mother was crazy. She'd just laughed and told him that everyone thought their mother was crazy, that her mother was crazy, too.

His, however, was crazier than most.

Cos hadn't been able to go into exact detail, though, because Kelly had turned pale green. She'd insisted she was fine—it was only morning sickness—but she'd closed her eyes and attempted to sleep through it, and they'd made the ride in silence.

It was obvious she was feeling much better now—she had color in her cheeks, and her blue eyes sparkled with amusement. There was no chance she was going to sleep away the ride out to Malibu, where she and Tommy were going to spend the next few weeks relaxing.

Allegedly.

This visit to his mom had served a double purpose. Tom hadn't wanted Kelly lifting anything as he moved their vacation gear into the beach house. This way, when Kelly arrived, Tom's truck would be completely unpacked. She could go right onto the deck, sit in a lounge chair, and sip a virgin daiquiri.

"You need to check with your mother's health insurance company," Kelly continued, and he forced himself to pay attention, "and make sure they're not paying for a nurse while you're getting an aide."

"Yeah," Cosmo told her. "Thanks." He glanced at her. "I'm sorry that my mother . . . you know. Embarrassed you."

Kelly laughed. "She didn't. Honest."

Yeah, he was the one who had been dumbstruck with horror.

She giggled. "You've got to admit, it was pretty funny."

He just shook his head. His mother had taken one look at Kelly's physical condition and had jumped to the absolute wrong conclusion.

Cosmo had had to spell it out for her—no, Kelly was not his pregnant girlfriend whom he was bringing to meet her in order to discuss plans for their impending nuptials.

But who was she? And what was she doing with Cosmo? And why couldn't he marry her anyway? So what if it wasn't his baby—they could have another of their own. Clearly the young lady was capable . . .

Christ.

"She's sweet," Kelly said now. "And obviously single-minded in her determination to have grandchildren." She giggled again. "And I thought **my** mother was bad."

He'd had to explain to his mom in precise detail:

Kelly was already married. To Tom Paoletti, the former commanding officer of SEAL Team Sixteen and his current boss at Troubleshooters Incorporated. And since Cosmo was loyal to Tom to the point of being willing to die for the man, it was highly unlikely he was going to follow his mother's suggestion and try to convince Kelly to leave Tom and marry him instead.

"I guess you haven't brought your girlfriend home in a while," Kelly said. She was snickering now. "Understatement."

"Yeah," he agreed. "Try never." He laughed, too, rolling his eyes. "What a nightmare that would be."

"No—" Kelly started.

He cut her off. "Yes. Can you imagine if I really liked someone and . . ." He imitated his mother's slightly breathy voice. "I know you said you don't really enjoy Broadway musicals, but if you'd just listen to this song in **Jekyll and Hyde** where Lucy—she's the whore, dear. How do you young people say it these days? That's right, ho. She's the ho who sings about hope. . . . Oh, isn't that funny? The hopeful ho . . . Let me play it for you, dear, fourteen times in a row. . . ."

Kelly was laughing so hard, she was gasping for air. "She's not that bad. And so what if she's passionate about her music—that's wonderful."

"Yeah," Cosmo said. "I know."

They rode in silence for several moments before Kelly burst out laughing again. "I just . . ." she said, but couldn't go on because she was laughing so hard. It took her a moment to compose herself enough to speak. "I'm not laughing at you or her or . . ."

He sighed. "It's okay."

"It's just . . . I was sitting in her living room, thinking so that's why Cosmo's so quiet. You grew up unable to get in a word edgewise. And when your mother's not talking, the music is up so loud. . . ."

"And you wonder why I never bring anyone to meet her?"

"Cos, come on, you really don't need to worry about that. Anyone who cares about you will absolutely adore your mother, too," Kelly told him. "It's so obvious that she loves you. Clearly she just wants you to be happy." She paused.

Uh-oh.

"Are you still seeing . . . oh, God, I'm blanking on her name," Kelly asked. "I'm sorry. You know who I mean—the accountant."

"Stephanie," Cosmo said. "No. That was . . . No. She took a job in New York." He shook his head. "That was never meant to be long-term."

She reclined her seat a bit in an attempt to get comfortable, turning slightly to watch him as he drove. "You told me you liked her."

"Yeah," Cosmo said. He'd told Kelly a lot of things that he probably shouldn't have in the past nearly two years that they'd been unlikely friends.

He was friends with Tommy's Kelly. Who would've thought that? It had all started when Commander Tom Paoletti had been held under house arrest, charged with the unlikely treasonous crime of providing weapons to terrorists—among other equally ridiculous accusations.

Kelly had been hell-bent on running her own investigation, determined to find the proof she'd needed to clear her husband's name. At Tom's request, Cosmo had started hanging around her, riding shotgun, so to speak.

And when she dug just a little too deep, they'd both been injured from a car bomb that was intended to keep her from digging further.

She'd had some serious internal injuries and he'd badly broken his leg. Their friendship had solidified as they'd helped each other with physical therapy after getting out of the hospital.

"I did like Steph," Cosmo told Kelly now. "I guess she just never got that attached to me."

How could she have? They never spent any of their time together talking. Well, she'd talked. He'd listened. And before he'd gotten around to telling her how he felt, she'd found a replacement and left.

"I'm sorry," Kelly said.

He shrugged. "It happens."

They drove in silence for a mile or so before Kelly said, "So."

Cos didn't dare look up from the road. He just waited for it.

And it came, of course. "Sophia Ghaffari," Kelly said.

He laughed, swearing under his breath.

"Tom mentioned that you came into the office and, um . . . noticed her," Kelly said.

"Tommy told me she just lost her husband," Cos countered.

"It's not a just," she said. "I mean, okay, it hasn't

quite been a year, but it's close. I don't really know her that well, but she comes across as being lonely. At the very least, she needs a friend. And if there's anybody I'd trust to take it slowly with her, it's you. I think you should ask her to dinner."

They drove for a mile. And then another. She just sat there, watching him, waiting for his response.

"I don't know, Kel," he finally said. Dinner. With Sophia Ghaffari. Jesus God.

"How about this," Kelly suggested, because she knew exactly what he was thinking. "A dinner party. This week. At the beach house. Me and Tom. And John and Meg—"

"No, no, no, no," he said. "No officers from Team Sixteen. No way. Don't get me wrong, I love Johnny like a brother, but in that kind of formal setting, he'd be Lieutenant Nilsson and I'd be S-squared, all night long." Even without Nilsson's presence, Cosmo would be inclined to sit down and shut up. He sucked at small talk. He was still rolling his eyes at his attempt to tell Mercedes how much he'd liked her screenplay. He didn't even like the woman. There was nothing at stake, and he'd still ended up sounding like an idiot.

"It wouldn't have to be formal," Kelly argued. "We could have a cookout—"

"It would be hard enough with Tommy there." Cosmo laughed his disbelief. "I can't believe I'm actually considering this."

"How about Vinh and Angelina Murphy?" Kelly was not going to let go. "They just got back from their honeymoon, and I've been dying to hear all about their trip to St. Thomas. You know Vinh, right?"

"Yeah," Cos said. "He's part of the team on this op in Hollywood. I've never met his wife, though."

"She's great," Kelly told him. "You're going to love her."

That was a given.

She pushed harder. "It's a plan, then, okay? I'll call Sophia and find out when she'll get back from Denver and—"

"Whoa," Cosmo said. "Wait. I need to think about this."

"Think fast," Kelly said. "Or else while you're thinking, Bill Silverman or Jazz Jacquette or, God, Izzy Zanella is going to beat you to it and ask her out first. You're always grumbling about how you don't get to meet the nice women until after they're married to your friends."

Always? Cosmo had uttered those words only once to Kelly, obviously in a moment of insanity.

"Can we stop talking about this now?" he asked, desperation leaking into his voice.

"Think fast," Kelly said again.

He could feel her watching him again as he drove. One mile. Two.

"What's on your schedule for later this afternoon?" she finally asked.

Thank you, Jesus. "After I drop you off in paradise," Cosmo told her, "I'm heading into L.A. Mercedes—the producer—asked the entire team to show up at some kind of meeting over at the studio at 1630."

"Mercedes Chadwick, right?" Kelly mused. "I've read about her, I don't remember where . . . **People** magazine, maybe? What's she really like?"

"Baby's got back," Cosmo said. "Her body could make a dead man dance." He could see that he'd surprised her, so he tried to explain. "She's this really intelligent woman, an awesome writer, but that's not what she wants the world to see. She hides behind her knockout body: cleavage set on stun and belly button ring always in full view—you know what I mean?"

Kelly nodded, sighed. "Yeah. I've met too many women like that in California, unfortunately."

"Most of the time, I don't like her very much."

She looked at him, eyebrows up. "And the rest of the time . . . ?"

Figures Kelly would pick up on the fact that he'd said **most** of the time . . .

"A five six seven eight!" Cosmo said, then sang a few bars of the instrumental riff of the opening dance number from **A Chorus Line,** and she laughed.

Yeah, Cosmo was far from dead. And where J. Mercedes Chadwick was concerned, he was just a little too ready to break into a dance.

Robin Chadwick looked incredible in his paratrooper uniform, his hair slicked back from his face in a classic forties style.

His scene had wrapped an hour ago. Any other star would have left by now, but several of their extras hadn't shown up and Robin was filling in, careful to keep his back to the camera at all times.

He stood with a small crowd of extras, all wearing period clothing, on a set dressed to look like a night-club in London in the late winter of 1945, listening as the director gave instructions for the upcoming shot.

Patty would've liked nothing more than to stand there, clipboard clutched to her chest, dreamily reliv-ing last night.

When she'd kissed Robin Chadwick . . .

He'd wanted more. He'd pulled her with him into the kitchen, into the darkness of the formal dining room that was never used and . . .

There definitely would've been more to relive this morning, if it hadn't been so late and his on-set call so early.

She'd caught him watching her when she arrived at the studio today. He'd smiled, and her heart had gal-loped in her chest.

She'd nearly gotten knocked over by one of the crew. "Heads up, watch out, coming through! Hey, you there, girlie with the time to stand still! Can we switch jobs?"

Outside of the actors, who spent most of their time waiting for action to be called, no one stood around on set. At least not on this set.

Patty had been running all morning, all through lunch, too—the one block of time that Robin, who was also one of the movie's producers, had been free. She'd felt him watching her, but she hadn't found more than a spare few seconds to give him a breathless hello.

Would this day ever end?

Patty put her clipboard under one arm as she carried two coffees—one black, one with extra milk and sugar—across the studio.

One of her many jobs was to make sure all guests to the set were comfortable—and that they stayed seated in a special area, out of the way of both actors and technicians.

Jack Shelton was here today, as was that FBI agent, Jules Cassidy.

With his stylishly short hair, trim athletic body, and soulfully dark brown eyes, Jules was nearly as cute as Robin. He'd told her when he'd arrived that Mercedes had called and asked him to meet her over here this afternoon.

That was news to Patty, but then again, as a lowly intern, she was often the very last to know.

After introducing them, she'd seated Jules next to Jack, hoping he wasn't one of those former military types who got all freaked out by the idea of an openly gay man. Because despite his advanced age, Jack was flaming. No doubt about it. Especially when he greeted Jules with "And aren't you just absolutely adorable?"

"Can I get you anything else?" she asked after delivering their coffee. When she'd approached, they were talking and smiling in agreement. The FBI agent didn't look as if he were eager to run screaming away. He was far cooler than she would have been—Jack Shelton made her nervous.

"Settle!" came the cry from the assistant director.

"That means you need to get comfortable fast," she quickly told Jules. Jack had been on set plenty of times in his long, weirdly colorful life, and knew the drill. "She's going to call action soon, and at that point you can't speak or even move—not even to shift your weight. I'm sorry, but is your cell phone off?"

Jules nodded. "It's on vibrate."

"Oh," Patty said. "No, I'm sorry, but even that makes too much noise. I'm going to have to ask you either to step outside or—"

His smile was warm and quite possibly a little flirtatious. My goodness, he was good-looking. "No problem." He turned off his phone. "Actually, I've been on a soundstage before, so—"

"And. . . ." the director called loudly, drawing the word out. Patty put her finger to her lips, then closed her eyes. "Action!"

They'd already filmed this very same segment—two lines of dialogue and a reaction shot—so many times that she took the opportunity to rest. And have her favorite daydream.

Robin, winning the Oscar for Best Actor for his portrayal of Hal Lord in **American Hero.** He'd take the stage and thank his sister and HeartBeat Studios, as well as his supporting cast. And then, right there, on prime-time television in front of billions of viewers, he'd ask Patty to make his life truly complete by marrying him.

Photos of her face with tear-filled eyes, her hand over her mouth in heartfelt surprise, would be on the front page of every industry-related publication for the next week and a half—followed by invitations to lunch and job offers.

Patty Leshane Chadwick, associate producer.

As for Oscar night, she and Robin would attend endless after-parties, schmoozing with everyone who was anyone in Hollywood. Then, as dawn lit the morning sky, they'd go to the best party of all—a private party at the beach house they called home, where they'd make slow, glorious love until they fell asleep, exhausted, in each other's arms.

Much in the way they were going to, tonight.

She was determined to make it happen.

"And cut!"

The set came to life again. Assistants and technicians who'd been frozen in place by the command to settle now prepared to shoot the scene again, moving the camera back to the starting point.

Patty turned back to Jules. "Were you part of the team investigating that Russell Crowe thing a few years back?"

He blinked at her with his enormously long, dark eyelashes. "Excuse me?"

"You'd said you'd been on set before, so—"

"Oh," Jules said, "right," as he realized she was continuing the conversation they'd started before the call for **action.** "No. No, I, um"—he cleared his throat—"lived with an actor a few years ago, and, uh, he was in this little indie movie that was filmed in New York, and—"

"Excuse me."

Patty turned to see one of the extras standing beside her, a young man whom wardrobe had dressed in an American Army Air Corps uniform, complete with captain's bars. It was pretty surreal that she knew that—just a few weeks ago, she hadn't been able to tell a Marine sergeant from a four-star Army general. Now she could actually read rank.

This captain wore his brown hair slicked back from his face, and he juggled his hat into his left hand as he held out his right to shake. "Hi. Miss Leshane. I'm sorry to interrupt—"

"Patty," she corrected him.

"Patty," he echoed with a warm smile. "I am sorry to bother you, but every time I've had a break, you've been on the phone, so, I thought this would be . . . We were just given five, so I thought I'd come say, well, hi. I'm Wayne."

"Wayne," she repeated. Oh, God, was she supposed to know a Wayne? Was there a special guest who was on set today as an extra? She was pulling a total blank.

He looked amazingly unfamiliar, with brown eyes and a nice smile, good teeth—of course all American actors in L.A. had good teeth.

"Wayne Ickes," he said, which sounded a small bell of recognition. She'd heard that name before, but where? "We spoke on the phone last night?"

Bingo. Right before Robin had returned home.

Right before that incredible, amazing, toe-tingling kiss that had turned her world, her life, her hopes and dreams completely upside down.

"College roommate's sister lives in Tulsa . . . ?" he tried, because she was still standing there, gaping at him.

"Yes," Patty said, realizing he was still holding on to her hand. "Right. Wayne. Of course. I'm sorry. . . ." She pulled her fingers free.

"It must be hard to recognize any of us," he said, giving her a good excuse. "You know, with the uniforms, and the hair . . ."

"Right," she said. "Yeah." He was sweating, poor kid. "You must be dying, wearing that, under the lights."

"Oh," he said. "No, it's not bad. It's kind of cool, actually. I mean, not cool cool, because it **is** pretty warm in here, but it's . . . See, this was my grandfather's uniform. It's the real thing. Which is probably why I was hired—because I had my own uniform. Not that I'm complaining. A job's a job and . . ." He rolled his eyes. "Sorry, I must sound like an idiot."

"No," she said. He was actually kind of cute, the way he was falling all over himself. She gave him a "gotta run" smile, but he mistook it for an invitation to keep chatting.

"My grandfather flew a B-29 Superfortress—a long-range bomber," he told her. "He was stationed first in India, and then in the Mariana Islands. This was his winter uniform—he rarely wore it, I mean, considering where he served."

"That is really cool," she lied. Her eyes had started glazing over at **long-range bomber.** It **would** have been cool if only there were more hours in the day.

Everyone had their own important story that they just had to share, but she had a list of forty things that she had to do **right now.** On top of that . . . She scanned the set, searching for . . .

Robin. He was finally coming over to her, working his way through the crowd. She met his eyes across the room, and he smiled and her heart leapt and . . .

"My schedule's nuts, too. I work over at Cedars-Sinai. The hospital. I'm an orderly. It's a good job—not the most glamorous, I know, but I like helping people and my boss is flexible. Anyway, I was thinking if you weren't busy one of these nights," Wayne was saying, flipping his hat over and over, "there's this great place that serves the best barbecued—"

"Excuse me," Patty interrupted him. **Weren't busy one of these nights**— what a joke. "I'm sorry, but I need to . . ." She pointed toward Jack and Jules. And Robin, who had made his way to them, and was shaking hands with both.

Wayne was immediately contrite. "Oh, no, **I'm** sorry. I didn't realize this wasn't—"

"I'm just so overwhelmed and . . . Did you need something? One of those forms for additional pay?" The costume department was providing an additional stipend for extras who came with their own period clothing. Someone named Carl Something had asked her for one of those forms about an hour ago, but now she couldn't find him to give it to him.

"No," Wayne said. "Thanks. I've already got that. I'll, uh, see you later."

Patty turned back to Jules and Jack.

And Robin.

". . . don't suppose you harbor some secret desire to become a movie star," Robin was saying to Jules, who was laughing and shaking his head.

"No, I'm happy right here on the sidelines, thanks," the FBI agent said.

"Oh, come on." Robin teased him the way he teased everyone. "You can't tell me—a guy with a face like yours—that there's not this part of you that doesn't look into the mirror and think 'I could be the next James Van Der Beek'—you know, thirty-something and still playing a teenager?"

"Yeah," Jules said, "thanks, but no thanks. My days playing a teenager are over. I did a number of undercover assignments, going into high schools, dealing with gangs. I just . . ." He laughed again. "No thank you."

"I'm not saying you have to play a teenager," Robin said. "Just that you could. It gives you range in terms of roles, you know?" He sighed. "It's just we're still looking for someone to play Jack and . . ." He turned to Patty. "Don't you think it's uncanny?"

She had no clue what he was talking about. Of course, anytime he got this close, all words—all thoughts—left her.

"Look at them," he continued. "Am I nuts or am I nuts?"

Patty didn't know what to say. But he was Robin—he didn't need agreement or acknowledgment or even confirmation that she'd heard him. Once he was running with something, he just kept going.

"Jack, my man," he said, "tell the secret agent here how overwhelmingly fun it is to make a movie."

"I do see what you're talking about," the elderly man replied. "But it takes more than a pretty face to make an actor. You, darling, more than most, should know that."

At last there was something she could say—a way to participate in this bizarre conversation. "Mr. Cassidy knows about making movies—he's been on set before," she told Robin. "His roommate is an actor."

"Was," Jules corrected, adding, "Not that he's not still an actor, because he is. We just no longer, um, live together."

"Come on, Patricia," Robin said. "Back me up here, baby. Don't you think Jules would make a perfect Jack? Haven't you seen those portraits of him in uniform? Jack, I mean."

Understanding dawned. Oh, dear. "I guess there's a slight resemblance," she said, unwilling to contradict Robin, even though she didn't see it at all. Although, okay, yes, both men were compact and trim—short, in blunt non-Hollywood-speak. But Jack was effeminate and Jules was hot.

He was also a high-ranking federal agent.

"Your sister called and asked me to meet her here." Jules now changed the subject. "Any idea what that's about?"

Robin shook his head. "It could be anything from letting you know that she had four hours free last night, so she flew to Idaho and personally took out the leader of the Freedom Network, so thanks, she won't need your assistance anymore, to maybe she noticed your uncanny resemblance to our Jack so she's drawn up a contract and filled out your SAG application for you, or—"

"Places!" came the call.

"Gotta run," Robin said. He shook hands with Jules again. "Think about it. As Jack, you'd get to do a big-screen kiss with me. How's that for enticement?"

He waggled his eyebrows at the FBI agent while, aghast and amused, Patty exclaimed, "Robin!"

Fortunately Jules Cassidy had a sense of humor— he was laughing.

Robin turned to face her, walking backward, away from them. "You're coming back to the office later, right? For the dailies?"

"If you want me to." She ran to catch up with him.

"I want," he said, and the heat in his eyes sent her heart into triple time again. He leaned closer to her and lowered his voice. "I have to talk to you, baby. Privately." He laughed softly, ruefully. "Which is going to be ridiculously hard with Janey breathing down my neck."

"Maybe," she said, and her voice came out little more than a whisper. She had to clear her throat. "Maybe you could come over to my place? I mean, later tonight?"

He made a sound, as if he were in serious pain. "God, baby," he said. "You're killing me. I don't think that's a very good idea . . ."

"I think it's a great idea," Patty whispered. "My place, at eight."

He didn't say yes, but he didn't say no, either. And then she had to turn away, hurrying toward the door as she saw Jane and her bodyguards enter. She could feel Robin's eyes on her all the way across the room, and she knew he'd be there.

Patty laughed aloud at her amazing good fortune.

"What's with the TV crews in the parking lot?" PJ Prescott asked Decker as he joined the team already gathered in the studio.

Cosmo was just a few steps behind him, and Deck waited for the SEAL chief to move close enough before he gave his response. "Ms. Chadwick's giving a press conference in just a few minutes."

Cosmo was unflappable as usual, but PJ's eyebrows rose. Deck himself had to shake his head at the absurdity of the words that had just left his mouth.

Nearly all the ops he'd ever been on had been covert assignments. First for the Navy SEALs, then for the Agency, and now for Troubleshooters Incorporated, almost all of his deployments had been quiet ones. As in no fireworks or twenty-one-gun salutes to celebrate going wheels up; no ticker tape parade upon return home. And no talking about where he was going or where he'd been to anyone, not even to his live-in girlfriend—back when he'd had a live-in girlfriend. Forget about holding a press conference.

But this was Hollywood. Tom Paoletti had warned Deck that this job might be a little different. Mercedes Chadwick was high profile. In fact, she actively sought the limelight.

The traditional response to receiving a death threat was to lie low. The average threatee went into hiding. Very few people sent out press releases about it the way Mercedes had done.

"It must be a slow news day," Murphy commented. The former Marine was sitting on some kind of packing crate next to Dave and Lindsey, the seventh and eighth members of Deck's team. Dave Malkoff was former CIA—enough said. And at barely five feet tall, with her timid-seeming, nearly constant smile, Lindsey Fontaine looked to be the least likely bodyguard in the entire history of personal security. But her seven very productive years with the LAPD proved that looks could deceive.

"This really going to happen outside?" Cosmo asked.

"Yeah," Decker said shortly. "Believe me, I advised against it. . . ." He shook his head again.

He'd advised against having a press conference today, period, let alone holding it anywhere but indoors. But apparently bringing the reporters inside would disrupt the movie's shooting schedule. And, also apparently, keeping to the schedule, as well as promoting this movie, were more important than a lot of things. Such as remaining not dead.

He'd urged Mercedes to give them more time to set this up. With a little advance notice, they could have done this in a way that guaranteed her safety. They could have requested a list of names of attending reporters from the various news agencies, run a security check on the individuals, set up metal detectors, searched all the equipment being brought in to a safe, secure, locked-down location . . .

She'd laughed and laughed. A list of names? For a press conference? Apparently the idea wasn't just to catch the news editors' attention with a fresh, different story, but to make it as easy and enticing as possible for the reporters to attend—not time-consuming and difficult. Because, gee, that lighthearted story about the baboon and the llama that appeared to have fallen in love over on the set of **Doctor Dolittle Part Seventeen** would suddenly seem pretty interesting, especially since it wouldn't take four hours of equipment searches to gather enough footage for a fifteen-second sound bite on the evening news.

Did Decker know how many movies were in production in this town right this very minute, all sending out press releases? Mercedes had asked him. Did he have a clue exactly how many production companies were vying for the media's attention, dying to create some early buzz about their project?

Apparently he did not.

They'd come to a compromise by erecting a tent just outside the studio door.

It was not the best setup, but it wasn't the worst, either. They'd be surrounded on three sides by the big, warehouselike windowless soundstages, and by a narrow parking lot on the fourth. With the tent overhead and several team members stationed on the roof, there was virtually no threat from a sniper. As for short-range attacks, everyone on the studio lot had to pass through the main gate and get checked in.

It didn't mean an assault couldn't happen. But it was far less likely.

"Sunglasses on," Decker told his team. "If you get asked a question by a reporter—any question at all, including, 'Is the sky blue?'—your answer is 'No comment.' Is that understood?"

He waited for a murmured acknowledgment from them all before he continued. "Radio-up, but let's keep the on-air chatter to an absolute minimum."

"Jesus," Dave said, his voice filled with wonder.

He was staring across the cavernous room, and Decker turned to see what had captured his attention so completely.

Mercedes Chadwick was walking toward them like a queen with her entourage behind her. The blond college girl with the clipboard trailed behind FBI agent Jules Cassidy, who followed Bailey and Nash, the last two members of the Troubleshooters team to arrive. Good. They were all here. They could get this over with.

"Jesus," Dave said again, his glasses all but fogging up. "Is that . . . ?"

Ah, yes, Dave hadn't yet met the client.

"That's her," Decker said.

She was crossing the enormous soundstage, with her miles of legs and her shiny, bouncing brown hair down loose around her shoulders in artful disarray.

Lips fully glossed, makeup applied to feature her exotic eyes and perfect, smooth skin, Mercedes was dressed in an updated version of the pin-striped suits Decker's great-uncle used to wear when he worked at the bank, but in place of trousers, she wore a skirt. At least he thought it was a skirt. It may have been a headband.

Her jacket was tailored to accentuate her very female form. Although it covered her belly button ring, it was held together in front by a single button set nearly at her waist, giving the jacket a deep V neckline.

Unlike Uncle Lloyd, Mercedes Chadwick was not wearing a crisply starched white shirt beneath her jacket. In fact, as far as Decker could tell, she was not wearing anything beneath her jacket at all.

Decker knew it was impossible for someone to move in classic movie slo-mo, but somehow this woman managed to imitate the effect. Not only that, but there was a nearly palpable wake of pheromones trailing behind her.

Beside him, Dave had managed to close his mouth.

The entire team had fallen silent as they'd put on their radios—miniature earpieces and tiny wireless microphones that attached to their shirts. There was none of the usual chatter or even "Testing one-two-three." For several brief moments, Decker could have sworn that Cosmo, one of the quietest and the least likely of all the men that he'd ever met to break into song, was actually humming a vaguely familiar melody under his breath. Was it that old Sly tune, "Dance to the Music"?

"Wow," whispered Lindsey, who hadn't met Mercedes yet, either. "She's tall."

Yeah, right. They were all standing there marveling at the woman's impressive height.

"Deck, hi!" Mercedes said in her musical voice. She could do sincere really well. So many other Hollywood types pushed too hard, overacted, and ended up fawning. She sounded genuinely pleased to see him. "Thanks so much—all of you—for coming out here this afternoon."

She held out her hand, and Decker shook it, and then he **was** marveling at her height, because she was towering over him. She hadn't been this tall yesterday, had she?

Decker shook Cassidy's hand, too, then introduced them both to Dave and Lindsey. He started in on the names of the rest of the team, but Mercedes cut him off. She remembered everyone without any prompting, making a point to shake their hands.

Each time she leaned forward, her jacket was on the verge of gapping. If she leaned just a little farther . . . Nope, not quite.

It was totally inappropriate and absolutely riveting, and Decker realized that that was the movie producer's intention. Her outfit, including her fourinch heels—height mystery solved—was designed to draw and hold attention. No doubt she knew exactly how far—to the millimeter—she could move before exposing herself to the world. She wasn't going to let that happen, but most people wouldn't realize it, and all eyes would remain on her, waiting, hoping . . .

He had to admire her for her understanding of human nature—as well as her ability to manipulate the system to her advantage. It didn't make him any less annoyed about the press conference, but it did drive home the differences between the two worlds in which they were used to operating.

"You weren't able to talk her out of this, either, huh?"

Deck turned to see that Jules Cassidy, the agent in charge of the FBI's investigation—the gay AIC; how had **that** happened?—had come to stand beside him. "No."

"I don't think it's likely there'll be trouble," Cassidy said, his gaze on Mercedes, too. He glanced at Deck. "Do you want to field any questions about security procedures, or should I?"

"You can," Deck told him, "as long as your answer is 'No fucking comment.'"

Cassidy smiled. "I'll be a little more diplomatic, but, yeah, that'll be the gist of it."

"Then be my guest," Deck said.

"Do I make you uncomfortable, Chief?" Cassidy asked—just whammo, balls out, point-blank—and no doubt calling Deck by his former military rank on purpose.

"Yes, but I'll get over it," Decker told him, because, yeah, as uncomfortable as he was with the idea of . . . Jesus . . . he'd liked what he'd seen of the guy's easygoing leadership skills so far. And how many times had he worked with an FBI agent who actually listened to outside input the way Cassidy did?

The expression that flashed over the other man's face made Deck realize that the honest answer he'd given was not one Cassidy heard all that often.

"Good," Cassidy said with a nod. "Excuse me." He turned away to take a phone call. He didn't thank Decker for giving him the respect that should have been his by right.

Which made Deck like him even more.

He turned away from Cassidy and back to Mercedes, who had ended up next to Cosmo. As Deck watched, she smiled up at the SEAL, leaning close as she clasped his hand and asked with what sounded like warm sincerity, "How's your mom?"

Cos, whose resting heart rate probably clocked in at about 22, gazed back at her expressionlessly as she added, "I was talking to Tess today and she said your mother broke her wrists—both of them? My God . . ."

He finally nodded. "Yeah," he said, providing no further details as he took back his hand. It was pretty obvious that he didn't think her worthy of the effort required to have a full conversation. "She's improving, thanks."

But Mercedes didn't seem to notice. "I'm so glad." She turned to look at Decker. "Are we ready to go?" But then she turned back to Cos. "You'll be close to me, right? When we go out there?"

Deck stepped forward and answered for him. "Actually, out of all of us, Richter is best positioned toward the back." The SEAL was on leave, and the Navy really couldn't tell him what to do on vacation, but Team Sixteen had a new commanding officer. Deck knew from experience that the last thing Cosmo would want was to piss off the top brass by appearing in a picture on the front of **USA Today.**

"Oh." She caught her lower lip between her teeth. "We can't cancel this, and we can't move it inside, so don't suggest it, but . . . I'm really nervous. I didn't think I would be, and . . ."

On the other hand, in any pictures taken, even if he was in the front, Cosmo would be one of a group. With his sunglasses on, he'd be unidentifiable.

"I know this sounds crazy," Mercedes said, "but . . ."

It wasn't crazy at all. When it came to protecting someone who'd received a death threat, there were all kinds of psychological elements in play. It was important to remember that the person being protected had been thrust into a strange, new, extremely dangerous and frightening world. They coped with that in a myriad of ways, some of which could seem irrational or even nonsensical.

Deck's policy was to do whatever was possible to lower stress levels for the client. If she honestly felt better with Cosmo by her side . . . He looked at Cos, who shrugged.

"No one's going to be looking at me," he said.

And wasn't that the truth. All eyes were going to be on J. Mercedes Chadwick. "Okay," Deck said, then nodded at his team. "Let's do it."

The SEALs had a word for a situation gone out of control.

Goatfuck.

Although, in this case, Cosmo was pretty sure this entire press conference had been choreographed by J. Mercedes Chadwick. She'd played them. **I'm really nervous. . . . I know this sounds crazy. . . .**

She knew exactly what she was doing. She was totally in control. On her way up the stairs to the platform, she'd asked, "Do you have a girlfriend, Chief?"

"No, ma'am," he'd told her curtly, not that it was any of her business.

"You do now," she leaned in close to say as they stepped onto the makeshift stage, and the camera lights blazed like the surface of the sun, flashbulbs exploding.

But the dance wasn't done. She caught a heel on something. Or at least she pretended to. Cosmo moved instinctively, reaching out to keep her from falling, and then there he was, holding her tightly, with her arms up around his neck, and damned if he hadn't completely walked into that one, like a fucking puppet on a string.

Flashbulbs continued to go off, particularly when her lips brushed his cheek—she freaking kissed him for the cameras. "You saved me," she said loudly enough for the reporters to hear. "However can I repay you? Hmmm, I bet we'll think of something."

The crowd laughed, and even as they approached the podium, even as Mercedes smiled and stepped up to the array of microphones, Cos could see that a large portion of those lenses remained aimed at him.

Decker pulled him into the back, but it was too late. At the podium, Mercedes was saying something about Troubleshooters Incorporated, making it sound as if she were partying around the clock with her own private squad of men who were half James Bond, half Chippendale dancer, which absolutely put the icing on the cake.

Yeah, she'd planned for this to happen.

And he was the goat who was getting fucked.

CHAPTER
FIVE

Jules was feeling the brunt of his jet lag when he pulled into the hotel parking garage.

The sun had gone down hours ago, and several of the bulbs were out overhead, making it darker and far more shadowy in there than it had to be. Or maybe the bulbs weren't out. Maybe they'd been unscrewed. Maybe the kid who'd tried to mug him wasn't the only one who used this garage as a crime scene of choice.

Although if someone dared to hassle him now, when he was tired and hungry and, okay, yeah, a little depressed about being in L.A. all by himself, partnerless in every sense of the word, they were really going to regret it.

Jules got out of his car, grabbing his jacket and his briefcase from the passenger seat, but before he even turned around, he was aware that someone was behind him—someone who had been sitting on the front hood of a car over in the corner of the dimly lit garage.

The local police had advised him to find another hotel. Apparently they were currently having an increase in hate crimes against gays in this West Hollywood neighborhood—an ongoing backlash from the marriage issue. It was kind of funny, actually, the idea that a love strong enough to create a desire for a deep, permanent, legally binding commitment between two people could get other people riled up enough to injure, damage, or even kill.

Usually in the name of God.

Jules shifted his things to his other hand as he reached for his sidearm, flicking open the snap that secured it in his shoulder holster.

Shoulder holster. He was wearing a fricking shoulder holster, the bands black against his blue shirt, surely visible even in this dim light. It was possible that whoever was about to try to mug him was the dumbest perp in the history of criminal intent.

He kept his weapon holstered while he turned, but the grip was solidly against his palm.

"Whoa! Easy there, J. Edgar!" Adam stood in front of him, hands slightly raised. "I thought you might not be too happy to see me, but come on. . . ."

Adam stood in front of him.

Adam.

Who'd lived in their apartment with his new boyfriend while Jules was out of the country. Who'd packed up and moved out with the famous last words, "You know, J., you've really got to learn to lighten up."

Adam, who'd said that he'd loved Jules, but apparently hadn't loved him enough.

"What are you doing here?" Jules asked. God, Adam looked good. Healthy, like he'd been working out and eating something other than his usual junk food crap. His dark hair was longer than it used to be and it made him look younger than his twenty-seven years—no doubt a calculated move for an actor looking for work. He was dressed in faded jeans and an expensive leather jacket worn open over a white T-shirt, his trademark biker boots on his feet.

Of course. Some things never changed.

"I saw you on the news, figured you'd be staying here," Adam said with a shrug and a smile.

They'd always stayed at the Stonewall when they came out to L.A., a hotel where the garage had an elevator, accessible by key card, that went directly to the room levels, bypassing the main lobby.

Adam knew quite well that if he wanted to catch Jules, he'd have to wait for him here, in the garage.

"That wasn't very smart," Jules informed him as he snapped his weapon back down. "How long have you been sitting in here? Hours?"

"Yeah, well, I know it probably looks creepy, like Adam the Stalker, but I wanted to see you and I had some lines to memorize. I'm auditioning for this play—"

Jules slipped his arms into his jacket, adjusted his tie. "I was mugged in this garage yesterday."

Adam took a step toward him. "Oh, my God, are you all right?"

Jules took a step back. "Yes. Why are you here? What do you need?"

"Wow, J., that's harsh."

"What. Do you need?"

"Fuck you, I wanted to see you. It's been years, and . . . Jesus, you're an unforgiving fuck."

Jules, unforgiving fuck that he was, just stood there.

"I thought we could have, I don't know, dinner," Adam continued. "You do still eat, don't you? I mean, everyone has to—"

"I'm tired. I'm going to have something in my room."

Mercurial as always, Adam slid easily from angry to mocking to seductive. He smiled, quirked an eyebrow. "Well, hey, that works for me."

"Does it work for Branford?" Jules asked, but quickly cut himself off. Shit. Bringing Adam's current live-in into this would only serve to make him sound jealous and petty. Which would stoke Adam's already inflamed ego. "Look, I'm sorry—I'm tired. It was . . . interesting to see you, but I really have to—"

"I'm not with Bran anymore," Adam told him. "I haven't been for about eight months."

And there it was. The reason Adam was here. He'd come back to try to mess around some more inside Jules' head. And while Adam was extremely talented when it came to creative sex, it was the mindfuck in which he truly excelled.

He knew that Jules had rules about certain things, that he refused to hook up with people who were in so-called relationships, as open as they might claim them to be. He knew Jules wouldn't so much as have dinner with him if he weren't single.

Except that wasn't what he'd said, was it? He'd merely said he wasn't with Branford.

"So who are you with?" Jules asked.

"Right now?" Adam shook his head. "No one."

"You've been alone for eight months?" His skepticism echoed off the garage walls and low concrete ceiling.

"Of course not." Adam laughed. "After Bran, I bounced for a while. Why? You want a list?"

Jules just looked at him.

Adam was single, Adam was single, Adam was single . . .

And Jules would be the biggest fool in the universe to think that anything they started tonight would end any differently than it ever had in the past.

"I've changed, you know," Adam said quietly, capable, as always, of reading Jules' mind.

"Yeah," Jules said. "Your hair's longer."

Adam laughed again. "That's not what I meant, J."

"I know what you meant, **A.,**" he said, mocking Adam's habit of using cute nicknames as terms of endearment.

Adam looked away, perhaps actually remorseful. "Sorry. I just . . . I'm sorry."

Jules sighed. "Look, I'm sorry, too. I'm tired—"

Just like with a wild animal, with Adam it was dangerous to show any sign of weakness, of softening. Remorse morphed into a fresh assault. "But you've got to have dinner." Adam took a step forward.

Jules took a step back.

"Come on, can't I even have a hug?" Adam asked. "I mean, we were together for two years. Surely I rate at least a friendly hug."

"I can't do this," Jules said, but as Adam stepped toward him again, he didn't move.

And then Adam's arms were around him. God, oh God, it was as awful as it was wonderful and he dropped his briefcase and held on to Adam tightly, wishing to Jesus that his memory could be selective and he could forget about all the terrible times, about the anger and the jealousy and the bitter frustration of knowing that no matter what he did or said, Adam was never going to change.

"God, J.," Adam whispered, "you smell exactly the same."

"You don't," Jules said, turning his head to avoid Adam's mouth, getting a kiss on his ear instead.

"Yeah, well . . ." Adam let him go and stepped back.

Was it possible that Adam was as shaken as he was by something as simple as a fully clothed embrace?

"I've changed, remember?" Adam continued, trying to turn it into a joke. "Look, let's just ignore the fact that we're both single again and go out and get something to eat."

It was Adam's thoughtless assumption that bolstered Jules' resolve to keep his distance. True as it was, it was still goddamn arrogant of the prick. "You're so sure I'm still single?"

Adam blinked, but then laughed. "If you're not, where is he? Upstairs? And if he is, why are you still down here, talking to me?"

"Maybe he's back home in D.C. Maybe he's got a real job."

"Bravo," Adam said. "A direct hit."

"Or maybe I just met him a few days ago," Jules lied as he bent to pick up his briefcase, as he brushed it off. "Maybe I'm at that place where I'm starting something new, and it's magic, and the last thing I want to do is risk that by—"

"Maybe you're full of shit."

Jules nodded. "Yeah, maybe I am. But here's something that's not a maybe: You're not coming up to my room tonight. If that's why you're here, you should just leave right now." His delivery was good. He almost believed it himself.

"I'm here to have dinner," Adam said again. "To catch up." He cranked up the sincere. "I care about you, G-man. I have no idea what's going on in your life. Suddenly you're this high-profile FBI guy all over my TV and . . . I want to hear about it. That's all this is."

Yeah, right.

"That Indian place right down the street is still open. Remember how much you loved their malai kofta and chicken vindaloo?" Adam continued. "Or if you want, we could go somewhere else. There's this new House of Thai—it just opened, about two blocks over. I've been wanting to try it for a while."

"I'm tired," Jules said for the umpteenth time. He was truly exhausted, physically from the jet lag. And now he was emotionally drained as well, goddamn it.

"Let's go with Indian," Adam decided.

Maybe his being so tired was why he quit fighting and let Adam pull him out of the garage and onto the sidewalk.

Or maybe it was because it had been too damn long since he'd had decent chicken vindaloo.

Robin had to call Patty.

It was after eleven o'clock. Somehow eight o'clock had come and gone without his noticing, and now he was over three hours late for their rendezvous at her apartment.

Three was the night's magic number.

It took him three tries to get the coin into the pay phone slot, another three tries to dial.

Only to find that he needed three dollars and eighty cents in coins to complete his call.

Not to mention the fact that the band had started playing and he couldn't hear a thing.

He staggered outside to the phone in the parking lot, only to find he'd lost his quarter.

He dialed anyway, calling collect. Patty, his angel, wouldn't mind.

She accepted the call, of course. "Robin, are you all right?"

"Hey, baby," he said. "I owe you a . . ." He struggled to find the word. To pronounce it. "Apology."

"Where are you?" she asked. "Why aren't you using your cell phone?"

"I lost it," he reported, as the world tilted and he had to cling to the privacy shield around the phone to keep from losing his balance as well. "I think I lost my wallet, too. And my backpack. Shit, my script's in there, with all my notes. . . ." He shook himself. "Look, babe, I can't come over. Cuz we'll have sex and then Janey'll be all mad at me. See, I knew if I came to your place, even just to tell you that we can't have sex, I wouldn't be able to resist because I'm so fucking in love with you—"

"Oh, Robin," she said, her heart in her voice, which made tears spring into his eyes.

"So I came out here and got faced because I knew if I did, Carmin would take my car keys away from me and then I wouldn't be able to get over to your place, only I forgot to call you to tell you that I wasn't coming, but that's a lie because I knew if I called you to tell you I wasn't coming before I was faced, you'd talk me into it because I just cannot resist—"

"Where are you?" she asked.

"—you. I cannot. Cannot. See, even just talking to you now makes me want to drive over to see you because I—"

"No!" Patty shouted through the phone. He had to pull the receiver away from his ear, she was so loud. "Don't you dare drive anywhere!" he heard her say, her voice tiny but clear through the telephone speaker.

"Well, I won't cuz I can't, baby," Robin told her. "Carmin has my keys." Whoa, shit, hey there, maybe Carmin had his wallet and his phone. His backpack, too. Wouldn't that be cool?

"Thank God for Carmin, whoever he is," she said. "Robin. Tell me. Where are you?"

"The Tropicana," he confessed, knowing she was going to come pick him up, knowing he was going to end up doing exactly what he'd tried so hard to avoid, knowing he was exactly the fuckup Janey thought him to be, but unable to do a goddamn thing about it.

"Thank you," she said. "Thank you. Stay there, okay? I'm on my way."

Robin hung up the phone and lost his balance, sliding down to sit on the asphalt with his back against the concrete block building. A skinny man with a barbed-wire tattoo and cigarette with the world's longest ash on the end came over to use the phone.

"I tried," Robin told him. "I really, truly tried . . ."

Jane was still awake when the personal security team made a shift change.

She was still writing that blasted dream sequence, books and personal accounts of the Normandy invasion out and open on her bed, filmed footage on DVD from the History Channel playing silently on her TV.

She heard a car drive up, heard the front door open, heard PJ talking to whoever had come to replace him in the hallway outside her rooms.

It was supposed to be Cosmo Richter.

Jane was more than half hoping that this afternoon's circus in the media tent had been the last straw for him—that he'd request reassignment or at least demand to be placed on out-of-doors guard duty and thus avoid all future contact with her.

But now she definitely heard his voice, and she knew that even if he was leaving, he'd come here one more time to administer a verbal ass-kicking.

She'd taken it too far today, no doubt about that. Decker had been angry, too. But oh, God, every news program in the country had carried a clip of her press conference, most of them in a "lighter side" type segment, with a headline that played with the words **body** and **guard.** She'd even seen a brief story on CNN, and they hadn't even had a camera there.

That kind of national publicity was worth just about anything.

So what if Cosmo Richter hated her now and was here tonight to tell her that to her face. Big deal. He'd disliked her from the moment he'd first walked into her house, smug, superior bastard that he was.

Of course, cool dislike was a little different from the hot anger she'd picked up from him back in the studio, after the press conference. She'd felt his eyes burning into her back as she'd taken a call from one of the suits at HeartBeat Studios.

By the time she'd gotten off the phone, Cosmo was gone.

He was here now, though, no doubt to share the exact dimensions of his hatred for her.

But, God, just wait until tabloid photojournalists caught up with him. And they would. Even when the interest of the so-called respectable news venues waned, the tabloids would work to keep this story alive.

Sooner or later, Cosmo would have microphones thrust into his face and be asked everything from his opinion about Mercedes' legendary bad relationship with her mother—frequent fodder for the rags—to his favorite sexual position.

He was really going to hate her then.

Jane heard PJ's truck start out in the driveway, heard him pull away.

As the soft knock sounded on her office door—the

knock she'd been both dreading and expecting—Jane had to face the fact that she was completely alone in this house with Cosmo Richter.

Okay, Robin, time to come home. It was nearly midnight and tomorrow was going to be another long day.

But Robin didn't come home. And wherever he was, he wasn't answering his cell phone.

Cosmo knocked on her door again.

No doubt he'd seen the light on in her room as he'd pulled up.

Of course, she could pretend to be asleep. It wouldn't be the first time she'd fallen asleep with the light on.

Except she wasn't asleep, and sooner or later she was going to have to have this conversation with this man.

She was heading for the door when her cell phone rang.

She rushed back to her bed to get it. "Robbie?"

"No." The voice on the other end of her phone was Cosmo's. He sounded the same as always. Quiet. Un-emotional. "You going to open this door, or you going to wimp out and pretend to be sleeping?"

"I considered it," she admitted, as she turned on the overhead light in her office and opened the door. She found herself face-to-face with the man's broad chest. God, her bare feet were a mistake. She had to get him sitting down as quickly as possible to get them on even ground. "But I figured we may as well get this over with."

" 'Get this over with'?" he repeated, closing his

phone and slipping it into one of the many pockets of his cargo pants. He smiled at her and it almost made him look pleasant and friendly—except for the fact that his eyes were flat and cold. "Are you sure we're talking about the same thing?"

"Come in. Sit down." She motioned toward one of the chairs in front of her desk. "Can I get you a drink?"

"Sure, why not? Got beer?"

Jane opened the little refrigerator in her office. It was filled with Dr Pepper, guava juice, bottled water, and . . . yes. Way in the back. "Is Fosters all right?"

She turned, bottle in her hand, to find that Cosmo had disappeared.

"Great," he called. From her bedroom?

"What are you doing?" she asked, going over to the door and . . .

Dear God. He'd taken off his shirt, revealing a chiseled upper body that gleamed in the dim light from both her TV and her laptop screen. He'd actually taken off his shirt, and was over by her bed, as if . . .

"What are you doing?" she asked again.

He was in the process of unfastening the fly of his pants, button by button. He stopped halfway, looking over at her, his lean face seeming to have as many angles and sharp edges as his body. With his short haircut, he was all cheekbones and those strange, pale eyes. "What? You said you wanted to repay me." He came toward her, making no effort to refasten himself—was it possible he wasn't wearing any underwear?—and took the bottle of beer from her hand. "Thanks."

He twisted off the top, took a swig as he went back to the bed, and made himself comfortable upon it, ankles crossed and one arm up and back behind his head. Lordy, lordy, he was outrageously well toned.

"So, come on," he said. "Get changed. Don't get me wrong—the sweat shorts are cute, but the T-shirt leaves a little too much to the imagination, if you know what I mean. Got anything in red? I really, really like red."

For a man who in the past had kept his conversation to sentence fragments, Cosmo Richter wasn't having any trouble at all finding words tonight.

"Okay," Jane interrupted him. "I deserve this. I know it, but thank you, that's quite enough."

"Enough? What? You don't want to . . ." He gestured between the two of them. "You're not gonna . . . Oh . . ." he said as if it were only just dawning on him. "You only want several million people to **think** that you're in here with a highly skilled, well-educated professional, having gymnastic sex all night long. I see. How disappointing."

Jane sighed. "Okay, when you're done being sarcastic, could you please put your shirt back on and, you know, button up, so we can finish the lecture out in my office?"

"What, is my being in your bed like this a problem for you?" he asked. God, he was furious. She could see his pulse drumming in his neck.

She cleared her throat. "It makes me uncomfortable, yes."

"It makes you un**com**fortable," he said. "And it never occurred to you that using me for show-and-tell this afternoon might've made **me** uncomfortable? Or am I not supposed to care? I'm just supposed to . . . to . . . what? Swagger around, getting high-fived and"—he made a thumbs-up gesture—"because the entire Los Angeles area—including my mother—thinks I'm screwing some famous, sexually adventurous movie producer, like it's some kind of extra special notch on my belt?"

He was serious. He was also on his feet, pulling his T-shirt back on, thank God, his movements jerky with anger.

"Do me a favor," Cosmo continued. "Give my mother a call. Tell her there's a difference between screwing and getting screwed. And that my role in your little game here is definitely only in the getting-screwed category. Maybe if she hears it from you, she won't go rushing out to buy a mother-of-the-groom dress."

Jane laughed. She couldn't help it. "You're upset because of what your mother might think?" The laughing was definitely a mistake. At least she didn't call him Rambo, too.

"What does your mother think of you, Mercedes?"

Okay, they were so not going to go there. Her voice came out a little too sharp as she said, "Look, I really am sorry if—"

He sat back down on her bed. He'd set his beer bottle down on her bedside table. He'd barely had any of it, but he didn't bother to reach for it now. "Yeah. I really believe you."

Her control slipped. She may have misjudged him on some levels, but she sure got smug and superior dead-on.

"Okay, yes, you're right," she told him. "I'm not sorry. Not even close. In fact, I'm celebrating. A whole hell of a lot more people know about my movie tonight than they did this morning."

"Because of your reckless defamation of a company whose entire future rides on its professional reputation."

What? Was he kidding? Defamation? Forget about the fact that he'd actually used a string of four-syllable words, defamation didn't even come close. She'd given Troubleshooters Incorporated an incredible boost in visibility today.

"Because of the positive spin I put on this entire god-awful situation!" she shouted. "I hate this, in case you haven't noticed! I hate having you here—you and your extremely noninvisible friends!"

He got loud, too. Who knew Mr. Silent was capable of such volume? "You think we really want to be here, protecting your selfish, worthless ass?"

What? "Oh, don't stop there," Jane shot back at him, glaring down at him. "Why don't you make the insult complete? Strike at the heart of every woman's insecurities and call it a giant ass, too, you smug son of a bitch!"

"Very good," he said. He even managed to applaud

mockingly. "Make it be about your body. That's always worked for you in the past, hasn't it? A major distraction . . . I hate to break it to you, J. Mercedes Chadwick—Jesus God, can you be any more pompous with the name thing, **Jane**?—but you could be standing here naked right now. I wouldn't give a good goddamn."

"Oh, oh, oh," she said. "**You're** mocking my name? **Cosmo?** I know you commando types have nicknames, but like, what? Was **Dickhead** already taken or something? What's your real name—no, no, let me guess. Stanley. Or, wait . . . I know—Percy. That's it, isn't it? Percy Richter."

"You done?" he asked flatly.

"Are **you** done?" she countered. "I have an important casting session tomorrow for the twenty-million-dollar movie that I'm producing and my worthless, **giant** ass needs to get some sleep."

"Great," he said. "Focus on the thing I didn't say. That is so goddamn typical of women like you—"

"Women like me?" Jane sputtered. She came as close as she'd ever come in her entire life to crossing the room and slapping another human being. "**Women** like **me**? You know me well enough to toss me into a subset? When did you get to know me, Percy? We've had, what? Exactly zero conversations? When did you ever say, 'Hmmm, Jane, what do you think about that?' or 'Hey, Jane, why does this movie you're making matter so much to you?' But maybe you didn't need to. Maybe when you sat outside my room last night, you managed to read my mind while I pretended to sleep—is that how you got to know me?"

Finally, she'd managed to shut Cosmo up. He was still glowering at her, but he was glowering silently now.

"As far as subsets go, you're the worst kind," she said. "I **have** met people like you before. You waltz into my world, and you think you've got it all figured out—that the entire Hollywood scene is so base and beneath you. You think you've got me figured out, too—you're so fucking judgmental. You don't bother to look beneath the surface. You think you know me? Honey, you don't have a clue."

Cosmo was definitely back to doing his silent thing.

" 'Gee, Jane, what is it about this movie you're making?' " she spoke for him, her voice dropped a register, mocking him. " 'I mean, it's only a movie. You really willing to die to get it made?' Why, yes, Percy, yes, I am—not that I think this threat is real. But you know what? If it were real, I wouldn't be doing anything different. I would still be working my worthless ass off to make sure that not only does this movie get made, but that this movie gets seen, because I believe it's a story people **should** see. I spent years—years—pushing to get the money to make this movie, and I am not going to quit now. I'm sorry if what I did and said today offended you. But I'd do it again, in a heartbeat, because we got so many hits on the **American Hero** movie website. Do you have even the slightest idea what that means? Tonight hundreds of thousands of people were introduced to Jack Shelton and Hal Lord, two wonderful and brave American men who fought in World War Two, two undeniable heroes who were prepared to make the ultimate sacrifice for their country, who helped make the world safe for freedom and democracy—who just so happened to be gay. There are people in this world who think that makes them less than, and . . ." She shook her head. "Of course, you wouldn't care about that."

He finally spoke. "How would you know?" he asked.

She laughed. "Yeah, right. How would I know? I forgot to ask you if you were a gay rights activist. Jeez, what was I thinking—I'm **so** sure a lot of you SEALs are. Get out of my room. Now. This conversation is over. Oh, and by the way, you are so fired."

Cosmo opened his mouth to speak, but he never got the chance.

A gunshot rang out—it had to be a gunshot; it was an unbelievably loud explosion-like sound coming from outside of the house—and he launched himself up and off the bed, tackling her.

Jane didn't even have time to let out a full scream as her back hit the rug, but somehow Cosmo managed to put his hand behind her head, keeping her from cracking it against the floor.

"Stay down!" he ordered even as he pulled out both a deadly looking handgun—where on earth had he been hiding that?—and the radio he used to touch base with Murphy, who was outside.

It was unbelievable. It was absurd. This man who had

been so furiously angry with her mere moments ago was now shielding her with his body. If someone wanted to kill her, they were going to have to kill him first.

It was crazy. It was stupid.

It was humbling as hell.

It was also hard to breathe—Cosmo's full weight was atop her. Not that she particularly cared right now—she was clinging to him, squeaking, "Oh, my God, oh, my God . . ."

Was someone really shooting at her?

"Report!" he ordered Murphy. "Hush, it's okay," he said to her. "I got you covered. I'm right here. I'm not going to let anyone hurt you."

"I think it was just a car backfiring," the former Marine's voice came back.

Of course. A car. A **car.** Jane started to laugh, pressing her face against Cosmo's very solid shoulder. God, having bodyguards could really make a person paranoid.

But Cosmo wasn't laughing. "No fucking way," he said. He looked directly at her, spoke directly to her. "Excuse me."

It took her a moment to realize he was apologizing to her for his language. As if she hadn't used that very word herself just moments ago. At this proximity, his eyes were really quite a remarkable color, with specks and threads of different shades of gray and even white woven in among the pale blue.

He spoke again into the radio to Murphy. "That was a rifle shot."

"I don't think so, Chief. I was out front—I saw

the car," Murph's voice came back, as cheerful as always.

"I know a rifle shot when I hear one," Cosmo insisted, and some of the relief Jane had felt at Murphy's pronouncement began to waver. Unless maybe . . .

"Yeah, my man, I do, too. But I'm telling you, I watched this car drive past. It was moving slowly, so I checked it out with field glasses. I got a clear look at it. A mid-seventies Pontiac Catalina, dirty white with a peeling black soft top—one of those old ocean liners, a real piece of shit. No windows were open—not on this side, anyway. If someone was firing a rifle, I would've seen a muzzle flash."

"Make a perimeter circuit," Cosmo ordered.

Maybe he was deliberately trying to frighten her. "I think you can probably get off of me now," Jane said.

"Sorry." He shifted his weight. "Keep your head down," he said, helping her into a sitting position but dragging her over next to the bed. "Stay back from the windows."

"Come on," she said, "you don't honestly think—"

"I didn't hurt you, did I?" His concern seemed to be sincere as he crouched beside her. He swore under his breath as he discovered the rug burn on her elbow.

It was bleeding a little and it stung, but she shook her head, pulled her arm away from him. "I'm okay. Look, you know, it was funny. Ha-ha, I was really scared, so . . . You win."

Was he even listening? Still crouching low, out of

range of the windows, he crossed the room, shut the door to her office, locking them in her bedroom. He spoke into the radio on his way back to her. "Murph?"

"There's nothing out here, Chief."

"You sure got the best of me," Jane said, starting to stand up. "But now—"

Cosmo grabbed a handful of her T-shirt and pulled her back down. "I said stay down," he ordered. "Call PJ back in," he said into his radio. "I want to walk through the house while he sits in here with Jane."

"Jane?" Murphy asked.

"Mercedes," Cosmo corrected himself, meeting her eyes only very briefly. "Ms. Chadwick."

"I'm on it," Murphy said.

Cosmo was looking at her arm again. "We need to wash that out."

Again, she pulled away. "What we need to do is end this pathetic game. Didn't you hear me? You win. I don't know why I believed you, but I did." She laughed at her own gullibility. As if this man, who didn't bother to hide his intense dislike of her, would really be ready and willing to risk his own life to keep her alive . . .

"You don't do anything without an argument, do you?" he asked, his disgust more than apparent. "Come on." He pulled her up and moved her swiftly toward the bathroom, carefully keeping himself between her and the bedroom windows—so that if someone were shooting at the house, any bullets that came through the glass would hit him instead.

Of course, he knew as well as she did that no one at all was shooting at either her or her house.

"I don't appreciate this," Jane told him icily.

"Yeah, no kidding," Cosmo said, closing the bathroom door behind them.

CHAPTER SIX

"So what's Mercedes Chadwick really like?" Adam asked.

Dinner was over. Throughout most of it, as well as their thirty-minute wait at the bar for a table, they'd talked about—what else?—Adam. The stage play he was auditioning for, the student film he'd done that had recently wrapped, the acting classes he'd enrolled in to try to make industry contacts, his sister, his mother, his brother the "fucking Nazi," the modeling job he did that he still hadn't been paid for . . .

Jules shrugged. "I don't know. She seems nice. Funny. I liked her brother. Good sense of humor— both of them."

"What's his name?" Adam asked. "Robert?"

"Robin."

"Right." He flagged down the waiter. "Bring us an- other round."

"No," Jules said. "Not for me. I'm all set, thanks."

"Are you afraid if you drink too much you'll lose your inhibitions?" Adam teased.

Yes. It was amazing how quickly the past two years

had just seemed to melt away. It was amazing how it all came rushing back—old feelings, old hopes.

God save him from old hopes.

"Just the check, please," Jules told the waiter.

"So dish more on Mercedes." Adam rested his chin in his hand. With his hair long and artfully mussed, he probably got carded all the time. He looked about as young as he'd actually been when Jules had first met him. "Is this death threat thing real?"

"I really can't talk about that," Jules said.

"What's it like on set?" Adam asked. "The grapevine says she's feuding with her director—that he's HeartBeat's boy and that she's not all too thrilled with some of his choices."

"I haven't met the director," Jules said. "And the time I spent talking to Mercedes—it was all about making sure she remained safe." The waiter returned with Adam's drink and the check.

The check.

Jules let him put it on the table between them, waited to see if Adam would pick it up—he had, after all, made the dinner invitation. But it was a stupid test, a ridiculous game. He knew it was stupid, particularly since the outcome was obvious.

What, had he actually thought Adam might have changed?

While he'd talked about a lot of different things going on in his life, his lack of mention of a day job had been pretty noticeable.

"How's the cowboy—sexy Sam?" he asked now. "You turn him yet?"

"Not even remotely funny," Jules shot back in pure disgust. "He's a friend of mine and a far better man than you'll ever be. If you speak his name, scumbag, you better speak it with the respect he deserves."

Former Navy SEAL Sam Starrett—undeniably straight and formerly homophobic—had recently married Jules' last partner in the FBI, Alyssa Locke. Both were working now for Tom Paoletti's Troubleshooters, although they were currently out of the country on another assignment.

Didn't it figure? Jules considered the two of them to be his best friends in the entire world. It would've been beyond nice to work with them again.

Instead, he got Lawrence Decker.

"Jesus, relax," Adam said. "It was a joke."

"You think perpetuating that myth is a joke?" The myth that gays had a constant agenda to "turn" straight men.

"What myth? It's no myth," Adam countered.

"God damn it, is everything a game to you? Do you have any idea what it's like to work in a world where—"

"J., J., J. . . ." Adam interrupted. "What just happened here? When did you lose your sense of humor?"

Part of it had vanished two years ago, when Adam had packed up and left and hadn't come back.

The rest of it had taken a serious hit two minutes ago, when all of that same old longing and self-esteem-crushing wishful thinking had grabbed Jules once again around the throat and made him dare to hope . . .

That maybe this time it would be different.

How many times would it take for him to learn that, where Adam was concerned, it was **never** going to be different?

Jules took out his wallet, flipped open the check. With a generous tip, sixty dollars would cover it. He pulled three twenties and slipped them in with the bill, put it back on the table. "I have to go."

"Jules, come on. I'm not done with my drink."

"I have to go." He pushed his chair back, picked up his briefcase. "I'm glad things are going well for you."

"Jules . . ."

He was about to turn, to walk away, but on second thought, he picked the check up off the table. He'd hand it to the waiter on his way out.

Because, just like old hopes that constantly bobbed back to the surface even after being scuttled in the most devastating emotional shipwreck, some things just never changed.

Patty had taken a cab over to the Tropicana so that she could drive Robin's car back to her place, so it would be here for him in the morning.

He was a mess, spending the entire trip home either apologizing or telling her how beautiful she looked and how much he loved her.

She had to help him out of the car and up the steps to her apartment. He tripped on the threshold and nearly managed to take them both to the floor of her living room. As it was, she lost her grip and he went down, his backpack flying.

But, typical Robin, it made him laugh. He was—if such a thing was possible—an adorable drunk.

"Do you really live here?" he asked from his vantage point on the floor. His speech was slurred. "Shit, this place is depressing. Look at this carpeting. God damn . . ."

"I don't get paid very much, remember?" she told him as she stepped over him. "It came furnished and it's in a decent enough part of town, so—"

She shrieked with laughter as he grabbed her legs and toppled her to the floor beside him. But then she couldn't laugh because he was kissing her, his tongue filling her mouth, tasting of whiskey, not that she cared. It was that whiskey that had gotten him here.

All of the anger and hurt she'd felt as eight thirty had rolled into nine and then into nine thirty had made her not only take a call from that extra, Wayne with the funny last name, but accept an invitation to have drinks with him tomorrow night. Why not? Robin had obviously forgotten about her.

Except he hadn't. He'd stayed away—or tried to, anyway—because he loved her.

"Oh, baby," he was mumbling now. "Oh, God . . ." He'd pushed his way between her legs and was rocking against her as he kissed her again and again. "Don't make me wait," he pleaded. "I need you right now. . . ."

This was it. It was finally happening. She and Robin were going to make love.

She helped him pull off her shirt and unhooked her bra, sliding the straps down her arms. But he was far more interested in the button on her jeans, so she un-fastened that for him as she kicked off her sneakers, and he grabbed the bottom edges of her pant legs and pulled hard, sending her sliding across the rug on her bare butt. She struggled to sit up, laughing. "Robin!"

"Jesus," he said, "Jesus!" as he somehow managed to get one of her legs out of her tight-fitting jeans, and then he was kissing her again, pushing her shoulders back down on the floor, his mouth hot and wet and hungry as he reached between them, fumbling with his own pants.

Patty pulled at his T-shirt, loving the feel of his taut muscular shoulders beneath the cotton but wanting to touch the smoothness of his beautiful skin. Except he didn't stop kissing her to help her pull it off. He just pushed between her legs and—

She gasped her surprise as he thrust deeply inside of her. It didn't hurt. On the contrary, what she felt didn't come close to pain. She was ready for him— but she just wasn't **ready** for him, with one leg still in her jeans, him still fully clothed, and them lying here on her living room floor instead of in her bed with her pretty-patterned sheets and romantic throw pillows.

"Robin!" My God, had he put on a condom?

"Oh, yes, baby," he said. Harder and faster, each thrust pushed her back along the floor until her head bumped the wall, and still he kept coming. "Yes, baby, oh God, oh God, I love you, too, baby—"

How could he have had time to put one on? "Oh, my God!" she said, reaching between them, trying to check to see if he'd covered himself and encountering only him. "Robin!"

"Oh, yes," he cried, "oh, me, too—baby, yes!" as her head hit the wall again and again, bang, bang, bang. Bang.

He collapsed on top of her. "Holy shit, that was great," he muttered. "Holy shit, holy shit . . ."

His voice was fading—he was, too.

"Robin!" she said, trying not to cry.

He didn't lift his head. "Wha . . . ?"

She wasn't sure what to say, what to do. "We can't sleep on the floor."

"Oh, yeah," he said, rousing slightly. "Yeah." He pushed himself up, off of her, out of her. "You got a bathroom? I should get cleaned up, get rid of this . . . uh-oh."

If Patty lived to be two hundred, she would forever remember the look of pure panic in Robin Chadwick's eyes as he'd realized they'd just had unprotected sex.

"I think I'm going to be sick," he said.

One leg still in her jeans, she scrambled to her feet and helped him hurry into the bathroom where she lifted the seat of the toilet.

If any small part of the evening's romantic potential was still alive, that clank of the toilet seat snuffed it out completely.

"Shit," Robin said, rubbing his forehead as he knelt there on her bathroom floor, as she grabbed her robe from the back of the door and slipped it on. She shook her jeans off and kicked them over toward the laundry pile in the hall.

Robin was trying not to cry, but the alcohol in his system was making it hard for him. She hadn't had anything to drink at all, and she was having some serious trouble herself. "Shit," he said again. "I always fuck things up."

Patty sat next to him on the floor and put her arms around him. "No," she said. "Shhh, Robin, that's not true."

"It was supposed to be different with you," he said, then lunged for the toilet, leaving her to wonder, This wasn't different . . . ?

"I've done a second circuit of the house," Murphy's voice came over Cosmo's radio, "and everything still looks quiet. PJ's on his way back—ETA ten minutes from now."

"Have him come directly inside," Cosmo ordered as he ran the water in the sink, testing it periodically with one finger, waiting for it to heat up. "Tell him to do a quick walk-through before he comes upstairs. And keep an eye on the street. I want model, make, and plate numbers for every car that goes past tonight."

"This is a total waste of time," Jane said. "You're taking this too far."

Standing there, on the verge of getting pissed off all over again, in nightwear that was radically different from the Victoria's Secret fantasy gown and robe she'd had on the other night, Jane looked nothing like the woman who'd charmed the reporters at that press conference this afternoon. Hair back in a ponytail, makeup scrubbed from her face, oversized T-shirt almost making her look skinny, elbow rug-burned and raw—she looked like her own very distant cousin, the family tomboy.

"Why do you do it?" he asked. "The bimbo slut thing?"

"Fuck. You!"

Oh, yeah. He was the one who'd cooled down, whose temper was back under control. She was still pissed off.

She'd latched on to the idea that his reaction to the gunshot they'd both heard—and it was a gunshot—was some kind of practical joke he was playing on her. "I have half a mind to call Tom Paoletti about this," she said icily. She had that ultra-chilling attitude down cold—like each word she spoke was a complete sentence. "Right. Now."

"He usually doesn't stay up this late—and his wife, Kelly, is pregnant. You'd wake them both." The water was finally warm enough, so Cos soaked one of her fancy washcloths and wrung it out before crossing the room and handing it to her.

This was some bathroom—almost larger than the bedroom in his apartment in San Diego. Jane was sitting on a chair near some kind of antique writing desk. A writing desk—in a bathroom. Oddly enough, it looked good there. It matched the old-style tile and fixtures.

Jane took the wet cloth from him, resentment radiating from her as she dabbed gingerly at her elbow.

"Besides," Cosmo added, "I'll be calling Tom about

this tomorrow. As well as writing a report. God help me."

"Not a writer, huh?"

"No," he told her.

"Figures."

He let her hostility roll off his back as he sat down on the edge of the claw-footed tub. "Look, PJ's going to be here in a few minutes. I have a few things I still need to say, so—"

"Tough. I'm not interested in listening to you," she said. "I have no intention of apologizing, so—"

"My father—my biological father—ran when he found out my mother was pregnant," Cosmo interrupted her.

She laughed. Scoffed, really. "What does that have to do—"

"Her parents kicked her out. Even the pastor of her church stopped being friendly when she refused to give me up for adoption," he continued. "Only person who stood by her, who made sure she had food to eat and a place to sleep, was this guy Billy Richter who worked as the town photographer—you know, he did all the weddings and school pictures. His full name was Cosmo William Richter. He went by Billy—he was named after his father who died in the war, in Guadalcanal. Everyone whispered about Billy, said that he'd been kicked out of college because he was homosexual, which in Findlay, Ohio, in 1972 was worse than being a serial killer. But Mom was always kind to him, and he repaid her first by giving her a job in his camera shop, and then by marrying her, because, well, it was Ohio, in 1972. But they were husband and wife only in name. Separate bedrooms, you know? In 1982 we packed up and went to California, where Dad met Uncle Riley, who moved in with us. We all shared a house, right up until I was a senior in high school, when Dad died from a car accident."

Jane had stopped her sputtering and now sat there silently, just looking at him.

So Cosmo held out his hand to her. "How do you do? I'm Chief Petty Officer Cosmo William Richter the third—named after my adopted father, the kindest man I ever had the honor of knowing. You ever get the urge to talk about gay rights or gay activism, I'm well versed in the subject—I'm straight, but not narrow. I'm a card-carrying member of PFLAG. I also have quite an extensive knowledge of musical theater and Bette Midler movies, and oh yeah, I can name every Barbra Streisand album ever made, in order of release date. I can also kill with my bare hands." He smiled at her. "In case you were wondering."

She didn't take his hand, so he pulled it back in. But she was definitely listening, so he kept going.

"PJ's going to be here in just a minute," he told her. "I'm going out to check the house, take a look at the road down where Murph said he saw that car. But first I have to clear up something that's kind of important to me. You implied back when we were, you know, both shouting and not really listening to each other that you believed your, um, actions during the press conference would benefit Troubleshooters Incorporated. You're dead wrong."

She opened her mouth, about to speak, but he stopped her. "Wait. Hear me out. I heard you out."

She waited.

"When I'm out there, working to protect you, the way I was at the press conference, I'm a personal representative of both Tommy Paoletti and his company. When you did what you did—using me as a prop like that—you implied that I'm engaging in unprofessional behavior."

She started to speak again, to argue, but again he stopped her with one hand. "I know there's lots of movies and books where, you know, the bodyguard and the client get busy, fall in love, whatever, but it's crap. Bottom line, it's unprofessional—that kind of contact. It's not romantic; it's wrong. My relationship with you is a business relationship. You pay Troubleshooters, Tommy pays me, I keep you safe. I don't care how good anyone is—you can't have sex with someone and be paid to keep them safe at the same time. It cannot be done. At least not by someone who considers themselves truly professional."

Across the room, Cosmo could see that Jane was on the verge of exploding. She couldn't keep silent another moment. "I was joking. It was a joke. Like, hubba hubba, check out the bod on my bodyguard. Nobody really thought—"

"Jane." He cut her off. "You're an intelligent woman. I know you know that people definitely **thought.** My own mother **thought.**"

She was subdued, but she still shook her head. "I just—"

"See, if I'm unprofessional, then Tommy and TS Inc. is, too. Tommy's most valuable asset is his reputation as the former CO of the best SEAL Team in the country, as an honorable man, as a professional. You know that saying? There's no such thing as bad publicity? Well, yes, there is. That's exactly what you gave Tommy this afternoon."

She looked up at him, finally meeting his gaze. "Then I'm sorry. I am. I really thought it would be a double win. I just . . . I didn't realize."

"Yeah, I know," he said. "And I apologize to you—for assuming that you did realize and that you did it anyway. I thought . . ." He shook his head and laughed. "Well, you know what I thought. You still want me off this team, just say the word, and I'm gone."

"Am I really in danger?" she asked. "I mean, what just happened here—that was . . . real?"

"I heard a rifle shot," he told her. "It's possible it was a blank or that it was fired away from the house—maybe only in an attempt to scare you, to scare us all." He asked the question he knew would be coming next, beating her to it. "Who would do something like that? I don't know. Was it the Freedom Network—or someone else who saw the news and thought they'd shake you up?" He smiled at her. "Maybe the producer making **Doctor Dolittle Seventeen** saw all the press you were getting and was jealous—wanted to make sure you didn't get a good night's sleep."

Jane smiled back. "You've been talking to Decker."

"Yes, ma'am. We share all information. There are

no secrets on an assignment like this—no such thing as private information," he told her. "We're doing more than providing personal protection, you know. We're actively investigating the e-mailed threats you've received—the ones that we perceive to be credible. One way to keep you from getting hurt is to find who-ever wants to hurt you before they can get close enough to do any damage."

"I read most of those e-mails," Jane countered. "They all sound alike—just . . . kind of crazy."

"If you want," Cosmo said, "I'll sit down with you and Deck and Jules Cassidy—you know, from the FBI. We'll show you the ones we think could be real trouble."

She swallowed as she nodded. "Okay."

He'd scared her.

Good. She needed to start taking this more seri-ously.

His radio crackled. "PJ's here," Murphy's voice an-nounced. "He's inside."

"Thanks," Cosmo responded. He stood, and Jane looked up at him.

"If you honestly thought there was a threat," she said, "then you really were ready to . . . to **die** for me?"

"No one's going to die," he told her as there was a knock on the door. He gave Jane a nod as he went out and PJ came in.

The knock on his door came after Jules had spent thirty minutes on the treadmill in the hotel's gym.

He'd pretended he was going to the gym in an attempt to exhaust himself, but while he ran, he was hit on five times—twice by the same barely twenty-year-old outrageously buff rap artist wannabe who called himself the White Boomerang. And as Jules took the elevator back to his room, he knew why he'd really gone down there.

It was because he wanted a reminder of everything he **wasn't** looking for—of everything he **didn't** want cluttering up his life. And he'd also gone there because even though he had no trouble at all declining sexual invitations from strangers, he knew that Adam wouldn't have been able to walk out of that room alone. He'd wanted to be reminded of that, too.

He opened the door with a towel around his neck, saying, "Look, kid, you get points for persistence, but I'm really not into pretentious children who—"

It wasn't the White Boomerang standing there.

It was Adam.

This was bad. This was very bad.

"Hey," Adam said.

Jules just shook his head. "No."

"You're saying the word," Adam told him, "but, you know, if I were directing you in a scene, I would have to tell you that the audience just isn't going to believe you because—"

"How did you get my room number?"

Adam leaned against the wall outside his door. "I used to live with an FBI agent, remember?"

Jules did remember. Vividly.

"Look, I'm not asking you to let me in," Adam said with total sincerity. Of course, he was an actor, so it meant nothing. "I just . . . I didn't get a chance to tell you about everything that's going on in my life."

Jules folded his arms across his chest, planting himself firmly in the open doorway, making sure his body language was a very clear noninvitation to enter.

Adam kept going. "I just wanted you to know that I've had this really great job for the past, I don't know, six months now."

"Job," Jules repeated. "Is it possible I just heard you say job?"

"Don't be an asshole." Adam was good at playing injured, but there was a new depth to his performance, a new vulnerability that Jules had never seen before. Was it possible . . . ? "This isn't easy to talk about. When I do, it feels like I've sold out—you know, given up on the acting. But it's not a career, J., you know, it's not. It's just a day job. Well, sometimes it's a night job, and the money's not all that great, but it's a job that I like, so . . ."

It was the lack of eye contact that did it—the fact that Adam didn't look at Jules at all, didn't check to see whether he was buying into the performance. And that made Jules dare to hope that it wasn't an act.

"Where?" he asked, squeezing the word past his heart, which was securely lodged in his throat.

"That's the cool part," Adam told him, finally looking up and meeting his eyes. He was almost shy about his own enthusiasm. "It's at this vet's office—you know, veterinarian."

"That's so great," Jules said. Adam had always bemoaned the fact that their apartment building had a no-pets rule.

"Yeah," Adam agreed. "I help run a doggy hotel—we don't call it a kennel, but that's what it is, you know, for people who need to go out of town and leave their dog someplace nice where they know they're going to be treated right. It's really pretty upscale. The dogs stay in these rooms that are nicer than my apartment, and two or three nights a week I stay over there, too. It's great, J.—we have regulars. You know, return customers and . . . My boss is okay. Mandy—she's cool. She's become a friend and—"

A door opened across the hall. "This reunion is touching, boys, but I'm trying to sleep. Do you mind?" Whoever he was, he closed his door forcefully.

Jules looked at Adam, who held his gaze only briefly before looking away.

"That's pretty much all I wanted to say," Adam said, more softly than before. "That and, well, I miss you." He was looking down at the floor again, and this time when he looked back up at Jules, there were actually tears in his eyes. "I've missed what we had." He straightened up. "Thanks for dinner. I'm glad you're doing well, too."

He turned away. He actually turned and began to walk away.

"Adam." Jules heard himself speak. With the part of

himself that remembered the pain, he knew that doing anything other than letting Adam leave was a terrible mistake. But that part of himself wasn't in control of his voice. Or his feet.

He stepped back, opening the door wider.

And he let Adam in.

CHAPTER SEVEN

Sometime last night, a truce had been called.

Decker sat in Mercedes Chadwick's downstairs meeting room with Cosmo Richter, waiting for her highness to appear.

Cosmo looked beat, but the undercurrent of anger Deck had noted after yesterday's press conference had vanished. Of course, it wasn't any wonder that the SEAL was tired—Deck had heard his account of last night's drama.

Cosmo had sat outside, in front of the house, in the dark, for hours. He'd made a list of every motor vehicle that had gone past, right up until dawn.

The road ended at a cul-de-sac a couple of miles past Jane's driveway, so there hadn't been all that much traffic.

There had been some, though.

After the sun had come up, after Cosmo had taken a brief nap, he'd spent quite a bit of time searching for evidence that what he'd heard had indeed been a rifle shot. Problem was, he'd found no shell, no bullet hole.

The intern came back in with mugs for them both.

The coffee steamed, too hot to let him do more than sip very cautiously. Decker set his mug down on the table next to his chair, on top of the file folder he'd brought with him.

Cosmo drank deeply, apparently needing that caffeine desperately enough to risk being burned. Decker could relate. He'd been there plenty of times himself—wishing he could have his coffee in an IV drip.

Cos had a file folder, too. Inside was his list of the ten cars and trucks that had driven past last night, including one—a dark-colored Ford pickup with a significant dent in the right rear bumper and a torn bumper sticker reading only ". . . ville Honor Student"—that was slightly suspicious due to its mud-smeared license plate. Cosmo had told Deck he'd only been able to make out a six in white against a dark background.

It was only slightly suspicious considering it had driven past more than two hours after the "incident." If there had been, indeed, an actual incident.

It wasn't too long after the coffee arrived that Mercedes swept into the room. Both Decker and Cosmo got to their feet.

"Sit," she said, "please, sit." So they sat. At least until she headed for the windows. "It's a beautiful day. Why didn't Patty—"

Cosmo moved to intercept her. "We closed the blinds."

She stopped short, looked from him to Decker and back, instantly understanding that they'd done it as a precaution. So that someone couldn't aim a weapon at the office window and wait until she walked into their sight and . . .

She was a smart woman, and she took it a step further. Until they eliminated the threat, she wasn't going to be spending much time outdoors.

"Well, damn," she said. "There goes my tan."

"Only temporarily," Cos told her. "The way this house is set up, we could construct a wall, create an area where you'll be able to go outside—"

"And take walks around the prison compound three times a day?" She shook her head in disgust. "No thanks."

"Think of this as short-term," he said.

"Yeah, I know." She met his gaze. "I'm sorry for complaining. It's just . . . frustrating."

"It must be."

So okay. Who was this apologetic woman, and what had she done with Mercedes Chadwick? She was actually wearing clothes today, too. Clothes that covered her. Mostly. Her T-shirt didn't quite meet the low-rise waistband of her jeans.

Still, it was an improvement. It was going to make it a hell of a lot easier to focus on their agenda.

"You look good in sneakers and jeans," Cosmo volunteered his opinion as they both sat down on the sofa, surprising the hell not just out of Decker but Mercedes, too. "Not stupid at all."

Obviously, they'd had a conversation about the producer's default four-inch heels.

She recovered first, laughing. "Yeah, well, I figured the 'bimbo slut' didn't need to attend this particular meeting."

Again, there was eye contact, as some kind of silent communication passed between them.

"Hey, didn't you go home?" she asked suddenly, no doubt noticing that Cosmo was wearing yesterday's clothes.

"Nah," Cos said. "I caught a nap, though. I'm okay."

"In your truck?" she asked, her voice dripping with horror, as if she were asking if he'd fixed the sewage problem by swimming to the bottom of the septic tank.

"I'm okay," he said again, this time with a smile. An actual smile.

Decker knew for a fact that the SEAL had taken naps in far worse places.

But Mercedes turned to him. "We have, like, ten extra bedrooms in this place. Why don't we make them available to your team?"

"That's very generous. As long as it's not an imposition," Decker said.

"It's not," she said. "Make sure everyone knows. I'll have Patty send a memo. No more truck sleeping."

That got a head shake along with another smile from Cos. Easy there, man. Two smiles inside one minute? What was next? Fire falling from the sky?

"Before we get started, I need to apologize to you."

Decker looked over to find that Mercedes Chadwick had focused her enormous eyes back on him.

Apparently an apology—which, when he'd walked in here this morning, had seemed about as unlikely as that rain of fire—was next.

"Larry," she said. "May I call you Larry?"

Decker cleared his throat. "Most people call me Deck."

"Deck," she said. "Right. Yesterday, at the press conference, I . . . I'm sorry. I really am. I had no idea that what I said would reflect badly on you and Tom and . . . I really do apologize. It won't happen again. Although I'm afraid the paparazzi are going to be circling for a while. If I go out—**When** I go out, and I have to go out. I can't stay inside forever. I have a movie to make. But when I go out, there's a good chance there'll be cameras. Some of them will be focused on, well, you." She included Cosmo in that collective you. "Whoever's with me. But mostly you." This time the **you** was singular, and aimed at the SEAL. "At least until next week's tabloids come out. When they do . . . Well, I'm working on making this thing with Cosmo go away."

"Thanks for the warning," Decker said. "We'll keep the cameras in mind."

"I am sorry," she said again.

"To be honest," Deck told her, "Tom and I had a long conversation last night, and I recommended we pass your case over to another security organization."

She nodded, even more subdued. "And yet you're still here," she pointed out. "What made you change your mind?"

He opened his file folder and pulled out the three

e-mails that Cosmo had recommended they show to her. She quickly read through them. They weren't more than a few sentences each.

Bitch,

You think you're so smart. You think you're going to get away with this? You may be smart, but I'm smarter. You're wrong about me—everyone's wrong about me, and you won't catch me. I will catch you, guaranteed. Clear your calendar—it's almost time to die. You'll be dead, and I'll be laughing. You'll be rotting, and I'll still be free.

"Sorry I'm late." Jules Cassidy, the gay FBI agent, came breezing into the room, followed by Mercedes' intern, who was running to keep up. "Traffic was . . . I left a little too late and . . . Good, you started. That's good."

"Can I get you coffee, Mr. Cassidy?" the intern asked.

"Yes," Cassidy said. "Please. Coffee. Excellent. Gallons, please, Patty. Bless you."

Was Decker the only person in California who'd actually gotten a good night's sleep? Even Patty the intern looked as if she were stumbling around in a fog.

Cassidy sat down, setting his briefcase on the floor beside him. "How far did you get?" he asked, and Deck realized the man was more than tired. He was emotionally fried.

Decker knew the symptoms well. He'd seen them in his own mirror a time or two. The strain he just couldn't keep from showing on his face. The red eyes, which were no fricking fair. A man shouldn't have to deal with eyes that made him look as if he'd spent days weeping, when in truth he'd spent every one of his waking hours making goddamn sure he **didn't** cry. The tension—shoulders, neck, back strung tight as a battleship's anchor cable.

There was stress, and then there was stress.

The kind that came from helping bury a friend . . .

Stress that came from mistakes that couldn't be fixed, from enormous loss that was irrevocable.

It fucking sucked.

So, yeah. He recognized emotionally fried when he saw it.

Something bad had happened to Jules Cassidy between last night and this morning.

"Bitch." Mercedes was reading the third and final e-mail aloud. **"You'll be news for a day, but then you'll be gone. You'll be dead, and I'll be here, laughing. They won't catch me. They'll never catch me. You'll be rotting and I'll still be free. You can't touch me, but I'll touch you."** She put the paper down. "So, okay. Aside from the different e-mail addresses, these are all obviously from the same person. I mean, the writing—the voice—is clearly the same, right? But what I don't get is how these are any different from the three hundred others we get each day."

Patty returned with Cassidy's mug of coffee along

with an entire extra pot that she placed on the end table. He managed to smile as he thanked her.

They all waited for the intern to leave the room and close the door behind her, and both Cosmo and Cassidy eyed Decker, obviously wondering who should take the point and answer Mercedes' question.

"Do you want to, uh . . ." Deck ordinarily would have just motioned for the FBI agent to take it away, but the man looked like he needed at least fifteen solid minutes alone with his coffee.

"Yes," Cassidy said much too crisply. "Certainly." He put down his mug, opened his briefcase, handed another sheet of paper to Mercedes, and gave a second copy to Deck. "Sorry, I only have—"

"That's okay." Cosmo moved closer to Mercedes on the couch so he could read over her shoulder.

This document was a copy of an e-mail sent from one of those free e-mail accounts. It started with a slightly different salutation, "Pigfucker," but other than that . . . Whoa-kay. The body of this message was identical—word for word—to the first of the e-mails Decker had just shown to Mercedes.

You think you're so smart. You think you're going to get away with this? You may be smart, but I'm smarter. . . .

"This was sent to ADA Benjamin Chertok on April 12, 2003. Thirteen days before he was fatally shot," Cassidy informed them. "He was murdered by an unknown assailant with a Remington 700P long-range rifle."

On the sofa, Mercedes looked up from the e-mail, directly at Cosmo. "Shit," she said.

Cosmo nodded. "Yeah."

"What's an ADA?" she asked.

"Sorry," Cassidy said. "Assistant district attorney. Ben Chertok worked in the Idaho Falls office. He headed a team of lawyers who had just successfully prosecuted John Middlefield—a prominent Freedom Network leader. It was a tax evasion case, with a huge penalty as well as a mandatory prison term. During the trial, the Freedom Network started an Internet smear campaign targeting Chertok. Two weeks after the trial ended, he was dead in his driveway, shot as he was coming home from work on a Friday afternoon."

"My God," Mercedes said. "Why haven't you arrested the entire Freedom Network?"

"It's not that simple," Cassidy said. "I wish it was. But we haven't been able to connect these e-mails to the Freedom Network, or even to Chertok's murder."

Mercedes looked from Cassidy to Deck to Cosmo questioningly. "But if you can't connect them, then . . ."

"This could be a coincidence," the SEAL explained.

"While we're as close to certain as possible that these four e-mails were sent by the same person," Cassidy clarified, "we have no proof that this e-mailer is the shooter who killed Ben Chertok. They could well be two different people."

"But . . ." Mercedes prompted him.

"Personally, I think it's one and the same," he admitted. He was sitting there, looking Mercedes straight in the eye, putting it all into plain-speak.

Deck had worked with both FBI and Agency personnel who refused to share guesswork with anyone. Until they could verify something as a fact, it didn't get talked about.

He preferred Jules Cassidy's all cards on the table approach. It was clearly the correct way to deal with someone with such a strong personality as Mercedes Chadwick.

"If it is," Cassidy continued, "if the e-mailer and the killer are one and the same, then we're up against someone who's killed before and gotten away with it. Not only that, but by sending you an exact copy of the e-mail he sent to Chertok, he wants us to know for sure that he's coming after you. In a sense, he's issued a challenge."

"This is not someone who's going to make sloppy mistakes," Decker told her.

"Of course not," she quipped. "God forbid Mr. Insane-o, my personal psycho, is actually of the careless variety."

"We're not going to let him or anyone else hurt you," Cosmo said quietly.

She looked at him, holding his gaze for several long seconds before she turned back to Decker and Cassidy. "But if he's got a Remington whatsis long-range rifle, isn't it likely that **some**one's going to get hurt?"

"Yeah," Cosmo told her. "He is."

Mercedes laughed as she nodded, but Decker could

tell that, as much as she wanted to, she didn't quite believe him.

As Jules let himself out the front door of Mercedes Chadwick's house, her brother, Robin, pulled into the driveway in a neat little Porsche Speedster that screamed **movie star.**

God, he had a headache. As he headed for his stodgy rental car, Jules searched his pockets for his sunglasses and slipped them on.

Not that they helped.

What he needed was sleep—at least six uninterrupted hours of it. But first he had to call his boss, Max, and verify that the FBI hadn't managed to trace those e-mails. Then he had to fax Cosmo's list of license plate numbers to Max's assistant, Laronda—what a total wild-goose chase that was. Maybe he'd put that off until later. Until after he'd checked out of his hotel room and checked in someplace else.

Someplace where Adam wouldn't be able to find him.

God **damn** it.

"Hey." Robin had opened the driver's side window several inches. He was sitting there, engine running, as he furtively motioned Jules over.

The man looked like shit. Worse even than Jules had looked this morning when he'd realized exactly what last night had been about. It was amazing, in fact, how someone as good-looking as Robin Chadwick could look so awful.

As Jules approached, Robin opened the window

wider, and Jeezus. The man reeked of alcohol. But it was last night's alcohol—partially sweated and puked out of his system, partly spilled on his clothes.

The good news about that—if there **was** good news about that—was that Jules didn't have to call his new friends in the LAPD and have Robin arrested for driving while intoxicated.

"Is she in there?" Robin asked in a stage whisper.

"Your sister?" Jules said. "Yeah, but she's getting ready to go to some meeting at the casting director's office—"

"No," Robin said. "Not Jane." He lowered his voice even more. "Patty."

O-kay. "Yeah," Jules said. "Patty's in there, too."

"Not so loud," Robin hissed at him, then swore.

"Don't want her to see you like this, huh?" Jules asked, knowing full well that it was more likely that Robin was the one who didn't want to see Patty. Period. Not right now, not ever again.

"Yeah. Yeah, um . . ." For an actor, Robin was really a dismally bad liar. Or maybe he was just too hungover to make much of an effort. "Hey, will you do me a giant favor—"

Jules shook his head. "No."

"Yeah, well, it's not like it's a hugely giant favor. It's more like a small and extremely easy giant favor. Very tiny in fact. If you could just go back inside, see if she's right by the door—"

"No," Jules said again, but it was as if Robin hadn't heard him.

"If she is, will you ask her to, I don't know, make

some copies for you or something? You know, to get her out of there so I can run upstairs without . . . ? No?"

About time he noticed that Jules was standing there shaking his head.

It was pathetic—doubly so, considering the entire presentation was coming at Jules in glorious Smell-O-Vision.

"What'd you do?" he asked Robin. "Wake up in some strange bed, all alone, with a note on the pillow telling you to help yourself to coffee and breakfast? Except the note wasn't signed, was it? So you had to find a stack of mail by the front door in order to figure out who you fucked last night."

Robin stared at him.

He wasn't sure if the wide eyes were because he'd gotten it all correct, or if Robin was surprised by the ugly edge of rancor that Jules couldn't keep from his voice.

"I was young and stupid once, too," Jules told him. Well, young anyway. Last night, when he'd let Adam in, he proved that he was still plenty stupid. "You have to talk to her, Robin."

Robin rubbed his forehead. "And say what? Hey, babe, gee, what happened last night? All I really remember is the part where I realized we didn't use a condom, and the part where I did the Technicolor yawn for some undetermined amount of time—somewhere close to, but just short of, forever. So, hey, was it good for you, too?"

Oh, Robin, Robin, Robin . . .

"And oh, by the way, baby," he continued with his

mock speech to Patty, "remember how yesterday I was dying to get my hands on you? Well, today I can't even **think** of you without feeling like I just might puke. Again."

Jules could relate. Right now, just the thought of Adam . . .

God **damn** it.

"I am **such** a fucking loser," Robin lamented.

"Yeah." Jules had to agree. "You really are. I was in the running for a while, you know, in terms of morning-after official loser status, but wow. That no-condom thing combined with the change of heart induced by slackage of desire? God, Robin, you're not just a fucking loser, you're a heartless, intern-fucking loser. What is she, all of nineteen? I'm pretty sure that makes you a scum-sucking, bastard-asshole, heartless, intern-fucking loser." He smiled at Robin. "I'm so glad I ran into you this morning. It really puts things into perspective for me. Have a nice day."

"Wait!" Robin turned off his car and clambered out, following Jules across the driveway. He moved in that hyper-careful, cringing, the-world-is-both-too-bright-and-too-loud manner of the super-hungover. "Are you really, **really** sure you don't want to star in a movie?"

What?

Heavens to Murgatroid, not this again. "Yes," Jules said. "I'm really, **really** sure."

"I mean, here we are, doing this huge casting search for the right actor to play Jack, only every time I see you, I hear this thousand-voice choir of angels, and I think, 'Holy shit, there he is.' " Robin squinted at him, using one hand to shade his eyes against the sun. "What is wrong with you? How could you be the one person in the United States who doesn't secretly want to win an Oscar?"

"Are you sure you're not in love with me?" Jules countered. "A hundred-voice choir—now, that says be in my movie. But a thousand angels . . ." He shook his head. "Gee, I'm sorry, sweetie, but I don't date actors. Not anymore. Too bad you didn't tell me this yesterday."

"Yeah, yeah," Robin said. "Ha-ha. You gay guys are so witty. Can't you just—as a giant favor—come to the casting session and—"

"We're back to giant favors, are we? No."

"I mean, just read a few lines, do a quick screen test . . ."

Jules unlocked his car door. "How can I say this to make you understand?" he asked. "Hmmm, how about: No."

"What if you—"

"Robin, sweetheart, you know how you made a whole fuckload of mistakes last night?" Jules told him. "Well, I did, too—only I didn't find out the particular bargelike size of my personal fuckload until about twenty minutes before I was scheduled to show up here for a very important meeting. So listen close when I tell you that I would rather stick a needle in my eye than go to your casting session."

"Shit," Robin sympathized. "What happened?"

"Someone like you happened," Jules told him.

"Someone who knew that I hadn't given up on my goddamn idealist dream of—" He stopped himself. What was he doing? This man was a stranger, and an obvious asshole to boot. Not to mention the fact that Jules was here in his official capacity. "Nice seeing you, Robin." He got into the rental car.

Robin got in the way of the door. "Is there anything I can do to, you know, help? I mean, if you want to talk or—"

Jules looked at him. "Like I'm going to take romantic advice from a man with vomit breath?"

"Sorry." Robin pulled the neck of his T-shirt up over his mouth. "Better?"

Jules rolled his eyes. "Go talk to Patty," he said. "Don't leave her hanging, thinking that it's real when it's not. She's a sweet kid and—"

"Robin! Hi!" There she was, as if on cue.

For a moment, with his back toward her, Robin closed his eyes, scrunching up his face in pain. Then he braced himself, plastering a weak smile on his face before he straightened up and turned around. "Hey, babe."

She was all aglow at the sight of him, poor little thing.

"You better hurry and get showered," she told him. She waved to Jules. "Mr. Cassidy, I called your friend—Adam. He's free so he's coming to the casting session. We haven't seen him before, so that's good, but . . . You might want to warn him not to get his hopes up too high. His résumé's a little sparse. We usually wouldn't even consider such a total unknown."

"Yeah," Jules said. "Thanks for giving him a chance. I, um, appreciate it."

Robin was looking at him, realization dawning. "You were on the news last night," he said. "With my sister. Weren't you?"

Yes, he was. And Adam had seen him on the news. Adam had seen that Jules was connected to the controversial movie **American Hero.** He'd recognized that this connection could quite possibly result in something he'd wanted for a long time—a chance to audition for rising-star producer J. Mercedes Chadwick.

Adam, being Adam, hadn't just called Jules up and point-blank asked for a favor. For old times' sake.

Possibly because the old times had been filled with lies and deception and relentless betrayals.

But most likely Adam hadn't just called and asked because he loved to play games. And here was a challenge. Win Jules back. Convince him to take yet one more chance on something he'd always wanted.

On the other hand, that really hadn't been that much of a challenge, had it?

It never had.

The sun had come up, and the new day had been so bright and filled with hope.

But then, after Jules got out of the shower, already late but too happy to give a good goddamn, Adam had said, "I've heard this rumor that Mercedes Chadwick is still looking for someone to play one of the leads in her movie."

It was a casual comment, but Jules had turned to look at him. Adam. Wonderful, amazing, gorgeously vibrant Adam—still in bed, hair rumpled, glint of beard on his perfect chin. And he knew. He suddenly knew.

For several seconds, time stopped as he replayed all the times last night that Adam had brought up Jules' current assignment. Even during dinner, he'd asked, "What's Mercedes really like?"

"Yes," Jules had finally answered Adam. "Yes, she is. There's a casting session this afternoon. Too bad you don't have a copy of your headshot and résumé with you."

Adam sat up. "Yeah, no—I do have one. Would you really do that?"

"You brought your résumé." Any doubt that remained was gone. Adam hated carrying a bag or a briefcase. He never walked around with more than his wallet in his pocket. If he'd brought his résumé, it was because . . .

Because his goal last night had not been to reconcile with Jules. His goal had been to snag an audition with Mercedes Chadwick.

"Well, yeah." Adam had surely noted the look on Jules' face, and he tried to make excuses. "I brought it to show you. I thought you might want to see it."

"But you didn't show it to me."

"It didn't come up." Adam smiled. "And since a lot of other things did—"

"Where is it?" Adam hadn't been carrying anything—an envelope, a folder—when he'd appeared in the hotel garage.

"Well, I, uh, I left it at the front desk for you," Adam said.

"You wanted to show it to me, so you left it at the front desk."

"J., I came here because I wanted to get back together. And I naturally thought if we **could** get back together, you might want to help me out by—"

"We're not back together," Jules told him. He picked up the phone, called the front desk for an overnight guest pack—toothbrush, razor, Visine, aspirin, replacement condoms. "Yeah, hi. Will you send a trick kit up to room 312?" He purposely called it by its less flattering name, which made Adam bristle.

"Oh, **that's** nice," he said. "Now I'm just a trick?"

That was all he'd ever been—a cheap one-night stand. Jules had just been too stupid to realize it. "Make sure you're gone before I get back." He put on his jacket and adjusted his tie in the mirror before he grabbed his briefcase and went out the door.

"So you go ahead and actually give this guy's head-shot to Jane?" Robin asked him now.

"Yeah," Jules said. "You know. For old times' sake."

He closed the door, put the car in gear. Opened the window. "Talk to Patty," he said again.

But as he pulled out of the driveway, he saw Patty and Mercedes—Jane, as Robin called her—being hustled into a waiting car by two members of Tom Paoletti's security team, leaving Robin standing in the driveway, alone.

CHAPTER EIGHT

Who was this guy? Jane skimmed the acting résumé that was on the table in front of her. Adam Wyndham was his name. According to this, he'd done next to nothing.

The casting director was out in the middle of the small studio, reading lines with the young actor—because Robin was still AWOL, damn it.

Patty was moving in and out of the waiting room, organizing the next group of auditioners, getting them ready to come in and read. When the intern slipped back through the door and into the studio, Jane flagged her down. "Patty, where's Robin?" First things first.

"I thought he was coming right over, but . . . he seems to be running a little late today." She blushed. "I'm sorry—"

"It's not your fault," Jane told her, but she had to wonder. Was it Patty's fault? This morning when she'd caught a glimpse of Robin out in the driveway, he'd looked as if he were just coming home, as if he'd spent the night somewhere else.

"Can I get you more coffee?" Patty asked, definitely not meeting Jane's eyes, definitely still blushing.

Oh, God. If her brother and Patty had . . . Last night . . .

Then it was entirely possible Robin had now gone into hide mode. Son of a bitch.

"I'm good," Jane told her, resisting the urge both to grab the girl by the shoulders and scold her for her stupidity, and to pull her into her arms and apologize for the tsunami of heartache that she didn't even realize was racing toward her. "Just tell me—where on earth did we find Adam Wyndham?"

"I'm sorry, is he awful?" Patty asked anxiously.

"No," Jane said, and it came out a little louder than she'd intended.

The actor—Adam—stopped reading and looked over at them. "Do you want me to try something different?"

Physically, he was Jack Shelton. His brown hair was too long, but that could easily be cut. Hazel eyes, boyishly handsome face, trim physique—he wasn't as slight as Jack, but he was close enough. He was certainly smaller than Robin, which was really all that mattered.

His résumé listed his age as twenty-four—which in Hollywood didn't necessarily mean anything other than the fact that he was over eighteen and under thirty. He could certainly play a twenty-two-year-old—Jane didn't doubt that. He was both adorable and charismatic. Even just standing there, waiting for someone to answer his question, he commanded attention.

For the first time since this casting session started—for the first time in months—Jane had real hope that she wasn't going to have to settle for either a talented actor who looked nothing like Jack Shelton or an untalented lookalike. Still, the idea of hiring someone with virtually no experience was frightening.

"Haven't you done anything that I've heard of?" Jane asked him as Patty hovered nearby.

He laughed, at ease with all eyes on him, revealing a dimple that was just too cute for words. "Not unless you count my high school drama club's production of **Midsummer Night's Dream.** I played Puck."

"Of course you did." Jane frowned down at his résumé. She wasn't familiar with his representation. How had he gotten in here?

Patty leaned close to say, "He's that FBI agent's friend."

Aha.

Amazing.

This sort of thing happened all the time. Whenever Jane met people who lived outside of the Hollywood world, it didn't take long before the requests for favors started. "Hey, my brother/cousin/friend/uncle/sister-in-law/niece is an actor . . ."

This was serendipitous. It was payoff for all the times she'd patiently sat through "favor" auditions with dreadfully awful actors whose friends and family had convinced them they were the next Kate Hudson or Jude Law.

Patty had agreed to see Adam Wyndham as a favor, and it turned out that instead the favor had been given to them. God bless Jules Cassidy.

"Have you ever done a screen test, Adam?" Jane asked.

He pretended to clutch at his heart and took several staggering steps backward. "Are you asking me to?"

"I think she's probably getting a little ahead of herself," Robin said.

Jane turned to see her brother closing the studio door behind him. Beside her, Patty managed to get even more tense. Son of a bitch.

"Sorry I'm late." He aimed the apology at Jane, then returned his attention to Adam. "Maybe you should read some lines with me, dude, before we go and waste any film on you."

Robin was being so uncharacteristically rude, Jane sat there, stunned, for several long, silent seconds. But then she leapt to her feet. "Please excuse us for a minute."

Grabbing her brother's arm, she pulled him with her into the bathroom and shut the door. "What the hell was that about?"

"I don't like this guy."

"But you haven't even seen him yet!" Jane could not believe this.

"I don't need to see him." Robin, one of the warmest, welcoming, friendliest people in the world, had definitely gone mad. "I know who he is and we don't want him in our movie, Janey. He's not very nice."

Jane waited for him to continue, but he didn't. He just stood there, looking at her as if he'd made a winning argument.

"That's it?" she said. "Not, he's a kleptomaniac, or he's got a serious drug problem, or he's a binge drinker, child molester, insane psycho stalker, serial killer . . . ?"

"He used Jules to get here," Robin said. Which would have been funny—those words coming out of that mouth—if this weren't so serious. "Adam Wyndham played the promise of reconciliation card when he found out Jules was working with us. Didn't you notice how upset he was this morning? Jules, I mean."

Truth was, this morning Jane had been a little distracted by the fact that someone clearly psychotic had sent her an e-mail that was identical to one sent to an attorney in Idaho who had ended up extremely, unquestionably dead.

Bullet-through-his-brain dead.

So, no, she hadn't noticed that Jules was upset—she hadn't noticed much of anything.

But okay, yeah, that wasn't quite true. She **had** noticed Cosmo. Steady and solid, quietly strong. She'd walked into her office, and at the sight of him standing there, part of her had been relieved. It was weird. She knew it wasn't rational. Logically, she was completely aware that she was just as safe with PJ or Murphy or Decker.

But seeing Cosmo . . . She couldn't deny that she was very glad he was there, very happy to see him.

Last night, Cosmo, who had every reason to hate her, had been ready to shield her from harm with his own body. He had been ready to take a bullet that was meant for her.

God.

Still, he'd managed to top that act of bravery by displaying an emotional maturity that was truly impressive, particularly among the no-neck set. Not that he didn't have a neck. In fact, he had a very, very nice neck. But he'd been mad as hell, and despite that, he'd actually stopped shouting and listened to what she had to say.

No doubt about it, when it came to Cosmo Richter, Jane had done a complete 180. Yesterday, she'd thought him arrogant, judgmental, and narrow-minded. Today, she honestly liked the man.

Enough to go through her address book of actors and directors and make a date with someone who was both male and available. Someone who wanted his public awareness quotient to increase. Someone who would benefit from the tabloid splash.

Someone like her old friend Victor Strauss, who was in town for the premiere of his latest project.

He was throwing a party tomorrow night at his house in Bel Air, and she would attend as his date. As usual, someone from one of the tabloids would crash the party and, using their cell phone to take a picture, would get a shot of Jane and Victor together again. **Together** together.

A first-rate director with two Oscar nominations under his belt, Victor was best known for his inability to keep his pants zipped. Which would add fuel to the paparazzi fire.

Which would, in turn, take the heat off Cosmo.

Who had slept in his truck last night.

Jane had indeed noticed at that meeting this morning that Cos was still wearing last night's clothes—that same snug T-shirt that he'd taken off while in her bedroom and . . .

Yeah. She'd noticed Cosmo.

". . . they used to be together," Robin was saying earnestly. "And when Adam saw Jules on the news—"

"Whoa," Jane said. "Wait a minute. Jules Cassidy gave us Adam's headshot and résumé. He couldn't have been that upset by—"

"Yeah, well, he was. He was feeling pretty used. I think he really loves this guy—who's a total shit, and I don't want to work with him." Robin crossed his arms. "He doesn't deserve this movie."

This was on the verge of bizarre. "Because he's a total shit?" she clarified.

"That's right."

"Which you, personally, know a great deal about, considering you're also a total shit—for spending the night with Patty."

Jane was only guessing, but he confirmed it when his "I will not give in" stance crumbled.

"I'm sorry, Janey. I really screwed things up. I'm such a loser." It was a too-familiar song.

Her brother had gotten way too good at sincere-sounding apologies. With his self-deprecating words, he seemed to take responsibility for his actions. But lately, those words were sounding a little too hollow. It was as if by granting himself loser status, he was allowing himself to go ahead and just keep on screwing up.

"Isn't it possible that Adam screwed up and that he's sorry, too?" Jane countered. "Read with him, Robbie. He's really good. He's so good he scares me. Give him a shot. If you honestly can't work with him, or if the chemistry's not there . . . But you know what they say about hate—it's very close to love."

"This is going to suck," Robin said. "For Jules, I mean. If we cast this guy, and he's on set, Jules is going to run into him all the time."

"Hasn't it occurred to you," Jane asked her brother, "that maybe that's exactly what Jules wants?"

Old Jack Shelton seemed to like Adam.

Robin sat with the two of them at HeartBeat Studios, waiting for the film crew to get their act together and shoot Adam's screen test.

Adam was flipping through the script—he hadn't even read the whole thing yet—and asking Jack questions about his experiences during the war.

"It wasn't hideously awful," Jack was telling him. "Well, it was a **war**—that part of it was tragic and terrible—but boot camp, joining the army . . . I was put in a barracks with dozens of other young men and I was in **heaven.** But it wasn't about sex. Don't misunderstand. It was . . . You see, I'd never played team sports. I'd never felt welcome either on the playing field or in the locker room. But after Pearl Harbor, suddenly I was allowed into a club I'd never had access to before. And then, when I was transferred into the Twenty-third, where quite a number of us **were** gay . . . My God. It was both thrilling and terrifying." He laughed and leaned closer, lowering his voice slightly. "Because it meant that someone knew my secret.

"D'you know, when I first joined the Twenty-third," Jack continued, "I was certain that Uncle Sam had transferred all of us not-quite-he-men into the same unit with the intention of wiping us out in one giant training accident."

"Really?" Adam had stopped looking at the script. He was watching Jack and subtly mimicking the old man's hand gestures, as well as his very manner of sitting and breathing. Except somehow Adam was translating it all into a young man's gestures, a young man's sitting, breathing.

Janey was right. The bastard was damn good.

When Robin had read with him back in the casting agent's office, the very air had crackled.

Not that that meant Robin was happy about casting him.

Of course, Adam still had to get past the screen test. Hugo Pierce or Pierce Hugo or whatever his name was had seemed good at first, too.

"Yes." Jack turned to Robin. "Which scene are you using for the screen test, Harold?"

Robin loved the fact that the old man called him Harold. It was almost enough to disappear the queasiness he'd been feeling all day. Almost.

"The one where your bunk mates are trying to figure out what everyone in the barracks has in common." He leaned forward to look across Jack, directly into Adam's eyes. Adam **did** have movie star eyes, hazel and luminescent. Janey was right. The bastard would light up the screen. "You only have a few lines of dialogue in this scene. We're looking for your reaction—your realization that you're not the only gay man in the room, not by a long shot."

"My God," Adam said, repeating Jack's words. "It was both terrifying and thrilling. It meant that someone knew."

It was scary—for a moment there, he **was** Jack. But then he dropped character and asked the old man, "You really thought they were going to, like, kill you?"

"A group of officers came into the barracks in the middle of the night," Jack told him. "They woke us up and marched us into the woods, where we were told to take cover, be silent, no lights, stay put. And then they left. Everyone in charge was just gone. I wasn't the only one who was alarmed, believe me. About an hour after we got there, we heard this incredible noise—engines revving, trees and brush being crushed and pushed aside, like some giant monster was approaching. It didn't take long before we realized we were hearing tanks moving into position in front of us.

"Gay bashing didn't have such a lovely name back then, but that didn't mean it didn't exist," Jack continued. "All of us there that night—that is, all of us who had come to terms with the fact that we were, indeed, friends of Dorothy, who'd gone on vacations or shared apartments with our 'cousins' "—he made quotation gestures in the air—"we'd all experienced some threat of violence because of who we were." He turned then and spoke directly to Robin. "When you've faced the possibility of having a two-by-four connect with the back of your head simply for showing affection to someone you care about . . . ? Well, trust me, being blown out of the woods by tanks didn't seem far-fetched."

"So what happened?" Adam asked, as fascinated as Robin had been when he'd first heard this story. As fascinated as Janey had been when she'd first met Jack. Robin could still remember how excited she'd been at the idea of telling his story, of making a movie about his life. "You didn't just stay there and wait to get blown up, did you?"

"We'd been ordered to stand fast," Jack told him. "It occurred to me that they were intending to fire artillery all around us so that those of us who ran would get killed. And it would be our own fault, **n'est-ce pas**? And of course fairies would be expected to run, wouldn't they? Silly fools—they didn't have a clue as to the courage it took to live in that homophobic society. As I lay there in that dirt, I figured we could show them a thing or two."

"Jack rallied the unit," Robin told Adam, because this was the part that the old man skipped whenever he told the story. The part where, even though he wasn't an officer, he'd assumed a leadership role. "He convinced the men to dig in and stay put."

"And so we lay there," Jack said, "nearly soiling our trousers, listening to those tanks move back and forth for hours that night."

"Did they really shoot at you?" Adam asked.

"Oh, no," Jack said. "It turned out that the officers in charge had no idea we would think ourselves in peril. They returned in the morning and cheerfully asked what we'd seen and heard. Of course, we'd seen nothing. We'd heard those tanks. They gave us a map and ordered us to go find them. So off we went.

"It didn't take long before we approached the edge of the woods. And there we saw a line of tanks out on the far side of a cow pasture," Jack continued. "Only it was very odd, because all night we'd heard tanks crashing through trees and brush, but there was no damage to any of the foliage. 'Go closer,' the officer told us, and so we went out of the woods. As we were about to cross a dirt road that cut the field in two, we could see there were two men standing over by the tanks—they were still quite a distance away. And these men, they bent down and picked up one of the tanks, and they turned it completely around so the gun turret was facing us. Two men—lifting an enormous tank?

"Well. We all stopped short. And then from down the road, kicking up dust behind it, there came a truck. Mounted upon it were enormous loudspeakers. And over the speakers the sound of tanks was blasting away."

"No way," Adam said, grinning.

"That scene's going to be a great visual in the movie," Robin told him. Janey was right about the bastard's smile, too. It made him shine.

"Our officers showed us the role—that of Ghost Army," Jack said, "that the Twenty-third would play in the war. If they had simply told us, 'You're going to use sound effects and rubber tanks filled with air to fool the Germans into believing we have a huge invincible army, we would have thought them certifiable. How could that ever work? **Fool** the Germans with their Panzers and storm troopers and mighty 88s? But now we saw how it could be done, how a handful of men—us—would be able to tie up tens of thousands of Germans troops, preventing them from attacking elsewhere."

"The Twenty-third also worked extensively with camouflage," Robin told Adam. "And optical illusions. They painted shadows of tanks on the sand to make high-flying German surveillance planes believe that the Allies had an enormous buildup of equipment in the desert. They broadcast fictional troop movements over radio channels that they knew the Germans listened to. They used the actors among them to plant false information in towns where they knew there were Nazi sympathizers."

"We were given assignments," Jack explained. "We called them **problems** and we were trusted to use our creativity to solve them. This movie focuses on the last few months of the war, when I was given the assignment of locating authentic German thread and buttons and delivering them to the OSS office in Paris. I soon realized I was assisting with the creation of realistic Nazi uniforms that were to be used by an Allied team on a very dangerous mission. They were going deep into Germany to try to find out whether or not Hitler had the capability to create a nuclear bomb."

"That's where Jack met my character, Hal, who was

a captain in the Airborne," Robin said. "He volunteered to be part of that suicide team. I guess he figured being shot by the Germans as a spy would pretty much put an end to his inner struggle with his homosexuality."

"So what was it that the soldiers in the Twenty-third all had in common?" Adam asked. "I mean, obviously you weren't all gay."

Jack laughed. "No, we certainly weren't." His cell phone rang, and he took it from his pocket, peering over the tops of his glasses at the caller ID. "Excuse me, boys, I really must take this." He started to stand, but Robin was already on his feet.

"Stay here," he told Jack. "I need more coffee, and I'm pretty sure Adam does, too."

Jack was already deep into his call with Scott, his partner—his latest twinkie, as he called him—as Adam followed Robin toward the craft services table.

"I'm at a real disadvantage," Adam said. "I wish I could have, like, a month just to talk to Jack before I do this screen test."

"Yeah, well, time crunch, you know? Do the best you can." Robin took a clean mug from the tray.

"I intend to." Adam watched as Robin poured the coffee, waiting for him to put the pot back onto the warmer before he took a mug himself. "Although, that's not my only disadvantage, is it? I mean, it's kind of obvious that you don't particularly like me."

Robin stirred milk into his cup. "How perceptive of you."

"It's also kind of obvious that Mercedes is really

into me. I mean, for this part. Obviously, since . . . Well . . . You know what I mean."

"She's desperate," Robin said. "We're down to the wire. The role needs to be filled. That's why she's ready to settle."

"Yeah," Adam said. "I guess so. Wow." He laughed, charmingly rueful. "Look, is there someone else you want for this part, that she doesn't particularly . . ."

"Yes, there is," Robin told him. "I think maybe you know him, too. Jules Cassidy."

Adam nearly dropped his coffee mug. But then he laughed again, this time in disbelief. He had a laugh for every occasion. "You're kidding, right? Because, you know, J. isn't exactly an actor."

"You don't think so?" Robin asked. "Because I happen to think he is. I think he's amazing."

"Okay," Adam said slowly. "I'm beginning to understand what this is really about . . ."

"He told me about last night." As Robin said the words, he had to push away an image that flashed into his head—Adam and Jules together. And God, he so didn't want to go there. If he was going to imagine two people having sex, at least one of them should be Christina Ricci.

But then his brain sent him a picture of Patty, on the floor, beneath him as they . . . Holy Jesus, had they actually done it on her living room floor, with most of his clothes still on?

"Of course he told you about it," Adam was saying. "He's Jules. He's honest about every-fucking-thing, and . . ." He laughed again, warmly this time, shaking his head as if they were sharing a private joke. "Man, all your PR is intensely . . . Whoever you've got working for you is aces. I really thought you were razor straight."

"I **am** straight."

"Right," Adam said in that tone that implied he so didn't believe it. "And you and Jules are just friends. Fine, play it that way—I don't care, Robbie. It doesn't matter, either way."

"Because you already got what you wanted from him, right?"

"Wow," Adam said. "You really think I'm a total prick, don't you? Yes, I wanted this audition, but I also wanted to get back together with him. I still do—and I'm going to. Have no doubt about it, Roberta. This morning was just a glitch. He misunderstood, and thought . . ." Another laugh, this one dismissive. "Whatever he thought, he was wrong, and I'll convince him of that."

"It sounded to me like he was through with you," Robin said.

"He'll get over it," Adam told him. "He always does."

"You know, that's the funny thing about **always.** He'll always come back, until one day he doesn't. Kind of like living forever—right up until the day you die."

"Deep." Adam toasted him with his coffee mug. "And okay, yeah. You win. If you're trying to freak me out, you did it. Congratulations. You want the bottom line? I had no idea how much I would miss him until I was living an entire continent away from him. But I did. I missed him. Badly. But do you have any idea what it's like to have someone love you that much?"

Robin thought of Patty, still in the casting director's office with Jane, of the note she'd left for him this morning. **I love you** with a heart in place of the O in **love.** She'd stayed with him all night as he puked his guts out in her bathroom. He didn't remember much of it, but he did remember Patty's cool hands against his forehead.

But what did that have to do with love?

He wasn't sure.

"It scared the hell out of me," Adam confided. Quietly. Intensely. Seriously. "So I ran away. But now I want it. I'm ready. I'm at a place where—"

Enough of the bullshit already. "If you really want him back—"

"I do," Adam said, oozing sincerity from every perfect pore.

"Unless you really fuck up the screen test," Robin told him, "my sister's probably going to offer you this role. If you want to send a real message to Jules, turn it down."

Adam laughed out loud at that. It was musical and infectious amusement, and it made heads turn toward them. "Yeah, I don't think so."

"You really think you can have it all?" Robin asked.

Adam dropped all pretense. "Actually, yes, I do."

"What if you had to choose?"

"But I don't." Adam poured himself more coffee. And changed the subject. "So what **did** they have in common? The men like Jack who were brought in to form the Twenty-third Ghost Army?"

Robin stood watching him for several long moments. "They all had extremely high IQs," he finally said. "For the record, I'm going to encourage Jules to stay away from you."

"You've got to do what you've got to do—it's a free world," Adam said lightly, pouring yet another cup and stashing some packets of sugar and creamer in the front pocket of his shirt. "But also for the record, sweetie pie, you're so not his type."

"I'm straight," Robin said again as Adam put his script under one arm and picked up both cups of coffee.

"Sure," he said with a wink as he headed back toward Jack. "Just keep saying that to yourself over and over. That'll make it true."

CHAPTER NINE

"I've got a date tonight," PJ Prescott informed Cosmo when he arrived at Jane's house shortly after midnight. "Please do whatever you can not to hear any rifle shots within the next thirty, forty minutes, will you? At least give me enough time to be too far away to turn around and come back here."

"A date after midnight?" Cosmo said, setting the paper bag that held his deli sandwich on the kitchen counter.

PJ smiled, checking his reflection in the glass on the microwave door, fixing his hair. "Best kind. No, seriously, my girlfriend Beth just heard . . . Well, she's in the Reserves and she got called up. She's heading out for Iraq in a few weeks. Any time we both have a few hours free, we try to connect."

"Man, I can't imagine," Cosmo said. He shook his head.

"Yeah. I wish I could go over there for her. Look, I've got to boogie. Security system's up and running," PJ informed him. "Although we're still doing a test on it every hour. You know the codes, right?"

Cosmo nodded.

"The brother's home tonight," PJ continued, heading toward the door. "He's up in his room. I haven't seen Mercedes since around twenty-thirty. Nash is outside. We've got security cams running in case your trashed-out Pontiac or mystery truck comes back. So unless you need something else from me . . ."

"Go," Cosmo said. "If we need backup, I'll call Decker."

"I love you, man." PJ was already gone. But then, "Oh, hey," Cos heard him say from the foyer. "I thought you were asleep."

"Yeah." It was Jane. She laughed. "Sleep. Good one, PJ. You're a very funny man. You going?"

"Yeah, baby, yeah, I'm out of here. Richter's in the kitchen, doing . . . what did you call it? Oh, yeah, his tall, dark, and brooding thing."

What?

Jane laughed again. "See you tomorrow night."

"And not one second earlier."

Cosmo heard the door open and shut and the sound of the security system being reengaged.

Then bare feet on the tile floor.

"Hey." Jane crossed to the refrigerator. Opened it. Took out an apple. Washed it off, then took a bite.

Her robe was cotton, and she wore it open over a tank top and boxers, her hair down loose around her shoulders.

"Brooding?" he asked.

She leaned back against the counter. Took another bite. "So, what's your all-time favorite movie?"

Huh?

She stood there, patiently waiting, just watching him.

"I don't know," Cosmo finally said after the silence had stretched on a little too long, even for him. "I'll have to think about it."

She laughed her disbelief. "How could you not know?"

He shook his head, shrugged. "It's not one of my FAQs. I like a lot of movies, but I'm not sure which one is my all-time favorite. Labeling something like that—all-time favorite—really puts the pressure on. So I have to think about it."

"F-A—?" she asked, but then answered herself. "Frequently asked questions." She took another bite and said, with her mouth full, "You actually get asked the same questions so often you think of them as FAQs?"

He shrugged again. "There are definitely some re-peats."

"Like what?"

His FAQs usually came from people that he met in bars. People who'd had too much to drink. The rest of the time, the people he met usually didn't ask him any questions at all.

Jane, however, looked extremely sober.

And again she waited patiently for his reply. Most people gave up after even a few seconds of silence.

But she just stood there, eating that apple and wait-ing him out.

"Mostly about being a SEAL," he told her.

"You mean, like, what's a SEAL?"

Cosmo shook his head again. "No, these days— since 9/11—most people know that."

"I'm not sure if I do. Not exactly. I mean, it's some kind of commando squad, right?"

"We're part of U.S. Special Operations Forces."

"Special Forces, like in **Black Hawk Down,**" she said.

"No," he said. "I mean, yes, those were Special Forces in that incident. But what they do is different from what we do in the SEAL Teams. Well, it's not **what** that's so different, it's **how.** See, Special Forces are part of Special Ops, but . . ."

She was trying her best to follow, but he could tell that he'd lost her. Damn. How did the senior chief explain it to civilians like Jane?

"Here's the deal," Cosmo tried. "Special Forces tend to go in in force—in large groups—weapons out and evident, if not blazing. They use those gunships, helos—helicopters—with massive firepower as air support, like what you saw in **Black Hawk Down.** A Special Forces assignment tends to be—not always— but it tends to be noisy. What we do in the spec ops groups or SEALs is we insert covertly. That means we go into a hostile city or country with stealth. Quietly. In small groups—usually six, seven men. We do whatever job needs to be done, like taking out a communications system, or pinpointing a terrorist hideout, or . . . maybe something like a hostage rescue. So we go in quietly, and we extract just as covertly. We leave

the city or country without anyone—well, almost anyone—knowing we were there, without a single shot
fired."

She'd stopped eating the apple and was actually
listening, her eyes glaze-free and locked on his face.
Damn, she did have pretty eyes. And gorgeous skin.
And a body that didn't quit. But did she understand?
There were servicepeople in the U.S. Military who still
got Special Operations and Special Forces confused.

"Here's a good way to keep it straight," he told her,
remembering the senior chief's concise explanation.
"When you think Special Forces, think of that gun-
ship. Think show of force. But with Special Operations—SEALs—it's all about the op. It's about getting
the job done as quickly and quietly as possible."

She nodded. "I think I get it."

"Good." He smiled. "Because I'm not sure I could
explain it any more clearly."

She turned away. "But . . . why seals?" she asked. "A
seal isn't exactly sexy. Not the way a wolf is. Or even an
eagle. Screaming Eagles—now **that**'s a sexy name."

What had just happened here? Cosmo, who made
a point never to miss anything, had definitely missed
something.

Jane kept her back to him as she crossed to the
garbage and tossed her apple core in the container
marked COMPOST as she kept up the chatter. "But
you're Navy—so okay, water . . . oceans . . . Sharks?"
She shook her head as she went to the sink and washed
her hands, still not looking at him. "Eh. Too often as-
sociated with evil. Dolphins . . . porpoises . . . Okay,

those don't work either—too friendly, too hard to say. . . . But how about stingrays? Rays. Yeah. They're much sexier than seals. Have you ever seen one?"

Cosmo just stood there watching her. Was she really brainstorming a name change for the Teams?

She crossed the kitchen again and dried her hands on the towel hanging on the refrigerator door handle. "They look kind of like those flying pizzas in **Star Trek**—you know, 'I am quite blind.' Where Spock gets infected and they use radiation to—" She stopped herself, allowed herself to glance in his direction. "Not a **Star Trek** fan?"

Cosmo wasn't sure what to say—she'd taken their conversation in so many different directions. And as she moved around the kitchen, her nightwear made for quite an eyeful. **I am quite blind,** indeed.

Her boxers bore images of characters from **Sponge-Bob SquarePants,** and she wasn't wearing any makeup at all. The gray tank wasn't designed to be at all alluring, yet . . . Tonight, SpongeBob aside, he found her unbelievably attractive in every way.

When the hell had that happened?

As she waited for him to respond, she self-consciously closed the front of her robe, tying the belt at her waist. God, had he just been staring at her?

Was that what just happened here? Something had definitely freaked her out. Yet at the same time, she didn't seem to be in any hurry to leave.

Star Trek, renaming the Teams . . . Cos mentally worked his way back to where she'd started. **Why seals?**

"SEAL is an acronym," he told her. Client, client, client. She was his client. Damn, it had been much easier when he'd seen her only as expensive and annoying arm candy. "Sea, air, land. We're trained to operate in those three environments."

"Well, that about covers it, doesn't it?" she said. "I mean, except maybe for outer space—or does that count as air?"

Why wasn't she going back upstairs? It was late; she had to work in the morning. "Hasn't been much call for us to do ops in outer space," he said.

"You know, ducks make more sense," Jane pointed out. "Seals don't exactly fly."

"Yeah, I'll be sure to bring that to Admiral Crowley's attention next time I see him."

She laughed. "Good."

And then there was silence. This time it was hers—and as she stood there, just looking at him, it was goddamn unnerving. What was she thinking? Cosmo honestly had no clue.

He cleared his throat. "Now that the security system is installed, I'll just be down here in the kitchen, so if you need me—"

"Have you ever killed anyone?"

He didn't let anything show on his face. He never did—or at least he was pretty sure he didn't, but now he had to wonder because she quickly added, "I'm not asking you that. It's none of my business, of course. I'm just . . . I'm guessing that's probably another question you get a lot."

"Yeah. It's . . . Yeah."

"Who asks it most?" she wondered, and he realized she was telling the truth. She hadn't asked it because she wanted to know the answer. "The women or the men?"

"Women," she guessed in unison with him as he answered. She laughed. "That's amazing. What are they thinking?"

Cos shook his head. "I don't know." It was always kind of weird when women he met in a bar—clearly trying to pick him up—asked that. Apparently, men with kill notches on their belts were hugely attractive to some women.

"What do you tell them?" Jane asked, but this time didn't wait for him to answer. "I would make up some huge number, like, 'Yup, just made my five-hundredth bare-handed kill last week. With one-forty-three slice-and-dices and fifty-seven double pops to the head, I'm up to the big seven-oh-oh, so not only did they give me a brand-new watch, but I also had enough body count points to get me a washer and dryer. It'll be delivered next week. Can't wait.' "

Cosmo laughed. "Nice."

She lowered her gaze with false modesty. "I'm a writer. It comes naturally. Feel free to use it."

"Usually I just excuse myself and walk away."

"Not into having sex with the ghoulishly, morbidly curious?"

He laughed again, but before he could answer, she added, "Don't give me that 'ridiculous question' laugh. You **know**—admit it, you **do** know—that some guys wouldn't care. Some guys—I'm not naming names: **Robin**—would gleefully use it to their advantage."

"Do you ever get approached by men?" she continued, completely comfortable again. Maybe he'd simply imagined that temporary oddness. Maybe it was just inside of his own head. Maybe it was a reflection of his own freaked-out status, brought on by the fact that when he looked at her now, he liked what he saw. A lot. "Any macho types who follow you out into the parking lot to see just how tough the Navy SEAL really is?"

He shook his head. "You planning to write a story about a Navy SEAL?"

Jane smiled at him. Leaned back against the counter again. "I can't help but notice how my life suddenly resembles a TV movie of the week log line," she told him. " 'Hollywood screenwriter is thrown into a world of intrigue and danger when her latest project, the too-honest story of a beloved war hero's hidden secret, sparks death threats.' I figure I better start thinking about it, yeah."

Cosmo couldn't tell if she was serious.

"How's your mom?" she asked. And meant it. Which brought a whole new source of weirdness into the room. Sometime between yesterday and today, they had become friends. At least she was treating him as if he were her friend.

"She's getting tired of having two broken wrists," he told her.

"I bet. How exactly did she . . . ?"

"New bifocals plus a storm that knocked some branches onto her deck. She tripped and fell—all the way down the stairs."

"Oh, my God!" Jane said. "That's awful!"

"Fortunately her neighbor was outside and saw it happen. Called 911."

"My God," Jane said again, honestly upset. "Can you imagine if the neighbor hadn't been there?"

Yes, he could. And he did. Far too often. "I was out of the country when it happened."

"Oh, Cos, that must've sucked."

"Yeah," he said.

"I can't imagine that," she said. "Going overseas the way you do, to some outrageously dangerous place and . . . PJ told me he was getting a taste of what it was like to be on the other end of that. His girlfriend's going to Iraq. He's pretty stressed out."

"Yeah," Cosmo agreed. "That's got to be tough."

"What exactly does **your** girlfriend do?" Jane asked.

Her question was a fishing expedition, asked so casually that he could practically see the beach chairs and cooler of beer.

Or was it? Before he could answer with "I already told you, I'm not seeing anyone right now—remember? My shift ends at 3:17. Wanna meet up in your room, get naked and—" she continued: "She works for Troubleshooters, right?"

"Uh . . ." Cosmo said. "Where did you hear that?"

"I was talking to Murph this afternoon, and I don't know, I guess it was when PJ showed up and mentioned his girlfriend going to Iraq . . . We started talking about Jimmy Nash and Tess Bailey, who are hot and heavy, and how difficult—or not—that must be. You know, working together 24/7. In contrast to Beth and PJ spending the next eight months apart. But Murphy mentioned he and Angelina were having dinner with Tom and his wife sometime next week and that you were going to be there along with someone named Sophia, who also works for Troubleshooters, and . . . Murph thought maybe you and Sophia were seeing each other."

Shit, Murph, send out press releases, why don't you? And what was Kelly doing, calling Murphy like that? She was supposed to wait for Cosmo's go-ahead. Didn't she realize that even if she called it a "friendly get-together," speculation would start?

Jane cleared her throat. "I'm sorry if what I did at the press conference made things difficult for you, and wow, I can see from your face that you are not happy that we were talking about this."

"She's not my girlfriend," Cosmo finally ground out. "She's just . . . Kelly—Tom's wife—was trying to make it easier for me to meet her and . . . Shit. Does **every**one know?"

"Oh," Jane said. "I don't—"

"Forget it," he said. This was so freaking perfect. Suddenly he was in seventh grade again. What a nightmare. "Excuse me. I didn't mean to—"

"What? Say **shit**?" she asked. "You're kidding, right? This counts as at least a **shit.** You like her, you ask for a little help getting together, and suddenly she's referred to as your girlfriend? No, no, Cosmo, believe me, that's a solid **shit.** If I were her, and I heard that, I'd think you were responsible for the rumors and—"

"Thanks so much for the comforting words."

"PJ says she's really pretty," Jane said. "All blond and Barbie-perfect."

"Yeah," Cos said. "She is. She's very . . . pretty." This was freaking surreal. In truth, he could barely remember what Sophia looked like.

"Murph says she's a kick-ass operative, that he worked with her in Kazbekistan, after that earthquake they had there? What woman in her right mind would willingly go to Kazbekistan? I mean, talk about courageous. She must be awesome."

Whoa. K-stan? Really? "Yeah," Cosmo said again. "She must be. I didn't, um . . . I didn't know any of that about her. I just . . . I don't know her at all. I was hoping to, you know, get to know her. I had one conversation with her, where I spilled my coffee on myself. I'm sure she thinks I'm an idiot, and after she hears . . ." He shook his head. "Talk about fated not to happen."

"What? Come on. That's defeatist bullshit thinking. It ain't over till it's over." Jane sat up on the kitchen counter. "Why not just ask her to dinner?"

How could they be having this conversation? How could this have happened? Cosmo just shook his head.

Jane didn't let it go. "Why not?"

"In case you haven't noticed, I'm not exactly a sparkling conversationalist."

"What you need to do is let yourself get really pissed off at her," Jane suggested. "Scream at her for a while, and then call a truce. That's what you did with me—and now you're holding your own just fine. Sure, there can still be a time delay when I ask you a question that you don't particularly want to answer, but now that I'm used to it . . ." She shrugged.

"It's not that I don't **want** to answer," he countered. "I just . . ." He shook his head.

"Why in God's name would you want to have a first date with an audience?" Jane asked. "You're either crazy or really brave."

Cosmo briefly closed his eyes. "It wasn't supposed to be a date," he said. "It was supposed to be, I don't know, mutual friends spending the evening . . . and it was a stupid idea, whatever it was supposed to be, because I'll just sit there and say nothing."

"Are you a virgin?" Jane asked.

He looked at her.

"Well, the way you're all complainy, it almost sounds like you've never even had a conversation with a woman before, let alone—"

"I'm not." What the fuck was **complainy**?

"I mean, unless you **are** a virgin, words must have been exchanged," she pointed out. "Obviously—"

"This is different," he said.

She leaned forward. "How?"

"This woman is . . ." He searched for the words. "She's . . ."

"Hot?" Jane suggested.

"No. Well, yes, but . . ."

"Sassy?"

He stared at her.

"Sorry, I was just reading a really ridiculous women's magazine, and they had this quiz, 'Are you sassy?' and if you don't want me to finish your sentences, snap to it." She actually snapped her fingers at him.

"Nice," Cosmo said. "She's nice, all right?"

"Oh, ew. Nice?" Jane looked as if she'd stepped in the kitty litter with bare feet. "Like, nun nice, or librarian nice, or—"

Jesus God. "Smart nice," he said. "Educated, intelligent, and . . . sweet nice."

As opposed to the not-so-nice women he usually dated—women who chased after him because they thought he looked dangerous, women who liked playing with fire. Desperate women who weren't exactly looking for someone to talk to.

Truth was, Cos usually didn't meet nice women. At least not until they were married to his friends. His problem was that he didn't often hang out where nice women hung out.

Of course, even if he did, even if he joined the library book group or the local gardening club, the nice women wouldn't approach him. And he wouldn't know how to approach them. **Nice weather we're having . . .** Christ. Just kill him now.

"Sweet nice, as in not the type to do it in the closet in the back room during halftime at the sports bar?" Jane asked him.

Cosmo laughed. "Yes."

"Well, okay. At least we got that straightened out, although you might want to rethink getting with someone that suffocatingly nice, because you **can** have both nice and the sports bar back room closet thing— it's a male myth that it's got to be all or nothing," Jane told him. "Ginger versus Mary Ann. Why do you feel like you have to choose between the two?"

"Do you ever sleep?" he asked her.

"The virgin or the whore," Jane said. "You asked me yesterday why I dress the way I dress. You know, when I go out in public. The fact is, the peeps want to party with the whore. Playing the virgin doesn't get me very far in my line of work." She mocked a TV news anchor's voice. " 'And today, in Beverly Hills, Jane Chadwick drew absolutely no attention to herself when, while wearing a drab business suit, she got seated in the very rear of the Grill on the Alley because no one recognized her.' "

Cosmo threw her question right back at her. "Why do **you** feel like you have to choose between the two?"

She stared for a moment, but then smiled at him. "Wow, you are a smart man, aren't you? Looks do deceive." She slid down off the counter. "I've decided that I'm going to help you with your Sophia problem."

What? "No," Cos said. "There's no problem—"

"Are you dating her?"

He didn't bother to answer.

"Then there's a problem, Romeo. And that was a Romeo, not a Rambo, so don't, like, get all huffy on me."

"Look, Jane . . ."

"We'll talk about it tomorrow. It's late and . . . Oh, my God, did I tell you we found our Jack?" She did a victory lap around the kitchen.

He couldn't help but laugh. "Congratulations."

"Thank you. Thank you. Thank you very much.

Some unknown named Adam Wyndham. He's a friend of Jules Cassidy and he's **amazing.** My movie's going to kick ass!" She danced her way toward the kitchen door. "I have to go write that ass-biting, double-boning, pain in the balls D-Day battle dream sequence. We're filming it next week. It's the only time we've got access to both the beach and a helicopter, so we need to do it then. Which means I really need to write it. Try not to be too loud down here, Cosmo. I mean, come on. Do you ever shut up?" She stuck her head back in the door. "Hey, I was thinking—if you want, you're welcome to bring your mom onto the movie set. I mean, if you think she'd be interested. It might at least help her pass the time until the casts come off."

"Thank you," Cosmo said. "That's . . ." She was already gone. He could hear her dashing up the stairs. ". . . nice of you," he finished even though she couldn't hear him.

It was unbelievably nice.

CHAPTER
TEN

"Excuse me, Patty," Decker called.

But Patty pretended not to notice that the security team leader from Troubleshooters Incorporated was bearing down on her. This was so not the right time for a conversation, let alone one with a man who clearly was on the verge of asking her for help or a favor.

Because she'd just spotted Robin. He'd finally come into the studio, barely in enough time to get into costume for his upcoming scene. If she hurried, she could catch him in the makeup chair.

She'd nearly escaped to the stairs when Decker caught up to her. "Patty, hi."

Darn it. She could hear Robin laughing and joking with Harve the makeup magician, his voice carrying up from below. Robin, who hadn't called her or come to see her last night, whom she hadn't so much as heard a whisper from since yesterday. Robin, with whom she hadn't exchanged a coherent word in private since they'd had unprotected sex on her apartment floor.

She forced a smile. "Oh, hi, Deck. How can I help you?"

He wasn't fooled. "Are you all right?" he asked, and of course, his kindness made her want to break down into a sobbing ball of tears.

She muscled through, blinking it all back. "A little overwhelmed today," she told him. "Things are crazy."

"I know the feeling. And I hate to add to your load," he said, "but Mercedes said I should talk to you about getting copies of your personnel records. I need info on cast, crew, caterers, extras—anyone at all who has access to the set."

Oh, God. There were, literally, hundreds of people involved in making this movie.

Decker correctly read the expression of horror that she couldn't keep from her face. "If you can just point me to the right computer," he reassured her, "I can download the information I need."

"No, you can't," she said. "Well, some of it's on the computer, sure. But I've got about a thousand head-shots and résumés of extras that we might use for crowd scenes—for the upcoming D-Day sequence. They don't get entered into the computer until they're actually scheduled and hired."

"A thousand." Dismay wasn't included in Decker's limited arsenal of facial expressions, but she knew he was feeling it now, too. "Well, let me get started with the people you've already hired," he said.

"You really think one of them might be Mr. Insane-o?" she asked, using Jane's irreverent name for the e-mail killer. But wasn't **that** a creepy thought.

Someone she'd had a conversation with could actually be a murderer, preparing to kill again.

"It's just a precaution," Decker told her. "Part of the process of the investigation."

"I'll copy the files you need," she said, about to add, "If you'll just give me twenty minutes . . ."

But then "Settle!" was shouted. And her chance of talking to Robin was gone, so she might as well do the copying now.

"Settle!" she echoed down the stairs, and closed the door, with herself on the non-Robin side of it. Motioning to Decker, she led the way through the door to the production offices—and nearly ran over who else but Wayne Ickes.

Oh, no!

She had so completely forgotten that last night she'd had plans to meet him for drinks. She'd been so wrapped up in Robin and all that had happened that she'd forgotten to call Wayne and cancel.

Instead, she'd stood him up.

There was no anger in his eyes, however, only concern. Which made her feel even worse. "I am so sorry," she told him. "Things got crazy busy last night and . . ."

"I figured it was something major," he said. "It's okay. I really need to get a cell phone of my own. I've been using a friend's and last night he needed it. How about—"

"Right now I'm in the middle of something very important," she said. She had to tell Wayne that she and Robin were a couple now, but she couldn't do it here, in front of Decker. That would be too cruel. "Maybe we can talk later?"

He took **later** to mean later today instead of later this decade. "Maybe at lunch?"

The way her day was going? Not a chance. "Maybe," she lied, just to get him moving. She turned back to Decker. "I'll get you those files now."

They left Wayne standing there in the hall.

"Boyfriend?" Decker asked as they went into the studio office.

"Gosh, no," she said after she'd closed the door, although it was clear that Wayne was auditioning for the role. It had been stupidly moronic of her ever to agree to go anywhere with him, but at the time, she'd been so angry with Robin.

"Another thing I need from you," Decker was saying, "is a list of all locations where you'll be filming. Mercedes mentioned something about some outdoor shots starting in a few days. My team will need to go out there to make sure it's safe enough for her to—"

"What? It's not safe at all!" Patty had thought Robin had succeeded in talking Jane out of accompanying the camera crew. "It's a night shoot," she told Decker, nearly breathless with anxiety. Was Jane crazy? Did she want to die? "It's in these woods. I helped scout the location. It's in the middle of nowhere. No offense, but there's no way even the best security team in the world could keep anyone safe out there. Not from a crazy man with a sniper rifle." She lowered her voice, glanced around to make sure her boss wasn't in earshot. "You can't let her go."

Decker nodded as he watched her sit in front of her laptop, which was locked to the desk with a security wire.

"I'll check it out," he told her as she keyed in her personal code and then began copying the personnel file onto a disk. "But my job isn't to restrict Mercedes' movements. As much as I'd like to, I can't forbid her from going someplace simply because I deem it too dangerous. I can advise and recommend, but ultimately the choice is hers. You'd probably have a better shot at talking her out of something like that."

"Believe me, I've tried." The computer clicked and whirred, and Patty pushed with her feet so her chair rolled over to the file cabinet. She opened the huge third drawer. "Here's our headshot file. This entire drawer." She could tell from looking at him that a thousand headshots and résumés took up a whole lot more space than he'd imagined. "Oh, and I've also got another stack—probably about three hundred more of these—at my apartment. I'll bring them in tomorrow."

There was a knock on the door, and Patty braced herself for the worst—another round with Wayne Ickes. But instead, it was the newest cast member, Adam.

"Excuse me," he said. With his hair cut short, he actually looked quite a bit like the photos they had of young Jack Shelton. "I'm sorry to interrupt, but I've got only five minutes and . . . You're Patty, right? I'm Adam. Hi. Mercedes wasn't sure and she thought you might know. . . . Are you, um . . . expecting Jules Cassidy today?"

Patty rolled back to the desk, where she'd put her

clipboard. "I don't think he's on my visitors' list, but you know, he's with the FBI, so he can pretty much flash his badge whenever he wants and—"

"He left town," Decker said.

"Really?" Adam was surprised. "Is he coming back? I mean, he **is** coming back, right? He helped get me this job, and I haven't had a chance to thank him."

"We need to thank him, too," Patty said. "You're terrific."

Adam beamed. "Thank you. You are so sweet. Hey, you wouldn't happen to have Jules' cell phone number, would you? He gave me his card with his new number on it and—silly me—I left it at home."

Patty accessed Jane's address book, which she kept on her laptop, and read the number off to Adam.

"You," he said, inputting it directly into his own cell phone, "are my new best friend." He headed for the door, but then turned back. "I'm not needed until after lunch. Will you do me a favor and give me a call on my cell at one-fifteen—in case I fall asleep?"

"No problem." Patty wrote herself a note and stuck it onto her clipboard.

"Thanks." Adam closed the door behind him.

Decker was looking at her, eyebrow raised. "I thought you were Mercedes' assistant."

"On a shoot with a bigger budget, he'd have someone of his own," she felt compelled to explain. "I don't mind doing whatever I can to help the actors."

"As if you don't have enough to do," he said.

The door opened. It was one of the crew. "Hey, Pattycakes, Mercedes is looking for you."

Shoot. The file was only ninety percent copied. "I'll be right there." Patty turned to Decker. "I won't have time to photocopy the extras' résumés until, well . . ." She sighed as she looked at her watch. Her chance of talking to Robin at all today was dwindling fast. "I guess I could probably start after we're done here tonight."

Another knock on the door. "Patty, catering needs to know how many cast and crew will be here on Saturday. They're willing to take a guesstimate, but they need the number in twenty minutes."

Oh, brother, where was the scheduling book?

"I'll have one of my team come in tomorrow and copy everything in the extras file," Decker told her.

"Thank you," she said.

He smiled. "Maybe that way you can get more than two hours of sleep tonight."

Patty laughed. "Yeah, wish me luck."

"File's done," her computer announced.

She popped out the disk and handed it to him, logged off the computer, grabbed the week's scheduling book and her clipboard, and ran to find Jane, praying that Robin was with her, because darn it, she needed to see his smile.

"I'm sorry, sir, the hotel's completely booked."

Jules gazed across the counter at the desk clerk. "No, you don't understand." It was nearly one o'clock in the morning. It was easy not to understand things at one o'clock in the morning. He should know. Throughout his life, his most stupid mistakes had taken place after midnight. "I have a reservation. I've got a confirmation number."

He fished in his pocket, pulled out his notepad, put it on the counter so the worried-looking clerk could read it for herself. He gave her his most reassuring smile, but as the young woman typed some information into her computer, her frown only deepened.

Which was not a good sign.

"I spent the day in Idaho," Jules told her. "So if I burst into tears, well, now you know why."

Nothing. Nada. No laughter. No smile even.

He was starting to wonder if she had a pulse when she finally glanced up at him. But she went back right away to frowning at the computer screen, worrying at her lower lip now.

"Irving, Idaho," Jules tried. "Which, believe it or not, is as dull as it sounds. So I'm ready for my luck to change. Something good's going to happen—I can feel it in the air. You're going to upgrade me to a suite, right?"

Either that, or he was on a roll of well-deserved bad luck. He'd brought it down upon himself by surrendering to Adam's smile again.

Again.

And again.

His own stupidity was astonishing.

He was like his own little special needs brother. **And this is Jules. Don't let him get near the box of Twinkies—he'll have too many and make himself sick. It's not his fault. He just doesn't have the brain power to realize—**

But oh, God, just **seeing** Adam again . . .

Jules had been living with a heart made of stone. When Adam had left D.C., he'd shut everything out, shut everything down. No pain, but no real joy, either.

He'd done more the other night than let Adam into his room, his life, his bed.

For the first time in years, he'd let himself truly **feel.** And God, how it all came flooding back—anger, hurt, resentment, pain . . .

Hope, joy, laughter . . .

Love.

He'd been going nonstop for the past few days. He'd had no time to think, to figure out what the hell he was going to do now, to at least try to order and organize all these untidy emotions he'd stuffed out of sight for so long.

All he wanted was to get to his hotel room and fall unconscious across the bed.

The young woman behind the counter shook her head. "I'm sorry, Mr. Cassidy," she said. "We don't have a room for you. This isn't . . . well, it's a confirmation number, but it's not yours."

It was one o'clock in the morning, so Jules didn't say anything right away. He just stood for a moment, absorbing her words, trying extra hard to understand.

"It's not mine," he repeated.

"I'm sorry, sir."

She actually looked truly sorry, so he kept his voice gentle. He even managed to smile. "Would you mind getting your manager"—he read her name tag—"Kaitlyn?"

She blinked at him. "It's after one in the—"

" 'Cause here's the thing," he interrupted, still smiling, but yes, he knew quite well what time it was. "I called and made this reservation at 4:14 this afternoon. See where it says that right here?" He pointed to the page in his notepad. "I spoke to someone named Colleen"—he'd also written that down—"who booked me a nonsmoking room. I gave her my Visa card number because I knew I would be arriving late. This is my notepad. This is my handwriting. Ergo, Kaitlyn, it's probably safe to assume that this would be my confirmation number."

She was tippy-tapping away on her computer keyboard again, shaking her head. "I'm sorry, sir, but our records show that someone from your office named Laronda called at eleven thirty p.m., transferring the reservation out of your name."

"Laronda." Jules laughed. Perfect. Unbelievably, fabulously perfect. "Into whose name was it transferred?"

Kaitlyn continued to be unswervingly apologetic. "I'm afraid I can't give out that information, sir."

As if he didn't know. "Is it Max Bhagat?" he asked. This was like a twisted version of **The Three Bears.** But instead of Goldilocks, it was Papa Bear's boss sleeping in that bed.

Kaitlyn's reaction was a solid affirmative. Apparently she hadn't yet taken the course titled Desk Clerk Poker Face 101. "I'm sorry, sir, I really can't—"

"I understand. I'll need my rental car brought back up from the garage," Jules told her as he reached for his cell phone, which he'd been carrying around turned off because Adam had somehow gotten hold of his number. As it beeped back to life, sure enough, there were about a half dozen messages from Laronda, who forevermore would be known as That Hotel Room Stealing Bitch. "Can you help me find a local hotel that does have a vacancy?"

He pushed the button that would let him listen to the most recent of Laronda's messages, holding up one finger to stop Kaitlyn from replying.

"Jules, where **are** you?" Laronda's rich voice chastised him. "You ought to be on the ground by now. FYI, I was just informed that the airline got you onto a different flight. Apparently you'll be arriving in Los Angeles after all, but now I've gone and given Max your hotel room, because the original delay wasn't going to get you out of Idaho Falls until the morning. Call me at home if you need to, but, honey, even I don't have powerful enough magic to conjure up a room for you in a city where every hotel is completely booked."

"How could every hotel in L.A. be booked?" It was a rhetorical question, but Kaitlyn answered it for him.

"There are six different conventions in town this week," she told him helpfully. "I could maybe find you something in Anaheim."

"These may or may not be words that chill the blood in your veins," Laronda's message continued, "but it looks like tonight you'll be bunking with the boss."

Jules laughed. No fricking way. Share a room with Max? She had to be kidding.

But she wasn't. "Call him when you get to the hotel," Laronda continued. "He's in room 1235. It was his idea. Call him, Jules."

Yeah, sure it was Max's idea. No doubt he'd had it handed to him on a platter, with a serious side dish of heavy guilt.

"How far away is Anaheim?" Jules asked Kaitlyn as he snapped his phone shut.

"This time of night, you can probably make it in about an hour," she told him, turning away to answer a phone that managed to ring soothingly.

His own phone rang, too, far more jarringly, and he checked the screen for the incoming number.

It was Adam. Of course. How else could Jules' evening get even more pathetically awful?

To start, he supposed that Kaitlyn **could** morph into a demon vampire like on **Buffy,** leap over the counter to sink her teeth into his neck, and—

Instead she smiled perkily, as only a Kaitlyn could at one a.m., and held the telephone out to him. "It's for you, Mr. Cassidy."

He put Adam back in his pocket, still ringing, and took the handset. "Hello?"

"I have a seven a.m. meeting." It was Max. His boss. The head of the FBI's most elite counterterrorist team. He didn't sound happy. Of course, these days he never sounded happy. "I'm sitting here, watching **Headline News** cycle around for the third time, waiting for you to turn on your cell phone—which, by the way, you better have a goddamn good reason for turning off."

"I do," Jules told him. "Sir. But you don't want to hear it."

"Try me," Max said. "But do it after you get up here. Room 1235."

"Yeah, um, about that . . ." Jules said slowly. No way could he share a hotel room with Max. It didn't matter that the man was relentlessly straight. Someone would find out and ugly rumors would spread. He couldn't let that happen. "Really, sir, it's probably not a good idea—"

"What are you going to do?" Max asked. "Sleep in your rental car?"

"Well . . . yeah."

Max sighed. "Just get up here, Cassidy. I'll take my chances. What am I supposed to be afraid of anyway? That you'll get some of your gay on me?"

"Sir, believe me, people can be pretty awful. They'll talk—"

"The hell with 'em."

Jules tried again. "Sir, your career—"

"Okay, look. It's your room. You come up here, I'll go sleep in your car."

"That's ridiculous," Jules said.

"Yes," Max agreed. "Yes, it is."

Jane's shiny black dress looked as if it had been painted on.

Cosmo had been waiting for quite some time when

the limo pulled into the driveway. Tess Bailey and Jimmy Nash were the first out, followed by PJ. They were all wearing dark suits—wherever they'd been, ties had been required.

Cos joined them, duffel bag over his shoulder, as Jane emerged. They surrounded her, diamond pattern. He was on her left as they hustled her to her front door.

Decker had told him she was going out tonight, but he hadn't gone into detail as to where.

Apparently, she'd been partying in the land of the painted-on clothing.

"Hi, Cos, how are you?" she greeted him, genuinely glad to see him. She smelled like cigarette smoke and wine. He caught only a faint trace of her now-familiar perfume.

"Fine," he said as he helped her inside, sticking close until the door shut behind them. PJ stayed outside, shouting an adios, racing to spend the rest of the night with his girlfriend. Tess and Nash, despite the security system that was on and working, left to do a quick search of the house.

"Any luck finding that car—or your truck?" Jane asked.

"No."

She knew it was bugging him. He spent a lot of time standing out in the yard, trying to get a feel for where the shooter had been when he'd fired that rifle. Trying to figure out where that freaking bullet might have gone.

It was starting to be a joke among the other members of the team. "Hey, Cos. Find that bullet?" "Any sign of your truck?"

Your truck.

Murph hadn't gotten a plate number for the car. It—like the truck's—had been obscured.

Probably intentionally.

But yeah, okay. Mud happened.

Tonight Cos had gone prowling again around the neighbors' driveways and garages.

There were twenty-three homes past Jane's. About a mile down, the road dead-ended. There was only one way in and one way out.

Cosmo had found that six of the ten vehicles on his list belonged to those neighbors. The seventh had had out-of-state plates. Eight was an eighty-thousand-dollar sports car that didn't meet the FBI's profile of the man Jane had dubbed "Mr. Insane-o." As for nine and ten . . . there was no sign, anywhere in the area, of either the beat-up Pontiac that Murphy had seen or "Cosmo's truck."

"How was your evening?" As if he had to ask. He could tell Jane was jazzed about something.

What he couldn't tell was how she could possibly be wearing underwear beneath that dress. And what the hell kind of fabric was it made of? It was so shiny it almost looked wet.

"Awesome! **What** an incredible night!" She sat on the stairs to take off her stilts. "Aren't you going to congratulate me?"

"Congratulations." Cosmo watched her rub her

feet as her already short skirt rode up and up and . . .
He turned to check the security system's panel of
lights, slipping his bag off his shoulder and onto
the floor. Everything looked good. Although, granted,
some things looked a little **too** good. "What am I con-
gratulating you for?"

"HeartBeat wants to put together a distribution
deal for **Fool's Gold,**" she told him, pulling herself to
her feet. "It's a romantic comedy Robin and I made a
few years ago. It's never been released."

"You made a movie without knowing you were
going to be able to distribute it?" he asked.

"Yeah." Jane grinned. "Crazy, huh? You have no
idea how many movies get made each year that never
see the light of day. The lucky ones go direct to video;
some just sit in the can and gather dust. It's definitely
a gamble. And my luck has been, well, less than, since
I refused to make **Hell or High Water Two.**"

About that . . . "Robin told me you could've had it
easy if you'd done the sequel—"

"And the sequel to that and the sequel to **that . . .**"
She rolled her eyes. "No. Thanks. I refused to be forever measured by a screamingly successful fluke. Wait.
That sounds like I'm bashing myself. For the record, I
think **Hell** was a terrific movie. The script was good,
and my actors rocked. The fluke was that anyone at all
saw it, outside of my film school professors. But okay,
it happened. Big-time. And yes, as a result, I had
plenty of offers—to do **Hell Two.** Except I didn't want
to write the sequel. And even if I did . . ."

Cosmo nodded. He got it. It would automatically be compared to the original, and how could it possibly compete?

"So I wrote something completely different," Jane told him. "Which flopped because since it wasn't **Hell Two,** it didn't get the distribution it deserved. Which meant I had to make **Fool's Gold** on my own. It took two years to raise the money—most of which was mine. Hooray for credit cards—which I'm still paying off." She gestured toward the metal pails that were scattered about the entrance hall. "Believe it or not, this is not just a quirky yet bold decorative choice."

"Yeah, I kind of guessed," he told her.

"Anyway, I did it, hoping that when I was finished someone would see the movie and want to distribute it. Which they didn't. See it, I mean. At all. By that point, **Hell** was so five years ago. Nobody was interested—I'd dropped off the map." Jane laughed. "This is a crazy place. I'm twenty-six years old, and I'm having a comeback. Which is how it all works here. Everyone's careers has highs and lows. So even when your movie doesn't get picked up right away, you just hang on and wait for the next wave. If you play it right, you get noticed again, and whammo, old projects get snapped up, and you can maybe recoup your expenses."

If you play it right. "The Party Girl Producer," Cosmo said.

"J. Mercedes Chadwick to the rescue." Jane pulled her hair up and off her shoulders and neck, giving him a better look at the details of that dress. And here he'd thought the front neckline was low. But now he could see that the opening in the back was held together only by three slender strips of fabric. It went all the way down to . . . Yes, she had a tattoo—it looked like the Chinese character for happiness—low on her back.

"God, I need a shower. Did you smell my hair? I usually go out by the pool during parties because there's breathable air out there, but this time I had to stay inside." She did a quick spin of joy. "Oh, Cos, it was wild—everyone made a big deal about closing the curtains, and I had so many people ask if they could get me a drink because the bar was outside. Sofia Coppola. Sofia Coppola got **me** a Diet Coke. It almost makes it worth it. You know, the whole psycho killer Mr. Insane-o thing."

Her enthusiasm plus that dress was quite the combination.

"You must be exhausted," Cosmo said. "As soon as Tess and Nash give us the all clear—"

"You're kidding, right?" she countered. "I am so wired. And there's actually something I was hoping you could help me with. If you don't mind."

Um . . .

Tess Bailey saved him for the moment, coming down the stairs. Nash was right behind her, looking svelte and sophisticated in his expensive, well-tailored dark suit. "All clear," Tess announced with a smile, looking none too shabby herself.

For the first time in a long time Cosmo felt underdressed and self-conscious about his clothes. Cargo pants and a T-shirt. Damn, he dressed like a fifteen-year-old.

"Touch base in five," he said as he closed the door behind them. Nash was off duty, but it wasn't likely he was going to leave while Tess was still here.

Cos turned back to Jane, hoping she was too tipsy to remember that she'd just asked him for some un-named favor. There was no doubt about it—Diet Coke wasn't the only thing she'd had to drink tonight. "You're good to go take that shower," he told her.

But she didn't start up the stairs. She just stood there, silent for a moment.

"So was that an evasive no?" she finally asked, lower lip caught between her teeth, visibly subdued. "It's okay if you don't want to help me—it really is. I just wasn't completely sure . . ."

Way to be the Grinch to her little Cindy Lou Who.

"I'm happy to help with whatever you need," Cosmo told her. And wasn't that the truth. "But why don't you shower first and, uh, you know, change. Meet me in the kitchen."

"That's why you're acting so weird, isn't it?" she said, realization in her voice.

What? He wasn't acting weird.

Was he?

"You hate this dress," she accused him.

She was so direct. Before he could figure out what to say in response, she added, "No, actually, you don't hate it. You just disapprove of my wearing it in public. That's what it is, right?"

And that he could respond to. "If you want me to be honest . . ."

"I do." She crossed her arms, which was distracting as hell, considering that neckline.

Cosmo focused. "I think there's more to you than your body," he told her. "I think you're selling yourself short, Jane. You walk into a room looking like . . . Well." He gestured to her. "What do you think people think when they see you?"

She knew where he was going and it obviously pissed her off. "They think, 'Golly gee, look at her—she must be wicked-ass smart.' What am I supposed to do, Cos? Wear a burlap sack? Just because God said, 'Hey, I have a good idea—let me make this one stacked?' Just because I refuse to starve myself? If I'm hungry, I'm going to eat! Screw you, Ally McBeal! And why am I responsible for other people's stupidity? If they look at me and can't see past my body, why is that **my** fault?"

"It's more than the way you dress," Cos said. "It's the way you act. The do-you-want-to-do-me-now-or-**right**-now? attitude. You perpetuate the myth."

She laughed. "Oh, that's perfect. **You're** lecturing **me** on perpetuating the myth? Your entire professional reputation is based on a myth. **How** many people did you kill while they were sleeping on some mountaintop on the other side of the world? Was it two hundred, Chief, or was it three? Nobody quite knows the number, and you haven't exactly stepped forward to clear it all up."

Jane had heard The Story. Of course she had.

"It was eighteen," Cosmo told her. "Total."

She took a step back, and he knew that, despite her taunting words, she believed what she'd heard about him. He didn't know why that should make him feel so disappointed, but it did and he was. In fact, he felt almost sick.

"Sorry," he said. "Somehow we always end up fighting. I didn't mean to . . . Congratulations on the movie thing. Really."

"We're not fighting," she countered. "This isn't fighting. The other night, **that** was fighting. This is healthy disagreement. You don't like my public image, well, tough shit, dude, because I don't particularly like yours, either. If you killed eighteen people, you must have had a reason for doing it. It was probably because they would've killed again, and they needed to be stopped or . . . There was a reason you did it. I don't care what people say about you— you're not a robot. It couldn't have been easy to do, and you couldn't have done it without feeling something. I don't buy into that. I don't. But most people do. And you just let them think what they want, don't you? You even kind of like it, because it keeps them at arm's length."

If. She'd actually said **if** he'd killed eighteen people.

She was standing there, gazing at him, scrutinizing his face, as if she were trying to read his mind.

Cosmo just let her look, even though he no longer knew what she might see in his eyes.

And then she asked him. Right to his face. "It's not really true, is it? That story . . . ?"

He didn't answer right away, but Jane just waited.

And waited.

He could have stalled until dawn, and she would've still been standing there.

"You're the first person who's ever asked me that," he finally admitted.

She was honestly surprised. "Are you serious?"

Cos nodded. "Not everyone's like you, Jane. In fact, hardly anyone is."

She narrowed her eyes at him. "I'll take that as a compliment, thanks."

"It was meant as one."

"So it's not true," she guessed. "Or is it? Because you haven't exactly answered the question."

"Take a shower," he told her. "Then come downstairs and I'll tell you what happened."

"Okay, you win." Jane raised her hands in surrender. "I'll go change. God, you must really hate this dress. For your information, I wore it tonight because it photographs well."

It was impossible not to watch her as she went up the stairs, and Cosmo had to laugh. Hate that dress?

She had no freaking clue.

CHAPTER ELEVEN

Jules carried his towel with him as he came out of the hotel bathroom. "I'll hang mine over here, on one of the coat hangers," he told his boss, who was sitting at the room's one desk, glaring at the screen of his laptop, chin in hand.

The TV was muted but still playing CNN. It was possible Max would leave it on all night.

And sleep with one eye open, watching it.

This was beyond weird—rooming with his boss. Please, Heavenly Father, don't let either of them fart tonight.

There were two beds in the room, one rumpled, one still neatly made. Jules pulled back the hideously floraled spread of the bed that was as yet untouched. From the looks of the other, along with Max's rather intense bedhead, it was obvious that he'd attempted to sleep earlier this evening.

Attempted and failed.

In all honesty, Max looked like shit warmed over.

And it was only partly due to his red plaid flannel pajama pants, faded Jimi Hendrix T-shirt that **clashed,** and his totally out-of-character uncoiffed hair. He had bigger than usual bags under his eyes, and although he wasn't known for being a smiler, his mouth and jawline were set on extra unhappy.

The man was a tension convention.

Of course, Max had never been particularly good at relaxing, but he'd been stress personified ever since his girlfriend, Gina, had left him. Or rather, since he'd let Gina leave.

Unlike when Adam had left Jules, if Max had gone after Gina, if he'd gotten down on his knees and begged her to come back, she would have. He might've been smiling right now, thinking of her waiting for him in their sweet little condo in Dupont Circle—no, wait, it was Jules who wanted to live in Dupont Circle, not Max.

God only knew where Max wanted to live.

Other than in a world free from terrorist attacks.

"Is that something I can help you with?" Jules asked his boss now.

Max glanced up. "No."

"You sure?"

"Yeah." He shut the laptop, but he didn't move out of the chair. "So why'd you turn off your cell phone today?"

And there it was. The question he'd been dreading.

When Jules first came into the room, dragging his rolling luggage behind him, they'd discussed all of the obvious topics.

What was Max doing in L.A.?

His being here had nothing to do with the Mercedes Chadwick case. He had a meeting in the morning with the Los Angeles office of Homeland Security. He caught the flight out before Laronda had discovered the dearth of hotel rooms.

What was new up in Irving, Idaho?

Zip. Jules had spent time with the Bureau's Idaho Falls office. He'd even taken an uneventful chopper ride over Tim Ebersole's Freedom Network compound. The area was being watched by the FBI, 24/7, same as it had been for years. There was no unusual movement today or even over the past few weeks, nothing out of the ordinary whatsoever.

Had Jules spoken to Peggy Ryan lately?

Apparently another suspicious e-mail had come in while Max had been on that flight to California. His second in command, a lovely but homophobic woman named Peggy, who preferred to pretend that Jules simply didn't exist, was getting it checked out. Jules should touch base with her in the morning.

O frabjous day! Callooh! Callay!

The things he and Max **hadn't** talked about included the fact that Jules' ex-lover, Adam, whom Jules had foolishly just slept with, had been cast as one of the leads in Mercedes Chadwick's movie **American Hero.**

They particularly didn't discuss how difficult it was going to be for Jules to be on set on the day they shot that big-screen kiss between Adam and the hottie of an actor playing Harold Lord—Robin Chadwick.

They didn't talk at all about the fact that Robin was

embroiled in a soap opera of his own making with his sister's personal assistant, Patty.

What a joke.

He and Max hadn't discussed the fact that Jules desperately missed his former FBI partner, Alyssa Locke, who was out of the country with her husband, Sam, in some no-cell zone. He didn't mention how badly he needed to talk to her—especially now—so he could confess that he'd fallen—again—under Adam's spell. He said nothing of how much he needed her, his best friend, to tell him that his slip had been only temporary, that he was now back on his feet, that he was strong, and it wasn't going to happen again.

That given enough time, all the pain he was feeling would fade to a manageable level.

Jules also didn't talk about the fact that he'd actually gone and called his mother earlier this evening, but that she'd been on her way out to a movie with her new husband, Phil, who pretended to be cool with the fact that Jules was openly gay but really wasn't.

Max was still sitting there, gazing at him, waiting for him to respond to his question. Why had he turned his cell phone off?

"You know the way Gina sometimes calls, and you run out of the room so that Laronda doesn't have to lie when she tells her you're not there?" Jules asked him.

Max closed his eyes and rubbed his forehead, the body language equivalent to **Oh, my holy Christ, I can't believe you brought up Gina.**

"Well, I've also got someone that it hurts too much

to talk to," Jules continued. For one wild moment, he was filled with hope that Max would reach out to him, that he would acknowledge this kind of weird half friendship they'd built over the past few years. That he would say, **Do you want to talk about it, because I would love to talk to someone about Gina, and I get the sense that you might understand. I miss her so much it sometimes feels as if I'm going to drown. Is that what it's like for you?**

"I'm sorry to hear that" was all Max managed to mutter as he turned out the desk lamp and threw himself into the other bed. "But you've got to make sure we can get in touch with you, Cassidy. Don't go dark side of the moon on us again."

He used the remote to turn off the TV, and the room was plunged into blackness.

Okey-dokey.

The silence was as suffocating as the pitch darkness, and Jules let it rest there, on his chest, for as long as he could.

Which wasn't very long at all.

"I guess you're not going to use my clever mention of Gina to tell me how she's doing or where she is," he finally said. "You know . . ." He imitated Max's FM DJ–like delivery: " 'Gee, Cassidy, funny you should bring up Gina. I just got an e-mail from her. She's back in New York. She's doing well, getting ready to go to law school.' "

"She's still in freaking Kenya," Max said, his smooth voice unusually rough. "Just drop it, all right? Don't make me regret letting you in here."

Letting him in here? The bastard had practically issued a presidential order demanding he share this room. But right now Max's inner cornered dog was snarling—Jules had hit a little too close for comfort.

He pushed himself up onto one elbow. "With all due respect, sweetie, why aren't you in Africa? If Adam loved me even **half** as much as Gina loves you—"

Now Max's voice was dangerously quiet. "I said drop it."

Again the silence seemed to crackle around them in the blackness of the room.

"Okay," Jules said, lying back down. "It's dropped." He waited, but Max said nothing. "Good night." Again, no response. "Sir."

Max didn't so much as move.

"Sleep tight, Mr. Bhagat," Jules added, just to drive home the fact that Max was missing out on a very real opportunity here to bond.

"I have a meeting"—Max finally spoke—"in less than five hours. With all due respect, **sweetie,** shut the fuck up."

"Butch Cassidy and the Sundance Kid," Cosmo said as Jane came into the kitchen, her hair still wet from her shower.

It took her a second, but then she remembered. Yesterday she'd asked him what his all-time favorite movie was. "Really?"

He'd been reading a book, and he put it down now, open and spine up on the table in front of him. It was a military history, nonfiction. Something about the Philippines during the Second World War.

"For true classics, it would have to be **The Philadelphia Story,**" he told her. "Katharine Hepburn floats my boat. And as far as more recent movies go, I'm a sucker for both **Apollo 13** and—don't hate me, I know it's a popcorn movie—**Air Force One.**"

"Yeah, I always liked the idea of a kick-ass president, too. One who's actually been in combat." Jane took the kettle from the stove to the sink, dumped out the tea she'd brewed far too many days ago, and washed the thing out. He liked Katharine Hepburn, huh? It was an interesting variation on the beautiful, blond, skinny Sophia-from-his-office theme, because ol' Kate had played smart-mouthed, high-society characters who were often sharply funny—as well as being bony-assed, beautiful WASPs.

Jane had the mouth, but her ass was about as far from bony as it could be—and what was she doing? Comparing herself to Cosmo's ideal woman? As if she were interested in him or something?

She crossed the kitchen on feet that still ached from too many hours spent in too-high heels, and began refilling the kettle with water from the bubbler. The answer to that was a depressing yes. She was definitely interested in the man. And not just interested as in, **Oh, you're a Navy SEAL with a rather odd name— that's so different from most of the men I know. How interesting. What on earth made you decide you wanted to do that for a living?** No, she was also **interested** interested.

As in interested in the possibility of long, lazy Sunday morning breakfasts in bed.

Jane glanced up to find Cosmo watching her. Provided, of course, that he wasn't a psycho who had lost control on some mountaintop in some unnamed country and killed eighteen people in cold blood.

She laughed at herself. A few days ago she would've believed him capable. His silence and watchfulness seemed to support the allegation that he was, indeed, a killing machine. When he wanted to, he could make his eyes look cold and flat.

But now she knew him. Not well—it would take more than a few conversations over the course of a few nights to really dig beneath his crunchy protective outer shell. But she definitely knew enough to be certain that if he had killed anyone, it had been because there had been no other option.

Jane also knew that if this were a perfect world, she would do whatever it took to get to know him much, much better—an effort that would surely culminate in many Sunday morning breakfasts in bed.

But the world wasn't perfect and her timing couldn't be any more wrong.

Cosmo was here in her kitchen not by choice, but because protecting her was his job. She'd also spent most of the evening making sure that, starting in a few days, anyone who came within ten feet of a supermarket checkout line would believe she and movie director Victor Strauss had a thing going on.

And if that weren't enough to keep her from letting her feelings get out of this still low, mostly curious idle, she'd promised to help Cosmo win the heart of his Sophia.

Petite, blond, bony-assed, beautiful, sweetly nice, and Barbie-doll perfect Sophia.

The bitch.

"So why **Butch Cassidy**?" she asked Cos now as she crossed back to the stove and turned on the gas.

He didn't answer—what a surprise—so she turned back to look at him. He had the strangest expression on his face.

"What?" she asked.

He shook his head. "Most people don't ask why."

"Is that your polite way of saying, 'Most people aren't nosy like you'?"

Cosmo laughed. God, she loved it when he laughed. "No," he said. "Most people don't care enough to ask." He scratched his chin. " 'Course, now that I've said that, I'm not sure I can explain why it's my favorite movie."

He was silent then, but she waited.

And waited. She just watched him.

"I guess," he finally said, "it's because it's funny and well written and . . . Because it's a movie about friendship. About loyalty and trust." He met her gaze. "They were a team. Butch and Sundance. When I was a kid, when I first saw this movie, I mostly hung by myself. I was really quiet and . . . shy, I guess. I think I probably connected with the Sundance Kid, because he was quiet, too. He was okay, so I was okay, you know?"

Jane nodded. His answer was so much more heart-felt and honest than she'd expected. So of course she lightened things up. "Good answer. Congratulations. You pass."

He laughed at that. God, he had an awesome smile. She was both dreading and dying to hear his version of that story she'd first heard from Alana in makeup. Alana, whose roommate used to waitress at some bar near the Navy base in Coronado.

Apparently Navy SEAL chief Cosmo Richter was frequently talked about by other sailors in hushed tones.

But not so hushed that Alana's friend hadn't been able to listen in from time to time.

The fact that no one—no one—had ever asked him directly about the legend seemed unbelievable.

On the other hand, maybe it didn't. He was huge, with arms reminiscent of those on her Terminator action figure. Only Cosmo's muscles were real.

And yes, she had seen him with his T-shirt off—hard to forget that. Everything underneath there was real, too. The man was ripped, and he had the height to go with the build.

And then there were his eyes. Startlingly pale blue in a face that had too many hard edges and sharp planes and angles to be called handsome.

If she were casting him in a movie, he'd play the bad guy. He had that type of face.

Except when he smiled like he was smiling right now . . .

When he did that, it was bad guy, good-bye. Hello, hero.

"So that was a test?" he asked.

"Well, yeah. Want some tea?" she asked, as she got her favorite mug from the cabinet.

"No thanks." He managed to say it without that little condescending laugh that implied real men didn't drink tea. It was another point in his favor, damn it.

She wanted to shout at him, **Stop being so attractive, will you?**

"There was definitely a wrong answer," she told him instead. "If you'd said, like, something that featured a chimpanzee, or **Laurel and Hardy versus Dracula—**"

"Okay," he said. "You're right." He laughed again, but this time she was busy rummaging through the boxes of herbal tea in the cupboard.

God save her from that smile. Last night his smile had made her stammer and babble like an idiot.

"So what's your all-time favorite movie?" he added.

Lemon Zinger. Alleluia, there was a God. There was one more bag left—not enough to brew an entire pot, but one couldn't be picky when it came to miracles. She tossed it into her mug.

"I'm a **Casablanca,**" she told him, as she turned off the heat under the kettle, filled her mug with water, and popped it into the microwave instead. "I love Bogey's Rick. What a great character. Forget about the symbolism, which rocks, and the fact that the movie is amazingly lit. Next time you watch it, check out the lighting and the camera shots. It's brilliant on a whole bunch of levels, but really, the reason I love it is Rick."

"I haven't seen it in a while," he admitted.

What was that on the floor? A duffel bag? **Richter** was stenciled on the green canvas side. "I watch it once a year," Jane told him. He must've been carrying it when he first came inside with her, but she hadn't noticed it then. She pointed at it, both hoping and dreading that it meant what she thought it did. "Moving in, Chief?"

"Mom went up to San Fran to visit some friends," he told her as the microwave dinged.

Jane took her mug over to the table, pushing the tea bag back down into the steaming water with her finger. Ouch, that was hot, but she was too lazy to go back for a spoon.

"They have tickets to see **Stomp,**" Cos continued. "The trip was planned months ago. She was going to cancel, but we talked her into going."

"Good for her." Jane sat down across from him, tucking her aching feet up underneath her, not sure what his mother's trip had to do with his overnight bag.

"She's having her condo repainted while she's gone. I volunteered to do it, but she showed me this picture from a magazine and . . ." He shook his head ruefully. "It's not a single roller job. It involves sponges and speckling. The painters had this block of days free, so . . . I'm not a fan of paint fumes, and since you'd said no more sleeping in my truck . . ."

"I did," she said.

"I can just as easily get a motel room if—"

"No, this was why I'd offered." But holy mama's boy, Batman. Was it really possible . . . ? That the big, tough, mean Navy SEAL . . . ? "So you, uh, live with your mother?" She tried but couldn't keep from sounding incredulous.

Cosmo let her think about the absurdity of what she'd just asked for several long moments while he just smiled at her.

"I have an apartment in San Diego," he finally said. "It's more convenient to stay at Mom's place while I'm working up here in L.A. I also gain visit points when I stay overnight. It counts big, even though we're both asleep. I love her, but . . ." He watched as she shifted in her seat, pulling her foot onto her knee so she could rub it. "There's a definite limit to how many Broadway show soundtracks I can listen to in a row."

She needed to get one of those foot bath things that her grandmother used to have. "And presumably at night the music is turned off."

"Either that or I'm unconscious," Cosmo said. "Although sometimes, just for grins, you should try dreaming to a programmed endless repeat of 'Dancing Queen.' "

"Eek."

And then there they sat, both just smiling at each other. Danger, danger, danger. Still, Jane couldn't look away. How could she have ever thought his eyes were cold?

And how come she didn't get these supercharged energy jolts when she talked with Decker, who was relentlessly single and very attractive in his own compact way? Or PJ, who had high flash and, despite his steady girlfriend, made no secret of the fact that he approved of Mercedes' miniskirts? He'd hinted more than once that his Beth was not a fan of long-distance love affairs and was intending to end their relationship upon her departure for Iraq.

And then there was her old friend, mentor, and ex-lover Victor Strauss, who had let her know that he would not be at all adverse to bringing the little fool-the-paparazzi game they were playing back into the bedroom. The only jolt she got from him was an awareness of how huge a mistake **that** would be.

This time Cosmo broke eye contact first.

But this time it wasn't because of the clothes she was wearing—flannel pj pants and an old T-shirt. Her makeup and costume were eighty-sixed.

As if he could read her mind, he asked, "Why do you wear them? Those high heels?" He gestured to the way she was rubbing her foot. "You're doing it wrong. It's really hard to massage your own feet—look at the way you're twisting your knee. It's going to hurt worse when you're done." He motioned for her to move her chair closer. "Let me show you."

He wasn't kidding. He wanted her to put her feet up on his lap.

So she did. And oh, my God. His hands were huge and warm, and his fingers were strong, and . . . Jane tried to keep her eyes from rolling back in her head.

"You need to get one of those heavy-duty electric massagers," Cosmo told her. "Press it against the ball of your foot, right here, and let it run for a while."

"I will," she said. "I'll get one." Once she signed that distribution contract with HeartBeat, she'd have some extra money. She'd spend some of it on herself this time before dumping the rest into **Hero**'s production.

"Or you could stop wearing the crazy shoes."

Or she could make sure he was here in her kitchen, every night for the rest of her life, when she got home from work.

"I made a choice," she focused hard and told him, "about how to get noticed in this business. Cos, I was a has-been at twenty-two." It had actually been her noisy breakup with Victor Strauss that had brought her back into the public eye. She'd taken the description the tabloids had given her—Party Girl Producer—and developed a whole persona to go with it.

"I got HeartBeat interested in backing a World War Two gay love story," she continued. "Do you really think they would have given me so much as a **meeting** if I hadn't made myself the person to be seen having lunch with? If I didn't dress the way I do?"

"How many meetings do you get with men who don't really want to have a meeting?" he countered. "At least not the kind with a spoken conversation."

She waved that away. "That happens to everyone in this business."

"But probably more often to you," he guessed correctly. "What do you do, Jane, when you show up at someone's office, and the man you're meeting with expects you to follow through with the fuck-me attitude and actually put out? Pardon my French, but I'm tired of dancing around what it really is. It's dangerous, what you do. What if you meet with someone who can't hear you say no because everything you've done up to that point has been a great big yes?"

"I don't do private meetings," Jane explained. "I always bring Robin. Always." She tried to sit up. "Hasn't it occurred to you that my so-called fuck-me attitude is really just confidence? Yes, I walk around trying to give off a vibe that says 'You want me.' As a producer, as a writer, hell, yes—I want to be wanted. But because I combine that confidence with clothing that shows off my body, you interpret my message as a purely sexual one. It's classic male thinking—if a woman so much as smiles at a man, he thinks, 'Yeah! She wants to have sex with me.' News flash: She might only be thinking, 'Gee, I like the color of that tie.' "

"You do more than smile," Cosmo said.

"No, I don't," Jane argued.

"Yeah, you do," he said. "You use eye contact to—"

"Oh, that's nice! What? Would you prefer I demurely avert my gaze when speaking to men?" She was pissed, and she pulled her feet away, which wasn't particularly smart because now she wasn't getting them rubbed.

"There's eye contact, and then there's eye contact," he said. "You know damn well what you do. You crank the sex to eleven."

"I crank the confidence," she countered. "You know, if I were a man you'd think, 'Ooh, he's commanding.' Or 'Wow, he's charismatic.' And you wouldn't think twice if I wore a wife beater or snug-fitting jeans. But because I'm a woman, you see the confidence combined with the outer package. And by the way, if I wore the exact same clothes but I had a different body, you'd think, 'Whoa, she's hip.' But because I have breasts and a butt, you see me and you think it's all about sex. That's pretty sad, isn't it? What, do you think I should wear a muumuu—cover myself completely? How about a veil while I'm at it? Oh, but even that's not enough, is it? God forbid there be eye contact. Better put a paper bag over my head!"

He was silent for a moment. But then he said, "Sorry if I offended you. I hear what you're saying, and, fair or not—and in my experience, life's not fair—I think you go too far. That's my opinion. But whether you're right or I am doesn't really matter. Bottom line, I'm concerned for your safety."

Was this guy for real? Thoughtful, sensitive, honest, intelligent, he actually seemed to listen to what she said. So, of course, instead of thanking him for his very genuine-seeming concern, Jane tried to turn it into a joke. "With two guards around me day and night, I think there's a good chance I'm safe."

"We won't be here forever," he pointed out.

"It just seems that way," she quipped, hating herself for not being brave enough to say what she really wanted to say. **So, hey, yeah, you won't be working here forever, but do you maybe think that there might be a ghost of a chance that when this job is over, provided things don't work out between you and perfect Sophia, you might be interested in kicking this friendship we've got going up to a higher level?**

Because, God, what if she said that and he said, **I'm**

sorry, but you've mistaken my polite concern for friendship, and when I'm gone, I am never, ever coming back.

"Have you noticed how we've talked about everything **except** the Legend of Chief Cosmo Richter?" Jane asked, because, please, God, maybe hearing the truth about exactly what happened to those eighteen very dead people would make her a little less interested in being this man's friend.

"Not quite everything," Cosmo deadpanned. But then she realized he wasn't kidding when he added, "I wanted to ask you about this night shoot you've got coming up. When does it start? Tomorrow?"

"Yeah, after dark." They were scheduled to start shooting the scenes from the beginning of the movie, where Jack first joined the Twenty-third. Robin had the night free—he wasn't in those scenes. Jane had been tempted to give Patty the night off, too, but she needed her intern on set. "I know what you're going to say. Don't worry, I'm not going to go out there and put my cast and crew in danger."

"Good."

"I'm not happy about it, though."

He nodded. "Yeah, but it's the right thing to do."

"I have to go shopping," she told him. "I thought I could do that tomorrow night. I need a new dress to wear to the premiere of **Fool's Gold,** and it occurred to me that the safest time to go is late at night, when stores are usually closed. There's a shop I like—the owner won't mind opening up for me after hours. Do you, uh, want to come? I thought maybe we could pick out something for you to wear to your dinner with Sophia."

Cosmo gazed at her, clearly trying to decide whether or not she was making a joke.

"I'm serious," she said. "You've been in the Navy for how long? Since high school, right?"

He nodded.

"I'm guessing the number of nice suits you have hanging in your closet would be . . . close to zero?"

"Suits?" Cosmo laughed. "Zero would be close, yeah. Not having to wear a suit and tie to work was at the top of the pro column when I decided to enlist."

"Yeah, well, wearing a suit to work and wearing a suit to impress the woman of your dreams and maybe even get laid as part of the deal are two entirely different things."

He wasn't wearing sunglasses. They were sitting indoors and it was night. But she recognized the look he gave her. Had he been wearing sunglasses, he would have been looking over the tops of them. He didn't say anything. He just gazed at her.

"Oh, sorry," Jane said. "I didn't realize we were pretending that your life was a Disney movie. Maybe she'll hold your hand." She batted her eyes as she smiled sweetly at him. "Better? I know you don't like the idea of dressing up, but if you want my opinion, a man with your height and build in a well-cut dark suit . . ." She fanned herself.

Elbow on the table, he closed his eyes as he rubbed his forehead. Then he looked up at her from beneath his fingers. "If you want to know the truth, it's not about like or dislike. I don't have the money right now for new clothes, no matter how badly I want to get . . ." He cleared his throat. Sat back in his chair. Crossed his arms. "Well, I have money, I'm just saving it for . . . See, Medicaid would only cover care for my mother if she went into a nursing home." He shifted in his seat. "That wasn't an option. I was going to do it myself. You know, take care of her. But she was mortified at the idea and . . . She doesn't know any of this, and you know, I **am** going to bring her onto the set after she gets back from San Fran—thank you for offering that—so I'm, you know, trusting that you won't tell her that . . . you know . . ."

"That you're paying for her at-home care out of pocket," Jane finished for him, her heart in her throat.

Cosmo nodded. "I don't know how long it's going to take, so until she gets the casts off and starts therapy, I'm not buying anything."

Game over.

There was no denying it any longer. Jane was totally crushing on this guy—whose life **was** a Disney movie. He was spending his savings to keep his mother out of a nursing home, and he said things like "Pardon my French," and couldn't even manage to utter the phrase "get laid" in front of her.

"You can borrow a suit from Costume," she told him past the lump in her throat. "Retro's in—you'll look amazing."

"I don't know—"

"I do," she said. "Don't argue. God, for a guy with a rep for being silent and deadly, you argue about everything. And speaking of that rep . . . I believe the question was, 'That story's not really true, is it?' "

Time stood still as he gazed at her, as she lost herself—just a little bit—in his beautiful eyes.

Finally—she had no idea how long they just sat there like that—he shook his head. "No," he said. "It's not true."

She knew it. She **knew** it.

"So what really happened?" Jane asked. She intended to sound matter-of-fact, but her words came out as little more than a whisper.

Cosmo looked down at the table, but she knew he wasn't seeing his book and her mug. He was millions of miles away. She held her breath for what seemed like forever. And when he finally looked back up at her, the haunted expression on his face was one she knew she'd remember for the rest of her life.

He nodded very slightly, as if he were answering his own internal question, giving himself permission to tell her something that she instinctively knew he didn't talk about often—if at all.

"You've heard The Story, so you know about the villagers," he said. "The bloodshed was—" He stopped. The muscle jumped in his jaw as once again he stared at the table, seeing what, God only knew.

Jane just waited, not daring to move, not even to reach across the table to take his hand.

"They didn't waste their bullets on these people," he told her quietly, not looking up. "It was all done with swords and bayonets and . . . I was helping with cleanup. Burials. The villagers who had been spared were overwhelmed—and some of the dead had no family members left alive to care for them. Some of them had only one and . . . I helped this old man whose entire family had been killed. Three sons and his daughter-in-law, his two grandkids—Christ, they were babies, Jane, and they—" He met her gaze for only the briefest moment before he looked away, shaking his head.

She leaned forward. "You can tell me," she said. "I'm pretty tough, you know, and it might help to talk about it."

"It won't." He was convinced.

"How do you know?" she asked, just as convinced that Cosmo had never told this story to anyone before.

He met her gaze. "They didn't kill them quickly. They took the time to be particularly brutal with the children," he told her, and she shut her mouth.

"The old man's daughter-in-law was still alive," he continued after another of those seemingly endless silences. "I don't know how, with her throat cut like that, but she opened her eyes and looked right at me, and it was, you know, **Jesus God.**" He shook his head. "It was unreal. I shouted for Lopez, our corpsman—medic, you know—but he'd gone with the others. It was just me and good old Frank O'Leary at that point. So Frank gets on the radio, calling in a helo to medevac her out of there, and I'm doing first aid, and oh my holy God, Jane, I don't know why she hasn't bled to death already—she's barely got a pulse. But then she starts fighting me. To this day I don't know where she found the strength, but she's trying to get to her kids.

Trying to . . ." He faltered, briefly closed his eyes. Pushed the words out. "Put them back together. Like she doesn't realize it's way too late."

"Oh, God," Jane breathed.

"Yeah." He cleared his throat. Rubbed his hand across the lower part of his face. "And the old man is begging us not to let her die, like we're God or something. O'Leary goes, 'Helo's coming, Cos, but the closest they can get is back at the insertion point.' " He stopped himself again, sensitive to the fact that the military jargon was lost on her. "We inserted into the area—fast-roped down from a helicopter, you follow?—about seven miles up a steep mountain trail. That's as close as the helo would come to pick us up. This village is right in the middle of a terrorist hot spot—the helo can't come this far east into the valley without providing an opportunity for undesirables to test-drive their black market grenade launchers."

Jane nodded because he was looking at her as if he wanted some kind of response. She **was** following him, but a nod was the best she could do. Words were failing her. Seven miles. Up a steep mountain trail . . . ?

"O'Leary's going, 'She's not going to make it, man,' except we've got a medical kit with the right equipment to . . . Well, see, I'm Oh." Unlike **insertion point,** he didn't explain what that meant. Clearly he thought she knew. "My medical training is pretty limited, but I'd seen Lopez do it before—"

"Hang on." She had to interrupt. "You're Oh?"

"Universal donor," he said, and she still didn't realize exactly what he meant until he added, "She needed blood and I'm type O. Technically, yeah, we're not supposed to do that. When we go overseas we get shot full of all kinds of shit—" He winced. "Sorry."

"Whoa—back up. Are you telling me that you . . . ?" Her mouth was hanging open.

"We didn't have any plasma. Some kits are equipped, but this one wasn't. So we hook up a tube, a direct line, you know, me to her and . . . Stop looking at me like that. It's no big deal."

Like hell it wasn't. Still, she managed to shut her mouth because incredulity bordering on hero worship was clearly something that made him uncomfortable. This story was hard enough for him to tell as it was. She didn't want to make it harder.

Or make him think she'd heard enough.

Indeed, Cosmo was looking at her again, muscle jumping on the side of his jaw, and again she got the feeling he was deciding just how much of the details he was going to reveal.

"We can tell it's helping because she starts fighting harder," he finally continued, so quietly she had to hold her breath to hear him. "She wants her kids. And the old man's telling her, 'They're dead,' but I stop him, because I know it's what's keeping her alive. You know?"

She nodded. That and the blood that he was giving her, directly from his veins.

"So I'm lying to her," he said, and Jane realized that his decision wasn't so much about how much to tell her, but how much he could bear to say. "Right to her face. I get the old man, who has some English, and he tells me the words for 'They're all right, they're going to be all right,' and coming from me, the almighty American, she buys it. She's hanging on to me, believing me, and I'm thinking, Christ, she's thanking me for saving her children."

Dear God, he had tears in his eyes.

"O'Leary picks her up, he's going to carry her because I'm, you know, a little shaky." Cosmo shook his head. "Only she doesn't want to leave her kids. We're afraid to give her morphine because even though her pulse is stronger it's still so low, and now I'm telling her that the kids will be safe with their grandfather. And she goes, 'My baby, my baby,' and she starts pleading with me. I don't need to speak the language to know what she's saying, but the old man tells me she's not going to leave without her two-month-old and . . ."

He stopped again, this time putting his hand over his eyes.

Jane couldn't move, couldn't breathe.

"So I carry her baby. 'Is he all right?' She can barely speak, but she keeps asking that. And I'm all, 'Yes, he's great, he's fine.' For seven fucking miles." His voice broke. "And I'm holding the pieces of him together. In case she looks back at me."

"Oh, God," Jane said. "Cosmo—"

"Don't!" He said it so sharply that, startled, she stopped short almost before she'd even realized she was out of her chair and heading toward him. He softened it by adding, "Please . . ." and she slowly backed up and sat down.

But she couldn't keep herself from leaning forward. "Cos . . ."

"Sorry. Just give me a—"

A beep came from his walkie-talkie or radio or whatever it was that provided a direct line to the guards outside, and he grabbed it and stood in one fluid motion, turning his back to her. "Yeah."

"Hey, Cos. Just checking in." Tess Bailey's voice was cheerful, as usual.

"Good," he said curtly. "Touch base again in ten."

"Roger that." And she was gone.

Cosmo stood there for several long seconds before he turned to face Jane. He'd managed to compose himself completely, except now he couldn't quite manage to hold her gaze. "Sorry."

"You're kidding, right?"

He shook his head, and it wasn't so much in agreement or disagreement, but rather as if he were shaking off the question. "So that's what happened. That's where I was when that warlord's patrol—all eighteen of them—were killed. O'Leary made me get on the helo, too. He thought I gave away too much blood, so he ordered me back in. I was young and stupid. I was convinced I was fine—never mind the fact that I kept getting tunnel vision going up that trail. Superman syndrome—you know? Guys who get it usually end up dead, but I was lucky. I had some Gatorade on the helo, convinced the medic I was good, and came back on the flip-flop. Heading down to the village, I lost my footing on the trail and fuh—" He cleared his throat.

"Freaking knocked myself out. Took, like, a seven-hour nap there in the underbrush. When I came to, it was morning. I staggered into the village, looking like hell, covered with blood. A few people made some incorrect assumptions about my previous night's activities."

"Which you never bothered to clear up."

Cosmo nodded, finally steadily meeting her eyes. "Yeah. I'm pretty sure it was the villagers who retaliated. But the rumor of the vengeful SEAL single-handedly wiping out three squads . . . See, even when the myth started, the number was seriously inflated. But that kept those villagers safe because the rumors didn't just spread among the Spec Ops forces. It's wild just how fast news can spread in a country without telephones or technology. So I didn't say anything to clear it all up."

"And O'Leary didn't, either?"

He shook his head. "No. He probably would have eventually, but he died a few years later, in a terrorist attack in Kazabek."

Oh, God. "I'm sorry."

"Me, too. He was a good man. A friend. I had the pleasure of helping clean up the cell that killed him." He sat back down at the table. "I've taken lives, Jane. It's an aspect of my job that I usually don't enjoy. But if I'd had the opportunity, I **would** have enjoyed eliminating those eighteen bastards who murdered children in front of their mothers. I would have fucking ripped them apart. Maybe that's another reason why I never bothered to stop the rumors. Excuse me."

"Cos," she said. "Come on, it's really all right. I'm a big girl. You don't need to censor your vocabulary around me."

He smiled, a rueful twist of his lips. "Yeah, it's just, you know, it's my mother's fault."

Jane couldn't help it. "God, you are too sweet," she said.

Cosmo laughed at that. "No, you don't get it. See, if I use, um, salty verbiage around my mom, well, she'll start using it, too. I knew I had to do something when she was asking about one of my teammates and she goes, 'Have you seen Silverman lately, Cosie? How is the little motherfucker?' "

Jane cracked up. "She did not!"

"Yeah, she did."

"Now I'm really dying to meet her." And suddenly that felt weird—her saying that she wanted to meet his mother. As if they were dating and serious. "When you bring her onto the set," she felt compelled to add.

"Maybe next week, after she gets back," he said.

"Great." She took a sip of her tea. It was barely lukewarm now. "Thank you. You know. For telling me. I know that wasn't easy—"

"It's late," he interrupted. "You probably have an early day."

It was and she did. But she didn't want to leave. She wrapped both hands around the mug, even though it was cool to the touch. "When your shift is done, feel free to crash wherever you like. Although some of those beds in the other wing are pretty decrepit."

"I'll be okay," he told her. "Good night."

Jane had been dismissed. He punctuated it by picking up his book, so she stood and turned toward the door, but then turned back. "I feel like I need to say something," she said. "To apologize to you on behalf of all of humanity. That you should have had to endure that—"

He lowered his book. "What I endured was nothing compared to what Yasmin lived through."

"Her name was Yasmin?" His account had been grim enough when the victims were faceless and nameless. She had to ask. "Did she live?"

Cosmo nodded. "Yeah. Much to her disappointment."

Jane could only imagine how awful it must have been for Yasmin to wake up in a hospital and discover that her husband and children were all dead. "God . . ."

He sighed, no doubt reading her mind, as usual. But he obviously didn't want to talk anymore.

Still, she lingered. "I'm just . . . I'm so sorry."

Cosmo lifted his book. "Sleep well."

"Thanks." She stood there uncertainly for several more moments, but he didn't look up again, and she finally headed for the stairs and her room.

Sleep well?

Snowball's chance in hell.

CHAPTER
TWELVE

Patty went outside by the smokers' tree, pretending she was on a mission to find the video camera operator who was working on a "Making Of" segment for the DVD extras, but in fact hoping to catch Robin as he was pulling into the studio parking lot.

"Anything I can help you with, Pattycakes?" asked one of the crew, a grip named Gary.

The rumor going around was that Gary's boyfriend—how weird was that?—had left him for Harve the special effects makeup wizard, which was doubly strange. Although all three men were out here right now, having a cigarette in what seemed to be a friendly enough manner, so maybe it was just gossip.

"Oh," she said. "Thanks, but . . ."

She craned her neck and . . . Yes! That was Robin's sports car pulling into the lot.

Except . . . Unless she was standing here having a conversation with someone, she'd look as if she were waiting for him.

But Gary had already turned back to Harve and Guillermo.

It was too late to take up smoking. Besides, if she came home with a nicotine habit, her mother would kill her.

Maybe if she just stood near Gary and the others and pretended to be listening . . .

Then Patty saw Cosmo, the Navy SEAL, in the parking lot, getting out of his truck.

This was perfect. She'd received voice mail this morning from Decker, telling her that Cosmo would be coming to the studio today to photocopy the extras' headshots and résumés. She could pretend she was waiting out here for him. Of course, as she greeted him, they could linger for a moment, at which point Robin would catch up, allowing them to walk inside together.

And she'd casually turn to Robin and say . . . what? **Why haven't you returned my calls?**

Bad idea. If she said that, she'd sound like a crybaby.

Maybe she should say, **Hi, Robin, this is going to sound crazy, and I know I'm paranoid, ha ha ha, but part of me is wondering if you're avoiding me.**

No. He'd come away from their exchange thinking that she was high maintenance. That was never good. Guys like Robin needed a low-maintenance girlfriend. Someone who wouldn't wig out if he didn't call for several days in a row.

Maybe, **Where've you been? I thought at least I'd see you at the dailies last night.**

Except that sounded as if she were accusing him of something.

Last night's dailies rocked. You were awesome. For a minute there I actually believed you had a real thing for Adam. Ha ha ha.

Yes, that was the perfect approach. Lighthearted teasing that also complimented his acting skills.

Except as Cosmo approached, five of the smokers broke away from the group. Patty hadn't paid attention to who was standing out there, but she realized now that she didn't recognize any of these people.

Four had cameras—digital video.

Shit! Paparazzi.

Including that scumsucker who freelanced for the nastier of the supermarket tabloids—what was his name? Mike Green. His one goal in life seemed to be to dish dirt on Mercedes Chadwick—and whomever she appeared to be sleeping with.

In this case, Cosmo.

The reporters were clearly lying in wait for him. They were holding their cameras behind them, waiting for him to approach before they pulled them out, so they could get high-quality close-ups.

There was only one thing Patty could do.

"Cameras! Reporters! Head down—cover your face!" she shouted, rushing toward Cosmo, trying to get between them.

Of course, now that the reporters knew that the jig was up, they rushed him, too.

"Is it true you're a Navy SEAL?"

"How long have you been seeing Mercedes?"

"What do you know about her rift with her mother?"

"How long, exactly, were you in Afghanistan?"

"I've heard that you've recently served in Kazbekistan and Iraq as well. Isn't this particular job—if you can call it a job—radically different from your duties overseas?"

"Yeah, and be honest now," Green called out. "Is Mercedes Chadwick really as good as they say?"

Cosmo had been hustling toward the studio door, but now he stopped. That was not good.

"No comment," Patty said, hoping he'd get the message.

But he didn't. He turned and faced them. His sunglasses covered his eyes, and that, combined with the hard edge of his jawline and grim mouth, not to mention his well-above-average height and muscular build, made for a very intense picture. This was not a happy man.

Patty held her breath. She should say something, step in, intervene.

For several long moments the potential for violence hung heavy in the air. He was going to beat the crap out of them all.

It was like standing in the middle of a Quentin Tarantino movie. This man was going to tear their heads off. And, bad person that she was, she was going to get to watch. With glee. **I didn't have time to do anything,** she'd tell Jane after it was all over. **It all happened so fast . . .**

But Cosmo just stood there until the questions finally stopped, microphones jammed in his face, ready to catch his every word—which was going to be a blistering **Fuck you**—she just knew it. After which he was going to give Mike Green the pounding he deserved.

"Get him inside." Patty looked up into Robin's bloodshot eyes. God, he looked awful, like he'd spent the night drunk.

Again.

He handed Patty the daypack he used to carry his script and stepped between Cosmo and the press. "If you have questions about **American Hero,** you can ask me. I'm associate producer Robin Chadwick. I also play Captain Hal Lord in the film."

Unfortunately, "Get him inside," only worked if Cosmo wanted to get inside.

It seemed he didn't.

Cosmo gently shook off Patty's hand and even pushed Robin to the side.

"Mercedes Chadwick's life has been threatened because some small-minded people don't like the movie she's making," he finally said, those sunglasses still trained on Green. "And you think the big news story here is who she's **sleeping** with?"

The reporter didn't back down. "Is it true you just met her a few days a—"

"I don't see how that's your business."

"So it's true," Green countered.

Cosmo smiled. It was not a friendly smile. "You

know, I have friends who died to protect your right to be an asshole." He glanced at Patty. "Excuse me."

Mike was not moved. "Isn't it true that with your military background, you have more in common with the patriotism and Christian values of the Freedom Network than with the, uh, shall we call them **questionable types** you're here to guard?"

"You're kidding, right?" Cosmo didn't get loud, he got quiet—and it was scary as all get-out. "You do any research at all on the Freedom Network, or d'you just swallow their propaganda bullshit whole, direct from their website? They aren't patriotic and they sure didn't get their doctrine of hatred from asking What Would Jesus Do. Freedom Network—my big hairy ass. Only freedom they're interested in is freedom for people who look just like them, think just like them, and believe only what they believe—"

"I think we're probably done here." It was Jane. Gary the Grip was the hero of the hour, because he'd gone inside to fetch her—along with Decker and Jules Cassidy and even old Jack Shelton, although God only knew what he could do if things got ugly. "Get these vermin off this lot," Jane ordered even as she took Cosmo's arm and, ignoring the babble of questions from the reporters, pulled him with her back into the studio.

The steel door clanked shut behind them. It was dark in the hallway—it took Cosmo's eyes a moment to adjust, even after he took off his sunglasses.

"I am **so** sorry," Jane told him.

"Whoa, I'm the one who needs to apologize," he countered. "I should've said 'No comment.' " He should've just kept walking.

"No, it's my fault completely," she said. "I started this. Damn it! It was supposed to be finished tomorrow when . . . But now those reporters are going to be all over you."

"I can handle them."

"Even when they follow you home, and try to trick your mother into an interview?"

"Trust me, they're not going to do that. Besides, she's still in San Francisco."

Jane was really worried. "You have no idea how low these creeps can go. You might actually want to call your mother's friends in San Fran and make sure someone's with her at all times."

Cos had to laugh.

"It's not funny." Now she was indignant, yet still looking at him with such concern.

"Yeah, it is," he told her. "After you meet my mother, you'll understand. She'd enjoy tangling with a tabloid reporter. I'd worry more that once she did it, it might become her favorite hobby. You know, shades of the little sister from **Philadelphia Story**? Mom would probably only speak in risqué iambic pentameter or maybe bawdy haiku."

Jane laughed, but he could tell that she still didn't buy it.

"That's a real turn-on, you know," she said. "Hearing the words **iambic pentameter** from the mouth of a man like you."

Good thing it was dark in there, because it was possible he was now blushing. A turn-on. Christ. Was she actually flirting with him or just being her usual irreverent self?

"A man like me?" he managed to ask. "I thought we were past the labeling stage."

"The subset I'm talking about is 'hotties who don't own a suit.' You have to admit you fall into the category."

Hotties? Did she really think of him as . . .

She was wearing heels again today, although they weren't as high as usual. Her dress was a pretty shade of blue, but it was neither low cut, aggressively short, nor of the painted-on variety, thank you, Lord Jesus. Still, talk about hot. The soft fabric hugged her curves and screamed to be touched.

Cos clasped his hands behind his back. "What, you think a man who doesn't own a suit and tie can't be well-read?"

Jane smiled. "No, just that men who are well-read are usually smart enough to figure out that most women like contrast. The cargo pants and T-shirt are a very nice look for you—don't get me wrong. But if you want Sophia to notice you, show up for your dinner party in a well-tailored suit."

Sophia. Damn. She was still trying to set him up with Sophia.

Whereas he couldn't stop thinking about last night,

when they had sat in Jane's kitchen and he'd foolishly told her about Yasmin, about the reality behind The Story.

Christ, he was the King of Bad Ideas—thinking he could tell her the truth, thinking she wouldn't go and reach for him when he did.

If he'd let her last night, she would have put her arms around him. And no way on God's green earth could he have sat there without holding on to her in return. And if he had done that . . .

Ding.

He would've been completely done, totally cooked.

He would've pulled her onto his lap. Or, okay, even if he hadn't, even if he'd showed amazing restraint and she'd only knelt on the floor next to him, her arms around his neck, her fingers in his hair. . . .

Ah, God.

His mouth would've been only inches from hers and . . .

Bad, **bad** idea.

Kissing the client while on duty was not good. Not good at all.

Cosmo took another step back now, farther away from her.

"So is that why you're here? To pick up that suit?" she asked.

Huh?

"From the costume department?" she elucidated.

"Oh, right, no." He had to laugh. "No, Jane, that's, you know, not . . . I'm not . . . I'm here because we're checking out everyone who has access to the set. It's time-consuming, but we have to do it. Process of elimination—make sure the guy we're after isn't right under our nose. I think I'm supposed to make copies of something."

"Of our extras casting file." Jane nodded. "I'll show you where it is, except, oh. You know what? Why don't you wait here for Patty."

"Oh, sure," Cosmo said. "Yeah, of course. You're busy. I'm sorry." He'd already been enough of a time drain, and no doubt a total pain in the ass.

"No," she said, moving closer. Close enough to touch his arm. Her fingers were cool against his skin, and it was all he could do not to jump straight up into the air. "It's just . . . we probably shouldn't spend too much time together in public. Alone, I mean. You know, 'Don't throw bouquets at me . . .' " She sang the opening lines to the old Rodgers and Hammerstein classic "People Will Say We're in Love."

She had a nice voice. It was nothing too special— she was certainly no Broadway diamond in the rough. It was just . . . sweetly pleasant.

"The cast and crew are prone to gossip. They don't seem to understand that a man and a woman can be friends," Jane continued. "And since I'm working hard to undo the damage from the press conference . . ."

She'd stopped touching his arm, but she was still standing close enough so that he couldn't breathe without smelling her subtle perfume. He couldn't tell what it was—only that there was a hint of vanilla in it. And coffee. And lemon and . . . She smelled delicious.

"Let's plan to meet at noon," she suggested, gazing up at him. "Down in Costume, where no one will see us. I'll get Jack to help pick out the right suit and . . ." She smiled, the outer edges of her gorgeous eyes crinkling. "What's so funny?" she asked.

Cosmo realized he was standing there smiling at her like a fool, just completely over the moon as far as she was concerned. The singing had clinched it.

Yeah, he was standing there, adoring her, despite the fact that she didn't see him as anything more than a friend.

Friends—yeah, right, Jane. Like this pull he was feeling was purely one-sided. Electricity practically crackled around them when their eyes met. That was not a one-sided side effect.

"What's the big joke?" she asked again, laughing a little, her eyes sparkling. "Share it, Chief. Don't hold back."

He almost did it.

He almost herded her back into the dark corner of that hallway, pressed her up against the wall, lowered his mouth to hers, and proved to her that there was way more than friendship between them.

Light flooded the area as the door to the outside opened. It reminded him of that time he had been wearing night vision goggles and someone suddenly turned on their truck headlights right in his face.

He fumbled to put his sunglasses back on. He was bah-lind.

And deafened by Patty, who was shrieking with laughter as she followed Robin inside.

". . . a minute there—ha ha ha—I actually believed you had a real thing for Adam," she was saying. She laughed again, much too loudly and merrily, but Robin didn't join in.

"Crap," he said instead, trying to see his watch in what was for him, no doubt, sudden dimness. "I'm late for makeup. Janey, this time it's not my fault."

"Get down there," Jane ordered him. "Go. Patty, stay!"

Robin took his backpack from Patty and went out the door.

"I mean, we can check them out, of course," Jules Cassidy was saying to Decker as they, too, came inside. Jack Shelton trailed behind them. "We **should** check them out—along with everyone who's been issued an open-ended press pass by HeartBeat."

"Please tell me I've misunderstood what you're saying," Jane interrupted him, "and that those clowns from the **National Voice** have not been given a press pass"—it was obvious from Jules' and Decker's faces that she hadn't misunderstood at all—"by those raging idiots at HeartBeat. Why would they **do** that?"

As Jack Shelton offered his opinion, Decker pulled Cosmo aside. It wasn't quite far enough from the others for a proper dressing-down. That would come later.

"There's some real irony here," his team leader told him.

"I know, Chief." Cos was known on the Teams for his ability to be dead silent. He was capable of going days—weeks, really—without uttering a single word. "It won't happen again."

"Next time," Decker said, "**if** there is a next time, you need to say 'No comment' and walk away."

"I will. I should have."

Deck wasn't done. "You don't touch them, Cos. You don't get within five feet of them. You lay hands on them, it's their payday. You know this."

He did. These bastards were experts when it came to never throwing the first punch. They were also card-carrying members of Litigation Nation, whose motto was "Sue first, figure out the damages later."

"Don't screw around with your career—or Tom's reputation," Decker told him.

"Heard and understood, Chief."

"Excuse me. If you're ready," Patty said to Cosmo, "I'll show you that extras file."

She was waiting by the door, radiating impatience, and Cosmo headed toward her. Still, he couldn't resist one last glance at Jane, who—hot damn—was watching him walk away.

He must have smiled, because she smiled back, and his heart did a slow somersault in his chest.

Friend, client—he didn't give a damn how their relationship was officially defined. Bottom line was that he loved it when she smiled. As much as he wanted to run his tongue over every inch of her naked body—or lie back and close his eyes while she did the same to him—he also knew he'd be perfectly happy just to sit in a room with her, talking to her, listening to her laughter, watching her smile.

She touched her watch and quirked an eyebrow.

Meet at noon, she'd said.

Cos nodded once. Oh, yeah. He remembered.

He was so there.

CHAPTER THIRTEEN

"Hey, J. Welcome back to the set!"

Robin turned to see Adam heading toward them. **Shit.** What was he doing here?

Robin was escorting Jules down the back hallway off the soundstage—the one that led to both Janey's and Patty's offices. They were in search of a quiet space with a power outlet where Jules could plug in his cell phone.

The FBI agent's battery had run out because he'd had to share a hotel room with his boss last night. The ensuing panic—What if he hates my underwear? What if he ate beans for dinner? What if he snores like Elmer Fudd and my laughter keeps waking him up?—had created a certain amount of brain fade.

Apparently Jules' formidable team leader, Max Something, was the result of a three-way between Emma Peel, Einstein, and the Energizer Bunny, with the possibility of a small, superpower-inducing nuclear accident tossed in.

Mysterious, brilliant, unstoppable, fabulous, fair-minded, tough, powerful, brilliant, brilliant, and, oh, had Jules mentioned that Max was brilliant?

The adverbs—or were they adjectives? Fuck it, Robin could never keep that straight. Whatever they were, they really flew when Jules described the man.

There was also this kind of quiet reverence involved in the utterance of Max's name that, for some reason, really pissed him off.

Robin was almost jealous.

Well, okay, he **was** jealous, but not in, like, a gay way. He was jealous because he could live to be 500, and no one would ever say **his** name with that amount of devotion and respect.

Except maybe Patty.

Who certainly wouldn't use the world **brilliant** four times as she attempted to describe him to one of her friends, so it just wasn't the same.

Crap, he still hadn't talked to Patty.

His plan was to set up a dinner date way, **way** in the future—claim they were both too busy to get together before then. That would get her off his back. He could use the breathing room to figure out what he was going to say when they did sit down together. Obviously **So, hey, remember how I thought I was madly in love with you? Well, I suspect it was only a virus because I'm feeling much better now** was not the right approach.

Although it was clear that running and hiding from her forever was not the solution, either.

It took up far too much of his time and energy.

When Robin had first led Jules into this hallway,

looking for a quiet place to make a phone call, the sounds of life coming from Patty's office had scared the bejesus out of him. But Patty wasn't in there, thank you, God. It was just Janey's Navy SEAL, Cosmo, using the copying machine.

"You can use Jane's office," he told Jules, focusing on the main problem at hand—the fact that Jules needed to make a call to Washington.

At least that **had** been the main problem before Adam appeared.

The big irony was that Robin had just finished telling Jules that they weren't filming any of Jack's scenes until tonight—the obvious subtext of his message being that he could relax. Adam wouldn't be around at all today.

Unless, of course, he made a special effort to come to the studio because he was hoping to bump into—who else?—Jules.

Cue Adam. Enter stage left. "Hey, J. Welcome back to the set!" As if this was Adam's movie, and Jules was his personal guest. As if Jules hadn't been here before Adam even walked into the casting director's office. As if Adam hadn't used Jules shamelessly just to get that audition.

Although, okay. Janey was right about the little shithead. He was a tremendously powerful actor. The few scenes Robin had already shot with him had been awesome. But when "Cut" was called, when the scene was finished and the AD dismissed them, Robin moved fast to get out of chat range.

Adam as Jack was terrific, but Adam as Adam was loathsome.

"Well, well," Robin said. "Isn't this an unpleasant surprise."

Adam ignored him. He'd apparently decided to go with the happy-go-lucky, absolutely nothing is wrong approach, as opposed to the repentant and apologetic grovel.

"How was your trip?" he asked Jules cheerfully. He always dressed like a gay Fonzie—faded blue jeans, pristine tight white T, leather jacket slung over one shoulder, biker boots.

As if he'd ever even been within spitting distance of a real motorcycle.

Yet it was clear he'd made an effort to look good today—his hair was carefully tousled, and the way he was carrying his jacket accentuated his well-defined biceps.

"I missed you," Adam continued, giving Jules more of that same big smile. "Did you get my messages? I'm sorry I called so often. I couldn't tell if I was getting through." He tossed his jacket over several sawhorses that had been stacked near the wall and continued the rest of the way with his arms outstretched. "How about my scoring this role of Jack, huh? Pretty amazing. Of course, I have you to thank, totally."

"Yeah, well," Jules said, lifting his briefcase, using it as a rather obvious shield to prevent Adam from throwing his arms around him in an enthusiastic embrace. "Congratulations."

"That's all you're going to say?" Adam was working his ass off to keep this light. He actually managed to make his eyes sparkle with amusement. "Congratulations? This is huge, J. This is why I came out to California—for a chance like this. And it's all thanks to you."

What a fool. Robin didn't know the FBI agent all too well, but it was beyond obvious that Adam's doing a face-to-face here, in public, at work no less, was the dead-last thing Jules would want.

"Gee, and here I thought you came out to California for the sex," Robin said to Adam.

Who turned and looked at him with wariness in his eyes.

What fun. He had apparently hit close to the truth with that sex comment, and now Adam was trying to gauge just how friendly Robin and Jules had become.

"Will you excuse us, please?" Adam asked him oh so politely.

"Not a chance." Except now Jules was looking at him in surprise, too. "Unless, you know, Jules wants me to go," Robin added.

There was silence then—well, if you could call the sound of that ancient copy machine running **silence**—while Jules stood motionless. Robin cursed himself for giving him a choice. It was obvious he had a serious weakness where Adam was concerned.

"This isn't the time or place for this," Jules said.

"Yeah, it sort of is," Adam said. "Considering I have no idea where you're staying and you won't return my calls. Where else am I going to get a chance to talk to you?" He must've decided there was a shade too much pissy whiner in his voice, because he stopped himself. Smiled a smile that was amazingly genuine seeming. "I have so much to tell you, J. Have you seen the script? I'm in almost every scene. And oh, my God, I'm actually doing an interview with **Out** magazine tomorrow morning and I just found this great new apartment and . . . It's unbelievable how much my life has changed in just a few days. Look, it's almost noon. Let's go have lunch. My treat."

For some reason, that made Jules laugh. But it faded far too quickly, and then all he looked was tired. "I can't. It's too late."

Adam played dumb. "No, it's not. It's only 11:45."

"You know that's not what he meant," Robin said.

Adam got hostile, which was pretty cocky considering Robin had at least forty pounds on him. "Why don't you let him speak for himself?"

"Why don't you start listening to what he's saying? Of course, you'll have to stop talking about yourself in order to do that." Robin made talky-talky motions with both of his hands. "Blah, blah, blah, me, me, me . . ." He was channeling Harve now. This was awesome. He had to call his agent and ask him to find another gay role. Someone who wasn't completely repressed this time.

"Fuck you!" Adam laughed as he said it, his subtext clear: What an asshole.

It took one to know one, didn't it, Tiny?

Robin straightened to his full height, which made him tower above Adam. He could crush the little faggot like a bug. He took a menacing step closer. Got loud. "Fuck **you.**"

Jules, shorter than them both, pushed between them, one hand on each to keep them apart. "Stop."

Cosmo stuck his head out of Patty's office, surveyed the situation, and disappeared again. Obviously, the SEAL felt that he wasn't needed.

"Are you seriously with this guy?" Adam asked Jules, incredulity pouring off each word. This time he didn't leave it to subtext. "What an asshole!"

Robin was aware as hell of Jules' hand warm against his chest, applying pressure, as if he could keep Robin from kicking the shit out of Adam.

He tried to take a step forward, but he couldn't—Jules was an unmovable rock.

A rock who shot Robin a warning look. "Don't prove him right."

Dude might've been short, but make no mistake, Robin was not going to get past him. Of course not. Jules was an FBI agent. He just happened to be a short one who smelled really good.

So okay, pushing Adam against the wall and making him beg for his life wasn't an option here.

Robin would have to use words to scare him.

"It's not serious yet," Robin said to Adam, complete with a much-too-sweet smile, right over Jules' head. "Jules and me. But maybe it will be—after tonight."

Both Adam and Jules turned and looked at him in surprise. He ignored Adam, making his smile warmer now as he gazed at Jules. Flirty. With a hint of I-dare-you. "I didn't get a chance to ask you, but I'm going clubbing tonight. Research, you know? Want to come?"

Jules laughed and somewhat self-consciously re-moved his hand from Robin's chest. He laughed again. Then held Robin's gaze. "Yes, actually. I'd love to."

Robin didn't let himself look away. Harve had told him so much was said via eye contact. Straight men didn't gaze into each other's eyes. Not for more than a very few seconds.

But hey, come on—he was acting here. And doing a damn fine job of it apparently, because that sure as hell was a spark of attraction in Jules Cassidy's pretty brown eyes.

The weird thing was, the man really did have very pretty eyes. Deep and dark, they were so brown that he had to look closely to see where the iris ended and the pupil began. Gazing into them was like looking into the far reaches of an outer space that was warm and welcoming, like diving into a bottomless pit of hot, melted chocolate, like . . .

Hey, there. Okay. Getting just a **little** too lost in the role. And yet he still couldn't look away. . . .

"J."

Jules ended up turning first, to look at Adam.

"It's never too late," Adam continued. "People change. **I've** changed."

Score. Adam had bought it—this completely fic-tional relationship between Robin and Jules.

"How's nine o'clock?" Robin asked Jules, loving the way it made Adam squirm. He reached out, adjusted the slightly rumpled collar of Jules' shirt, touching without quite touching. It was a technique he used all the time when he was trying to pick up a woman at a bar. "You want me to pick you up at your hotel, or should we meet at the club?"

"I'll meet you there." Jules glanced at Adam, and Robin knew he didn't want the shithead to know where he was staying. Wise move, kemosabe.

"There's this place called Big Dick's over on Santa Monica—"

"I know where it is," Jules cut him off with a laugh. "You're kidding, right? That place is so . . . tacky."

"Isn't that the point?" Robin turned to Adam. "Aw, gee, too bad, **A.,** you can't come—you're filming the tanks in the woods scene tonight." He delivered a big, fake sigh. "What a shame."

"Fuck you," Adam said, yet the message that Robin received loud and clear—just how very worried he was—was broadcast by the way he was standing with such obvious and insolent lack of concern.

"It's almost noon—I need to call Peggy," Jules told Robin. "Are you sure it's okay if I use your sister's office?"

"Positive," he said, making his smile extra warm for Adam's benefit. "Go ahead in. And if I don't see you later, J., I'll see you tonight."

For a moment there, Robin was convinced that his use of Adam's cute little nickname for Jules was going to make the son of a bitch pop a vein.

Instead, Adam smiled—tightly—and asked Jules, "You still working with Peggy Ryan? That must suck." He turned to Robin. "Let's just say she's not exactly a contender for this year's Open and Affirming Award from GLAD."

Again with the subtext. **Look at how well I know my J.—I'm familiar with the people he works with.** This son of a bitch just wouldn't give up.

"But you've got to admit, Max **is** pretty wonderful. And so brilliant." Robin countered with a message of his own: **Jules has talked to me about his work, too.** "He makes up for Peggy in spades." He only suspected that was true—Jules hadn't said a word to him about this Peggy Ryan. Of course, what Adam didn't know could be used to drive the bastard crazy.

Cosmo Richter chose that moment to emerge from Patty's office. The sound of the copier had stopped.

Adam clearly hadn't noticed when the SEAL had popped his head out of the office earlier. Now he gave Cosmo a full once-over, obviously checking for a tell-tale rainbow keychain trailing outside of his pants pocket. Or a triangle tattoo on his massive biceps.

Dude made Adam's gym arms look practically atrophied.

"Dream on," Robin murmured to him. Still, he could understand the fascination. The guy looked like he could bench-press a refrigerator. "He's straight."

It was hard to tell if Adam was seriously interested in the SEAL, or if he was only playing the "I don't care—you didn't really hurt me" card for Jules' benefit. "No one's completely straight," Adam said. Obviously he didn't care whether or not Cosmo overheard him.

"Are you finished in there?" Jules asked Cosmo, clearly preferring to use Patty's office instead of Jane's for his phone call.

"Just taking a break for, uh, lunch," Cosmo told him, glancing at Robin and Adam, too.

As they all watched—well, he and Adam watched; Jules had already gone into Patty's office and shut the door behind him—Cosmo opened the door leading downstairs.

"Studio cafeteria's the other way," Adam said helpfully.

The SEAL paused. "Yeah, I know. I'm . . . Costume department's in the first level of the basement, right?"

"Yeah. I'll show you where it is," Adam volunteered.

"I think I can probably find it," Cosmo told him.

"You strike me as the type who can find whatever you're looking for," Robin heard Adam say as he followed Cosmo down the stairs.

Way to get the shit stomped out of you—hit on a Navy SEAL. Although, truth be told, Cosmo seemed tolerant enough. He'd been very cool with Jack—the real Jack, that is.

So maybe Adam wasn't about to be killed. He was, however, gone. Which was good. Let him stay as far away from Jules as possible.

Adam's disappearance also provided Robin with the opportunity to make absolutely sure Jules understood that all that prolonged eye contact had been part of his act.

"She isn't going to like that," he heard Jules say on the phone in the other room. The soundproofing out here was for shit. Then, "So you're actually suggesting we shut down production? Doesn't it bother you, even a little bit, that the Freedom Network'll see it as a win?" Another pause. "No, I'm not accusing you of—" Jules sighed. "No, ma'am." A longer pause. "No, ma'am. I'll make sure she's aware of your recommendation, yes. But I also intend to call Max and—"

"Hi! Oh, my goodness, I'm sorry—are you waiting here for me?"

Patty.

Just perfect.

She came through the studio door and was bearing down upon Robin with her clipboard and kneesocks and freckles and clogs—a bizarre combination he'd found so alluring just a few days ago. Amazing what a little time and distance could do.

"Hey," he said. "Wow," he said. "Uh, yeah . . ."

Patty swooped down upon him and kissed him. It would have been a full tongues affair if it had been up to her. He was the one who kept it both dry and short.

He kept her from noticing that he hadn't truly kissed her by saying, "It occurred to me that we better make plans to have dinner together—to, you know, put the date into our Day-Timers."

She lit up and he felt like a total asshole. Still, he plunged on. "We're both so busy, it's probably going to be a few weeks before we find a night that we both have free. Do me a favor, will you, babe, and send me a copy of your schedule?"

"We're probably going to get rained out tonight," she said, "which means—"

"Oh, hey, sorry, tonight's not good for me," Robin said quickly. "I've already made plans to do some, uh, more research. You know, prep for playing Hal. Being Gay 101."

"We could meet when you're done," she suggested.

"Um . . ." Robin searched for a reason why that wouldn't work. He suspected that **Because I'll be totally shitfaced and unable to drive** wouldn't cut it.

Jules rescued him, using that very moment to throw open the office door. "Where's Jane?" he asked. He had on what Robin thought of as his Detective Joe Friday face. Mega serious.

"She's down in Costume with Jack Shelton," Patty said, wide-eyed. "What's going on?"

"There's been another e-mail. Find Decker," Jules ordered Patty. "Have him meet me down there."

She dashed off—for which he owed Jules, big-time. On her way out the door, she nearly ran over an actor dressed in uniform. "Not now, Wayne," Robin heard her say.

The extra, a kind of goofy-looking Tom Hanks type waved to them. "Hey, Jules, how's it—"

"Hey, sorry, Wayne, we're kind of busy." Jules waved back, then grabbed Robin's arm, pulling him into Patty's office and kicking shut the door. "This place is crawling with extras today."

"Yeah, we're filming part of the big love scene this afternoon. Not mine—the hetero one. Virginia and Milt." Thank God. He was not at all ready to film any of the intimate scenes between his character and Adam's. That was going to be unbelievably hard to do.

Jules was blinking at him. "A love scene with seventy-five extras?"

"They were a little unconventional, Gin and Milt," Robin said. He laughed. "Look at your face—you believe me. I'm kidding. The scene starts in a crowded bar. Janey wants this solitude in the midst of chaos thing. You know . . ." He sang. " 'I only have eyes for you, dear. . . .' "

"I need you to get them all out of here," Jules said. "The extras. And the crew. Now."

Robin laughed again, but then stopped. Jules was not kidding. In fact, Robin had never seen him more dead serious.

"Anyone who hasn't had a proper background check," Jules continued, "and—"

"You're talking about shutting down production," Robin interrupted. "I don't have the authority to—"

"Who does?" Jules asked, then answered in unison with Robin, "Jane. **Shit.**" He opened the door. "We better find her."

"She's not going to shut this movie down." Robin followed him out into the hall. "No way. Just because we got another crazy e-mail from Mr. Insane-o?"

"He's in town," Jules said. "We have reason to believe that as of seven twenty-five this morning, Mr. Insane-o is here in Hollywood."

"The navy blue, I think," Jack said, "although we won't know for sure until he tries them on."

The elderly man clapped his hands at Cosmo from his perch in the director's chair that Jane had dragged down to this main costume room. She knew that his hip was bothering him, although he'd never mention it.

"Out of those awful cargo pants, Mr. Richter," he continued. "I swore when I left the service I would never gaze upon that particular shade of olive drab again, and here I am making a movie filled with it. But to have you walk in, wearing it by choice . . . ?"

As Jane watched, Cosmo looked from Jack to Adam and finally over at her as he took the wooden clothes hanger and dry cleaner's plastic-covered suit from her hand. "Is there someplace I can—"

Jack cut him off. "Trust me, there's no one in this room who hasn't seen even the most ungodly worn-out tightie whities. Don't be shy."

"Yeah, um . . ." Cosmo said, and Jane realized the problem as he met her gaze again.

She'd thought it had been a too-close-to-laundry-day incident—that night he'd come into her room and started to pretend to unfasten his pants. But apparently, she had been wrong. Apparently, Cosmo Richter was neither a boxer nor a briefs man.

She started to laugh.

How . . . interesting.

Jane swung two rolling racks that were jam-packed with WWII-era Marine uniforms, cutting off a small corner of the big basement.

"Instant dressing room," she said briskly, because, oh my God, the big bad SEAL was actually embarrassed. He was blushing.

It was adorable.

Or maybe a more accurate way to put it was that she adored him even more because of it.

Patty had told her about the way he'd faced down the tabloid reporters when they'd asked a question that particularly disrespected her. **Is Mercedes Chadwick as good as they say?**

Although dear sweet Cosmo, by trying to defend her virtue, had done exactly the wrong thing. By stopping and talking to the reporters—even though it was only to reprimand them—he'd revealed that he was vulnerable to their pressure. He'd let them know that they could get under his skin. Which they would try to do again. And again and again.

Which was unacceptable. It was intolerable.

Especially since they were close—so close—to having it all disappear. Especially since Jane had worked so hard to make it all go away.

Especially—damn it!—since she'd taken all of her young, tender, fledgling feelings for this incredible man and stomped them relentlessly back.

She wasn't involved with him. She wasn't going to be involved with him.

And tomorrow the **National Voice** would hit the racks in the grocery store checkout lanes—she wouldn't legitimize the tabloid by saying it would hit the newsstands—with the pictures taken at Victor Strauss' party.

When those pictures came out, Cosmo would be, like, so fifteen minutes ago.

Except now that he'd given this interview, maybe he wouldn't be.

Jane would have to call Victor again. Ask him to visit her here on set. Have a lot of people see her bring him into her office and close the door. Send out for lunch.

And as for Cosmo . . . She was wrapping him up, putting a bow on him, and sending him special delivery to Sophia, the bitch, who goddamn better appreciate what she was getting.

"I would have dressed for the occasion if I'd known I was going to be putting on a fashion show," Cos said quietly, so the others couldn't hear him, as he went inside the area she'd partitioned off.

"Actually, you're not putting on a show," she countered, pushing the clothing racks against each other, sealing off the corner and giving him privacy from at least the chest down. "You would be if you weren't getting changed in here." Oops. There was a definite gap where the two metal poles met. Or rather, didn't meet. "I'll just stand in front of this," she said.

"Thanks." But he didn't wait for her to turn around. Sure, he had his back to her, but he just dropped his pants and . . .

Well, golly.

Nice . . . legs.

She turned and found Jack watching her watch Cosmo, his elegant eyebrows raised. Amusement made his eyes dance.

Jane shook her head at him. He had an interview

later today with the entertainment reporter from some small cable news station. She didn't doubt for one moment that he would be asked about Mercedes Chadwick's relationship with one of her bodyguards. Which really pissed her off. The reporter would be sitting there with a man who'd fought in WWII, a hero who'd helped save the world from Nazi oppression, and instead of talking about that, they'd discuss behind-the-scenes dirt on the Party Girl Producer.

Which was Jane's own fault, wasn't it? This was the image she'd used to get back into the public eye. She really shouldn't complain when her hard work paid off.

So okay. Jack would get asked about her.

But if Jack mentioned seeing any kind of spark between Mercedes and Cosmo, that would only add to the fire the SEAL had rekindled this morning.

What Jack had to do instead was mention that Cosmo already had a girlfriend.

"What the . . . ?"

Since she'd definitely heard the sound of a zipper, she turned back.

Cosmo was looking at the cuffs of the shirt that she'd given him, trying to make sense of the fact that they flopped down past his wrists.

"You need cuff links," she said, rolling back one of the racks and coming to his rescue.

The dismay on his face made her laugh. "Can't I just wear a regular shirt?"

She dug in the jacket pocket for the links—cheap, gold-plated, and engraved with the initials C.F.K. Charlene from Costume swore up and down that

Orson Welles had worn them during **Citizen Kane.** "Do you **have** a regular shirt?"

"Yeah," he said as she folded back the right cuff and hooked the link in place. "It's cool. It's black and it has a skull on the back, along with this red and orange flame. . . ."

Jane stared up at him. He was kidding. Wasn't he? "And you are so completely conning me, aren't you?"

He broke down and laughed. Damn, he had some smile. "I've got a few plain white shirts in my closet, too."

"Too? You mean along with the hideous skull-and-flames number?"

"Show a little respect," Cosmo said. "Chicks dig the skull and flames."

He made no effort to button his shirt. He was just standing there with it hanging open, so she began buttoning it for him. There was only so much half-naked Navy SEAL that a person could bear. "Don't tell me— it's your lucky 'wear it and score' shirt. I hate to break it to you, Cos, but I think you're probably getting laid in spite of the shirt—not because of it."

Again, Cosmo laughed, and as she smiled up into his eyes, something fluttered deep in her stomach. Ah, jeez, she was in trouble. She liked this man a little too much. As he tucked his shirt in, she called, "Adam, will you see if Charlene has a belt?"

"Sure thing, boss."

She had to keep this all business. She knelt in front of Cos, checking the length of the pants, adjusting the lightweight wool, pretending that she wasn't hyperaware of the solidness of his legs beneath the thin fabric. "I think the length is perfect, although it would help if you were wearing shoes. Do you have dress shoes?"

"I did, but I lost them last time I went to New York City." He glanced over at his work boots. They lay where he'd kicked them off, clunky and enormous, like two empty cardboard boxes. "I could just—"

"Don't finish that sentence. Don't even **think** it. Jack, are there any dress shoes in mega huge out there?" she called.

"Charlene says no, but you know how she lies," he called back. "I'll find some."

"My feet aren't that big," Cosmo said mildly.

She tipped her head back and gazed up at him. "How does one lose one's shoes?" From this perspective, he looked gigantic. And gorgeously elegant, the crisp white of the shirt a nice contrast to his tanned skin.

He smiled down at her. "I know what you're thinking, but it's not that exciting."

"Oh, yeah?" Jane said. "What am I thinking?"

"One-night stand gone bad, right? Livid femme fatale throwing my shoes out of a twentieth-story window?"

"How else do you lose your shoes?" she countered. "A weird paddling mishap in Central Park? Yeah, like I'm going to believe **that.**"

"Airline lost my luggage," Cosmo told her. "I never got it back."

"Oh," she said, making a face. "That's very disappointing."

"Sorry."

"If you want, you could bring that skull-and-flames shirt over to my place sometime," Jane told him. "I could throw it out my window, while shrieking, 'You cad!' Although, I'm only on the second floor, so the dramatic impact might not be the same. As well as any potential damage to the shirt. I suppose I could always cut it to shreds with my scissors first."

"That's very kind of you," he said, laughing.

Damn, he looked good, even without a belt and shoes, even with his jacket off.

It was funny—extremely muscular men often looked bulky when they wore a suit, and there were all kinds of costuming tricks and illusions to make them look more triangular rather than like a refrigerator wearing clothes. But Cosmo didn't need any help. His waist and hips were trim. Almost too trim for these pants.

"Are these too loose?" she asked.

"Nothing a belt won't take care of."

"Yeah, but you don't want to do an accordion—you know, get all bunchy up here." She rose up on her knees, reaching to see for herself how oversized the pants were, her fingers inside the waistband. Holy God, the man had zero body fat. He didn't have a tummy—he had a wall of solid muscle. There was a good two inches of extra room, and she chewed on her lip as she considered their options. The zipper pull was sticking up, and she pushed it down, then adjusted the fabric of the fly. "I think we'll need to see what it looks like with the belt. When trousers aren't pleated like this, the front is supposed to lie flat—"

"Which it's not going to do if you keep that up," Adam said, startling them both. She'd forgotten he was standing there.

Jane yanked back her hand which, yes, had been lingering on the front of Cosmo's pants. "Sorry." She got to her feet. Now she was the one who was blushing. God, what an idiot.

She took the belt from Adam, handed it to Cosmo, pretending she wasn't flustered. "I've helped tailor more than my share of costumes," she said. "My specialty is hemming—I think probably because you can't really screw it up too badly. I used to do hair and makeup, too. See, if a movie is low budget enough, a producer has to learn to do just about everything."

Great, now she was babbling.

"Stunts?" Cos asked, fastening the buckle.

"Okay, maybe not everything," Jane conceded.

Jack appeared with a pair of shoes. They were less like cardboard boxes and more like elegant leather canoes. "These should work." He looked at Cosmo. "Oh, my."

Oh, my, indeed. Perfect timing, too. "Let's talk for a minute about Sophia," she said for Jack's benefit as Cosmo slipped his feet into the canoes.

"Sophia, eh?" Jack said, turning to look at Jane. "All this effort is for a **Sophia**? Not for—"

"Yes, Jack, it most certainly is." She kept him from saying "a Jane." "Brilliant, beautiful, brave Sophia. Right, Cos?"

She took the suit jacket from the wooden hanger and held it out for him, shaking it slightly when he didn't move right away.

Cosmo shrugged into it, glancing back over his shoulder at her. "I don't really know her," he finally said.

"Isn't that the point of having dinner with her? To get to know her?" Jane smoothed the fabric of the jacket over his amazing shoulders. "This fits like it was made for you." She handed him the tie that Jack had picked out—blue with a jazzy pattern.

"I don't know who Sophia is, but frankly, I hate her," Adam said.

Jane could relate. Up to this moment, she'd been nursing this foolish fantasy that after **Hero** was in the can, after the death threats became yesterday's news, after her life returned to relatively normal and her encounters with paparazzi dwindled back down to once or twice every six months or so, she'd call up Cosmo and say something like, "Hey, remember that lucky shirt you told me about a few months ago? With the skull and flames? What do you say you put it on and come on over and see what happens? Wink, wink, nudge, nudge."

But now she knew that wasn't going to happen. Perfect Sophia was going to take one look at Cosmo, and . . .

Jane would call in a few months, sure—to congratulate him on his upcoming wedding to the woman of his dreams.

Damn it.

Jack was watching her, one eyebrow askance, so she smiled brightly. "From what I've heard, Sophia sounds lovely. She and Cos both work for Troubleshooters Inc., so they must have a lot in common."

"Too much in common makes life boring," Jack intoned. "The relationships that I've seen work—the ones that seem to last the longest—are opposites. There's more to talk about. The sex is better, too."

"In that case," Adam said, batting his eyelashes, "Cosmo should forget about Sophia and hook up with me. I'm his exact opposite." He pulled back the clothing racks so that Jack could sit down again and not be left out of the conversation.

Adam was not only a wonderful actor, but also considerate, charming, and quite funny. Jane didn't understand why Robin had such a huge problem with him. It was particularly weird, since it was so unlike her brother to hold a grudge for more than five seconds.

"I was thinking more in terms of our Jane," Jack said to Adam.

She made herself laugh at that, as if it was as absurd a thought as Cosmo paired with Adam. "Yeah, thanks but no thanks, Jack. Cos and I are friends. Period. Don't start believing what you read in the tabloids. Cos and I are hot and heavy, a two-headed baby was born speaking ancient Latin and Greek, and a doctor in Latvia has cloned Elvis."

"What's going on? You going to be in this movie, Cos?"

Jane looked up to see Lawrence Decker standing in the door.

"Just a lunch break, Chief," Cosmo said as Deck came in. Patty, Robin, and Jules were right behind him. "I'd mentioned to Jane that I didn't own a suit so—"

"He needs a suit so he can take Ms. Sophia Wonderful to dinner," Adam said. It was so obvious to Jane that he was pretending that Jules' presence didn't affect him in the slightest.

"Really?" Decker said. He looked at Cos. "You and Sophia are, um . . . ?" He shook his head, looked at Jane, pointed over his shoulder with his thumb toward the stairs he'd just come down. "Is this the main access to this area?" He pointed across the room. "Where does that door lead?"

"Hallway to a costume storage area. This basement's huge," Cosmo answered for her. "There are a number of other exits: six different stairways going up, and four going down to a sublevel."

Decker motioned to Jules. "Would you . . . ?"

The FBI agent went to the other door, opened it, and checked outside of it.

"What's up?" Cosmo asked before Jane could.

"There's been another e-mail," Robin said. "Janey, the FBI were able to track this one. It was sent from a Kinko's, here in Hollywood. The one right down the street."

CHAPTER
FOURTEEN

S o this was how a movie love scene was filmed. It was remarkably unromantic, with bright lights and instructions to the actors called out by the director.

"Keep your right shoulder down, Virginia, or we're going to get another nipple in the frame."

"Legs closer together, Milt. We want only your butt in this shot, no hairy surprises."

Jesus.

Good thing Decker had his back to the action. Of course, that was the only way Mercedes would let him into the studio.

She'd cleared most of her cast and crew from the set. The multitude of extras had all been sent home, much to Deck's relief.

Although she probably wouldn't have done that if the actor and actress who were playing Milt and Virginia hadn't agreed to shoot their big love scene several days earlier than scheduled. But they had, so here they were, with a skeleton crew filming two naked forty-year-olds pretending to get their groove on.

Deck, of course, would have been much happier if everybody had gone home. Everyone except Mercedes and the Troubleshooters team. Mercedes had to stick around—at least until Cosmo called to say that they were finally ready for her. He'd taken a team back to the producer's house to clear out fifty years of clutter from the garage so they could drive the producer directly inside upon arrival at her home. No more hustling her out of the car and up the front steps in clear view of anyone with a hundred-fifty-dollar rifle scope.

Not with their man's latest e-mail saying, "I'm closer than you think."

Sadistic bastard.

The FBI had swarmed over that Kinko's, dusting for prints, hoping to find footage from a surveillance camera.

No such luck. The Kinko's camera had stopped working early that same morning—no mere coincidence, of that Decker was sure.

They'd located the computer the e-mailer had used to send the message. They also got his name and credit card number, which was, of course, fake and stolen.

The stolen card had been taken sometime in the past three days, somewhere here in the greater Los Angeles metropolitan area.

It wasn't much to go on.

Both the Troubleshooters and the FBI had interviewed the Kinko's counter help. There had been three people working at 0725 this morning, but none of them could put a face on the e-mailer. Youngish—maybe. Average height—maybe. Brown hair—maybe.

"We get a lot of students early in the morning, this time of year," the most senior of the staff, a woman all of twenty-two years old, had said apologetically when Deck had talked to her.

Apparently, their man was white and male.

And surely clever enough to know not to go back to that Kinko's, where the FBI were installing their own surveillance device—one that couldn't be tampered with.

After Cosmo's team finished clearing Mercedes' garage, they would drive to the studio, checking out any locations along the route that might be used as a hiding place by a shooter with a sniper rifle.

Church towers, office building roofs, hillsides . . .

Unless they could convince Mercedes to lie low for a few days, they were going to have to map out other routes to the studio, and never take the same one twice.

But what they really had to do, first and foremost, was catch this son of a bitch.

Then Deck could return to the world he knew best—a world where the words **we're going to get another nipple in the frame** weren't used very often.

If at all.

Cosmo Richter, too, could go back to Coronado, to SEAL Team Sixteen, where he belonged.

He was a good man, a good addition to the Troubleshooters team. Decker didn't dispute that. He was just so . . . tall. So striking looking in that goddamn classy suit and tie.

He was such a perfect physical match for Sophia, whom he obviously had the hots for. Why wouldn't he? She was beautiful and intelligent and . . .

She was actually having dinner with him. Cosmo must've asked her out, and she must've said yes.

Which was a good thing. Cosmo was a good man. He'd be good for her.

Decker looked like shit when he wore a suit. He could never find one that fit right. Not at a price he was willing to pay.

"Okay, cut, cut!" the director called. "I'm not getting enough here. This restraint is not what I want, people. You're holding back. Where's that passion I saw yesterday?"

"How about trying something a little different?" Deck heard Mercedes suggest. "How about we get the audio back up and running, have quiet on the set, and let our actors do this scene the way they want to do it."

The director wasn't happy. "That's not the way I—"

"Here's the thing, Len." Mercedes put a hint of steel into her voice. "We've done it your way for nearly three hours. My actors are getting tired. This time, we're going to do it their way."

"This isn't—" the director started to say, but Mercedes stepped close and spoke quietly into his ear. Deck couldn't make out the words, but whatever she said shut him up. Patty then intercepted, pulling him down near Decker, to show him what looked like a mock-up of the movie poster.

"Grab a PowerBar, get dressed, get restyled," Mercedes ordered the two actors. "Everyone else take five, then get this shot set up again. Deck, are you still here?"

"Yes, ma'am," he called.

"Come on over here, will you?" she called back. "Forgive me for not getting up, but my feet are killing me. New shoes. Want some coffee?"

"No thanks, I'm good."

Mercedes was sitting in a director's chair with her name stenciled on the back, part of a cluster of similar chairs positioned near a video monitor, slightly behind the camera. In front of the camera, the soundstage was set up to look like the shabby elegance of a Paris hotel room, circa 1945. Stage lights, attached to bars way up high, as well as enormous metal frames—trees, Mercedes had called them—holding huge spotlightlike fixtures, provided atmospheric lighting.

"Sorry to make you sit out there with your back to the action," Mercedes said, tipping her head back to look at him. "It's just . . . Can you imagine being an actor filming a love scene with people watching?"

"No," he admitted. "I can't. Not under any circumstances."

She nodded, gesturing for him to sit. "What I'm trying to do is make my actors feel as safe as possible, so—"

"Excuse me, Jane. I'm sorry . . ." It was Patty of the clipboard. "Victor Strauss left a message—I know you were waiting for his call. He can do lunch either tomorrow or the next day."

"Tomorrow," Mercedes decided. "Call him back,

make sure he knows to meet me here at the studio. Oh, and tell him to bring flowers—something wildly romantic."

Patty nodded, making herself a note. "Also . . . the FBI is here. Jules and another man. I'm not sure, I think it might be his boss. Max Something . . . ?"

Decker sat up. Max Bhagat was here?

"Let them in but make sure they know we've only got about ten more minutes of break," Mercedes told Patty, who nodded and trotted away, already making that phone call.

Mercedes turned to Deck. "What are the chances they're here to tell me they found a clue at the Kinko's and have already taken Mr. Insane-o into custody?"

"It'd be nice it if were that easy," Decker agreed.

Bang! Crash! Thump!

Deck leapt to his feet, scanning the soundstage, not all of which was lit. **Screeee!** What the hell?

Mercedes stood up, too. "What—?"

Whump! Crrrrrsh! That sounded like smashing glass and it seemed to be coming from overhead, as if the giant at the top of the beanstalk had dropped her serving tray and—

Shards of broken glass and pieces of metal were falling onto the set, raining down on them from above. Decker grabbed Mercedes even as he looked up into the lights, trying to see what—or, Jesus, who—the fuck was up there.

Whump! Crrrrrrsh!

"Look out!" someone shouted. "Oh, fuck!"

"Ow!" Mercedes exclaimed, but Deck didn't know

if that was in response to the spraying glass or his grip on her wrist as he instinctively dragged her back toward the door, because—oh, fuck indeed—there was a piece of lighting equipment that had somehow broken free from the overhead pipes. He could see it swinging up there like a wrecking ball, knocking into other lights and held in place by God only knew what—possibly only its electrical cord.

"Look **out**!" This voice was completely panicked, and Deck turned to see—oh, **big** fuck!—that one of those lighting trees—this one a towering steel pipe with seven or eight large lights attached like branches at the top—was falling, gathering momentum.

He and Mercedes weren't quite in danger of being crushed—they'd have two or three feet of breathing room even if they stood still. Except that thing wasn't just going to lie there quietly when it hit the stage. Deck tried to move her faster, farther away from the point of impact, dodging sound equipment and set pieces.

She was shouting something—his name was part of it, but he had no clue exactly what she wanted. He just yanked her in front of him, shielding her with his body as that thing hit the stage with a thundering, screeching, floor-shaking crash.

The stage lights exploded and some broke free from the tree, bouncing wildly across the set.

Deck pushed Mercedes toward shelter behind a parked forklift as a flying piece of metal whizzed past his ear.

Man, that was too close for—**Crunch.** The force of

something solid connecting with the back of his head pushed him forward and down to the floor. He took Mercedes with him, still trying to shield her, as the world went to black.

As far as nightmares went, Jane had written a doozy.

Cosmo leafed through the pages of script that she'd given him to read as he ate dinner at the picnic table outside the sandwich shop.

This was the big favor Jane had asked the other night—asked and then forgotten about. She'd wanted him to read this nightmare D-Day battle sequence that she'd written. It was, quite literally, a bad dream that the character of Jack had after meeting and falling in love with Hal Lord.

Jack, who was in the Twenty-third, had never been in direct combat. Hal, however, was an officer with the legendary 101st Airborne—the Screaming Eagles. He'd parachuted into France on D-Day. Hal had been in the thick of it, and Jack had persuaded him to talk a little about that hellish battle.

Much in the way Jane had gotten Cos to talk about his wartime experiences.

"You're the first person to read this," she'd said as she'd thrust the pages of script at him, right after Decker had put the soundstage into lockdown mode. She wanted to know if Cosmo thought it "worked."

As if he knew anything about screenplays.

He did, however, know quite a bit about war.

In the scene Jane had written, Jack dreamed he was part of the Normandy invasion. He ran up the beach, under enemy fire, fighting fiercely for every step he took. There were notes in the margin: "Check with Harve—can we get enough blood packs and other special effects makeup to make this look realistic?"

It was a nice way to fight a battle—with fake blood.

The scene had a dreamy quality to it. Some of the battle sequences would be in slow motion, some in silence with a voice-over from Hal, obviously from that heartfelt conversation he'd had with Jack.

Everett was standing inches away from me. Cosmo read Hal's words. **The Germans must've zeroed their 88 right in on us. The blast knocked me down, took away my hearing for a few hours, but that was it. I was all right. A few bruises. But ol' Ev . . . We found his legs. His boots. That was all we sent home.**

Heavenly Father.

You pray because you don't know why he died when you didn't. And you pray because the guilt brings you to your knees. Because the grief of losing a friend becomes a brief flash of sorrow that you push away—to focus on keeping your other men alive. After a while, you start pretending that you don't know their names, that they aren't your friends, that you don't give a crap if they live or die. But you do. And you remember every single name, every single face, for the rest of your life. . . .

Well, she got that part right.

There was another voice-over in this scene, too. A journal entry from Virginia, the American costume designer who'd been called in to help create the Nazi uniforms needed for that dangerous mission into Germany. In Janey's screenplay, Gin had surprised herself by falling in love with the group's team leader, Major Milt Monroe.

Seeing Milt take command yesterday, when those boys were killed by that sniper, made me realize—I will now be able to visualize his death.

I will be able to picture a blue sky sparkling behind him as he is hit by bullets, his blood spraying as he falls but then gets up again, falls and gets up again, refusing to quit fighting even as he breathes his last.

God!

Damn You! Where are You? End this war now!

Why do You hide when thousands of men, thousands of Jacks and Hals and Miltons, die in every battle?

They are not government issue, off some assembly line, as much as we pretend they are—these American men and boys who sacrifice so much so that others may be free.

They're called replacements, the new boys who come to fight. But they, like those who fell before them, were born to mothers and fathers who treasure them—not as one of many, but as someone unique, someone irreplaceable.

Someone loves them, even if You don't! Someone, somewhere, will bleed for them forever.

As I have already begun to bleed for Milt.

"I'll get there as soon as I can."

Cosmo looked up from the script to see that PJ was

on the phone again. Like Cos, his clothes were grimy from clearing out Jane's garage. He was no doubt talking to his girlfriend, who seemed determined to drive him completely crazy before she left for Iraq. "I know." He rolled his eyes at Cos. "I **know,** Beth. Look, honey—" He sighed. And moved the phone away from his mouth, covering the receiver with his thumb. "You just about done?" he asked Cosmo.

Who was sitting there with half of his sandwich still uneaten.

"Five minutes," Cos told him. Damn it, he got mustard on page four. He wiped at it with his napkin, but it left a grease mark. Great. Way to make sure Jane knew that he was a total slob.

Phone to his ear, still listening to Beth, PJ went next door, to the 7-Eleven. Lindsey, the third member of the Troubleshooters Trash Removal Team, was sating her raspberry Slurpee jones. No doubt PJ's intention was to hustle her along, too.

Shaking his head, Cosmo flipped to page five. The images in this scene skittered and changed, similar to the way a dream hopped randomly from one place to the next—and suddenly Jack was participating in a charge on a German pillbox. The fighting was violent, but the position was finally taken.

That was when Jack saw movement from the corner of his eye—a young German soldier. He fired before he realized the kid's hands were up in surrender, and the man fell. And wasn't that a total wartime nightmare—Jane got that right as well.

But for Jack, in his dream, it got even worse. He

moved closer and to his horror saw that the German soldier was, in fact, Hal.

Jack dropped to his knees, trying to stanch the flow of Hal's blood. But it was mortal—this wound he had inflicted upon the man that he loved. And it was too late. Blood flecked Hal's lips and the light in his eyes faded as he reached up to touch Jack's grimy face.

"You can't save me," he whispered as the battle once again raged around them.

At this point in the movie, Jack awakened with a gasp, in the dark, breathing hard, horrified—only to see Hal sleeping peacefully beside him.

The symbolism was nice. It was a good scene. And Janey had really managed to capture the nightmarish chaos of battle.

Janey. Damn. He was starting to think of her as Janey.

He was so totally screwed.

"Cos!" PJ was back, Lindsey on his heels. "Check this out! I'm in the **National Void.** In tomorrow's paper, no less. The 7-Eleven must've gotten it early."

He threw the tabloid—the **National Voice**—onto the table. Cos grabbed his can of Coke to keep it from getting knocked over and . . .

There was a picture, right on the front page, and indeed, PJ was in it, in the background, his sunglasses making him just another indistinguishable Man in Black. The focus, however, was on Jane, who was laughing, gazing into the eyes of an older man who was holding her close.

Very close. They might have been dancing. Or

maybe they were just standing there. With his hands on her ass. With him nanoseconds from locking lips with her.

"This must've been taken last night," PJ said.

Cosmo had to clear his throat, which didn't quite erase the sensation of having been hit in the chest with a bowling ball. He somehow got his vocal cords working. "Yeah." Jane was wearing that same little black dress.

"I mean, not that you can tell who it is, which is good, but I know it's me." PJ was just a little too thrilled by this. "Cool, huh?"

The caption read, "Party girl producer J. Mercedes Chadwick with old flame, director Victor Strauss."

Old flame? How old?

There was no article—except, wait. There was. It was just a paragraph in some kind of gossip column that ran along the side of the page.

From the horse's mouth: Caught with his hands in the cookie jar on his first days back in town after a seven-month shoot in Spain, Victor Strauss was quoted as saying that his off-again, on-again relationship with hot property J. Mercedes Chadwick is "serious this time. I'd be a fool to let her get away again." Might those be wedding bells we hear?

Lindsey was reading over Cosmo's shoulder. "I didn't realize Jane was dating Victor Strauss. I know she really wanted him to direct **American Hero,** but he wasn't available. He's cute—in kind of an older guy, nerdy, extremely rich and famous way."

Cos had seen some pictures flying around the Net of himself and Jane at that press conference. In most of them, he'd looked pretty damn detached. There were a few that had been taken exactly when he'd grabbed her to keep her from falling, when he'd held her tightly against him and . . .

He knew there had been a moment when he'd reacted in a less than professional manner, because the cameras had caught it on film. There had been an expression of undisguised anger on his face.

Of course, in those photos it had read as desire. Which, come to think of it, may well have been in his eyes at that moment, too.

But only for a split second.

"He actually has an Oscar," PJ told Lindsey. "That party we went to was at his house—it was on this little shelf right outside his bathroom, like it's the first thing he wants to see after he takes a dump in the morning. It's not as big as I thought, but it's heavy."

In this picture, however, Strauss' undisguised hunger for Jane was not a fleeting, temporary emotion.

But okay. Even though a picture was said to be worth a thousand words, the message could well be misinterpreted or misunderstood. Maybe Jane and this famous director were discussing their next project.

PJ laughed. "I should know. I stood outside that door for about ten minutes while Jane and Strauss had a quickie."

Lindsey laughed. "Are you kidding? In the bathroom, in the middle of a party? Go, Jane!"

Or maybe they weren't talking business at all.

"They probably thought they were being discreet by not going into the bedroom, which would've raised some eyebrows," PJ said. "His house wasn't that big and there were people hanging out in there."

"The alternative would've been him coming over to her place, which might be kind of weird for Jane, because there we all are, you know?" Lindsey said. "Day and night, nonstop."

"I know it would make me self-conscious," PJ said, "if I were her and I wanted to get it on with some rich guy who could probably further my career and give me a giant diamond—cha-ching!—as part of the deal."

Cosmo couldn't stand it any longer and he stood up. "Show a little respect."

"What?" PJ said. "I'm not being disrespectful. I'm just saying. I'm sure Jane likes the man. It sure as hell seemed that way last night, if you know what I mean."

His appetite was gone. Cos threw away the uneaten half of his sandwich as he started for his truck. He had to get out of here. Shit, he had to get out of L.A.

Lindsey poked PJ in the arm as they followed him into the parking lot. "Yeah, you're just jealous. You thought you had a chance with her. What, did you really think that a woman who dates famous movie directors would be interested in dating a bodyguard? Dream on."

"I'm not talking dating," PJ said. "I'm talking doing

the dance of looove, getting a little of that ten-minute bathroom action, although for sure I'd settle for five in the linen closet." He paused. "I'm kidding—you know that, right? I don't want some incriminating sound bite to work its way to Beth."

"Because she knows you well enough to know that you're kidding on the square," Lindsey countered.

"What the hell does that mean?"

Cosmo was spared the rest of this freaking annoying discussion when his cell phone rang. The number was Tess Bailey's—the Troubleshooters team's XO. "Richter."

She didn't waste words. "Code red. There's been an incident at the studio. Deck and Jane are hurt."

The world went still around him. Except Lindsey was saying, " . . . when you say you're kidding, but you're really not."

"Code red—quiet!" he ordered them sharply, but Tess stopped talking, too. "No, Tess. Go."

"We need you down here," she told him. "Now. Wait— Wait, hold up . . ."

PJ and Lindsey were already scrambling into the truck. "They've had action at the studio," Cos told them.

"No fucking way," PJ said. "Casualties?"

"Deck and Jane. I don't know details," Cosmo reported as he slammed the truck in reverse and backed out of the parking space.

"Dear God," Lindsey breathed.

Tess came back. "The ambulance is going to drive

right inside through a garage bay—shit, why didn't we know about that before? A freaking garage bay here on the soundstage, and we've been rushing her in through the door—"

"Where do you need us?" Cos interrupted her, his truck already in gear. First things first. But Christ, if they needed an ambulance over at the studio . . .

"The hospital," Tess told him. "Cedars-Sinai. Meet us there. ER entrance. Keep that freaking door closed!" he heard her bellow as she cut the connection before giving him any further information.

"Which way to Cedars-Sinai hospital?" he asked, and PJ looked up from checking his sidearm and over at Lindsey, who'd lived in L.A. all of her life.

"Left, and then left again at the light," she said, then hung on to the dashboard for dear life as Cos burned rubber leaving the parking lot.

As the ambulance pulled up to the hospital, Jane could see that Cosmo was already there. He looked grim—and grimy. Of course, he'd been cleaning out her garage.

The rest of the team was there, too. Well, except for Jules, whom they'd left back at the studio with his boss, Max Bhagat, and a crew of investigators from the local FBI office.

Amidst the chaos, Jane had exchanged somewhat absurd pleasantries with Max, the leader of one of the world's most elite counterterrorist teams, while they waited for the ambulance. "Nice to meet you, Ms. Chadwick, I'm Max. No, don't shake my hand, keep applying pressure. Hang on, don't move—let me get this big chunk of glass out of your hair. . . ."

"Do they know I'm okay?" Jane asked Tess Bailey, the Troubleshooters' answer to Wonder Woman, who was riding with her.

But Tess was on the phone again. She made a "hang on" gesture.

Of course, maybe Jane was getting ahead of herself. That worried look on Cosmo's face could have been for Decker, who was right behind them, in the second ambulance.

Much to her relief, Deck had come to and was lucid. His teammates practically had to sit on him to keep him from leaping to his feet and running up into the catwalks to see if foul play was involved.

He had a zillion questions. Were the falling lights intentional? Was this a murder attempt by Mr. Insane-o, her crazy e-mailer?

Jane found it very hard to believe this had been anything but an accident.

A miraculously well-timed accident, too. Imagine if it had happened in the middle of filming the love scene—that would have been awful enough. But, God, if it had happened before they'd changed the schedule, with all those extras on the soundstage . . . As it was, with only a few people on set when the accident happened, they'd been unbelievably lucky.

Only two people injured, and both superficially.

Of course, head injuries were tricky. Jane would feel a whole lot better about Decker after he'd been examined by a doctor. Tess had thought he must've been hit by the end of an electrical cord as it whipped past. It had struck him hard enough to both temporarily shut out his lights and break the skin.

Which must've hurt like the devil.

Although, if the actual stage light had hit him, he would be beyond feeling pain. Jane still got wobbly-kneed when she thought about that.

"Sorry," Tess said, closing her phone as the ambulance pulled to a stop.

"Make sure they get Deck inside first," Jane told her.

"You know he would never agree to that," Tess said. "You'll be going in first. And quickly, too, as soon as the doors open."

"But I'm not bleeding." Jane lifted the makeshift bandage she was pressing against her arm and . . . Okay, not quite the truth. "I'm not the one with the possible acute subdural hematoma."

Tess lifted her eyebrows. "I didn't realize you had medical training."

"I don't. I used to write for a soap opera."

Tess laughed. Then, "Here we go," she said as the ambulance door opened. The entire security team surrounded Jane's wheelchair as she was hustled toward the hospital.

Cosmo managed to look even more grim as he took in the blood on the front of her dress. "You all right?" he asked as he looked hard into her eyes, no doubt checking to see if she'd gone into shock or was harboring a secret head injury of her own.

"Yes," she said. "I'm fine."

He gave her that over-the-top-of-the-nonexistent-sunglasses look that she'd come to know so well, the one that said "Oh, really?" so clearly she could almost hear it, and she started to laugh. But, oh God, instead it came out sounding an awful lot like a sob.

She was not going to cry. J. Mercedes Chadwick did **not** cry in public.

"I was cut by flying glass," she told him, told them all. It was easier to aim her words at Murphy or PJ than to face Cosmo's concern. She somehow even managed to sound breezy. "I stopped applying pressure, but it was deeper than I thought. What a mess."

But then they were inside, wheeling her into the hospital, past the admissions desk. The team fell back—Tess was the only one who stayed with her.

"Janey!" Robin appeared, out of breath. "I got a message on my cell saying you were here and— Holy crap, what happened?"

"We had an accident," she said, looking back at Cosmo, who was standing there, by the desk, still watching her. "One of the bigger lights broke free from the pipes."

"Oh, my God."

Jane told her brother what had happened as the paramedics wheeled her around a corner into a small hospital room. As she left Cosmo behind. The paramedics made all these noises like they were going to lift her out of the chair and onto the hospital bed, and she interrupted her story to say, "My legs are fine. I can take it from here."

"Glad to hear it, dear, but you look like you've lost some blood, so we'll keep a hand on you while you get up there," the cheerful ER nurse told her.

"Thank you," Jane said as she scrambled onto the bed, pretending it had been easy. Jeez, this dress was totaled, she was light-headed, and her legs were still way too rubbery.

"Let's take a look," the nurse said, and as Jane pulled her bandage away, Robin turned green. Even when they were kids, a simple skinned knee could make him feel faint.

Tess, on the ball as always, pushed a chair behind him, and he practically fell into it.

"Have you had a chance to look at Decker?" Jane asked the nurse.

"Jane, I'll keep you updated," Tess answered for her. "He's gone over to, well, I don't know exactly—X-ray maybe. The doctors here will be checking him out thoroughly. Nash is with him and, I promise, as soon as we know anything, you'll know, too."

"Keep pressure on that," the nurse told Jane. "You're going to need a few stitches, hon."

"I was afraid of that," Jane told her. "I'm a real baby. Can I have general anesthesia?"

The nurse laughed as she bustled out of the room.

"She thinks I'm kidding," Jane said.

Robin was pale. "So **now** are you going to take these death threats seriously?"

"This was an accident," she told him.

Tess spoke up. "I think it's still a little too early to say whether this was accidental or intentional."

Perfect. Way to give her little brother another reason to get lubed tonight. Drink, drink, and drink some more, for tomorrow we may die.

"I thought my psycho killer was a brilliant and cunning psycho killer," Jane countered. "Isn't the idea of rigging a studio light to maybe fall—**maybe**—in the hopes that the intended murder victim—me—will be sitting directly beneath it at that exact moment, a little, well, double dumb-ass stupid, not to mention about as cunning as a stone?"

"The goal might've been to cause trouble on the set," Robin said. "Or shut down production—which, oh by the way, Miss Smarty Pants, it did."

"It's possible it was designed to put us off guard," Tess suggested. "Make us think that the danger was inside the studio. We all come running outside, he's set up on the roof of some nearby building, and when he's got a clear shot . . . bang. That's why we came over here to Cedars-Sinai. There are hospitals closer to the studio, but we didn't want to take the chance he was set up somewhere, waiting for you."

"That's so creepy," Robin said.

"And astonishingly paranoid," Jane added.

"We call it careful," Tess told them. "One of the things we're going to need from you is a list of everyone who was in the studio earlier today. We had a lot of extras in this morning—people new to the set."

"Patty's already getting that list for Jules Cassidy," Jane said.

"Jules is here?" Robin tried to interrupt, but she spoke right over him.

"But the thing is, Tess, the crew is union. There are rules about who goes up on those catwalks." Jane looked at Robin. "No, Jules is back at the studio, looking for 'clues.' Which he won't find because there aren't any." She turned back to Tess. "My gaffer is good. He wouldn't have let some random extra wander around up there. I think the fact that the safety chain was intact is proof that it was an accident. That chain did what it was supposed to do—it kept the light from falling. If someone went up there to do mischief, they would've eighty-sixed the chain."

"Unless they had a limited amount of time up in the catwalk." Tess was fairly serene about her job-induced paranoia. "Jane, I know you don't want to hear this, but we really want you to lie low for a few days—"

"You mean, hide at home, cowering under my bed?"

"I mean stay someplace where we're sure you're safe for a—"

"I'm safe when I'm home, and I'm safe at the studio," Jane said, her blood pressure and her voice both starting to rise. "That's what we all agreed. I'm not safe on location—I've already given that up, which is both terrifying and infuriating, since I've got a director who needs 24/7 supervision by the Creativity Police, otherwise he's not going to make my movie, he's going to make his, which is going to **suck** because his involves ignoring my actors completely and—"

"Jane," Robin said. "Lenny's not that bad. Breathe, okay? I keep picturing blood starting to geyser out of your arm, like something from a Monty Python movie."

"Robbie, we're re-creating the Normandy invasion in just a few days. Okay, yeah, on a much smaller scale than Steven Spielberg might've done, but I'm going to have to miss that and that makes me very unhappy!"

"An alternative solution might be to shut down production for a few weeks," Tess suggested in an oh-so-innocent tone that matched her girl-next-door face. She looked as if she should be hosting a Tupperware party, not taking over team leader duties for Decker, who was off in another part of this hospital, getting his head examined.

Jane gave her a variation of Cosmo's "oh, really?" look. "You **know** that's the last thing I'd consider doing. We shut down—they win."

"They kill you," Tess countered, "they win."

She had a point. "If they kill me," Jane said to Robin, "use the insurance money to make sure this movie gets made."

"Jesus, Janey . . ."

The happy nurse reappeared. "The doctor's on his way down. I may not be able to give you anything for the pain, hon, but I have someone out here who's eager to come in and see you." She winked. "I know he'd make me feel better if he held my hand. . . ."

Cosmo. Jane closed her eyes. God, yes. A dose of Cosmo's solid presence was exactly what she needed. "Please send him in."

"Of course, I'm a big fan of his movies," the nurse said, and Jane opened her eyes.

Ah, crap. She wasn't talking about Cosmo. She was talking about Victor Strauss.

What was he doing here?

Although, on second thought, it wasn't really that big of a surprise that Patty had turned a near-death experience into a promo op. After all, she'd learned from the master.

It was hours, at least, before Cosmo's official shift began, before Jane could sit in the kitchen with him and have a cup of tea. And maybe, while in his comfortingly solid presence, safe in the knowledge that, unlike most people, he didn't want or expect anything from her, she could be Jane for a while. And instead of laughing off the fear she'd felt, she could admit that for several terrifying moments she'd thought Decker was dead.

Her eyes filled with tears—God, she needed just a few minutes away from the relentless BS of her extremely public life—but she blinked them back.

She might as well make these hours count.

Jane pasted Mercedes' smile on her face and prepared to make her visit to the hospital part of the big show.

"Patty!"

She stopped short at the sight of Wayne Ickes. Coming at her from the end of the hospital corridor, dressed like the Good Humor man. God help her.

For several seconds, she actually considered turning

and running. Maybe she could pretend she hadn't seen him. Maybe . . .

"Are you all right?" he asked. Too late. God, she did not need this right now. "I was up in the children's ward when I heard what happened."

That's right, he'd told her his day job was at Cedars-Sinai. Of course this was where they'd come. And of course he was working this shift. She could **not** win today.

Today? Try this week.

Although, she had to give herself a high five for providing the news cameras—already gathered out in front of the hospital—with a very nice shot of Victor Strauss rushing in to see Jane. It was more proof for the tabloids that the two were romantically connected.

She'd been on the phone with Victor—he'd told her to call him by his first name, and he always took her calls, which was sweet—when the accident happened.

"I'm fine," she told Wayne.

"I heard Mercedes needs stitches."

"Just a few," she said. "She's getting ready to leave. And Deck's all right, too. He's not staying overnight, either."

"Too bad," Wayne said. "I could've gotten them extra Jell-O with their dinner."

She stared at him. Was that supposed to be funny?

"Sorry," he said. "Dumb joke. Look, I've got to get back to it—I need to leave early to get to the shoot tonight. I'm in the tank scene with Adam, you know."

"It's raining," she told him. He must not have checked his voice mail yet. "It's been canceled."

"Oh," he said, disappointed. But he brightened right away. "Well, in that case, you want to go to a movie?"

Was he kidding? "I'm **just** a little busy tonight," Patty told him, already walking away, unable to keep the sarcasm from her voice. "My boss was in an accident. I need to make myself available."

"I'm sorry. Of course," he said, following her. He just didn't quit. "But in the event she goes home and gets Percodaned up . . . Well, you know where to find me."

She certainly did. And it therefore should follow that she knew where to go in order **not** to find him.

And then she should have just done it. She should have turned to him and said, "Here's a clue, Wayne. After I spend the evening making sure Mercedes is comfortable, I'm going up to her brother's bedroom to wait for him to come home. Naked. In his bed. Because I'm sleeping with him—we're involved. So now **you** know where to find **me**."

But she didn't have time for the potential fallout. Knowing Wayne, he'd petition for a chance to audition to be her leading man—to prove himself just as capable in bed.

Which wouldn't require all too much effort, considering.

Instead she made a beeline toward Cosmo and Murphy, who were deep in discussion. Normally she avoided Cosmo—his eyes were just too weird—but she desperately needed to de-Wayne.

"My seabag's still there," the SEAL was saying to Murphy. "I'll come by to pick it up, but not until later. You know, I really appreciate this."

"No problem," Murphy said.

They both turned to look at her.

"Excuse me," Patty said. "I'm sorry. Message from Jane—she's almost ready to go." It was more than likely that they'd already heard this from Tess, but Wayne was lingering, still watching her, and she needed to say **some**thing.

Murphy smiled at her. "Thanks, Pat. We're on it."

Cosmo actually spoke. "How many stitches did she need?"

"Six." Over his shoulder, she could see Wayne finally disappearing down the corridor. Thank goodness.

Cosmo nodded. "That's not too bad. She had a scrape on her leg—did they get that cleaned up, too?"

Patty hadn't even noticed the scrape. "I don't know." She began backing up.

"Tell Jane I'm taking Cos's shift for him tonight," Murphy said. "She likes to know who's where and when."

"Sure," Patty said, but she wasn't even quite sure what she was agreeing to because, oh, my God, Robin was here. "Robin!"

He was talking to someone on his cell phone, and he stopped short when he saw her. He glanced back in the direction he'd come from, then . . .

Patty's stomach twisted, because as she watched,

Robin squared his shoulders and resolutely waited for her to approach him.

Which was exactly what she'd done when she'd seen Wayne.

Robin was running and hiding from her, the same way she was running and hiding from . . .

Oh, dear God.

She was Robin's Wayne.

A pain in the ass. A relentless pursuer. A clueless fool, except in her case, she was even more foolish.

She'd actually thought "I love you" meant "I love you," not "I want to screw you once, then never see you again."

Patty didn't wait for Robin to get off the phone. She didn't wait for a moment alone. She didn't wait for jack.

"FYI," she told him before she marched away, loudly enough for the nurses at the desk to overhear, "I've had **much** better sex all by myself."

CHAPTER
FIFTEEN

H e shouldn't have come.

Jules stood under his umbrella, on the sidewalk outside the club, wondering what the hell he was doing here.

He supposed he was here for the same reason that he packed clubbing clothes in with his staid suits, shirts, and ties every time he traveled. He was here because he believed that sooner or later, he'd meet someone who would finally make him forget Adam. Except it was raining and tonight's shoot was canceled, which meant Adam would be here soon—if he wasn't already inside.

So was Jules here because of that, or despite it?

Should he go inside or walk on by?

The bass drum beat a steady pulse, both audible and palpable from where he stood, even though the door to the club was tightly shut.

A cab pulled up, and Robin Chadwick emerged, his golden hair gleaming. He hurried right past Jules and into the club. As the door opened, music escaped: Tony Orlando and Dawn, "Knock Three Times," remixed to a steady dance beat. It was oldies night—just his freaking luck.

Hello, God, was that a message from You? Was it a sign—both Robin breezing past and the Tony Orlando thing, Mother help him—telling him to go back to the hotel and watch the latest Hugh Jackman movie on Pay-Per-View? He wouldn't have to worry about bothering Max—his boss had gone back to D.C. on the red-eye.

Jules now moved out of earshot of the crowd of men who were smoking, huddled under an awning to stay out of the rain. He took out his cell phone and speed-dialed number one. Alyssa Locke's cell phone. As he expected, he was beeped over, almost immediately, to his best friend's voice mail. She and her husband, Sam, were still off saving the world.

"Hey, sweetie, it's me," he said into his phone. "I'm in West Hollywood, standing in the rain—which is freakish, because how often does it rain here?"

The door opened again, and "Love Will Keep Us Together" leaked out, as if God were saying "Run! Run! Run for your life!"

"If that's not pathetic enough," Jules continued with his voice mail message, "I'm outside of Large Richard's—yes, Grande Ricco's, Giagantimo Ricardo's, Biggus Dickus, aka the scene of the crime—about to go on a date with a man who's so deep in the closet he didn't recognize me in my club clothes, and yes, that's right, children—hello, Sam, I know you're listening, too—I actually used the terrible, horrible D-word. I actually said yes to a date during a moment of severe blue-eyed-hottie-induced fever, only now that I'm here I want to go home because you know how you never really liked Adam and you thought he was bad for me? Well, hip-hip-hooray, this guy's even worse, and I know it, and yet I'm here, and that's so fucked up."

As Jules took a breath, the door opened again—**Hear with your heart and you won't hear a sound. . . . Just stop, 'cause I really love you, stop . . .**

"What's even more fucked up is that I've seen Adam again. He's making all these **let's get back together** noises, and, God help me, I'm actually considering it. Which means I probably shouldn't be calling you, I should be calling some certified therapist, although I know what he'd say, he'd say, **Hmmmm,** which'll do me a fuckload of a lot of good, because what I really need is to be told to go back to my malodorous hotel room before I do something stupid. More stupid.

"Lately my stupidity index has been pinned at one hundred percent. I keep waiting for myself to put in for a transfer to the L.A. office because, what the hell, you know? Living with someone I know will hurt me versus living with no one at all? At times of sheer stupidity like this, it seems like a tough call.

"Anyway, this is probably costing you, like, four million quatloos, just to play this message back, and, God, I wish you were here. Be aggressive out there, keep each other safe, and thank you for letting me bitch and moan. I'm really okay. I'm not going anywhere. I just needed to whine. I'll talk to you before I do anything rash. More rash. Shit. Call me if you get a chance, will you?"

Jules snapped his phone shut, turned around, and nearly bumped into Adam, who was standing just behind him, in the rain. He'd been listening, but for how long, God only knew.

Actually, God and Adam both knew.

And Jules had a small clue from the fact that, despite his lack of umbrella, Adam wasn't very wet yet.

Adam gave him another. "You're actually considering moving to L.A. to live with Robin Chadwick?" He'd obviously not heard his own name mentioned, and thought . . .

Jules had always found it strange that Adam could be so jealous, considering his inability to be faithful.

He didn't say anything in response to that ludicrous question. The fact that Adam could imagine Jules spending the night with him and then, just a few nights later, seriously think about moving in with someone else spoke volumes about how well Adam truly knew Jules—as in not at all.

All those years of everything from casual friendship, to tentative courtship, to serious relationship . . . Obviously Adam hadn't been paying attention.

"He's late," he pointed out. Meaning Robin.

"He's already inside," Jules said.

"He's a lush, you know," Adam said, as if that were some kind of breaking news story.

"He's struggling with some issues, and drinking too much, so yes," Jules countered, "I do know."

"This thing with you? He's experimenting."

"Yeah, well, so am I." Just showing up tonight was one big-ass major experiment. Jules started for the door to the club, since the alternative was flagging down a cab. If he did, Adam would try to jump into it with him.

Try? Who was he kidding? Adam wouldn't just try, he'd succeed. And then where would they be?

Adam grabbed his arm. "Let's not go inside," he said. "Let's go someplace else. I know this great restaurant around the corner—"

"I told Robin—"

"Fuck him." Adam winced. "Poor word choice. Look, I just want to talk to you, J. It's noisy in Big's. If we go to Diablo's, we can—"

"Talk about what?" Jules asked.

Adam wasn't listening. ". . . have some sangria. And I've heard the guacamole is—"

"I don't want guacamole," Jules said.

"Oh, but **this** stuff is great. Everyone who's anyone goes there and—"

"What do you want to talk about, Adam?" Jules interrupted. "You have exactly three seconds to give me an overview, or I'm outta here."

"Jeez, J., relax, will you?"

"One."

Adam laughed. "You're counting?"

"Two."

"Jesus. I guess I thought I'd start by—I don't know—by listing all the reasons we should get back together."

Jules laughed, but his heart was in his throat. God, was he really such a wuss that he would be moved so much by such a small acknowledgment of affection? "You . . . actually have a whole list?"

As always, Adam knew when he'd hit emotional pay dirt. He took a step closer, gave Jules that smile that he couldn't resist. "Number one is because . . . you still love me."

Yeah, right. Now his heart was in his throat for an entirely different reason. Disappointment. What a typical Adam thing to say. **You still love me** was number one. Not **I still love you.** Son of a bitch.

Adam didn't realize that he'd already leapt on top of the loser button with both feet. "Number two: You know me better than anyone on this planet, and despite that you still manage to like me."

"I sense a certain theme," Jules said, pulling his arm free. "Let's count the ways Jules loves Adam. Thanks, but no thanks. I've got better things to do. Robin's waiting for me."

"Robin's at the bar, chatting up the bartender, who is twenty-three years old, gorgeous, and female," Adam said. "Big tits—just his type. You know, I spoke to some of the crew on set. He goes out clubbing in West Hollywood under pretense of research, drinks until he's half-blind, and then fucks whoever's available—providing they're female. I don't know what game he was playing this afternoon, but—"

"That's so sweet of you to want to protect me from people who go out clubbing, drink themselves half-blind, and fuck whoever's . . . oh, wait," Jules said. "I suddenly realize why that sounds so familiar."

Adam actually managed to look embarrassed. As he should have been. "I've changed."

"So you've said," Jules told him. "Far too often for

me to take you seriously. You'll forgive me if I don't open a bottle of champagne to celebrate this particular accounting."

"So what am I supposed to do?" Adam asked. The rain on his face made him look as if he were crying, but Jules knew better.

"Talk is cheap. You want me to believe you? You're going to have to prove it."

Jules opened the door, but before he stepped inside and was swallowed up by a club mix of "Gypsies, Tramps & Thieves" at five million decibels, he heard Adam say plaintively, "How the fuck do I do that?"

Robin was at the bar, watching the door, groovin' to Cher, when he saw Adam come in. Typical. The sleaze-bag was chasing after that hot-looking shorter guy who was dressed all in black, who'd been out front under an umbrella, and—

Holy crap, the hot guy was Jules.

He'd spotted Robin, and he was heading for him, weaving his way through the crowd with Adam—of course—in hot pursuit.

Jules was wearing his hair differently. It was styled and funky, and very non–federal agent.

Between the two of them, both remarkably hand-some men, they were drawing a lot of attention from Big's regulars. Except Jules didn't notice it. He wasn't looking at anyone but Robin.

Adam, however, liked having all those eyes on him. He slowed down, made eye contact around the room, put a little extra swagger into his strut.

But then, probably because Robin was grinning at
how different he looked, Jules smiled and Adam disappeared. Poof. Just instantly gone, like a star in the sky
when the sun came up.

"I walked right past you outside," Robin shouted
when Jules got close enough to hear him over the
music. He handed him the chocolate martini he'd ordered when he first came in. "I didn't recognize you.
Where's your tie, FBI?"

Jules winced then leaned close to say into Robin's
ear, "Not too loud with that in here, please."

As always, he smelled incredibly good.

"Sorry." Robin motioned for Jules to come closer
again and said into his ear, "Is that a 'don't ask, don't
tell' thing, or . . . ?"

"It's a testosterone thing," Jules told him. He took
a sip of the drink. "Yikes. That's got some kick.
Thanks, I think. See, there's always someone who
wants to pick a fight with the federal agent."

"Are you sure they just don't want you to cuff 'em
and slap 'em around a little bit before tucking them
into bed?"

Jules laughed. "I never thought of that. God, I
hope not."

Adam was several feet down the bar, trying to get
himself a drink. He glanced over frequently, clearly annoyed that they were having this private conversation,
standing so close together, mouth to ear and ear to
mouth.

So Robin kept it going. "You know, it's not too late.
We've only filmed a few of the scenes with young

Jack—they'd be easy enough to reshoot. Just say the word, and we'll give Scowlface over there his walking papers."

Jules was not amused. He put his already empty glass down on the bar. Hey now, he'd finished that rather fast. Much stress in his life? "If you're going to start this again . . ."

"I won't," Robin said. "Relax." He pushed both of their glasses toward the bartender, signaling for a refill, then leaned toward Jules again. "You know what my problem is?"

"Yes, I do, sweetie, but you won't want to hear it."

Robin waved the comment off. They were talking about Adam here. "I hate his fucking guts." He looked up, and sure enough, the little bastard was watching them, so . . .

Jules cracked up. "Excuse me, I don't think I know you well enough for you to lick my ear."

"Sorry." Robin grinned back at him. "Adam's so easy to torment, and I've got a little swerve on," he shouted over the music.

"A little's putting it mildly," Jules agreed. Meanwhile Adam was getting more and more pissed off. Now it was because they'd gotten a refill from the bartender, and he hadn't even managed to place his order. Robin handed Jules his glass, made a show out of toasting, while Adam steamed.

This was fun.

"I had a few with dinner—I had to take the edge off," Robin said. Well, okay. The edge plus a fairly large portion of the center. "Today was a total suck-fest." He caught himself. "Although, I guess in a gay bar, that's not necessarily a bad thing."

Jules was laughing again, which was nice. "I shouldn't have another," he said, taking only a tiny sip of his drink. "These days I've been sticking to wine, so my resistance is down and—"

Robin caught his finger in the belt loop of those black pants, pulling Jules even closer, which—score!—annoyed the shit out of Adam.

"If I asked you to dance," Robin said loudly enough for Adam to hear, especially since the prick had come closer, "would your evil twin have to come onto the dance floor, too?"

Jules glanced at Adam, looked down at Robin's finger still hooked around his belt loop, then up into Robin's eyes. "This is probably a good time for me to tell you that Adam knows," he shouted over the music. "You know, that this is just an act. That you're not . . . we're not . . ."

Robin toasted him, clinking their glasses together again. "Yeah, well, hey, there's a first time for everything, right?"

It was supposed to be a joke—he'd meant it as a joke, with the double bonus of making Adam crazy—but this time Jules didn't laugh. He didn't pull away, but he did put his drink down on the bar as he sighed.

He gazed out onto the packed dance floor for a moment, rubbing the back of his neck as if he were tired. And when he looked back at Robin, his eyes were serious. "Just so there's not any miscommunication here, you need to know—I don't mess around with guys who get drunk so they have an excuse all ready for the morning after."

Adam, drink in hand, had stepped closer. "I do," he said.

It may have been another joke gone bad, or it may have been a real attempt to wound—a reaction to his hand, which was still holding on to that belt loop. Robin wasn't sure.

Either way, it was a direct hit. Jules closed his eyes briefly. "Yes, I know, Adam," he said. When he opened them, he forced a smile at Robin, but it didn't manage to hide his hurt. "And now Robin knows, too."

"Why do you say shit like that?" Robin asked Adam. "All you're doing is proving that you don't deserve him."

"**Deserve** him?" Adam laughed. "Like he's some big prize? Let me warn you, friend, he's possessive as hell—"

"Yeah." Jules had obviously reached his limit. "I tend to get a little riled up when we go on vacation and you have sex with some stranger in the back room of a dance club, exactly like, oh, say, this one."

Oh crap. Robin winced. So that was why Jules hadn't been keen on coming to this particular club.

"And gee, **A.,**" Jules continued, leaning hard on the nickname, "who was it who paid for the airline tickets to Los Angeles, the hotel, and every meal we ever ate?"

"Gee, I guess that would be you, J., and you didn't let me forget it for a single second, did you?"

"So let me get this straight," Robin interrupted. He looked at Adam with disbelief. "You think Jules is possessive because he was upset when he found out you had sex with someone else?"

"So I got a little carried away," Adam said. He mocked Robin. "I guess I had too much of a swerve on. 'Sides, it was just sex." He nudged Robin with his elbow. "You know how that is, don't you, bro?"

"Well, on that lovely note," Jules said. "I think it's probably time to call it a night. I'm—"

"Touch me again, douche bag," Robin said with his best Russell Crowe scowl, "and you'll be sorry."

"You mean like this?" Adam shoved him hard, and Robin's drink sloshed down Jules' T-shirt.

"Shit!"

Despite the dousing, Jules managed to catch Robin before he went off the barstool. And he grabbed his arm, too, keeping him from swinging at Adam.

"Don't do this!" he warned Robin, then turned to the other man. "You want to fuck up your movie career? You want to spend the night in jail, in the drunk tank with the worst of the homophobic psychos from the entire L.A. area? Keep it up—you're right on track. In fact, you might as well call Jane right now and tell her to replace you, because after the beating you'll have no teeth and be blind in one eye. But hey, it's okay. The dogs you take care of won't mind the scars."

Something shifted across Adam's face, and Jules made a noise that he tried to turn into a laugh.

"Oh. Right. That was a lie, too, wasn't it?" he continued. "That new day job that you love so much? Jesus Christ, Adam! And you wonder why I don't even want to **look** at you, let alone **talk** to you? Fuck you and your fucking lies." He turned to Robin. "And fuck you for using me in this stupid game you're playing."

"Jules—" Robin tried to grab him, but Jules shook himself free.

"J.!"

Adam started to go after him, but Robin blocked his route. "Haven't you done enough damage?"

As he watched, Jules took the most direct path to the door—through the dance floor instead of around it.

"Haven't **you**?" Adam countered. "He's serious, you know. He's not going to touch you. He's a Boy Scout." He stepped closer, too close. "I, however, will do whatever you want, whenever you want."

Time seemed to hang as Robin stared into Adam's eyes. The motherfucker was serious. It was more than a little scary. "In your dreams."

"Maybe, maybe not," Adam murmured. "Can't wait to shoot that love scene. When's that scheduled for? Day after tomorrow?"

Robin didn't hit him. It would have taken too much time. "Follow me and I'm quitting," he warned Adam as he scooped his backpack off the floor. "If I quit, filming grinds to a stop, the movie doesn't get made, and you're back to being nobody."

Plunging into the crowd, he followed Jules out the door.

Cosmo had just gotten out of the shower when his cell phone rang.

He could see from the caller's number that it was Jane.

He dropped his towel and fumbled his phone open, praying that something else hadn't gone wrong. "Richter. What's happening?"

"You," Jane said, "suck. That's what's happening."

What? "Are you all right?" he asked, ready to . . . what? Charge out of his motel room to come to her rescue, naked?

"Where are you?" She spoke right over him as he dripped across the room, looking for his pants. "I was counting on you being here, and I could maybe understand if something had happened with your mother, but Murphy said he didn't think so. Is she okay?"

He found his pants, but he stopped before he jammed his still-wet legs into them. "What?"

"Your Mo-Ther," Jane enunciated. "Is she all right? Did she fall down again? Is she sick? Did she—"

"She's still in San Francisco. She's fine—I just spoke to her on the phone. Jane, what—"

"Forgive me for disturbing you."

"You weren't disturbing me."

Silence.

Cosmo looked at his phone. What the . . . ? She'd hung up on him.

He called her back. "You weren't disturbing me," he said as soon as she picked up.

"Look, I'm really sorry I bothered you," she said. "I just thought . . . I was worried something bad had happened, and . . . Are **you** all right? Why aren't you here?"

Interesting question. Cos let it sit for a minute as he finished drying himself off, unsure how to answer. Physically, he was fine. Emotionally . . .

Emotionally, he'd been steamrollered. "Today was a difficult day."

"No kidding," she said. "I was counting on tonight being a little less . . ." She stopped. Cleared her throat. Started over. "Cos, what's going on? Aren't we friends?"

Oh, Christ. He closed his eyes. Didn't answer. Didn't say, **No, Jane, no, we are not friends.**

He also didn't ask what the fuck she was doing on the phone with him. Hadn't she brought Victor Strauss home with her? Was he already asleep, the insensitive shit?

She kept going, even though her voice wobbled. "Because I thought we were friends, and that you might be a little interested in knowing how I'm doing. At the very least, how many stitches I needed—"

"Six," he said. He knew all about her stitches. He knew the size thread they'd used. Jesus, he knew the middle name of the doctor—Constanza Manuela Puente—who'd done the stitching.

There was silence then, he couldn't even hear her breathing, and he checked the phone to make sure she was still there.

She was.

And then he heard it. The slightest catch of a breath.

Jane was crying. Softly, so he wouldn't hear, but she was crying.

He had to sit down.

"I was so scared," she said, but before he could sympathize—**Yes, that must have been awful, watching those lights topple, having to run to get out of the way, please, Janey, don't cry . . .**—she added, "He was just lying there, on top of me." She faked a laugh—it was really quite good. "I never really understood before what people meant when they said **dead weight,** but now I do. He was so heavy, so . . . limp. Then I saw all the blood, and, oh, Cos, I was sure he was dead—"

She was talking about Decker.

". . . and I knew if he was, that it was my fault, and God, he's such a better person than I am, and now you're not here to tell me that it's okay, it all worked out, because he's not dead—"

"He's not dead, Jane. It **is** okay."

She laughed again, but this time she didn't do such a good job of it. "I know. Thank God. Look, I'm sorry. I'm neurotic. You don't need this on your night off. I'll let you—"

"You want me to come over?" Cosmo asked, closing his eyes and cursing himself as soon as the words had left his lips.

"Could you?" she asked so quietly he almost didn't hear her, so much hope loaded into two little words.

No way could he say no. "Yeah." He stood up, pulled on his pants, slipped his feet into his boots, knowing full well that he was going to regret this.

Going to? Shit, he already did. "Hang on." He put down the phone, pulled on his T-shirt. "I'm back."

"Where are you?" she asked.

"I got a motel room," he admitted as he grabbed his keys from the top of the TV and let himself out into the parking lot. "It's not too far from you. Maybe five minutes. I'm getting into my truck right now, okay?"

She was confused. "But all your stuff is . . . I thought . . . Aren't you staying here?"

"Yeah . . ." He backed out of the parking space. "Well . . ." Christ, just say it. "I needed to not be over there tonight. I, um, needed some space."

"Oh, God," Jane said. "I'm sorry. I've been . . . I shouldn't have asked you to read those pages of script—"

"No," he said. "No, that's not . . . That's not why."

He could practically hear her thinking, trying to figure out what she'd said or done or . . . She was so ready to take the blame for everything. So he told her. "I didn't want to be there when you brought Victor home with you."

"Victor Strauss?" she said. "I know a lot of people think he's a little too abrasive, but . . . I didn't realize you knew him."

"I've never met the man," he said. "I just . . ."

"What?" she said, frustration in her voice after the silence had stretched on for too long.

Apparently, he had to spell it out for her. "I didn't want to have to sit in the kitchen while you were . . .

upstairs . . ." No, be more exact. "In your bedroom. With him. **With** him, you know? With. Him."

Was that clear enough? Or did he have to be even more specific?

Jane said it for him, wonder in her voice. Wonder that rapidly morphed into gleeful amusement. "You switched shifts with Murphy because you thought I was going to run through the second floor of the house with Victor, shrieking, 'Do me, big daddy, 'til the cows come home'?"

Cosmo closed his eyes as he sat at a red light, listening to Jane laughing and laughing on the other end of the phone.

"Oh, my God," she said. "Oh, my **God.** I thought you weren't here tonight because you didn't like me. But . . ." The wonder was back in her voice. "You're not here because you **do.** And you must've seen . . . You saw that picture in the **Voice.** Cos, you gigantic idiot, I planted that. What are you doing, believing something you saw in a tabloid? Haven't you learned anything this past week? Victor Strauss is a friend of mine. He agreed to pose as my latest fling to take the heat off of you."

Well, didn't he feel stupid. Stupid and . . .

"Cosmo, where are you?" Jane asked.

Relieved. He was incredibly relieved. The lead weight he'd been carrying in his stomach since this afternoon was gone, leaving behind this rapidly expanding sense of . . .

"I'm having an emergency," Jane said. "You have to get over here right away. Do you hear me?"

Hope.

"Cos, are you still there?" she asked.

"Yeah," he said, signaling for the turnoff that would take him up through the winding hills to her house. "I'll be walking in the door in about three minutes." Fewer, if he floored it.

"That's good," she said, her voice warm in his ear. "That's really good. Because I can't kiss you through the phone." She laughed. "At least not the way I want to."

She cut the connection.

And Cosmo floored it.

"Jules! Wait!"

Jules didn't stop walking. Shit, he'd left his umbrella in the club, at the coat check. But no way was he going back for it now. The rain was lightening up anyway.

Besides, his T-shirt couldn't get much wetter.

"Jules!" It was Robin who was following him, so he stopped. Turned. Waited impatiently, arranging his face into an expression he hoped was neither hostile nor disappointed. He was going for polite yet not particularly friendly, but alcohol tended to affect his ability to be subtle.

He shouldn't have had one martini, let alone two.

"Sorry about your shirt." Robin was out of breath from running after him. "And I'm so, **so** sorry about . . . I should have called you when I realized it was raining, because of course that meant Adam would show up."

"It's not your fault." Jules started walking again.

"No, but I should've anticipated it, and it **is** my

fault that . . . Well, you were right," Robin admitted, trailing along beside him. "I was having a little too much fun, trying to make Adam squirm. Can we please get out of this rain? You want to maybe go get something to eat?"

"No. I'm tired. I'm going back to my hotel." He wanted to find a cab, but every one that went past was taken. God damn rain.

Robin didn't give up. "If you really want to go, you should, but if . . . Well, I was hoping we'd have a chance to . . . I really wanted to . . . See, here's the thing. I have this scene coming up that I'm a little anxious about, and Adam's not giving me any help at all. Or maybe he's giving me too much help—I'm not sure—but . . . I'm just trying to get a feel for this role I'm playing—you know, Hal Lord."

Jules stopped dead and turned to look at Robin. Unbelievable. "You want me to give you insight into playing a man who was so deeply in the closet, he even lied about who he was to himself? I can't help you there. I was out at seventeen. I was the president of my high school gay-straight alliance. Try looking into your bathroom mirror, Robbie. You might find something mighty interesting there."

Someday he'd have a good laugh about this. He just knew it.

"I know you think that I'm . . . And I know I've been adding to the whole charade by . . . But it's all just an act, Jules."

"Yeah, lots of straight guys lick my ear. It happens

to me all the time. Men falling at my feet . . . Yeah, right." He rolled his eyes.

Robin met his gaze and held it. "I was paying attention in there. I don't think you realize this, but you could have anyone in that club. **Any**one. So what are you doing, carrying a torch for that asshole?"

Jules started walking again. "You haven't exactly seen him at his best."

"On the contrary. I've seen him act. He's amazing," Robin said. "But he really seems to get off on hurting you, which makes him an asshole in my book."

"Yeah," Jules said. "In mine, too. And yet . . ." He sighed. "There's a side to him you haven't seen. And when he's there, in that place, when he's the closest to at peace that he can manage, you can't help but fall in love with him."

They walked for a while in silence.

"I could. I could help it," Robin finally said. "I'm never going to fall in love with him. That's a given."

Jules laughed. "That's the kind of line where, if we were characters in a movie, we'd cut to a scene of you and Adam getting married."

Robin didn't find that very funny. "Thank God we're not in a movie. Look, this walking in the rain is certainly a novelty, but isn't there maybe someplace we could go to just sit and talk? Maybe get something to eat? Your choice completely. My treat."

Jules looked into Robin Chadwick's very blue eyes. He was tall and handsome and still young enough to have to stagger into the gym only a few times a week to keep in shape. He was kind and funny and sincere. He was also an alcoholic and an actor and a known player who probably lied his ass off without blinking when it suited him. Oh, yeah, and the big bonus—he insisted he was straight.

"Did you know that Jack wasn't Hal's first gay relationship?" Robin asked him.

Really?

"Ah, see—now I've caught your interest," Robin continued. "Yeah, there was more to ol' Hal than meets the eye. Look, let's just get out of the rain—"

"Are you offering me a bribe?" Jules asked. "Come out with me—not in a gay way, because we both know you're not gay"—right—"and I'll tell you this story?"

"No," Robin said. "I didn't mean . . . The story's not that long or exciting, anyway. Hal went to Europe the summer after high school and while he was in Berlin, he met this boy, Miguel—the son of one of his father's business associates. It was a textbook 'blame it on the alcohol' incident. Hal got tanked and 'accidentally' had sex with Miguel. He had the whole litany of excuses at his fingertips. It was just that once. It wasn't his fault. He didn't know what he was doing. Of course it got a little harder to convince himself of all that after he met Miguel again. They got together two more times before Hal boarded the steamship home.

"Hal told Jack that, at that point, he alternated between **I was drunk** and **No one ever has to know.**"

"From what I've read about Hal Lord's father," Jules said, "it was probably more along the lines of **I better never let anyone know.**"

"Yeah." Robin smiled ruefully. "**I'll just go home and spend the rest of my life hiding who I really am.** That's the way I'm playing the character. He knows exactly who and what he is, but he's chosen to lie about it. Deceit, denial . . . and terror. He's lived every day of his life in fear that someone will discover his secret. And then he meets Jack and he can't stay away. He tries, but he just . . . can't."

Jules looked at Robin, walking beside him with the misty rain glistening in his hair. God, what was he doing? How much of a masochist was he, anyway? A huge one, apparently, because the truth was, he would have been happy to walk all night, gazing at those perfect cheekbones and those blue-blue eyes, just letting Robin's beautifully modulated voice wrap around him.

He should run. He should shout, "Gotta go," and dash off down the street. After a block or two, Robin would fall back, unable to keep up. The man looked good, but it was only skin-deep. His wind was for shit.

And yet Jules didn't run. He just kept walking.

"So no bribe, see?" Robin told him. "And no pressure, either. No pressure, no bullshit, no ulterior motives. And no hard feelings. If it's still no, you don't want to, you want to go back to your hotel, that's okay with me, too."

Jules looked up and saw that they were approaching

a Mexican restaurant. He didn't recognize it from the last time he was in town—it was probably that new place Adam had tried to bully him into going to.

And, ah, the irony of his going here with Robin was just too good to pass up. "I've heard this place has great guacamole," Jules said.

Robin's smile was dazzling. "Well, good," he said, and held open the door, letting Jules go in first.

CHAPTER SIXTEEN

Three minutes wasn't a whole heck of a lot of time to get ready.

Jane washed her face, looking up into the bathroom mirror with despair. She'd rinsed off the mascara tracks made by her tears, but her eyes still looked swollen and red, as if she'd been crying.

Which she had been.

Shit.

She held a cool cloth to them for as long as she dared, then quickly applied some makeup. If she kept the lights dim, Cosmo would never know.

She did a quick circuit of her bedroom, scooping several days' worth of dirty laundry off the floor, throwing it into the closet, kicking one last sock underneath the bed.

She caught sight of herself in the mirror over her dresser—yeesh. She knew he liked her like this—dressed down, casual—but her skinned knee and elbow made her look like a clumsy twelve-year-old. And he was **not** going to like the bandage on her arm.

Not at all. It stood out, pristine and white, against the dark of her gray sweat shorts and blue tank.

She wasn't going to be able to hide it. The only option was to make it less obvious.

Or to distract the crap out of the man.

Jane dug through her dresser drawers, coming up with yoga pants just long enough to cover her knees and a tank that were both gleaming white. She quickly changed, shoved her other clothes under the bed, and . . .

Okay. Without underwear, this might be a little too distracting. She put her favorite beach shirt on over it—lightweight, white, and long-sleeved . . . Perfect. It even covered the bandage.

She was brushing her hair when she heard the front door open, along with the now-familiar sounds of the alarm system as Cosmo punched in his entry code.

She went into the hall and out onto the landing, and he glanced up at her as he . . . Went into the kitchen?

Jane had to laugh. Well, wasn't that terribly anticlimactic? So much for the great big running-through-the-field-in-slow-mo, Hollywood-moment kiss.

"Hey." She heard him greet Murphy.

"Yo, Cosmic-wonder! I didn't expect you 'til later, man."

"Change of plans," Cosmo said. "I just wanted to let you know I'm in the house. I may end up, uh, crashing here tonight. You know, downstairs."

Not if she had anything to say about that.

"No problemo. Just . . . if you've got a sec, you

might want to go up and give a howdy to Jane-ski. Was her light on? Is she still awake?"

Yes, she most certainly was.

"I guess Patty forgot to tell her that we changed shifts," Murphy told Cos, "and even though she was really nice about it, I could tell she was a little upset when she found out. It threw her, you know? She's had a tough day—go be nice to her, okay?"

Go be nice to her. Jane had to laugh. God, she could only hope.

Cosmo laughed, too. "I'll do my best."

Oh, my.

And there he came. Out of the kitchen, over to the stairs. He was moving swiftly now—definitely a man on a mission. Up the stairs. She retreated back into the darkness of her office, her heart pounding. Any second now, and he was going to grab her and kiss her and . . .

"White's not a real good color for lurking in the shadows," he said, slowing down. "Unless you're not trying to hide."

"I'm not trying to hide." Her voice sounded out of breath, as if she were the one who'd just double-timed it up the stairs.

He stopped just outside of her door. The hall light was behind him, and the shadows made it impossible to see his face. "May I come in?"

"Please." Jane switched on the desk lamp. That was better. She turned and he was closing the door behind him.

Locking it.

He was wearing the same clothes—T-shirt and

cargo pants—that he'd had on over at the hospital. But he must've taken a shower right before she called, because his hair was still damp. He'd shaved, too—his lean face was smooth.

He looked delicious.

He was looking at her as hungrily as she was looking at him, and when their eyes met, he smiled and said, "This is a little weird, huh?"

Jane nodded, backing away. Please, God, don't let her lunge at him and start tearing off his clothes before they'd had at least a half of a conversation. "Thank you for coming over," she managed to say.

His smile faded as he watched her put distance between them. "If this is too weird," he finally said, "or if you've changed your mind—"

"No!"

He smiled again at her ferocity and stepped toward her, and . . .

She hastily crossed to her refrigerator, which was safely behind the desk. "Do you want a—"

"No," he said, and they were back to staring at each other. "Thank you," he added. "Why are we being so polite, and why are you running away from me?"

"I'm afraid to get too close, because I really want to, like, jump you. Really," she added for emphasis.

"Okay, good," he said. "I thought for a minute you were suddenly shy, and that was freaking me out."

She laughed—a loud burst of disbelief. "Shy? Me? Oh, Cos, no, I'm just standing here, hoping and waiting for the perfect moment to say . . . well, see, it's something I'm really dying to say to you . . ."

Cosmo, a true gentleman, lobbed the perfect straight line back to her, like a big fat slow pitch dead over home plate. "I'm listening."

Jane smiled at him. And took off her overshirt. The look on his face, the sheer heat in his eyes made her giddy and she laughed. It was possible he didn't even see the bandage on her arm, especially when she kept it kind of hidden behind her.

She waited a moment or two, until he was looking back into her eyes, until she was sure he really was listening, and then she let him have it. " 'Do me, big daddy, 'til the cows come home.' "

Jane was pretty certain that there was nothing on earth quite as satisfying as the sound of a quiet man laughing his ass off.

Cosmo laughed so hard he had to sit down, and she laughed, too, just watching him. It was then he blew her away just as thoroughly.

"I am so fucking crazy about you," he told her.

And Jane had to sit down, too, but it wasn't because she was laughing. "Really?" It came out as little more than a breath of air.

But he heard her. And he nodded. "Pardon my language. I didn't mean to—"

"I don't think you're allowed to apologize for that one," she said.

He wasn't done. "I've never met anyone that I've wanted to be with as much as I want to be with you, Janey," he told her.

Aw, God, don't cry, don't cry. Jane had to blink hard, because damn it, she was welling up all over again.

And he still wasn't done. "Remember how I said it was stupid how, in the movies, the bodyguard always falls for the woman he's supposed to be protecting? Well, it's not stupid that he'd fall for her. Not if she's anything like you—successful and smart and funny and beautiful. What's stupid is she's single, you know? That she doesn't have a boyfriend or a husband. Like, what? She's just sitting around, being wonderful, waiting for the chump of a bodyguard to show up?" He shook his head. "That's why I believed it when I saw that picture of you and Strauss. It just didn't seem possible you weren't already committed to someone else. I thought . . . especially when you started in on the whole Sophia thing . . ."

"I thought you liked her," Jane said. "And I wanted those reporters to leave you alone." Reporters who would be following him around again if any hint of this came out.

Cosmo knew what she was thinking. "I can handle reporters."

They were sitting there, across her desk from each other, as if they were having a business meeting. She reached for him and he sat forward and intertwined their fingers, just smiling at her, as if this was all he'd come rushing over here for—a chance to hold her hand.

But then he caught sight of her bandage and frowned. "How's your arm?"

She met his gaze. "The doctor said I just might live," she told him, "if I can find someone really courageous and very strong to have sex with me all night long."

He grinned at her again, shaking his head. "Seriously, Jane . . ."

"Seriously, Cos," she said. "I had six stitches. My arm's a little sore. But it's nothing compared to—" She stopped.

He knew, and finished for her. "The scare you had when you thought Decker—"

Jane released his hand, stood up. She'd already told him too much. Somehow it was different when she'd thought he was only interested in being friends. "Is it okay if we don't talk about that?"

"Of course," he said, but she could tell that he was worried about her.

This was supposed to be fun. **She** was supposed to be fun. She wanted to make him laugh again.

He stood, too, watching her, his concern still apparent in his eyes.

She wanted it to vanish. She supposed she could have walked around the desk and kissed him, but . . .

God, first kisses, first times . . . They were so tricky. There was so much pressure for everything to be perfect.

"So I've been reading about Navy SEALs," she told him, taking as wide a berth around him as possible, making sure she didn't get too close as she headed for the bedroom. "You know, for my future movie-of-the-week bio-pic. And I have some questions for you."

He laughed. Score.

"Yeah, I know you're probably thinking, 'What the fuck?' I know you wouldn't say that in front of me, but you're thinking it. According to my research, that's something sailors like to say, and SEALs are sailors. So you're thinking, you know, 'WTF, I thought we were going to do the horizontal mambo, and she has **questions**?' But really, I'm just keeping the conversation going until we can get into the bedroom, because I know that as soon as I touch you, I'm going to go up in flames, and I really don't want our first time to be on my office floor. Or on my desk. I mean, how would I ever get anything done again with that kind of vibe coming off of it?"

"Jane . . ."

"What I can't figure out—and maybe you could help me with this—is the difference between a goatfuck and a clusterfuck. Every time I read anything about SEALs, about an operation that went wrong, it's referred to as a clusterfuck. Except sometimes it's a goatfuck. Which is worse? And is there some kind of chart that lets you know which one it is? 'HQ, this is Lieutenant Jones. We have a clusterfuck—no, wait, make that a goatfuck. Repeat, goatfuck. There are only seven terrorists hiding in the woods, not eight.' "

Cosmo caught up with her just as she went through the bedroom door, his fingers warm against her arm. "Jane."

She turned to him. "I guess the bedroom floor would be—" **Okay,** she was going to say, but she didn't get a chance to finish because he kissed her.

Thoroughly.

He didn't hold back. He covered her lips with his own and kissed the hell out of her. His tongue was in her mouth like it belonged there, and oh, sweet God, it most certainly did.

It was a kiss of possession, hot, hard, and demanding, but the demand he was making was not for her to submit. On the contrary. It was clear that he wanted her to give as good as she got.

It was an open invitation for equal opportunity passion.

So she took it and ran, angling her head, giving him better access to suck the very soul out of her body, so she could kiss the hell out of him, too—harder, deeper, longer. . . . **I see your bid and I raise it a million.**

He started making a sound and it took her a moment to realize that he was laughing—which left her thrilled and terrified, because, dear God, she wanted him to kiss her like this forever.

But nothing could ever really last that long.

Sure enough he pulled away, and there they were, both breathing hard. But—wonder of wonders!—they weren't on the floor.

Only because he was holding on to her shoulders with both of his hands, keeping her at a distance. She was gripping his arms—they were all she could reach. He was solid and smooth beneath her fingers.

It didn't seem possible, but it had to be—they'd just had zero body contact. During that entire long, amazing kiss, he'd touched her only with his mouth.

Imagine what he could do to her with his hands, with his—

"Here's what we're going to do," he told her now. "I'm going to let go of you. We're going to walk over to your bed in an orderly fashion, and I'm going to help you out of your clothes very slowly and carefully, without hurting your arm or pulling off that bandage. Jane, are you listening?"

Jane nodded. "Orderly. I can do orderly. But I should probably also tell you that I am **so** lying, and that I have a new goal in life, which is to get you inside of me as quickly as humanly possible."

He laughed, a hot burst that matched the fire in his eyes, but then he got very serious. "Here's the thing," he said. "I would rather not make love to you if there's a chance that I might hurt you. I would rather wait. I'd rather walk out the door, get into my truck and drive away—cursing the entire time, yeah, but . . . So unless we can do this—"

"We can," she told him. "Look." She let go of his arms and backed away, trying to appear orderly. She'd do damn near anything to keep him from leaving.

Cosmo released her, and she kept going. "I am moving slowly and carefully," she said, as she reached down and pulled the hem of her shirt up and over her head, as she stretched the fabric so it didn't come anywhere close to her bandage.

Of course, after she was done, she was standing in front of him bare-breasted, and the look in his eyes was . . .

Jane turned away, arms across herself. "No fair looking at me like that until we're on the bed, and we're done with the slow and careful part."

"Whoa," he said. "Jane. There's no slow and careful **part.** Or maybe I should say that if we do this, there's no part that's **not** going to be slow and careful."

Still with the "if."

As for the slow and careful, he was so wrong about that. But Jane didn't bother to argue, because he was taking off his own shirt, and then his pants, and . . . oh, my **God.** Jane started to laugh.

It wasn't what she'd normally do when faced with a lover's naked body for the very first time, but there was no way Cosmo would misunderstand and suffer a blow to his self-esteem.

Not a chance.

"It's when you're not talking that you're most dangerous," he said, glancing over at her. "I know what you're thinking—"

"Then you know that all language has left me except for **please, please, please. . . .**" She started for him.

He moved out of range and growled at her. He actually made a sound that was half growl, half laughter. "Stop or I'll leave."

"Yeah, you look like you really want to leave." She took another step toward him—just a little one, testing him.

He took a step back. "I didn't say a word about **want.** I'm serious, Jane. We do this my way, or I'm out of here."

She lifted her foot.

He picked up his pants.

She backed down. There were other ways to win

this game. She wriggled out of her yoga pants and climbed onto the bed, arranging herself artfully. "Oh, wait," she said.

She slid off the bed and rummaged through her bedside cabinet, searching for a condom, making sure he continued to get an eyeful.

He was laughing. "You're making this so much harder than it—"

"Good, the harder the better." She turned to face him, triumphant, condom in hand. "Since you can read my mind, you also know that I love it hard." She put the condom between her thumb and first finger, flicking it toward him like the paper footballs she used to make in seventh grade.

He caught it. Good reflexes. "Jane."

"Love it," she emphasized.

"I have an idea."

"Love. It. Love-it."

Cosmo had the world's best poker face. He was pretending that he was unmoved by everything she was doing and saying. His body, however, was not as good at bluffing. "Get back on the bed," he said evenly.

She gave up seductive and tried reasonable. "Cos. You're not going to hurt me. Look, my arm is **very** far from my—"

"Get on the bed."

"Okay," she said. "Okay, I have an idea, too. We could tie my wrist to the headboard, so that we both know where my arm is at all times, and then we could go ape-shit wild and—"

He reached for his pants.

She got on the bed. "You suck," she told him. "You weren't even listening. It was a good idea."

He laughed. "I promise, after your arm heals a little, to tie you up. Or swing from the chandelier with you. Or do it doggy-style up on the roof. Whatever you want. Right now, though I'm going to make you relax if it's the last thing I do. On your stomach."

"I love a masterful man," she said, complying. "The ordering me around thing is driving me mad with desire, Chief. Which is about as far from relaxed as possible, by the way."

"It doesn't have to be," Cosmo said. "Desire works really nicely with relaxed." He put his pants up on her other pillow, where he knew she could see them as he climbed onto the bed.

As he climbed onto her.

He straddled her, half sitting on her thighs, his knees on either side of her hips, his hands holding down her shoulders so she couldn't wriggle and turn to face him.

Which, of course, she tried to do.

"Don't move," he said quietly, leaning forward to speak into her ear. "First thing you need to do to relax is be still."

His breath was warm against her cheek, his chest warm against her shoulder blades. She could feel his arousal, too, heavy against the small of her back, and she moaned. She couldn't help it.

"Trust me," he said. "Do you trust me? We'll get there, I promise. I swear. I give you my word."

"Unless 'my word' is your nickname for your—"

"Shhhh," he said, laughing. "Try not to talk."

God, it felt so good, what he was doing to her. His hands were so warm and strong as he massaged her back, her neck, her shoulders. He kissed her, too—beneath her ear, at the nape of her neck, on her shoulder blade—places she never realized would feel so good to be kissed.

Cosmo had given her his word.

So Jane surrendered.

And somehow he could tell that she was finally done fighting him, because he no longer held her down.

He moved off of her, but it wasn't so she could turn over—it was so he could work his way slowly down her lower back. "You're so beautiful," he murmured, his hands on the very part of her he'd once called worthless.

This was not a coincidence. She'd added **giant,** and he hadn't forgotten that.

"I think you're perfect, Janey," he told her now, his quiet voice thick with emotion—this man some people thought of as a robot. "You're unbelievably sexy."

For a man who so often used silence to his advantage, he sure knew how to make words count.

He kissed and stroked his way down and then back up her legs, careful of her skinned knee and . . .

Jane didn't move much—she knew better than that—but she did open herself to him, just a little. An invitation. Don't forget to work your magic here . . .

Cosmo laughed. And turned her over. But he still didn't touch her where she wanted most to be touched.

Instead he started all over again. From the top. Straddling her hips. He smiled down at her, as he did his wonderful relaxation thing on her face, her neck, her throat, her shoulders.

Her breasts.

He leaned forward to kiss her, and as she lost herself in the softness of his mouth, she couldn't do it. She couldn't not touch him. His hair, his arms, his back—ah, God, he felt so good, so solid beneath her hands. He didn't seem to mind—until she reached between them and . . .

Cosmo lifted his head. "Hey."

"I'm moving very slowly and carefully," she told him.

He laughed. "Yeah," he said, his eyes half-closed as she stroked him. "I noticed."

"This is very relaxing for me," she said, loving the fascinating mix of soft and hard, loving that look in his eyes.

"Ah, Jane," he breathed, "if you keep that up . . ."

"I have an idea," she said. "This one's good, so listen: We skip to the part that you promised we'd get to—"

He laughed as he kissed her mouth, no doubt thinking that would distract her while he gently moved her hands up over her head. He was right, it did, and by the time he released her wrists, he'd once again shifted off of her, which moved him out of her reach.

By then she was floating.

Drifting . . .

His kisses trailed lower and lower until . . .

Yesssssss . . .

He touched, kissed, stroked, without ever increasing that maddeningly slow, deliberately lazy pace.

He tasted and looked, too—God, it was a turn-on the way he took his time to really look at her, as if she were the most beautiful woman he'd ever seen.

It was—all of it—like something from a dream.

A really good dream.

She floated, she sighed, she drifted, she flowed.

Her eyes were closed as he shifted on top of her, as he . . .

Jane opened her eyes to find him watching her as he finally filled her, as he . . .

"Cosmo," she breathed.

He smiled, watching her face as he moved inside her so slowly—God it felt so good—as he pushed himself even farther. . . .

She tried to tell him more, she wanted even more, but all that came out was a sound of pure pleasure. It made him laugh as he still watched her, heat in his eyes, as he still moved so slowly, so deeply.

Deeper.

She moved with him, content with his pace, and time seemed to stretch even more. Stretch and bend and curve in on itself until all that existed was now, this wonderful, amazing **now** that was Cosmo's eyes and Cosmo's smile and Cosmo's so obvious desire for her—such a powerful emotion transformed into the physical. His mouth on her mouth was a wonder as he kissed her again. His body against hers, inside her, that slow slide out and then home again, a miracle. And a miracle. And a miracle and . . .

She could have gone on like this forever. As it was, she had no idea how long they'd been . . .

Except when she opened her eyes, she did know.

Cos's arms were shaking slightly, his muscles standing out sharply as he held himself above her, as he kept himself from crushing her.

And he wasn't smiling anymore. His eyes were closed and the expression on his face had changed to one of complete concentration. Crushing her wasn't the only thing he was keeping himself from doing.

"Cos," she managed to say, and he looked at her. "I'm not sure . . . I'm quite relaxed yet. Can we . . . start back . . . at the beginning?"

It took several seconds for the fact that she was kidding to penetrate. But when it did, he laughed, and she could see that he was completely undone.

"God, Janey!" he said, still laughing.

He threw all his weight onto one arm and reached between them to touch her—somehow he'd already learned exactly, exactly where—and if his laughter hadn't already pushed her over the edge, she would have had no choice. As it was, he took her higher. She came with him, in glorious, beautiful, joyous slow motion, pulling him down so she could cling to him, so she could kiss him and kiss him and kiss him.

It took her forever to catch her breath, to drift back to a place where she could once again speak.

She opened her eyes to find Cosmo watching her.

"Hi," she said, still giddy. "Wow."

He smiled, and her heart expanded even more. She actually felt it growing, right there in her chest.

I love you seemed so mundane, so overused, so terrifying to admit, but she wanted to say something to him. To tell him . . .

"That orgasm you just gave me was defective," she said.

He laughed, but he didn't say anything. He just waited for her to continue.

"Orgasms are . . . well, you know how when you're in the middle of one, you always think, this one is it? This one is so special? The gleaming, golden, perfect O? Only afterward, it fades away like all the others. Which actually turns out to be a relief. Like, ooh, thank God, I don't have to spend the rest of my life following **that** loser around begging for another of those really good ones." She touched his face, tracing the lines that appeared next to his eyes and mouth when he smiled. "But this time it really was special. So don't freak out when I start following you around, okay?"

He kissed her, and it was so tender, she thought for a moment that she'd gone and slipped and said too much.

Like, **And don't be a loser and go and break my heart.**

No, she hadn't said it—and she wouldn't say it.

But just to make sure, she changed the subject. Which wasn't hard to do with a man who didn't spend much time senselessly chattering away.

"I've been thinking," Jane said. "And I haven't been able to figure out . . . Where exactly is it that the cows go all night?"

Cosmo blinked at her, and then laughed as he made the connection. Cows. 'Til the cows come home.

"And what kind of irresponsible dairy farmer," she asked, "would let his cows just wander around—"

Cosmo kissed her again. And flipped her—carefully, of course—onto her stomach.

"Obviously," he said, "we need to do a little more relaxation work."

CHAPTER
SEVENTEEN

Murphy was in the kitchen when Cosmo came in for breakfast.

"Whoa," Cos said. What was he still doing here?

"I'm double-shifting," Murphy told him before he could ask. He looked up from the piles of paper—computer printouts and reports, from the looks of them—that he had stacked in front of him on the table. "Sleep well?"

Um. "Yeah," Cosmo said, opening the cabinet in search of a coffee mug.

"PJ and Beth had a thing—not a fight, a thing. That's a direct quote," Murphy explained. "So I stuck around."

"You should have called me," Cosmo said.

"Hmmm," Murph said. "Yeah, I guess. It just seemed silly to use the phone when you were sleeping right down the hall. Except, you **weren't** there. Very mysterious. At first I thought you were out in the yard, still looking for that bullet, but then I realized that I would have heard the alarm go off and then back on as you went through the door."

Damn. He knew he should have gone back to his own room a whole hell of a lot sooner than he had. Cosmo poured himself a cup of coffee, keeping his back to the former Marine.

"It's really not my business," Murphy said. "Except now it sort of is my business, because I'm wondering how much of this is my fault. I believe what I said was 'go and give her a howdy,' but maybe I'm not up on the latest Caucasian slang, so—"

Cosmo turned to face him. "It's not your fault."

Murphy gazed at him. "Again, it's not my business, but if I were in your shoes—"

"I've already called Commander Paoletti, left a message that I need to talk to him sometime today," Cosmo told him. He had to figure out the right thing to do—morally, ethically, professionally. Continuing on as things were wasn't an option. Certainly not without bringing Tommy Paoletti up to speed. To some extent, anyway.

Cos had called his mother this morning, too, asked her to stay in San Francisco a little longer.

"Then before I tactfully change the subject and never speak of this matter again," Murphy said, "I want to say, **Dude**! You are **so** the man. Not only is she a walking wet dream, she's unbelievably **nice.** I just have to know, though—"

"Is it possible to tactfully change the subject after you're dead?" Cosmo mused as he took a sip of his coffee.

"Right. So. Guess I'll never know." Murph cleared his throat. "Angelina and I are having pizza tonight with Tom and his wife up in Malibu. You know Kelly Paoletti, right? She claims she wants to see the photos from our honeymoon. Is she serious or just being polite? I need to know whether to conveniently 'forget' to bring them."

"She means what she says," Cos told him. "Bring 'em."

Murphy nodded. "Maybe we'll leave 'em in the car at first."

The walkie-talkie squawked. "We've got a limo pulling up," Nash said from his post out in the yard. "We expecting anyone?"

Murphy looked at Cosmo, who shook his head. Not that he knew of. Of course, he and Jane hadn't done all that much talking last night. They certainly hadn't discussed the morning's schedule.

"Let me check with Jane." Murph got to his feet, and Cos followed him out toward the entry hall.

Where Jane was coming down the stairs, on her phone. ". . . your level of concern is . . . I hear what you're saying, but . . ."

She was dressed in one of her J. Mercedes Chadwick suits—the jacket with the deep V-neckline that she'd worn to that first press conference. With her hair artfully arranged up and off her neck, with makeup on and wide-legged pants covering her scraped knee, she looked very different from the wild-haired woman he'd made love to last night. So self-assured. Coolly in charge. Distant. Unattainable. Too perfect to be human.

"I hear you," she said again. "Yes . . . Yes, but . . ." Whoever she was talking to wasn't giving her a chance to speak, and she put steel into her voice. "Well, then they don't have to come and see the movie, do they?"

Something was up.

"It's Jack Shelton's limo," Nash's voice came over the walkie-talkie.

"He's here now," Mercedes told whomever it was she was talking to. "He stopped at the studio and picked up Patty. She's got a tape of the interview."

She caught sight of Cosmo leaning against the wall, just watching her, and for a second—just for a second—she looked vulnerable. Like a part of her hadn't expected to see him again. Certainly not this morning, and maybe not ever. It was followed quickly by a flash of pure relief, and then a very warm smile that made memories of last night come rushing back with a vengeance.

"I have to go," she said into her phone. She rolled her eyes and stuck out her tongue. "Yes, I'm well aware that we'll be talking more about this later." **Shit,** she mouthed silently. She listened, shaking her head for several more seconds. "Khhhhh," she finally said, making bad cell phone connection sounds. "I can't khh-hhhhh oo say-khh-ng. Khhhhhhhhh." She cut the connection, but kept talking, as if she were still addressing the person on the other end of that phone call. "You're welcome to talk until your ass turns blue, but

I'm not making the changes you quote unquote **require** because this is my movie, not yours, you brain-dead maggot." She smiled at Cos again. "Good morning."

"Problem?" he asked.

"Oh, just a little one. HeartBeat's on the verge of pulling their funding." She gestured to her clothes. "That's why I'm dressed for battle." She came closer. "You know, you could've left a note." She was far more upset than she was pretending to be, and she pulled up short and laughed. "Whoa, where did that come from? Sorry. Stress levels are already way too high today and it's not even nine o'clock."

"I'll, uh, go outside and see what's holding up Jack," Murphy said, punching the code for the front door bypass into the alarm control box.

"I didn't have anything to write with," Cosmo told Jane after Murph shut the door behind him. "Or on. I'm sorry. I didn't think—"

"It's really okay," she said. "It's not like I have any right to—" She laughed again. "I just wish you'd stayed. If you had, I wouldn't've answered the phone. We could be up there still, gloriously ignorant of the impending shitstorm."

"What shitstorm?"

She stepped close enough to slip her arms around his neck, pulling his head down for a kiss. "Want to go upstairs?" she asked. "I bet we could make each other come in sixty seconds. We'd be back in the kitchen before Jack even put sugar in his coffee."

It was such a J. Mercedes Chadwick thing to do—

use sex to distract. Cosmo was a little thrown. And a little intrigued, he had to admit. Was J. Mercedes just Jane with fancy clothes and makeup? Or was there more to the masquerade?

She kissed him even more deeply and—whoa—reached down to wrap her fingers around him, right through his pants.

Mission accomplished. Cosmo was completely and utterly distracted.

He found himself glancing over at the stairs, and Jane laughed because she knew he was actually considering that sixty-second thing.

"How's your arm?" he managed to ask.

"Completely, miraculously healed." She wiggled her eyebrows at him. "There's a chandelier in one of the upstairs rooms just perfect for swinging on—"

But the doorknob rattled—thank God for Murphy—and Cosmo let her go. He stepped back. Adjusted his pants, or at least tried to, while she smoothed her jacket and fixed her hair.

He knew there was something he wanted to ask her. Something that didn't have to do with getting it on. Oh. Yeah. "What shitstorm?"

"What are we going to do?" Robin asked, swatting the video camera away. Whose brilliant idea was it to tape this meeting for the "Making Of" video? And who the hell had invited Adam here? The actor playing Jack was the last person Robin had expected to see in Janey's conference room when he'd staggered out of bed this morning.

But because of a recently unearthed interview Jack Shelton had given several years ago in which he'd been scathingly critical of the U.S. President, HeartBeat Studios had been inundated by people e-mailing, phoning, and faxing to protest the production of **American Hero.** Even though it was clearly an organized campaign led by the Freedom Network, there was no denying it—HeartBeat was now officially spooked.

They had called and asked that Jane edit out the gay romance between Jack and Hal. In fact, they'd prefer it if she took Jack out of the movie altogether.

" 'Please consider making our recommended changes,' " Jane repeated now. "It was a request, not an order."

"You're not considering it, are you?" Adam asked, trying hard not to look worried.

"Maybe we **should** think about it," Robin said. He wasn't serious. He just wanted to see Adam's reaction.

The other actor didn't say a word—after all, that video camera was running—but the look he shot Robin was a resounding **Fuck you.**

The phone rang again, as it had been ringing every three minutes since this meeting had started. "Excuse me," Janey said, and took the call.

Adam moved several seats closer to Robin. "Have fun last night? Chasing Jules around the city in the rain?"

"Yeah." He had, actually. The quiet restaurant had been a nice change of pace from the relentlessly loud music in the dance club. "We found this place that had really awesome sangria."

Score. Adam was extremely unhappy at the news that Robin had successfully talked Jules out of flagging down a taxi. But the cameras were rolling and even though the lens was aimed at Jane, Adam was visible in the background. So he smiled. "Great."

And then Janey got off the phone. "No more phone calls," she told Patty, who was making a point to avoid all eye contact with Robin.

Which was fine with him.

"Decker's outside," Patty announced. "He's looking for Cosmo. Have you seen him?"

"He left a while ago. He said he had some errands to do at his mother's apartment up in Laguna Beach," Jane said, then smiled. It was a strange smile, dreamy and distant, as if she were suddenly somewhere else, somewhere a lot more pleasant than this controversy-filled conference room with the curtains drawn. She'd been smiling like that a lot this morning, even while she was talking to some numbnuts on the phone.

Adam stopped Patty before she went back out of the room. "I've been meaning to ask—tomorrow's shooting schedule hasn't changed, has it?"

"The damage to the studio should be cleaned up by later this afternoon," Patty reported.

Oh, crap. Really? He'd thought he had a reprieve. Robin cleared his throat. "I'm not sure I'm going to be ready for those scenes." He turned to his sister. "Can we push things off a day?"

"I'm ready," Adam said.

Jane sighed, frowning, pulled back to harsh reality.

"Robbie, God, you've had way more time than Adam to prepare—"

"These are not easy scenes," Robin defended himself.

"You're just freaked out by the kiss," Adam said. "Come on. Come here, right now. Let's just do it." He popped a breath mint. "Once you get rid of the mystery, you'll be—"

"Excuse me," Jane said. "I'm sorry, this isn't helping. You need to rehearse? Rehearse. But later, please."

Adam smiled at Robin. "I'd love to rehearse later. What do you say? Six o'clock, my place?"

Robin resisted the urge to hold his fingers up in the shape of a cross. Not in this lifetime. "Sorry, I'm booked," he lied. He checked his calendar. "How's . . . never? Is never good for you?"

"Aren't you just **so** funny," Adam said.

"Look, I don't know why you're here, but I'm here to help Jane," Robin said.

"Yeah, you're a big help," Patty muttered as she left the room.

"Here's what we're going to do," Jane said. "We're going to record our own interview with Jack, run it on our website. I was going to ask both of you guys to give the interview, you know, ask the questions, but I've changed my mind. It's just going to be Adam."

"Why?" Robin said, which was stupid. He didn't really want the extra work.

Jane ignored him. "I'll give you a list of questions," she told Adam. "We're going to focus on Jack's years in the service, on the fact that he's a World War Two veteran, that he risked his life fighting for freedom and democracy—that no one has the right to accuse him of being unpatriotic."

"That's a great idea," Adam said.

Jane turned back to Robin. "We're already several days behind, what with the accident and the weather. You need to go and do whatever it is you need to do to prepare for tomorrow's scenes."

Robin stood up. "But—"

"Go." Jane pointed to the door.

Fine. He went. He'd do what he needed to do—which meant that there was a very large gin and tonic in his immediate future.

Jane had just hung up the phone and put her head down on the desk when someone knocked softly on her office door.

"Got a minute?" It was Decker.

She sat up. "Oh, my God. How **are** you? I didn't expect you back today."

"I'm fine. I was fine yesterday," he told her, actually managing to look embarrassed. Or maybe it was sheepish. "I'm sorry about scaring you—I really didn't need to go to the hospital at all."

"Yeah, that's right," she said, gesturing for him to sit. "You're a former SEAL, right? I've been reading up about you guys. You like to cauterize your own wounds, pull out bullets with your teeth, stitch yourself up—that sort of thing, right? Although stitching up the back of your own head might be a challenge even for you, the mighty Decker."

He laughed as he sat down across from her. "I didn't need stitches. It was a surface wound—a scrape. Heads bleed a lot."

"Gee, if I'd known that, I would have demanded you help sweep up the studio last night. And then paint my house. Wash my car, mow the lawn—"

"How are you?" he asked. "Besides sarcastic, that is." He zeroed in his steady gaze on her. "Is there something going on that I should know about?"

Other than the fact that she'd had the most incredible sex last night with a man who scared the mother-loving daylights out of her?

How could Cosmo be so perfect?

The answer to that was easy: He couldn't possibly be.

Which made the next question obvious. When was he going to spring it on her—his fatal flaw?

Jane had made a list of possibilities in her head. Everything from the ridiculous: His mother wasn't really in San Francisco but instead was chained in his attic—to the realistic: He was totally incompatible with her Hollywood lifestyle—to the downright paranoid: He'd never really stopped hating her and last night was some kind of pathetic payback for her behavior at that first press conference.

Although as far as punishments went . . . Suffice it to say, she couldn't wait to be punished like that again.

Except, to be honest, when she'd woken up this morning all alone in her bed, she'd had a bit of a panic attack. Where had Cosmo gone? **Why** had Cosmo gone?

She'd thought they'd connected on a stay-all-night level. On a make-room-for-me-in-your-closet-'cause-I'll-be-here-for-a-while level.

The lack of a note had freaked her out. And the fact that she'd freaked out about it made her even **more** freaked out.

Because it was obvious that she cared too much.

Which meant that when she finally found out that missing yet vital piece of information—that terrible, unfixable flaw of Cosmo's that she hadn't yet discovered; that thing that would blow up their fledgling relationship—she wouldn't simply be able to laugh and just have fun. She wouldn't be able to shrug and enjoy the nonstop sex phase, even though she well knew there'd be no serious relationship phase.

Although, no doubt about it, with this man, the nonstop sex phase could go for months. Years. Decades, if she had anything to say about it.

She sighed, remembering the way he'd smiled into her eyes as he'd—

"Jane?"

Whoops. Decker had asked her something. "I'm sorry . . . ?" Her voice came out sounding a little breathless.

"Are you having some kind of problem with Cosmo Richter?" he asked. But before she could stammer out any kind of response, he added, "Because I got a call from Tom Paoletti, asking me if there was something going on—something that would trigger his resignation."

What? "Whose resignation?"

"Richter's."

Jane sat back in her chair. Cosmo had quit? Like, quit? Like, "Hi, Tom, how are you, I quit"?

Here was a fatal flaw she hadn't considered—that he'd meant none of what he'd said. Ever. But especially last night. **I'm so fucking crazy about you. . . .**

Deck was watching her closely. "You haven't, um, clashed with him again?" he asked.

Clashed? **Clashed?** She couldn't speak. She could barely think.

This put a real cow-patty frosting on a total cesspool of a day.

"I know there was some tension at first between the two of you," Decker continued, still watching her. "Differences of opinion and personality—that sort of thing. I was under the impression that you'd worked things out, and had even become, well, friends."

"Yes," she managed to say. "Friends." Her head was spinning. It was quite possible she was going to be sick. She forced a smile instead. "No, there's been no . . . clashing. . . . Are you sure he **quit**?"

"Apparently this is as much of a surprise to you," Decker said. "That's good. I was a little afraid something had happened last night that I'd missed by being out of the picture. I haven't spoken to Richter yet— I'm not sure where he is."

"He told me he . . ." She had to clear her throat. "He was going to Laguna Beach."

"Maybe this has something to do with his mother," Decker said.

Without calling Jane first to tell her about it? She

had to get this straight. "He just quit. Without giving Tom a reason why?"

"No," Decker said. "He left a message with Tom, requesting they meet this evening. But he gave him a heads-up—he wanted to give him as much time as possible to start looking for a replacement."

A replacement. God.

Jane arranged her face into another smile, hoping that would hide her gritted teeth. "Sorry I can't be of more help. I don't know anything about it." She picked up her phone, and he recognized that as the dismissal it was and stood.

"I'll let you get back to it."

"Thanks," she said. "Do me a favor and close the door behind you?"

He did, and she stopped smiling. She also speed-dialed Cosmo's cell phone number.

Okay. Relax. Be calm. Give the man a chance to say, "Hey, I was just about to call you. My mom fell off a trolley and broke both her legs, too, so I have to go up to San Francisco, but I'll be back, because I am so fucking crazy about you. . . ."

She was beeped over immediately to his voice mail.

"Richter. Leave a message." **Beep.**

"Hey, Cos, it's me. Jane," she added, hating herself for doing that, as if he wouldn't recognize her voice after he'd spent the night listening to her moan his name. Except God, what if he didn't? What if . . . ? Don't go there, don't go there! She made herself sound bright. Cheery. "Call me when you get this, will you?"

This was just a rumor until she heard it from Cosmo.

She sat at her desk, staring at her phone, willing it to ring, willing him to call her back. Right. Now.

. . . or from Tom Paoletti. Talking to Tom could, quite possibly, clear things up, too.

And, of course, she had a different reason to talk to Tom, since HeartBeat's threats to pull out of their distribution deal meant that Troubleshooters Incorporated could well be out of a job. There was no way Jane could afford to keep paying them.

She rummaged in the desk drawer where she tossed business cards. Tom's was in there, near the top. His office number was on the front—but that got her an answering machine. His cell number bumped her over to voice mail, too.

On the back of the card there was another number, written in her own handwriting. It must be his number at home. No, wait, that wasn't home. He'd told her he was spending a few weeks on a vacation of sorts, renting a house on the beach in Malibu, right on Pacific Coast Highway. When he'd given her that number, he'd said, "Don't hesitate to call."

So she stopped hesitating.

A woman picked up. "Hello?"

"I'm sorry to bother you," Jane said. "I'm trying to reach Tom. This is Mercedes Chadwick."

"Oh, hi, Mercedes. I'm Kelly, Tom's wife. It's not a problem at all." Jane could hear laughter in the background, as if there were some kind of party going on.

"He's here, but he's out on the beach, talking with one of his men. Is this urgent? Do you need me to—"

"No, no," Jane said. "I just . . . Is it . . . By any chance is he with Cosmo Richter?"

"That's right, yeah, you know Cos," Kelly said. "I can try to signal them from the deck if you—"

"No," Jane said. "Thank you, but . . . Do you expect them to be very long?"

"They better not be," Kelly said. "No, no, Murph, put it over here. **Here,** on the counter. It's greasy on the bottom. Sorry about that. The pizzas just arrived and—hang on . . ." She covered the mouthpiece of the telephone, but Jane could still hear her. "It's on the refrigerator door. Get a glass for Sophia, too, will you?" She came back. "I'm sorry—"

"Sophia's there?" Jane asked, the words escaping before she could clamp her teeth shut over them.

"Oh, do you know her, too?" Kelly said.

"Blond and perfect, right?" Jane asked through clenched teeth. Son of a bitch—the **son** of a **bitch**!

Kelly laughed. "I guess you know her."

How could this be? Cosmo couldn't—he wouldn't—do this. And yet here he was. Right after spending the night in Jane's bed, he sure as hell looked as if he were now sniffing his way down Sophia's perfect little blond garden path.

God **damn,** but she always picked the total losers. "Motherfah—" she said, catching herself just in time.

"Excuse me?" Kelly asked.

Jane cleared her throat. "Tell Cosmo—" No. No.

Don't assume. Never assume. Until she spoke directly to Cosmo, until he said, "Yes, Jane, you idiot, I've totally played you. All those heartfelt conversations in your kitchen, the sweetness of my kisses, the whole tears in the eyes bit—a total act to get you into bed. I am scum. I am rotting scum. I am the worst of all the losers you've foolishly chosen, because you actually, stupidly thought I was different. Which makes you the biggest loser of all. But really, that's not news to you, is it?"

"Shall I have Tom call you?" Kelly asked, with that "oh, my goodness, are you nuts or is it Tourette's?" tone in her voice.

"Do you have an attached garage?" Jane asked because, damn it, she was through putting her life on hold for some lunatic with a computer who would probably never venture out of his mother's basement. She'd had enough of rearranging her existence for some clever hacker who'd somehow gotten hold of those e-mails that had been sent to that dead lawyer in Idaho.

"I'm . . . sorry?" Kelly asked.

"You're staying in Malibu, right? I was thinking of spending some time up there," Jane lied, "and I'm looking for a house to rent, but it's got to have an at-tached garage." Which meant she could go from her garage here in Hollywood to Tom and Kelly's in Mal-ibu without ever stepping outside. Which meant she would be safe from her imaginary killer's imaginary bullets.

"Um, yeah," Kelly said, sounding more and more

perplexed. "This place is really nice. It's right on the beach. There's a two-car garage, actually."

"Fabulous," Jane said. "It's on Pacific Coast Highway right? Number . . ." God, the street numbers up there had to be huge. "Seventy-two thousand and . . . ?" she guessed, picking a number out of thin air.

"It's in the twenty-threes," Kelly said, which was good enough, considering Cosmo's truck would be parked in the driveway. "If you want, I can get you the name of the rental agent who handles—"

"That'd be wonderful," Jane said. "Thanks so much!"

She cut the connection before she did something stupid, like start to cry into the ear of a total stranger.

She was going to Malibu, where she'd give Cosmo the chance to tell her to her face why he was quitting, and why he was attending a pizza party with Sophia-the-perfect on the evening after he'd shared Jane's bed.

It was serendipitous, because if his answer **was** "Because I'm scum," Jane could use the opportunity to warn Sophia.

Because no one, not even women who were perfect, deserved to be hurt like that.

Jane grabbed her purse, a scarf, and dark sunglasses and thundered down the stairs.

"I'm going out."

Decker looked up to see Jane standing in the

kitchen doorway. He laughed—for about half a second. But then he stopped because she wasn't kidding. "Jane. Wait. You know that's not a good idea."

"Tell me," she said, holding his gaze with an intensity that was alarming, "that you know—without a doubt—that this threat is real. Tell me you're convinced, absolutely, that I'm in serious danger."

"Well," he started, stalling, because it was obvious she was upset.

"Yes, Jane, the threat is real," she persisted. "If you truly believe it. . . ."

But he didn't. He wasn't convinced. "It's not that cut-and-dried. Until we have more information, we need to treat this as if it's—"

But Jane had already turned away. "Feel free to come along and throw yourself between me and any stray bullets," she said as she headed for the garage, putting the scarf over her head—like that was some kind of useful disguise.

"Wait," he said again. "Stop. Where are you going? Are you going to the studio?"

Jane didn't stop. "I'm going to Malibu."

What? Why? "Okay," Decker said. "Hold on. Let's slow down here. You know I can't tell you what to do, but I can certainly recommend that—"

She got into her car.

He got in beside her. "Jane. I don't know what's in Malibu—"

"My life," she said, her eyes flashing and her knuckles white as she gripped the steering wheel. "My life is in Malibu. And in Hollywood and Beverly

Hills, and all those 'dangerous' locations where my movie is being made without me! It's not locked up here, in this stupid house! How long am I supposed to hide from some loony tunes psycho e-mailer who probably isn't even a real threat?"

Decker nodded. "I can understand your frustration, but taking these temporary precautions—"

"Temporary?" she said. **"Temporary?"**

"Yes, temporary. Look, I know what you're feeling. Everyone goes through it. There's even a name for it— prison fever. It's when the anger catches up with the fear, and protective custody feels more like a jail sentence—"

"How long is my sentence going to last, Deck? Four months? Six to twelve? Two to four **years**?"

"I don't know," Decker told her. "You know I don't know. What I do know is you need to take a deep breath and let me make some phone calls, set up backup, arrange this for you—for tomorrow."

"Tomorrow." She laughed. "Want to hear something really funny?" she asked. "HeartBeat is going to kill our deal and pull their money because I won't cut those pesky gay people from my movie. 'The World War Two drama is just as compelling without Jack Shelton,'" she said, pitching her voice to sound deep and stupid. "'The director agrees with our assessment—that the movie doesn't lose a thing by removing the controversial material.' Fuck! That! I'm not changing anything. So tomorrow you won't be here anyway—I'll be on my own."

Decker shook his head. "Jane, we'll work something out—we're not just going to quit."

For some reason that made her laugh, but again it wasn't a "ha-ha, you're funny" laugh. It was more of the "oh, my God, I can't believe you said that" variety.

"I can't afford you." She reached up to hit the button for the automatic garage door opener that had just been installed. "You better get the bill for this equipment submitted to HeartBeat tonight."

Deck grabbed her wrist. "I should drive. You should be in the back with your head down."

"Yeah, right," she said. "Then we'll go where you want to go, which won't be Malibu. Nice try, Smokey. I'm driving."

"Start the car first," Decker told her. "Then open the door. Move fast. Floor it as soon as possible—I'll tell you when the car'll clear the garage door." He now spoke into his radio. "Nash! Stay out of the driveway. Is there traffic on the street?"

They were all exiting the house like this now, every time any one of them left, even if it was just to run to the store to get cream for their coffee. Put their car into the garage, close the door, wait a few seconds, get an all clear from the street, and Starsky and Hutch it out of there.

The goal was to keep the shooter guessing and off balance. Had Jane left the house? Was she in one of those cars? All of the info that the FBI analysts had given them suggested that their man worked alone. Kind of hard to follow every car that left the driveway and keep an eye on the house, all at the same time.

"Everything's quiet," came the reply. "Nothing's moving. What's going on?"

"Open it," Decker told Jane, and the garage door went up. "Go," he said. They hit the street, tires squealing, as he told Nash, "We need a little air."

Jane headed west.

"What's in Malibu?" Decker asked her.

But she didn't answer. She just drove.

CHAPTER
EIGHTEEN

Jules' cell phone woke him.

His nap had lasted all of seven minutes.

The FBI office was still in the process of reviewing the list of extras, actors, and crew for **American Hero.** Reviewing and analyzing and checking via computer. Hoping someone's name would come back with a big red flag saying "homicidal psychopath."

For most of the day, Jules had stood around with his head up his ass, waiting for the analysts' results.

Just after lunch, he'd attended a meeting in which the cause of the accident in the studio was determined to be a mystery. Officially, they still did not know if it had been an intentional attempt to disrupt filming— as opposed to yesterday, when their inability to figure it all out had been unofficial.

Later tonight, after dinner, Jules would be meeting with Lawrence Decker—who was already back to work after yesterday's hospital visit. Topic of discussion: how to find the crazy e-mailer before he killed Jane.

After checking out the usual suspects from the Freedom Network, they had exactly zero leads. Or maybe they had four hundred thousand leads, considering that Cosmo had left a message on Jules' voice mail, asking for two lists. One was of all people living in the Western U.S. who owned ancient white Pontiacs. The second was of owners of dark Ford pickups with a six in their plate number.

Like those lists wouldn't take two weeks to print out and four dump trucks to deliver. Sheesh.

All the emotional drama of the past few days had seemed to catch up to Jules all at once this afternoon. He'd left the analyzing in the hands of the analysts and gone back to his hotel to catch a short nap before an early dinner.

His plan was to stop back in the office and see if there was any new information that he could bring to tonight's meeting. Unlike some FBI agents, he didn't have a problem saying "We just don't know." But it could get old after the seventeenth time inside of five minutes.

He now scrambled for his ringing cell phone. If this was Adam, he was going to throw the phone across the room.

But it wasn't Adam. It was . . .

"Robin Chadwick," Jules said as a greeting, as he sank back into bed. "What's up?"

Robin was part of the reason he was so tired. Although they hadn't stayed too long at that little Mexican restaurant in West Hollywood, Jules had been out later than he was used to these days. And coming on top of the week that he'd had—a too-generous dose of both Adam and the great state of Idaho . . .

He and Robin had talked for about a half hour about the movie industry, favorite films, acting techniques.

Then they'd spent nearly twice as much time talking about Jules' work, about Alyssa, about how hard it was to lose an FBI partner, about how glad Jules was that Alyssa's marriage hadn't meant an end to their friendship.

Robin was unbelievably easy to talk to. He asked questions, digging deeper as he strove to truly understand everything Jules had to say. He was genuinely interested.

Unlike Adam, who would start checking out the waitstaff when Jules talked about work.

Okay, that was a little too harsh. The truth was that Adam had always been jealous of Alyssa. He only pretended to be bored when Jules talked about her.

"I'm really sorry to bother you," Robin said now, on the other end of the phone. "But I could really . . . I need . . ." He sounded upset.

Jules sat up. "You're not bothering me."

Robin took a deep breath, let it out fast. "I need a giant favor, but it's too much to ask, so I'm just going to hang up and pretend I never called—"

"Whoa," Jules said. "Wait. Robin. Talk to me. Don't just assume. You know, some people's giant favors are other's insignificant no-big-deals. Try me."

There was silence from Robin's end.

"You still there?" Jules asked.

"I'm standing outside your door," Robin finally said. "May I come in?"

Well, didn't that surprise the screaming bejesus out of him? "Uh," Jules said.

"Yeah, see, never mind—"

"Wait!" Jules leapt out of bed. Scrambled for his pants. Flung open the door.

"Oh, crap." Robin stared at him, at his rumpled hair, his bare chest. "You were sleeping. I woke you."

Jules closed his phone. Smoothed down his hair. "That's okay. I'm okay. A little underdressed . . ." He finished fastening his pants while Robin watched, which was a little weird.

"Nice abs. I can't believe you keep a six-pack like that hidden under a suit."

Jules rolled his eyes. "No, I don't want to be an actor. Don't start. Let me grab a shirt and my shoes and we can go down to the bar—"

"I've already had a couple drinks," Robin said.

No kidding.

His blond hair was charmingly rumpled, and his tie was about as loose as it could get without being undone. He should have been relaxed, and he leaned against the door frame in a nonchalant manner, but Jules could see that he was wound pretty damn tightly.

"Irish courage," Robin continued. "My mother was Irish. Maureen O'Reilly—can you believe it? Jane's mother was Greek. Dad's third wife came from Mississippi. Four was from Australia. Number five is Russian. She's actually won the longevity award, but her days are numbered—Dad's planning a trip to Taiwan."

Well, okay, then. "Let me grab a shirt," Jules said again. He motioned for Robin to hold the door, but he must have misunderstood, because he took it for an invitation to come in. As Jules took his shirt from the back of the desk chair, the door closed with a **cachunk.**

"Wow," Robin said, and Jules knew he'd seen the scar on the back of his shoulder.

Which meant he was still looking, still checking him out.

"What happened to you?" Robin asked.

"Hazardous duty is part of my job description," Jules told him. "I'm thinking about getting a tattoo to cover it. Something cute, like Bert and Ernie or Big Bird."

Robin laughed.

And wasn't this just perfect. He was alone in his hotel room with Robin Chadwick, who was way too charming and attractive even though he was half-drunk at 4:58 in the afternoon.

"Just out of curiosity," Jules asked as he buttoned his shirt. "How did you get my room number?"

Robin fished into his pocket and pulled out a piece of paper. He held it out, and Jules took it. It was a receipt. From this hotel. For breakfast. Jules had charged the meal to his room—he'd written his number on it.

"This was in with the money you gave me last night," Robin told him. "Stuck between two bills."

Oh, shit.

Jules had insisted on going dutch. Robin had put the bill on his credit card and pocketed the cash Jules had given him for his share, without looking at it. At least not at the restaurant. Apparently he'd found this receipt later.

Found it and surely wondered . . .

"I wasn't sure it was intentional," Robin added, "or . . ."

"It wasn't."

"Yeah, I didn't think so," Robin obviously lied. "It was actually stuck to a five-dollar bill. I think with maple syrup."

Jules nodded. "The waitress was rushed when she brought the French toast. The plates bounced when they hit the table. Big splatter factor."

"So now I've completely embarrassed us both," Robin said. "Because you think that I think that you gave that to me so that I'd come here—"

Enough dancing. Jules went for point-blank. "Why **did** you come here?"

"We're shooting a scene tomorrow," Robin said. "It's the first scene where Hal and Jack kiss and . . ." He cleared his throat. "I've never kissed another man before, and somehow the thought of it being Adam . . . I was hoping maybe you wouldn't mind. . . ." He was embarrassed. "Forget it. I'm sorry. It's stupid."

He was hoping Jules could be his first. It was so unbelievably sweet.

"I mean, who the fuck cares, you know?" Robin

continued. "I'm acting, so I'll just kiss him. It doesn't mean anything. It doesn't—"

Jules stepped closer and kissed him.

It was nothing profound, just a light brushing of lips against lips, but it was enough to shut Robin up.

He stared at Jules, all gorgeous cheekbones, blond hair, and haunted eyes.

"Not quite as terrifying as you thought, huh?" Jules said.

But Robin shook his head. "That's not, uh . . . The scene is, um . . ."

Jules nodded. "More intense?"

"Yeah."

"Tongues."

"Oh, yeah," Robin said.

Jules nodded. "Who, um . . . ?"

"I kiss— **Hal** kisses Jack," Robin said. "It's, uh . . . You know, so it's clear that he's the pursuer."

"Not some innocent victim of Jack's insidious gay agenda," Jules said.

Robin actually managed to laugh. "Yeah."

"So, um, you must've given some thought to the, uh, blocking. That's what you actors call it, right? Blocking?"

"Yeah," Robin said, scratching behind his ear. "Screen kisses are different than, you know, real-life kisses—you want to be able to show the emotion, so you kind of tip your head back and keep your face open. . . ." He tilted his head to demonstrate. "Either that, or the cinematographer puts the camera lens right in the middle of it, and . . . Either way, it's bizarre."

"So how are you going to do it?" Jules persisted. "What kind of kiss is it? Is it, like, lunging? Zero to sixty in a flash, or . . . ?"

"We've got one like that in a later scene," Robin said. "This one, the one we're doing tomorrow, is sweet. Very romantic. Tender. At least it is when it starts. By the time we fade to black, it's pretty, um . . . **Hungry,** I guess is a good word for it. Starving, actually, because here's this guy who's been sitting on his sexuality for, like, seven years. At least that's how I'm, um, planning to play it."

"Well, okay," Jules said.

Robin didn't comprehend. "Okay?"

"I'm ready when you are."

Robin laughed. Then stopped. Swallowed. "Really? I don't know. . . ."

"This is why you came here, right? And you're always saying I should play Jack. So . . . I'm Jack. What's my line?" Jules asked. He knew he was playing with fire, but he so didn't give a shit. "What's the dialogue right before the kiss?"

"I don't know."

"How could you not know?"

"Well, because it's Jack's line, not Hal's. Hold on." Robin dug in his backpack. He'd actually brought a dog-eared copy of the script and flipped to a heavily marked-up page. "The scene takes place in Jack's room. Hal's there. He's brought a coupla bottles with him, and they're drinking and talking. What if–ing. You know. What would you be doing right now if you were back home? What would you choose if you were given three wishes? And that's when Jack fesses up. He doesn't want to go home. He wants to stay there, in Paris, with me—Hal—forever.

"I'm too drunk to run away," Robin continued, "but not drunk enough to pretend I don't understand. And I say . . ." He read from the script, " 'What's it like? Not being afraid someone will find out? Not being afraid to admit it, even to yourself?' And you say . . ."

He pointed to the script, and Jules read the line. " 'I guess I was more afraid of dying without ever having lived. I am who I am. There's a peace that comes with acknowledging that.' "

"And I get really quiet and say," Robin said, " 'If I knew—for sure—that I was going to die, I'd spend my last days locked in here with you.' And I laugh, but it's not because anything's particularly funny. In fact, it's so fucking pathetically sad—what I'm thinking, what I'm figuring on doing. See, it's right after this scene that I—that **Hal** goes and volunteers for that suicide mission into Germany. But right now he tells Jack, 'I'd gladly die for that—for a chance to really live, even just for a day or two.' And that's when he does it." He cleared his throat.

Jules nodded. And waited.

Robin cleared his throat again. "Okay." He looked at the script again for a moment, then put it down. He closed his eyes, took a deep breath, and let it out in a rush. When he opened his eyes, it was wild. He was still Robin, but there was a calmness to him that Jules recognized as belonging to someone else. To Hal.

"I'd gladly die for that," Robin said. It was Hal's line, in Hal's voice, with its soft southern accent. "For a chance to really live, even just for a day or two . . ."

There was such emotion in his eyes, such love. It took Jules' breath away.

Or so he thought.

Until Robin leaned down and kissed him.

It was the sweetest, most gentle kiss he'd ever shared, and not only did it **really** take his breath away, but it also stopped time.

Then Robin pulled back, just a little, just enough to meet Jules' eyes, to look down at Jules' face, his mouth, before he lowered his head to kiss him again.

All hesitation was gone, then, as Robin licked his way into Jules' mouth, as Jules melted into his arms. Melted and then, God, **melted** was so not the right word for it. He had his arms around Robin, too, wanting to get close, closer. He was kissing him back, harder now, deeper, Jesus . . . He could taste Robin's hunger and longing and more, God, he wanted more, he wanted . . .

This. He wanted this. Please, God, he wanted this man, he wanted this to be real, not some game of pretend he was playing with another goddamn fucking actor.

Jules pulled back. He broke the kiss, wrenching himself out of Robin's arms.

"Sorry," Robin said. "Sorry! Shit! Sorry, I didn't

mean to . . . Fuck, that was way too much. . . . That was my fault."

"No," Jules said. "No, it wasn't. Too much I mean. It was just a little . . . too much. Yeah, I guess it was. Considering . . ."

"I get lost in the part, and—"

"Yeah," Jules said. "I was kind of picking that up. I think you probably shouldn't rehearse this scene with Adam, because he won't stop when he should, um, stop."

"Right," Robin said. "Yes, I'll definitely make sure . . ."

"Other people are around," Jules suggested.

"Yeah. Yeah. Thanks. Good." Robin's hand was shaking as he reached up to push his hair back from his face.

Jules put his own hands in his pockets so he didn't act on his urge to reach for him. "I don't know if this is going to make it better or worse, but . . . That was amazing. It was absolutely, unbelievably, fucking amazing."

God, he could tell from Robin's face that his words made it worse.

The hotel phone rang—his wake-up call. Perfect timing.

Robin practically jumped out of his skin at the shrill sound.

Jules picked up the receiver and dropped it back into the telephone's cradle.

"I'm having dinner in the restaurant downstairs," he said, trying to be nonchalant, trying to ignore the fact that Robin was inching toward the door, ready to run away as hard and as fast as he possibly could. "If you don't have plans, I'd love it if you could—"

"That sounds great," Robin said, surprising the hell out of him. "Thank you, I'd appreciate the chance to, you know, do more research."

Research.

Jesus.

"Well, okay," Jules said. "Let me grab my tie." He also needed to check his face for beard burn in the bathroom mirror, put a little lotion on if he needed it.

Yeah, he needed it.

Robin did, too.

Jules brought his moisturizer with him out of the bathroom, squirted some into Robin's hand. "Chin," he said.

Robin looked into the mirror on the closet door. "Oh, fuck," he said, looking more closely. "God, I never thought of that. Thanks." He let out a laugh, and it was just on the verge of hysterical. "See, I'm learning as I go. This is valuable information."

Right.

Valuable information.

No doubt about it, as far as "I'm not really gay" excuses went, now Jules had heard them all.

"You know that I take this very seriously, sir," Cosmo told Tommy Paoletti as they stood on the beach. "And the opportunity to make this kind of money is . . . I appreciate it very much."

"I know," Tom told him.

"I'm just not . . . comfortable," Cosmo said, "being on the payroll for this particular job."

"There are lots of other—" Tom started.

"I'm not looking for reassignment," Cosmo told him. "I intend to, um, stay as close to Jane—Mercedes—as possible until we catch this asshole. And, uh, afterward, too. . . ."

Tom laughed as he looked out at the sunset. "Okay. I'm finally getting the picture. It took me a while, but . . . Okay. Holy shit, but okay."

"I need to apologize," Cosmo said. "For behaving in a less than professional—"

"You don't need to—"

"I do," Cosmo insisted. "The client should be off limits, and I failed to . . . I have no excuse. But Jesus God, I'm smitten, sir."

Tom carefully kept his eyes on the horizon as he nodded. "I can see that." He was silent for a few moments. "You know, Cos, when Kelly told me she was pregnant—it was unplanned—I thought I'd reached a point in life where nothing could surprise me anymore. The impossible could happen—it **had** happened too many times—so just throw any and all expectations and assumptions out the window and enjoy the ride." He turned to face Cosmo and held out his hand. "This is a surprise, but it's like the one Kelly gave me—one of the nicer ones. I wish you the best, Chief. I wish you'd stay as part of the team, though. I don't have any problem with what you and the client do on your time as long as you're discreet."

But Cosmo shook his head as he shook Tom's hand.

"I don't want there to be any misunderstandings between Jane and me. She's . . . amazing. I want to make
sure she knows that I'm serious."

Tom laughed at that. "Because you're so frivolous
the rest of the time?"

Cosmo smiled. "She doesn't know me that well
yet. I just . . . have to do it this way. I'm sorry,
Tommy."

Tom slapped him on the back. "You're forgiven."

"Thank you," Cosmo said. "Now. With that said, I'd
like to be kept in your information loop. Because I am
going to find this motherfucker before he hurts Jane."

Robin was freaked. Out.

He sat in the hotel restaurant, across the table from
Jules, pretending that he wasn't on the verge of a nervous breakdown. He couldn't even read the menu. He
just sat there, holding on to it, while Jules asked the
waitress about the seafood special.

He held the menu until his drink came, and then,
after ordering somewhat randomly—a salad, a steak—
he held on to his drink. "I'm going to need another
pretty soon," he told the waitress.

"Please don't be offended," Jules said after she left
to place their orders. "I wouldn't say this if I didn't care
about you, but you may want to consider the possibility that you have a problem with alcohol."

"Yeah, but no," Robin said. "See, Hal drank a
lot, so . . ."

Jules gazed across the table at him. "That's why you
drink? Because Hal drank?"

Robin focused on his glass, the ice, the whiskey. It was too unnerving to gaze back into Jules' eyes. It was even more unnerving to find himself staring at Jules' mouth, remembering what it had been like to . . . "Yeah."

Jules laughed. "That's such a load of shit, and you know it."

"You said yourself that you're not an actor," Robin pointed out. "You have no idea what it takes to get into character, to actually become someone else. You have to give up part of yourself so that the person you're playing can really come alive."

How could they just sit here, talking like this, after . . . Was Jules still thinking about it, replaying it, remembering?

"So, in order to play Hal," Jules asked, "you're giving up the sober part of yourself?"

Kissing a man was different from kissing a woman, but not that different. Although the embrace—**that** was different. Jesus Christ. Robin had become aroused almost instantly. And Jules certainly must've known it—how could he not have?

And God, he was still . . . He still wanted . . .

Something. He definitely wanted something, he just wasn't sure what.

"Are you all right?" Jules asked, concern in his eyes. Concern and kindness. "You want to talk about it?"

The waitress chose that moment to bring over their salads, and Jules smiled up at her, thanking her, watching until she was out of earshot before he spoke again.

"You're freaking because you got turned on, and

you know that I know it," Jules guessed correctly. "Why is that such a bad thing? I'm flattered. I'm actually feeling pretty good about myself right now—sexy enough to rev up the straight guy, you know? And if you're worried that I'll say something to—"

Robin couldn't keep it in any longer. "Do you think I'm gay?"

Jules didn't answer for several long seconds. "That's not a question I can answer for you," he finally said. "What I do know is that you've been spending a lot of time doing, well, something that feels an awful lot like pursuit. You know. Of me."

Pursuit? "What, a straight guy can't be friends with—"

"I have plenty of straight friends," Jules told him. "I'd be happy to file you in my address book under friends, comma, straight. But you keep giving me signals that say you aren't going to be happy if I do put you there, so . . ." He shrugged.

"I love women," Robin said.

"I do, too," Jules said. "I just don't want to have sex with them."

"Have you ever . . . ?" Robin asked.

"Yeah," Jules said. "When I was in college. With a friend. Experimenting."

"And, what?" Robin asked. "It didn't work? You couldn't . . . ?"

"Oh, I could, and I did. It was sex," Jules told him. "Yee-hah, you know? I was nineteen. What was that line? 'I would have fucked a tree if I could've.' " He laughed. "She was hot. She was wonderful, too. I loved her to pieces, but . . . something was definitely missing for me."

Missing for me . . . missing for me, for me, for me . . .

"Still—" Jules kept going, as if he didn't hear the reverberation, as if he were completely unaware of the profound significance of the words that had just left his lips. "I probably would've tried to fake my way through a hetero relationship, marriage even, if I didn't have the parents I had."

Something was definitely missing for me.

Jules broke a breadstick in half, ate a piece while Robin downed the rest of his drink and tried to listen.

"They were really supportive of me," Jules continued. "My dad managed to be . . . Well, he died when I was fourteen, which was rough, but . . . He wrote this letter that my mom gave me when I came out—you know, when I first told her I was gay. Turned out they both knew before me." He laughed. "I must've been a flaming five-year-old."

Something was definitely missing for me.

"But they loved me. They made me feel safe and secure about who I was, and just kind of sat back and waited to see if I'd figure it out. When Dad got the news that he needed to have the triple bypass, he, uh, pretty much knew his chances of coming out of surgery were slim, so he wrote this letter to me, telling me that he knew I was gay, and that although he wouldn't have wished this for me—because it meant my life was going to be tougher than he'd wanted—he also knew that this was the way God made me, this was the way

I was supposed to be. He wrote that he loved me, he would always love me. And he hoped I'd find someone wonderful to spend my life with, maybe even have the chance to get married and have a family of my own someday."

Something was definitely missing for me.

There were tears in Jules' eyes, and he forced a smile, blinking them back. "Yikes. Sorry, I don't talk about him very often. I just thought you might want to know that coming out doesn't always have to be traumatic. Like it was for Adam—getting kicked out of the house when he was sixteen. His father still doesn't talk to him. I can't imagine that. I can't imagine having a child and . . . What's your father like?"

Robin shook his head. "I don't really know him." He sent Robin a birthday card every year—on Janey's birthday.

As he watched, Jules ate more of his salad. "What would he say, do you think, if you told him you were, you know." He met Robin's eyes. "Gay."

Something was definitely missing . . . All his life, something had been missing.

But it hadn't been missing when he'd kissed Jules.

Robin had to hold on to the table with both hands.

"You okay?" Jules asked.

Robin shook his head, no.

Jules put down his fork. "You want to go? We can go. We should probably go." He looked across the room, searching for their waitress.

Robin had had sex more times with more women than he could count. Beautiful women. Hot women.

Smart, sexy, successful women who could have written how-to books on keeping men satisfied in bed. He'd started when he wasn't quite fourteen, and by age twenty-four he'd had more sex than most men had in their entire lives.

And yet it all paled in comparison to that amazing, incredible, mind-blowing kiss he'd shared less than an hour ago.

With another man.

Robin stood up. "I'm sorry, I have to—"

Jules stood, too. "Sweetie, wait for me."

"I can't." He bolted for the door.

Jules caught up with him, caught his arm. "Robin—"

"Don't touch me!" Jesus, he'd shouted that. In the middle of a restaurant.

Everyone was staring. The waitress and maître d' both hurried over. "Sir?"

Jules held his hands out, low in front of him, as if confronting a dangerous animal. "It's going to be okay. You're going to be okay. I promise you. You just need to slow down, take some time—take a lot of time, take as much as you need—to figure things out. You know, it's possible that you're going to be happier when—"

Robin did the only thing he could do—he turned and ran away.

Because after kissing him, Jules obviously thought—no, he didn't think, he **knew**—that Robin was gay.

Sophia Ghaffari was even prettier than Cosmo had remembered.

As he got himself a cup of coffee and carried it back with him into the beach house's spacious living room, Kelly Paoletti widened her eyes at him. Her unspoken message was very clear. **Why aren't you talking to her?**

He just shook his head.

He'd stayed silent through four slices of pizza, biding his time before he could make his excuses and leave, eager to get back to Jane's.

To Jane.

Murphy's wife, Angelina, was telling a story about the rustic hotel where they'd stayed in St. Thomas on their honeymoon. When it had rained, a river flowed through their room, from the bathroom and out the door.

She was a perfect match for Murph, quick to laugh, with a sparkling smile and long, dark hair. She was as tall and as full-figured as Jane, too—no petite little thing to be doubly dwarfed by Murphy's bulk.

". . . palmetto bugs the size of baseballs," Angelina was saying. "I swear, there was one with two heads. We slept with the light on in the bathroom, because the thought of running into Push-me-Pull-you Junior in the middle of the night was just too awful."

"Two heads?" Sophia was skeptical.

"One on each end," Angelina insisted. She looked at Murphy. "Back me up here."

"I saw it, too," Murphy said. "Although I'm still not sure it wasn't two separate bugs doing some kind of kinky bug thing."

"Bugs don't have sex," Angelina said. "Okay? Let's

start right there. They lay eggs. It's all very noninteractive."

Kelly motioned for Cosmo to join her in the kitchen. Good timing.

"I have to go," he told her as the door swung shut behind them.

She was stunned. "What's wrong with you? This is fate—you coming here to talk to Tom on the same day that I just happen to invite Sophia—"

"You just happened to?" he asked.

"Well, I may have overheard Tom leaving a message, asking you to come out here tonight. . . ."

Cosmo hugged her—which was very weird. It was like hugging with a basketball between them. "I love you," he told her. "Thank you so much, but . . . You know how I said I really didn't like Jane—Mercedes Chadwick? Well, I got to know her, and . . . She seems to like me, too. . . ."

Her eyes widened, and she laughed. "Really? Oh, my God, she called here tonight, looking for Tom."

"She did?"

Kelly nodded. "It was a little strange. The phone call. I mean, I'm sure she's nice, but . . ."

Cosmo took out his cell phone, dialed Jane's number. "She called me, too, while I was talking to Tommy, but when I called her back, I couldn't get through."

"Are you sure she's . . ." She paused, then said tactfully, "You told me once that you seem to attract women who are, well . . . You used the word **freaks.**"

"No," he said, laughing. "She's not like that. What I meant was . . ." His phone was having trouble finding service. Cosmo moved a few feet to the left. Much better. "Most women are . . ." He searched for the right word. "Cautious around me. Sometimes it seems like the only women who, you know, try to, um, meet me have an issue or two or maybe a slightly nasty streak or . . . But Jane's . . . You'd like her."

Kelly didn't seem convinced.

Cos tried again. "I can talk to her, Kel. I've . . . told her things I've never . . ." He shook his head.

"I just don't want you to get hurt."

"Yeah, me, too." He dialed Jane's number again and it finally rang.

Out in the living room, the conversation had moved from bug sex to Angelina's pictures from their trip.

Kelly pushed open the door and poked her head out of the kitchen. "I want to see them."

"They're in the car. Are you really sure . . . ?" Angelina said as—shit—Jane's cell service bounced him over to her voice mail.

"Yes. Get 'em," Kelly told her. "I'll be right out." She turned back to Cosmo, who was closing his phone. "No luck?"

He shook his head as the screen door screeched open and banged shut as Angelina went outside. "I already left a message. I don't want to, you know, inundate her. Two messages inside a half hour . . . Look, I have to go," he said again. "Before the pictures come back inside. Thanks for the pizza and, well . . ."

"The misguided matchmaking?" she finished for him, and the kitchen window shattered with a crash.

Gunshot!

Two of them, three . . .

Cosmo grabbed Kelly. What the **fuck**?

There was screaming, the screen door slapping, shouting—Murph's voice, **"No!"** as he raced outside.

Four gunshots, five!

Tom's voice: "Kelly!"

Cosmo already had her on the floor, careful of her pregnant girth, shielding her. "In the kitchen!" he shouted. "Kelly's safe!"

Murphy was still screaming, "No! **No! Angelina!**"

"What happened?" Kelly said, her voice shaking. "Vinh. My God, is Vinh . . . Cosmo, where's Tom?"

"We need an ambulance!" Tom roared, his voice coming from the front of the house. "Now! Cosmo!"

"Stay down," Cos ordered Kelly. "Stay on the floor—do you understand?"

"For God's sake, I'm a doctor. You have to let me help!" she shouted back at him, struggling to get free.

Sophia burst in, blood on her shirt, skidding on the broken glass. "Where's the phone?"

She saw it before Cosmo did, nearly ripping it off the wall in her haste to dial 911. "Murph and Angelina have both been—" The operator must've picked up because she cut herself off. "We need an ambulance and the police," he heard her say as he ran for the front door, and oh, Jesus God . . . "There's been an attack, a shooting," Sophia reported. "We have two people seriously wounded. You need to get here fast."

———

"What was that?" Jane asked as she followed Pacific Coast Highway north. Explosions. A bunch of them, in a row.

"Gunshots," Decker said. "Drive. **Drive!**"

He stomped on her foot, pressing it down on the gas pedal, and the car lurched forward.

Except then she saw Cosmo's truck, parked near Murphy's and . . .

She jammed on the brake with her left foot, because, oh God, oh dear God, Murphy was in the driveway, lying beside someone else. Tom was kneeling next to him, or had he fallen there? Had he been hit, too? She couldn't tell. All she could see was blood. So much blood.

Please, God, don't let that be Cosmo lying there with Murphy.

Jane threw the car into park and opened the door and ran toward them. "Cosmo!"

"What's she doing here?" Tom was incredulous as he looked up at Jane.

But Cosmo wasn't on the ground. He was coming out the door of the house, a hugely pregnant woman on his heels.

"Oh, Jesus God!" he said as he saw Jane, saw Murphy. "Get down!" he shouted at her. He spun to face the pregnant woman. "Get back in the house!"

Murphy was holding on to a woman. A woman whose long dark hair was matted with blood. Oh, God, oh, **God . . .** The woman was dead. How could she be anything but dead?

"Kelly, get down or get inside!" Tom roared, and the pregnant woman dropped to the ground, crawling toward him on her hands and knees.

Decker was several steps behind Jane, and he pulled her down to the pavement, shielding them with Murphy's car.

Her knees were in a puddle of blood.

"I'm now certain," Decker told her, "that the threat is real. Keep your head down!"

"Angelina," Murphy gasped, blood flecking his lips.

"Sophia! Grab the first-aid kit from under the kitchen sink!" shouted the pregnant woman—Kelly—who was next to Tom. "Help me," she ordered him.

"God damn it," he said to her. "You're pregnant."

"What, you just noticed that?" she shot back at him. "I'm a doctor—I'm not going to sit inside and let them die."

"Come on, man," Cosmo said to Murphy. "You've got to let go of Angelina so we can help her." He was down on his knees, fearlessly helping Tom and Kelly try to stop the bleeding. "Where's that first aid kit?"

"Murph," Tom said. "Did you see where the shooter was?"

"One," Murphy whispered. He touched his watch.

"Ambulance is on its way." A blond woman came out of the house carrying a plastic case—a first aid kit—that she gave to Tom as she ducked down behind the car, too. She was covered with blood. She had to be Sophia. God, had she been shot as well? "The emergency operator wants everyone inside as quickly as possible. Can we move them?"

"Are you hurt?" Decker asked. He was looking at Sophia.

"Shooter's probably gone by now," Cosmo said.

"What can I do?" Jane asked. "Is there anything I can do?"

"Stay down," Cos barked at her.

Distant sirens. Approaching . . .

"Angelina . . ."

"She's all right, Murph," Cosmo said. "She's hurt but she's going to be all right. She's strong—you know she's strong." He looked up, met Jane's eyes briefly. "You've got a pretty nasty chest wound, man. You've got to lie still or you're going to drown yourself."

Oh, dear God . . .

"Sophia," Decker said, grabbing the blonde's arm and all but shaking her. "Are you hurt? Were you hit?"

She shook her head, no. Smiled tremulously. "Nice to see you, Deck. It's been a while."

Decker seemed to know Sophia quite well. Apparently everyone did. As Jane watched, he pulled her into his arms and hugged her, hard. But only for a second, because then he was over next to Tom and Cosmo, helping them.

The sirens were getting louder.

"What can I do?" Jane asked again.

"Get inside the house," Tom ordered. "Sophia, get Mercedes inside. I need someone to update the emergency operator."

Sophia grabbed Jane's arm, pulled her to her feet, and hustled her toward the door. She was stronger than she looked.

"Keep her covered!" Cosmo shouted.

"Deck, when the ambulance arrives, I need you with me." Jane could hear Tom's voice, even from inside the house. "The shooter was positioned at about one o'clock, probably somewhere across the street."

Sophia picked up the telephone, which was off the hook and dangling from the wall.

"We've got two multiple gunshots—the worst is a chest wound and a head wound," Sophia told the operator. "The female looks bad. We can't move her."

"Oh, God, no," Jane whispered.

From outside, Tom bellowed, "Did somebody call Jules Cassidy?"

At last. Something she could do. Jane got out her cell phone—which was beeping. She'd just received voice mail from Cosmo. She cleared the screen and dialed.

CHAPTER NINETEEN

Robin puked in the bushes alongside the Malibu beach house for the second time.

It was the bloodstains on the driveway that got to him.

Or maybe it was the two gin and tonics he'd chugged on an empty stomach.

After sucking face with his gay lover.

Okay, well, maybe that was an exaggeration. Jules had made it pretty clear that he wasn't interested in being part of what he called Robin's science project. What he **was** interested in, Robin wasn't sure.

After he'd run out of the hotel restaurant, Jules had chased him down to tell him that Vinh Murphy and his wife had been shot in an attack meant to kill Jane.

The drive up here to Malibu had been tense. Jules had spent most of it on the phone, thank God, talking to the local police, the local FBI, and even his boss, the magnificent Max Bhagat, who was back in D.C.

The reality of what had happened—someone had tried to kill his sister—didn't hit until Robin saw the blood.

At which point he'd had an intimate conversation with the shrubbery.

He'd eventually gone inside to see Janey, but she was bustling around the beach house, cleaning up the broken glass and helping Kelly, Tom's very pregnant wife, pack up her things. Some friends—a man who looked like his nose had been broken once a year starting when he was fourteen, and his much younger, much prettier wife—were helping, too. They were going to take Kelly back home to San Diego.

The vacation is definitely over when the dinner guests get gunned down in the driveway.

Robin had explored until he found the liquor cabinet. He poured himself a tall one, then leaned against the wall and watched for a while. Mrs. Broken Nose—her name was Teri—had quite the trim little body. Under normal circumstances, she was the type he would've made a play for—cute as hell and married to an ogre.

He'd spent some time mentally undressing her, but Mr. Broken Nose didn't give him a second glance. The man was not worried by Robin's obvious attention at all.

No doubt he'd picked up a huge gay vibe from him. God.

Robin had gone back outside, where the sight of that blood on the driveway had sent him to the bushes for round two of tonight's puke-a-thon.

Jules was standing with a group of men—police, members of Troubleshooters Incorporated, and other FBI agents. He was clearly in charge, but he glanced over as Robin came up for air, and he excused himself.

And came over. "You okay?"

"Yeah," Robin told him, sitting on the steps that led into the house. He took a solid slug of whiskey to rinse his mouth, but it seemed such a waste to spit it out, so he swallowed.

"Easy there," Jules said. "You sure that's going to help?"

Robin was sure of nothing anymore. It was all he could do not to start crying.

Jules sighed and sat down next to him. "Maybe you should go back inside."

And risk having Janey fold him up and pack him in one of the Paolettis' suitcases? No thanks.

"How did this happen?" Robin asked, clinging to his glass. "How did this guy know Janey was going to be here?"

"He didn't, sweetie." Jules' eyes were so sympathetic, so warm and kind. "Best we can figure, he followed Murphy when he left your house this morning, caught sight of Angelina, and followed them up here, thinking she was Jane. From a distance, someone could make that mistake."

"You're kidding, right?" Robin said. "Isn't Angelina black?"

"She's Latino," Jules said. "She's got slightly less olive in her skin tone than Jane. They really do look quite a lot alike."

"That's so fucked up," Robin said. "I mean, just because they look alike . . ."

"Yeah," Jules said.

"Is she going to die?" Robin asked. "Angelina?"

"She's in surgery right now. She's pretty badly hurt."

"And Murphy?"

"Same," Jules told him. "Although he doesn't need brain surgery to pull through, so his chances are slightly better. Still . . ." He shook his head.

Robin couldn't hold it back any longer. He put his head down and started to cry. That could've been Jane. As it was, Murphy and his wife . . . God, they'd just gotten married. Murphy had told Robin about Angelina. "My woman," he'd called her. She did combination security and counseling at some kind of teen center. Murphy made her sound like a cross between Mother Teresa and Lara Croft. And now, because some nutjob didn't like the movie he and Janey were making, she was having brain surgery.

"It's times like this that being gay sucks," Jules said quietly. "Because even if you wanted me to, I couldn't put my arm around you. Not here, in a work situation." He stood up, putting distance between them, as if, despite his words, he needed help resisting temptation. "I shouldn't have brought you up here. That was a mistake. You didn't need this on top of everything else. I'm really sorry, Robin."

He started toward the other agents and officers.

"Jules."

He stopped. Turned back.

"I don't know what I want," Robin admitted.

Jules gave him a tired smile. "I do," he said. "For the first time in years, I know exactly what I want."

As he turned and walked away, Robin could've sworn he heard him laugh and say, "Adam who?"

When Cosmo went inside the beach house, Jane was washing the dishes.

She was standing right in front of the kitchen window.

He grabbed her and pulled her into the other room, dripping soap bubbles across the floor as he asked from between gritted teeth, "Are you **out** of your fucking **mind**?"

She stared at him, wide-eyed. "I'm just trying to help."

"How?" he asked. "How does it help if you die now, too?"

"The curtains were closed!"

"They're thin—you can see through them from the street."

"I didn't know," she whispered, her eyes filling with tears.

Cosmo pulled her into his arms and held her tightly. "Christ, Jane, what are you doing here?"

"I'm so sorry," she said, clinging to him. "I'm such an idiot." She started to cry. "When I drove up and saw Murphy, and I didn't see you, and I thought . . ." She pulled away from him, wiping her face, her eyes, using sheer will to stop her tears. God damn, but the woman hated for anyone to see her cry. "Tell me you didn't know Sophia was going to be here."

Sophia? Holy God. "I didn't," Cos told her. "Is that really what you thought? That I was—"

"Are you really quitting?" she asked.

How the hell had she found that out? He had been

planning to tell her tonight. "Yeah," he said. "I am. Because it felt wrong to be paid to protect my, well, my girlfriend. If you don't mind that label. I hope you don't. I hope I'm not assuming too much. . . ."

She didn't understand. "So instead, you're just going to leave?"

"I was hoping you'd be okay with me moving in," Cosmo explained. "Not into your room," he quickly added. "Into your house. Into, you know, the room I've been using."

"But I thought you needed the money."

"Not as much as I need you to be safe." He steeled himself against the new flood of tears in her eyes. "Jane, what were you thinking tonight? You shouldn't have left your house. You should have waited for me to call you back. It was reckless and . . . stupid. I know you're not stupid."

"I didn't think it was real," she said, wiping her eyes before her tears could fall. "The threat. Not really. I didn't . . . I wanted . . . I made sure there was a garage. You know. Here. So I wouldn't have to walk outside."

"It sure as hell looked like you were walking outside to me. Stupid thing number two—leaving the car when you knew there was a shooter in the area. Decker said he told you to drive but you stood on the brake. What the fuck? Excuse me, but—"

"I thought . . ." She turned away.

"It's not just yourself you're putting in danger when you don't follow the instructions of the trained professionals who have been hired to keep you alive," Cosmo said. She had to hear this. "You want to take a stroll down Rodeo Drive in broad daylight even though we tell you not to? Well, when you go ahead and do it anyway, we're going to be right beside you. You won't be the only one to die."

She stood with her head down, arms wrapped around herself as if she were cold. "I'm so sorry," she whispered.

He reached for her, putting his arms around her, but it was like hugging a stone statue. "This isn't your fault," he told her. "What happened tonight. You know that, right?"

She breathed a laugh of disbelief. "Yeah, right."

"It's not—"

"You know, I am stupid," she said, stepping out of his arms. "I thought you weren't calling me back because . . . I thought you were quitting and you were running off with Sophia. I thought you weren't ever going to call me back." She laughed. "God, I'm an idiot."

Christ, she was serious. "Janey, how could you think, after last night, that I'd—"

"It was too perfect," she said. "Nothing's that perfect. Although God knows I try to be. . . ." Again she fought her tears and won. "Has Decker called from the hospital?"

"Just to say Angelina's gone into surgery. They're trying to stabilize Murphy a little bit more."

"She looks like me." Jane turned to look at Cosmo, anguish in her eyes. "You said it's not my fault—"

"It isn't."

"—but he shot Angelina because he thought she was me, didn't he?"

"Yeah," he told her. "That's what we think."

"At first I thought it was my fault because he'd somehow followed me," she said, "but Tom told me he—the gunman—was in place, probably in the neighbor's yard, before I even left Hollywood. That he must've followed Murphy. So okay, that's good. Angelina and Murphy aren't going to die because I was jealous and stupid, but . . . It's still my fault."

"It's your fault that someone crazy picked up a gun and shot people? You can't take responsibility for that." Cosmo could see that she didn't believe him.

She hugged herself again. "If Angelina dies . . ."

Cosmo reached for her. "Janey, it's really okay if you cry."

But it wasn't, because Tommy Paoletti came in. "Excuse me. I'm sorry. . . ."

Jane pulled away from Cosmo, wiping her face. "Any news?"

"Not from the hospital, no," Tom said. But Cosmo could tell there was something, and it wasn't going to be good.

"We were right about the shooter," Tom continued. "He was firing from that open window across the street. And you're going to love this, Cos. We've got four different sightings of your mystery vehicle in this area this evening."

"Oh, my God," Jane said.

"The truck?" Cosmo asked.

"The Pontiac Catalina—a white wreck with a peeling black soft-top. It really stood out in this town."

That didn't make sense. After thinking about it pretty much nonstop for days, Cosmo had recently become convinced that the truck was the vehicle they should be looking for.

"One woman reported seeing it parked on her street, about a quarter mile from here, during the time of the shooting," Tom told them. "She was keeping an eye on it—if it was still there in the morning, she intended to call the police."

"Anyone get plates?" Cosmo asked.

"No. And no one could give a description of the driver, either." He looked at Jane, and Cosmo could tell from the expression on his face that there was more news, but Tommy was pretty sure Jane wasn't going to like it.

"Whatever it is, sir," Cosmo told his former CO, "she needs to know."

"Yeah," Tom said. "Jane, the shooter left behind a note. He's our e-mailer."

"Oh, fuck," she breathed. "You mean, Mr. Insane-o?"

"Yeah," Tom said. "He was in the house across the street—he fired from a second-story bedroom window. A rifle shell casing was left in the room. On top of the note. I suspect ballistics is going to prove that both the bullets and that casing came from the Chertok murder weapon."

Oh, fuck, indeed.

"The note was an e-mail," Tom said. "You know,

printed from a computer with an e-mail heading? It was sent to Jane's e-mail address, from our guy's Hotmail account. Today's date. Subject line said, 'Remember me?' "

And the e-mail itself? Cosmo took Jane's hand, and she clung to him.

Tom didn't look happy. "The message said, 'Oops, thought it was you.' "

"What?" Jane was horrified.

She wasn't the only one.

"He's saying, what? That he knew it wasn't me?" she continued. "That's what that means—oops? That it wasn't mistaken identity, that he shot Angelina—that he planned to shoot Angelina—as part of his sick game? I mean, he had to plan it—he'd printed that e-mail out in advance, right?" She looked from Tom to Cosmo, as if imploring them to tell her she was wrong.

But she wasn't. "There's more," Tom said grimly. "This is both good news and bad news. He didn't just print it out, he sent it, too. You received an electronic copy as well. And he made sure—like with the e-mail sent from that Kinkos—that we could trace the origin computer.

"To where?" Cosmo asked.

"It was sent from the **American Hero** offices at the soundstage," Tom told them, "at HeartBeat Studios."

What?

"When?" Jane asked. "Today? We had only a few people over there today."

"It **was** sent today," Tom said, "but it was programmed—scheduled to be sent—like in some kind of flash session. The sender didn't need to be present. In fact, we're pretty sure he wasn't."

"But he definitely gained access to the studio," Cosmo said. "Right? At some point? Which means he had to come through the main gate—get checked in."

"Yeah," Tom said. "But we have no idea when. The FBI's compiling a list from HeartBeat, but over the past couple weeks, thousands of people went through that gate."

"If he was at the studio . . ." Jane was terribly upset. "Why didn't he just kill me there?"

"No escape route," Cos said.

"Because he wouldn't have been able to get away," Tom clarified. "And because he really seems to like playing games."

"Shooting Angelina and Murphy is a **game**?" Jane pulled away from Cosmo. She walked out of the room and into the bathroom, shutting the door behind her. God forbid she cry in public.

Tom met his eyes. "Maybe you should get her home."

Cos nodded. As if that would help.

"We'll need to meet later," Tom said. "I want Jules Cassidy there, but he's going to be tied up, probably until the morning."

"Morning's good," Cos said. That would give him some time with Jane. Time to try to make her understand that this wasn't her fault.

Tom nodded. "I'll get the car into the garage."

"Get her brother, too, please, sir," Cos said. "If you don't mind. I want to make sure he's contained."

Tommy shot him a look. "Good luck with that."

Robin folded himself into the backseat of Janey's car for the ride back to Hollywood.

Jules had barely glanced up when he'd said good-bye—he was busy being official and investigative. Although when Robin looked out of the rear window, Jules was definitely watching their car drive away.

Holy Jesus, he needed a drink.

The Navy SEAL was driving Janey's car. He kept looking over at her as if he were worried about more than just her physical safety. She finally reached out and took his hand—well, wasn't that interesting?—as if she were the one comforting him.

"I guess you're not gay," Robin said.

Cosmo gave Robin a long, pointed look in his rearview mirror. "Guess not," he finally said.

About three miles passed before Robin spoke again. "I might be gay," he said.

Jane turned and looked at him. She was obviously exhausted, with dark circles beneath her eyes. "Are you drunk?"

"I might be drunk," he agreed, "but I don't think the being gay thing changes with blood alcohol levels. Although I could be wrong. I seem to be less gay when I'm drunk. Or maybe just more willing to fuck any-body. And by anybody, I mean women. I've never . . ." He shook his head.

"Robin, if you're playing some kind of freaky method acting game, like you are now Harold Lord all the time, 24/7, just stop, all right?"

"What if he's serious?" Cosmo asked her.

Janey rolled her eyes. "He's never serious."

"What if this time he is?" Cosmo looked into the mirror at Robin again. "What you're supposed to say is, 'So what? Gay, straight, bi—it doesn't change a thing. You're my brother and I love you.' "

Robin wanted to cry—those words coming from this big, tough sailor. Jules' voice echoed: **Coming out doesn't have to be traumatic.** "Nobody ever said anything like that to Hal. And he knew no one ever would. He would have lost **every**thing. Not just his family, but his career—his entire future."

"That must've been hard for Hal," Cosmo said quietly. "Having to face that."

Janey looked back at Robin again. "How could you be gay? Every time I turn around, you're with a different woman. You're, like, the least gay person I know." She glanced at Cosmo and smiled. "Well, except for you."

The reflective heat from that front-seat eye contact nearly scalded Robin. Well, hey now. And good for Janey. She hadn't had sex in . . . Jeez, it was probably years.

"Don't you think it's weird that I've never had a steady girlfriend?" Robin asked her. "I mean, not since middle school."

"That doesn't make you gay," Jane said. "That

makes you a selfish, commitment-shy asshole. Didn't you just have sex with my personal assistant? My very female personal assistant?"

"Yeah," Robin said. He'd been thinking about that a lot and was pretty sure he'd figured it out. "I thought I was in love with her, but I think I was just in love with the fact that she was unattainable. I couldn't have her, so I wanted her. And I was horny, too, so . . ."

"You suck," Jane said. "You are, like, the lowest scum on the bottom of the pond."

"Today I'm in love with Jules Cassidy," Robin said, mostly to see what it would sound like if he said the words aloud. It wasn't true. It couldn't be. He wouldn't let it. Besides, he had no idea what real love felt like. Everything he'd felt in the past—the intense need—always faded away too fast.

He was definitely feeling something powerful now, although it may have been indigestion from drinking whiskey on a newly emptied stomach.

All he knew for sure was that he couldn't stop thinking about that kiss. Although he supposed that didn't make him gay. Just obsessive.

"You are **so** screwed up," Janey said as he closed his eyes and relived the surprising softness of Jules' mouth, of the sensation of crisp cotton shirt beneath his hands, the hard body beneath that. . . . "I hope he stays away from you, because all you'll do is hurt him, too. He's a really nice guy, Robin. Are you listening to me?" She snapped her fingers at him. "Focus. Do **not** play your make-believe games with him. He won't know it's not real."

"Jane," Cosmo said.

"He's just being a jerk," she said. "He doesn't mean any of this."

Cosmo looked at her. He didn't say anything, he just looked, and she sighed with exasperation. "Gay, straight, bi—it doesn't change a thing. You're my brother and I love you," she rattled off, "but if you continue to mess with people I care about, you selfish prick, I will make you sorry you were born." She laughed her disdain. "Like that threat has ever stopped you before."

Well, of course not. Because he was in a perpetual state of being sorry he was born. Always so freaking dissatisfied. Always looking for something that he couldn't identify, let alone find . . .

Had he found it tonight in Jules Cassidy's eyes? **For the first time in years, I know exactly what I want. . . .**

Holy crap, what a total lose-lose situation.

Entertainment Weekly had called Robin "a sex symbol waiting to happen" and "one of Hollywood's hottest rising stars." He could take gay roles like that of Hal Lord and be thought of as "daring" and "edgy." But if he **was** gay, he'd **only** get gay roles.

He'd be stereotyped. Labeled. And eventually he'd get no roles at all.

He'd sink back into a life of obscurity. Or worse.

Pretty boy. Homo. Little faggot.

God, he remembered far too well the sheer terror as the older boys, the bigger boys, grabbed him in the middle school hallway, pushed him into the bathroom, and locked the door. They threw him to the floor, and he'd pressed his cheek against the cold tile as he cowered in the corner, flinching from their taunts, praying that they wouldn't do more than kick him. Because if they bruised his face, his father might notice and ask what had happened, and he couldn't tell him he'd gotten beat up again—he couldn't bear the shame.

Little faggot. Little faggot. Little faggot . . .

Then, almost overnight, it all changed. Jane, the least likely guardian angel on the face of the planet, had swooped down and rescued him. It took her over a year, but she got him transferred to her town, to her school district. She dressed him up, taught him how to walk and wear his hair, how to stand.

And then it was Kimberlee Novara who had taken him into the bathroom and locked the door. "Do you want me to?" she'd asked, and it never occurred to him to say no. Truth was, he didn't want to say no. He'd liked the way she made him feel. And when word spread around school that she'd done what she'd done, he was a hero. The same boys that would have beaten him up a year earlier were slapping him on the back. Inviting him to hang out after school.

Kimberlee was obnoxious and stupid and not particularly attractive, but "going out" with her didn't mean they spent a lot of time together. At least not time spent talking. When Robin went to her house, she'd take him down into her playroom and . . .

Sex was sex. And most of the time the lights were off.

Kimberlee turned into Ashley, who turned into

Brianna, who turned into Lisa, Tawanda, Jacki, Christy, Deena, Susan, Chloe, Mara . . .

And no one called him **little faggot** ever again.

How could he even consider going back to the abuse, the disrespect, the relentless fear?

Janey was probably right—he was just getting too caught up in this role. He was spending too much time as Hal. And despite his sister's casting choices, he'd somehow identified Jules as Jack. That was what this was about.

Robin wasn't gay—he was just an incredibly talented actor who truly lost himself in his part.

"Are we filming tomorrow?" he asked Jane. "Or are we shutting down production because of . . ."

She shook her head. "God, I don't know."

"Don't shut down," Cosmo said.

"It seems so disrespectful to just continue, as if—"

"It's not," Cosmo said. "If it were me in the hospital, I'd want production to continue. Don't let this guy win."

She nodded. Looked back at Robin. "Yes, we're filming tomorrow."

Ah, shit.

"All right." Robin unzipped his backpack, took out his script.

He was as ready as he'd ever be for that scene with Hal and Jack's first real kiss. But there was another scene they were filming tomorrow, too, and it had a kiss as well. Jesus, all he was doing, all movie long, was kissing fuckin' Adam Wyndham.

"I hate this movie," he said.

"Right now, I do, too," Janey said.

Tomorrow's second scene was Hal and Jack's big farewell. In it, his character gave a letter to Jack. It was sealed in an envelope upon which was written the cheery message, "Open in the event of my death."

The contents of that letter would be revealed toward the end of the movie via voice-over.

Robin flipped to that page in the script, dog-earing it. He'd read the letter several times in the morning, right before shooting the scene. Because even though the audience wouldn't hear it until later, the words Hal had written had to show on his face.

He held the script up so the page caught the glow from the headlights of the car behind them and he could read.

Dearest J., the letter started. Huh. He'd never really noticed that before. It was kind of funny, in a pathetic way. J. was what Adam called Jules.

God, he had to stop thinking about him.

By the time you read this, I will be gone.

I may be killed in battle, or a prisoner of the Germans, or safely on my way home to Alabama.

Whichever outcome fate chooses for me, the man you know and love will be dead. He must die—if not in body, then in spirit. If he does not fall in battle, I must do the deed and cast him, and you with him, my dearest, from my heart forever.

If I am truly dead, please do not grieve

for me. With you I finally knew happiness. Your love was a gift I never expected to receive. What we shared made my life complete—I left this world with no complaints.

If I should survive the war, please forgive me for not being strong enough.

Please do not write. I will not answer you. Do not come to see me. I will not know you. And you will not know me—the man you loved is gone.

The only place he will live on—and I fear his days are numbered—will be in your heart.

Respectfully,
H.

Robin's reaction, when he'd read that letter back when Janey had first shown him this script, was that Harold Lord was truly conflicted. What a terrible choice he'd had to make.

Now he wasn't so sure that the man hadn't simply been a flipping coward.

Cosmo brought a cup of tea into her bedroom.

It was enough to make Jane's eyes flood with tears. Again.

God, she was on the verge of tears at the drop of a hat. Never mind that she'd allowed herself to let loose in the shower for a solid fifteen minutes after they got home. Cosmo probably could have come into the room to discuss the weather and she'd well up and start sniffling.

"Any word from the hospital?" she asked as he set the mug on the table next to her bed.

"Not yet," he said without the slightest trace of exasperation, even though she'd asked the very same question ten minutes ago. He sat down on the edge of her bed. "Janey, it's really okay if you cry."

"No, I'm all right," she said. "I'm just . . ."

"What?" he asked, pushing a lock of hair behind her ear, his touch unbelievably gentle. "Talk to me."

Jane just shook her head. How could this be real? Guns and bullets and people getting shot—that was make-believe. It was Hollywood magic. In her world, the director would've called cut, and Murphy and Angelina would have stood up, laughing and joking, and gone to shower off all the pretend gore before joining friends for a late-night snack.

In her world, wars were fought with prop guns that didn't really fire, with bags of fake blood, with latex body parts.

In Cosmo's world, death and destruction were commonplace. Danger was a given.

Right now he was checking out the stitches in her arm, making sure she was okay. Stitches like that were nothing to a man who knew how to administer first aid to a sucking chest wound.

"We're so different," she told him.

He smiled. "I was just thinking how alike we are."

God, if he thought she was like him—brave and strong and solidly determined—she really had him fooled. Here sat another victim to the famous J. Mercedes Chadwick charm.

She did the only thing she could do. She made a joke. The alternative was to start crying and never stop. "Yeah, people always mistake me for a Navy SEAL."

Cosmo laughed, and she had to force back a fresh rush of tears. Which was crazy. She loved making him laugh. It was her new favorite pastime.

Except now he'd stopped laughing and was looking at her with such concern in his eyes. She reached for the mug so she didn't have to keep up the eye contact while she worked to will her latest bout of tears away.

"All this must seem so surreal," Cosmo said quietly.

"Yeah," she agreed as she took a sip of tea.

"How can I help you?" he asked.

Jane had to laugh, because—amazingly—he meant it. The most attractive man she'd ever known was offering her his complete support. She tried to imagine Victor—or any of the losers she'd dated before—uttering those words and . . . Nope. She couldn't do it.

She tried to imagine one of them giving up a well-paying job for her. Or bringing her a cup of tea. Or throwing himself in front of a bullet for her.

The thing about it was, she wasn't worth dying for. She was nothing like him—and sooner or later Cos was going to figure that out. The knowledge made her throat ache.

"Talk to me, Janey. Tell me what you need," Cosmo implored her.

She put down her mug because the tea wasn't helping, and she reached for him. "You," she said, her voice catching pathetically. "Cos, I need you."

He didn't hesitate. He kissed her.

And that was good because that meant his eyes were closed, too, and he couldn't see the tears that leaked out from beneath her eyelids.

And her ragged breathing could well be the result of passion, couldn't it? Either way, he didn't mention it as he joined her on her bed, stopping only to help her kick free from the sheet and blanket that covered her.

She reached for the light, needing total darkness, but he got there first, switching off the lamp for her.

There was a rustling sound then, just for the briefest moment, then, God, he was back, kissing her again. His clothes had vanished, and the sensation of all that smooth skin made her desperately want . . .

Yes. He knew what she wanted. She tried to wipe her eyes with her T-shirt as he helped her pull it over her head, but it was futile since her tears kept on coming.

She knew he wouldn't fail to notice her wet cheeks or the salty taste as he kissed her, but he didn't pull away, didn't stop, didn't so much as mention it. He just murmured, "It's okay, Jane. It's all right," as he kissed her again and again.

"Please." She only had to say it once. He'd already covered himself, protecting them both, and as she lifted her hips to meet him, he pushed inside her, no games, no delay.

She'd learned last night that he was an exquisite lover, possessing an incredible sensitivity, an ability to empathize that took her breath away. He was capable of turning sex into an art form.

But what she needed and wanted right now, however, was a good old-fashioned shagging.

Which was exactly what he delivered.

She let herself cry, really cry, as he rocked her, as she clung to him, as she gasped and sobbed her release.

And then he held her, just silently stroking her hair, as she cried herself out.

It was later, much later, before she realized, before she lifted her head to ask, "Did you even . . . ?"

She heard him smile in the darkness. "I'm all right," he told her. "Go to sleep."

CHAPTER TWENTY

Patty's mother wanted her to come home.

She had about a million messages on her voice mail. The phone just would not stop ringing as the story about the shooting in Malibu hit the news.

She'd dressed for the crowd of reporters that she knew would be waiting outside the studio, and she'd read a brief statement that Jane had e-mailed her. Production would continue despite last night's tragedy. Both victims of the attack remained in critical condition. Security on the lot would be increased.

Jane's message to her had been just as succinct. Help make sure the filming went smoothly today.

Not an easy assignment for her, considering Robin was here.

She'd passed him on his way down to makeup. He looked awful—another day, another hangover. What a jerk.

She wasn't sure what got into her, but she stepped in front of him, forcing him to stop.

He met her gaze only briefly. "I deserve whatever you have to say," he admitted. "I know it."

It was obvious he felt awful—or at least he was acting as if he felt awful.

She wanted him to feel worse. "My period's late," she told him, even though it wasn't true.

That did the trick. The pure horror in his eyes would've made her laugh if she weren't so angry with him.

Patty left him stammering some kind of apology. Was **I'm sorry** really the correct response to that news? Jerk.

She felt considerably cheered when one of her voice mails was from Victor Strauss. He'd called her himself, too, instead of relegating the task to his PA.

"Everyone's probably calling to see how Mercedes is doing," his message said. "But I thought I'd check on you."

He was so sweet.

It was enough to give her the strength she needed to call Wayne Ickes and ask him to stop by the studio so they could talk.

He was early, of course, knocking on the door to Jane's office, where Patty was sitting behind the desk. It was much nicer than her own, and Jane wasn't using it today.

"I was actually a little surprised you weren't on set, in the thick of things," Wayne said, sitting down across from the desk.

Patty had been for a while. But the electricity that Adam and Robin were creating for the cameras was just a little too freaky to watch. She knew it was acting, but still. "With Jane working from home," she

told him, "there's an unbelievable amount of administrative work to do."

He nodded. There was so much hope in his puppy
dog eyes as he asked, "So, what's up?"

Like she was going to say, "Wayne, the way you follow me around endlessly and pathetically is just so romantic and appealing, I've decided I can't wait another
moment. Come have sex with me behind Jane's desk."

"I owe you an apology," she said instead.

He laughed. "Uh-oh, that sounds like the intro to
the 'let's be friends' speech."

Patty nodded. "It is. I'm sorry I didn't tell you this
sooner but—"

"You want to just be friends," he finished for her.
"Even though you're not seeing Robin Chadwick any
longer?"

She laughed. "How did you know?"

"Oh, come on," Wayne said. "I saw the way you
looked at him. I also saw the way he was avoiding
you." His gaze softened. "That must really hurt, huh?"

"Actually," she said, "I'm more angry—and mostly
at myself. He's so . . . immature."

"I'm very mature," Wayne said. "I hold a very important, very grown-up job in a hospital—"

"Nice try." Patty laughed. "Seriously, Wayne, I'd
love to be friends with you."

"Friends it is," he said. "See, wasn't that easy?"

It had been. Far easier than she'd imagined. He had
such a nice smile.

"I'm already kind of on the verge of seeing someone

else," she admitted, thinking of Victor's voice mail message.

"That's good," he said. "Forget about what's-his-name."

Her phone rang. She glanced at the number. "Darn it, that's my mother," she told him. "She's, like, calling every hour. She wants me to come home. As if I would, you know?" She answered, "Hold on, Mom." She covered the receiver with her hand. "I really have to take this so that I can tell her, 'Nope, I haven't been shot yet,' " she said. "Sorry about that."

"That's okay." Wayne stood up. "Thank you for being so honest. I'll see you around."

"I'm glad you came by," she said as he shut the door behind him.

Funny thing was, she honestly meant it.

"How's Kelly?" Jane asked as Decker followed Tom Paoletti into her conference room.

"Doing well, thanks," Tom replied.

Deck knew what Tom didn't say was that he himself might never recover from last night's attack. The fact that Murphy and Angelina were in a hospital ICU, fighting for their lives, was bad enough. But having the violence of his work follow him home, putting his wife and his unborn child at risk . . . He hadn't put it into words, but Decker knew Tom was seriously shaken.

He wasn't the only one.

Jane looked exhausted. Cosmo also appeared not to

have had a lot of sleep in the past few days. He was in the corner of the room, making a pot of coffee. He nodded a greeting to Deck.

Their early morning meeting had been pushed to noon, mostly due to Jules Cassidy's busy FBI schedule.

He breezed in now. "Sorry I'm late." Jules set his briefcase down on the conference table and opened it up. He glanced around the room. "Are we all here?"

Decker did a head count. Tom, Nash, Tess, Lindsey, Dave, PJ, Cosmo, Jane, Sophia . . .

Sophia?

Decker crossed the room. "What are you doing here?" he asked her, even though he already knew.

"Replacing Murphy," she told him.

He shook his head. Unbelievable. "Considering I'm team leader, didn't it occur to you that you might want to ask me first?"

"I have fifteen minutes, tops, to do this," Jules said loudly. "So if we can all sit down?"

Decker sat next to Sophia. "This isn't going to work," he told her quietly.

"I apologize in advance for having to run out of here," Jules told them, "but I have a meeting down-town. I'm sure you're eager to hear about the ballistics report." He passed several copies of the document around. "Yes, yes, and yes. It's the same gun that killed ADA Ben Chertok in Idaho—a Remington rifle, model 700P, reportedly stolen in 1999 from a Davis T. Carter, who was living at the time in Seattle, Washington."

Decker flipped through the report. There were no surprises in it.

"There were no fingerprints on the shell casing, which was exactly what we'd expected," Jules continued. "The note left at the crime scene was printed with an older model ink-jet printer. The paper is as of yet untraceable. I doubt we'll get much from that—it's pretty standard twenty-pound-weight copy paper. No watermarks, no chocolate-doughnut fingerprint upon it. There were no prints in the house that the shooter broke into, either. So much for a quick and easy end to the case."

Sophia reached to take the report from Decker so she could look at it. She smelled impossibly good. "Murphy's my friend, too," she said quietly.

"What **do** we know?" Jane asked Jules.

He sighed. "Well, we know that whoever he is, he had or has access to your soundstage at HeartBeat, so we have his name or alias on one of our lists of cast, crew, and studio employees who've been past the front gate within the last few weeks. Unfortunately, there are thousands of names on that list.

"We're pretty sure he's good with computers—but these days that doesn't make him anything special.

"We're also pretty sure that, considering his ability to shoot," Jules continued, "—and he's either very highly skilled or a lucky novice—he's been practicing. A lot. We're compiling a list of visitors to local firing ranges, both regulars and out-of-towners. Of course, we're cross-referencing every list of potential suspects with our main list from HeartBeat. And we may find nothing if he's driving out to do his target practice in the desert." He paused. "We also know that you should not go anywhere, Jane, until we catch this guy. And you should stay away from your windows, too."

"So, what?" Jane was not happy. "I hide inside while he shoots my security team? Or my friends? Or my cast, or—"

"I'd like to suggest," Tom interrupted, "that we move you to a different location. One that's not just safer for you, but for the team as well. A hotel, for example, where we can monitor everyone coming onto or off of a floor."

"An alternative," Jules suggested, "might be for you to leave the area—the country, even. Temporarily, of course."

As Decker watched, Jane shook her head. "No. I'll go to a hotel if you really think that'll keep the security team safe. Although I have to be honest, at this point all my money is in the movie. I don't have the funds for much more than a Motel Six."

"I'll put in a request to HeartBeat," Tom said, "of course."

"Yeah," Jane said. "About that. I didn't get a chance to tell you last night, but yesterday HeartBeat was making noise about dumping me, just completely pulling all financing."

Tom sat back in his chair. "Why would they do that?"

"They want me to cut the movie out of my movie," Jane replied. "I haven't heard anything from them today, though, so . . ."

Tom nodded. "Well, we're not leaving you hanging.

We're in this to the end, whether they pay us or not." He smiled ruefully at Jane. "Please don't let HeartBeat know that."

This was supposed to be easy money. The irony here was very intense.

Jane was clearly deeply moved. "Thank you," she whispered.

"At the very least, sir, let's bring all security inside," Cosmo suggested. "We can watch the roads and the grounds from the attic windows, but we won't be such obvious targets."

"Good. And eyes open," Tom told them all. "Stay alert, even after your shift ends. Take the long route home. Let's make sure our families are safe."

If Murphy had been paying attention when he left Jane's house yesterday morning, he might have noticed that he was being followed. As team leader, Decker should have reminded him. God **damn** it.

Sophia handed him back the ballistics report. Somehow she knew exactly what he was thinking. "It's not your fault, Deck."

He just shook his head.

Jules' phone rang. "Excuse me, I have to take this," he said, standing up and moving out into the hall.

"It's not," Sophia persisted. But then she laughed softly. "You blame yourself for everything, don't you?"

He couldn't look at her. Goddamn it, Cassidy, get back in here and get this meeting moving again . . .

"You shouldn't," Sophia said. "What happened between us—"

"Should never have happened," he cut her off, forcing himself to meet her gaze. Jesus, he dreamed about those eyes, her face. . . .

That mouth.

She'd been living on the street in a third-world country, hiding from a war lord who'd put a price on her head. She'd used sex to try to distract him, fearful he was some kind of bounty hunter who would turn her in.

Usually utterly non-distractible, Decker had let things go much too far.

"It wasn't real," she told him now, her eyes so earnest as she gazed at him. "Deck, really. You've got to let it go. It didn't mean anything."

It didn't mean anything.

She had no freaking clue.

Jules came back in, pocketing his phone, saving Decker's ass. "Sorry about that. Where were we?"

"Nash and I are willing to move in here for the duration," Tess volunteered. "Dave and Decker, too. There's plenty of room." She turned to Jane. "If that's okay with you."

Jane nodded. "This is going to sound so **Charlie's Angels,** but can't we catch this guy by setting a trap? By using me as, well, bait?"

"We've already started thinking about that possibility," Jules said. He looked at Cosmo. "Easy there, you. We wouldn't use **you,** Jane, but rather someone who looks like you. A trained FBI agent wearing your clothes and a wig—"

Jane was already shaking her head. "That's unacceptable. I don't want to do that. If anyone's going to be bait, it's going to be me."

"And that's unacceptable to us," Jules told her, rummaging in his briefcase again. "I'm sorry, gang, I have to go. Obviously we're still plugging away, cross-referencing all our databases, as well as creating lists of people our analysts feel might warrant an interview."

An interview. They were going to talk to the people on that list, one by one. Knock on their front doors and ask to be allowed inside.

The FBI had to follow the rules. Warrants were necessary before houses could be searched.

But the members of TS Inc. didn't have to follow those rules. As civilians, they could use their . . . special skills to get inside houses and look for the killer. Of course, another name for "getting inside houses" was breaking and entering.

Because of that, the TS Inc. team also needed to use their "special skills" to keep from getting caught.

Jules took a file from his briefcase. "I have a list of every actor, extra, or studio employee who ever lived within fifty miles of Seattle, where the weapon used to shoot Murph and Angelina was stolen. A list of every actor, extra, etc., who ever registered a weapon." He tossed each list onto the table after he read its heading. "A list of every actor, et cetera, who has ever served in the military. A sublist of former military personnel who had sharpshooting or marksman training. And, just for shits and giggles, a list of every actor or extra who filled out costume information and claims to own their own Nazi uniform."

"What?" Tom couldn't believe that.

"Yeah," Jules said. "Does it mean anything? I don't know. I suppose owning one might come in handy if you do a lot of work in World War Two films. It doesn't necessarily mean that you goose-step in your basement or invite friends over regularly to read aloud from **Mein Kampf.** However, it did seem like something that might warrant some attention."

Cosmo was already over at the table, flipping through the pages of each of those reports. "You got a list of everyone who appears on two or more of these lists?" he asked.

"No," Jules said, "but I will absolutely get that for you. That's a good idea. I do, however, for you, Cosmo, darling-sweetie-cupcake, have two other lists—actors, extras, and studio employees who own white older model cars with a black soft-top, similar to your Pontiac mystery vehicle, as well as a list of actors, et cetera, who own a dark-colored truck with a number six in its license plate. Frankly, after your Pontiac surfaced in Malibu, I'm not sure why you're still interested in the truck, but from now on, if you want something, I'm making it a priority." He looked around at the Troubleshooters team. "No more jokes about Cosmo's mystery car or the endless search for that bullet, is that clear? In fact, I think we all owe Chief Richter a very humble apology."

He snapped his briefcase shut. "With that, I must run."

"Deck." Tom had noticed him sitting near Sophia.

"Sorry, I should have mentioned Sophia's request to help out. To fill in for—"

"I'm sorry, sir. That doesn't work for me," Decker said. "Unless you insist."

Tom was surprised, but he quickly recovered. "Of course not. You're the team leader."

Sophia wasn't happy. But before she could say anything, Decker excused himself and got the hell out of there.

Cosmo's favorite time of day for a well-executed B&E was late morning, when most people were at work and the kids were in school. But early afternoon worked well, too.

If the lock on the front door was too challenging, he'd drop through an open bathroom window, take a quick cruise around the house.

Looking for something that didn't sit right.

Searching for hiding places—good locations to stash a stolen Remington rifle and ammunition. Everything from the traditional—a loose floorboard beneath which was a hidey-hole—to the more creative—false backs built into closets—to the literary—a hole in the drywall hidden behind a poster of Sarah Michelle Gellar or Jennifer Aniston, à la Stephen King's **Shawshank Redemption.**

He was going down the list Jules Cassidy had given them—extras who owned Nazi uniforms.

It seemed as good a place to start as any. And it was significantly shorter than the other lists.

He was up to L—Carl Linderman. A good German name, but it had nothing on Richter.

Carl lived in an apartment on the first floor of an older house that was perched on a postage stamp–size lot in a neighborhood where the houses were ridiculously close together. It had been easy to get inside. The lock on his door was one that could have been compromised by a kindergartner.

Carl lived in one-bedroom, stale-aired squalor. A card table was set up in the dining area off the kitchen, along with a pair of folding chairs. A tattered sleeping bag was open on an air mattress in front of a small television set, but that was it for the furniture in the living room. In the bedroom there was another air mattress, another sleeping bag.

A couple of duffel bags were filled, but only with clothes. Standard jeans, cargo pants, T-shirts. This guy dressed a lot like him. Only there were two different sizes of clothing—one set quite a bit larger than the other. There were two people living here.

The Nazi uniform in question was cut to fit the smaller of the two. It hung in the closet, under dry cleaner's plastic. There were several other recently cleaned suits hanging there, too.

Pizza boxes, fast-food and candy wrappers, beer cans, overflowing ashtrays, and dirty laundry were everywhere.

There was nothing hidden—at least not that Cosmo found.

A telephone wire led from the outlet on the kitchen wall to the card table, as if someone had sat there using a laptop computer, accessing a dial-up Internet connection.

A copy of the shooting script to **American Hero** was on the kitchen counter, but that was it. There were no books, no magazines, no photographs, no personal items at all.

It was as if this apartment were being used only as a place to eat and sleep.

Which wasn't really that strange—lots of people came to Hollywood to become actors. They spent all their time auditioning or doing extra work, or working some pathetic low-paying day job to cover their rent.

Before he let himself out the door, Cosmo looked out the window to make sure no one was outside— that the inhabitants of the upstairs apartment hadn't just come home. Movement from behind what looked like a kitchen window in the house next door made him pause. But a closer look revealed that the window was open and what he'd seen was a curtain moving behind the screen.

He slipped out of the front door, locking it behind him.

"Who are you?" an elderly-sounding voice came from that open window. **Shit.** It had been more than a curtain moving in the breeze that he'd seen. "What are you doing here?"

One option was to run. Just book it out of there.

Another was to take advantage of someone who probably spent a lot of time noticing what went on outside of her kitchen window.

He turned to face the old woman, arranging his

face in a smile. "Carl lost his script—you know, for the movie he's in? He asked me to come by and see if he'd left it here." He held out his empty hands as he shrugged. "No luck."

"Carl," the woman repeated. "That the fat one or the skinny one?"

This was definitely a test that he had a fifty-fifty chance of failing. "Skinny," he guessed, remembering that uniform hanging in the closet.

She seemed satisfied and opened up her back door to peer out at him. "Who are you?"

"Name's Percy," he told her. "Me and Carl go way back. In fact, I came out to L.A. on his recommendation. He says he's doing real well, but you'd think if that was the case, he'd be able to afford some furniture. Dude lives like a nomad. Has he been in this place for long?"

"Just a few weeks," she told him.

"Ah, maybe that's it," Cosmo said. "No time to furniture shop. Nice meeting you, ma'am." He turned away, but turned back. "Hey, you wouldn't happen to know if he's still driving this big ol' Pontiac battle cruiser?"

She shook her head. "He's got a truck."

"Black?" he asked.

"Red," she said.

"Have a nice day," he told her. So much for that.

On to the next.

Robin sat at the bar, squinting into his seventh drink. Or was it his eighth?

He was at that point in the evening where counting became irrelevant.

"I thought I'd find you here."

Adam. Of course. Just his luck. He was still wearing his hair like young Jack's, which was disconcerting to the bit of Hal that lingered inside of Robin.

It was hard to be someone else for hours and hours and then just expect to return to normal when shooting wrapped. Robin didn't understand how some actors could just snap their fingers, reclaim their bodies, and go home after a hard day's shoot.

He needed a good six, seven drinks to calm down both himself and whoever was rattling around inside his head this month.

In this case, Harold Lord. This role was either going to kill him or bring him everything he'd always wanted.

Now, if only he could figure out just what that was. Fortune and fame as Hollywood's "hottest rising star"? Or . . .

"I've already seen way too much of you today," Robin told Adam, working hard not to slur his speech. He was good at that—not sounding drunk when he was toasted.

Adam laughed, his pretty eyes dancing. More than his hair was Jack's. Instead of his usual tight jeans and gleaming white T, he was wearing military-style pants and an army-green shirt. He balanced himself on the brass foot rail, but his boots were slippery, and he slid off, bumping into Robin. Obviously intentionally. He caught himself with a hand on Robin's leg, then draped his arm around his shoulders. "I haven't seen quite enough of you, so where does that leave us?"

"It creeps me out when you say things like that." Robin pushed him away. Although the part of Robin that was still Hal kept him from pushing Adam too hard.

"Pretend I'm Jack and you're Hal."

"No."

"I know—pretend I'm Jules."

"Leave me the fuck alone." Robin ignored Hal, pushed Adam harder.

The bartender scowled at them. "Take it outside or in the back. Fight or fuck, but don't do either while you're sitting here."

"Two more of what he's having," Adam ordered. "And keep 'em coming. We'll be good, I promise." He faced Robin, elbow back on the bar. "Come on, Robbie. It wasn't **that** bad today, was it?" He laughed. "We sure fogged up the fart's glasses."

"The director's name is Lenny," Robin said.

"Yeah, like he's your best friend. I read the trades— I know he came with the distribution deal from Heart-Beat. Did you know his claim to fame is a laxative commercial?"

"He's done a bunch of movies," Robin countered. "Look, just . . . go be negative somewhere else. He's doing fine."

The bartender delivered the drinks and Adam took one, shoving the other toward Robin. He raised the glass. "Here's to finishing what we started, hot stuff." He took a sip. Licked his lips.

Robin closed his eyes. "Get away from me."

"I'm kidding. Come on." He took another sip. "Although, seriously, can't you admit, just a little, that you enjoyed—"

"Here's how it works," Robin told him. "Hal's in love with Jack. I'm playing Hal, you're playing Jack. It's called acting."

"Why do you hang out in gay bars, I wonder?" Adam asked, obviously changing tack. "Why are you here tonight, Roberta? You had to know I'd be here, too."

It was a good question. One Robin didn't have an answer for. He'd thought about going over to the hotel where Jules was staying. Sitting in **that** bar. Both hoping Jules would come in and hoping that he wouldn't. Instead, he'd gone out with Harve and some of the other guys from makeup, and wound up here.

Where, in retrospect, yes, it made sense that Adam would find him.

Adam, whom he'd made out with for hours this afternoon, while cameras rolled. Adam, who'd taken advantage of the fact that Hal was in control to put his hands all over him.

All over him.

Hal had loved it.

Hal had gotten so freaking aroused, he'd practically embarrassed them both right there on the soundstage.

Hal, who despite eight drinks—or was it nine now? Holy Jesus, Robin was running out of fingers and Hal still would not leave him—Hal, who seemed to have retained possession of a certain part of his anatomy, was damn near ready to drop to his knees and beg for Jack to touch him like that again.

Except Jack wasn't here. Adam was.

"Okay, here's a question maybe you **can** answer, drunk boy," Adam said, finishing his drink and signaling the bartender for another. For both of them. "I couldn't help but notice that Mercedes' initials were forged—and badly, I might add—on those revised pages of script. You know, the handshake version that we filmed today."

Oops. "You noticed that, huh?" Robin said.

Adam laughed. "What, you thought maybe I wouldn't?"

"You know how HeartBeat Studios wants us to cut Jack Shelton out of the movie entirely?" Robin asked. "Obviously, one option would be to cut the Hal-Jack relationship, which is stupid, right? It's the heart of the movie. So what I've started doing—don't tell Janey— is working with the director on a 'compromise.' " He made quotation marks with his fingers. "We're writing a second version of each 'questionable' scene. This keeps Jack in the movie, but really downplays his relationship with Hal. It's become a 'friendship' instead."

"So you're cozying up to HeartBeat and rewriting your sister's movie without her knowledge?" Adam said.

"No, see," Robin said, "I'm, like, a double agent. I'm **pretending** to work with HeartBeat. We're still filming Janey's script; we're just doing this other version, too. HeartBeat thinks we're considering the changes they want—they're happy. The word leaks out to the public that we've made some changes, the shouting dies down. And maybe even this guy Janey calls Mr. Insane-o, maybe he disappears, too."

"But she doesn't know anything about this?" Adam asked.

"She's a little distracted right now," Robin told him. "What with Murphy and Cosmo."

"Oh, shit, what happened to Cosmo?" Adam was seriously upset.

"No," Robin said. "Nothing. I mean, Janey happened to him." He looked at his watch, but he couldn't read it. Not a good sign. Still, it had to be pretty late. "They're probably playing Little Red Riding Hood and the Big Bad Wolf right now. Or whatever Janey's into. I'm kind of just guessing based on the fact that we're related." Whoops, that came out sounding sort of flirty. Hal watched Adam for his reaction.

There was none. At least not to that. "God, you scared me," Adam said. "You asshole." He laughed, tossed back his drink. "Whew. I needed that. God. I thought the body count was going up or something. The thing with Murphy . . . Man. And his wife? That's bad shit."

"You should've seen the blood on the driveway," Robin said.

Adam was silent for a moment, just looking at him. "Was Jules there?" he asked. "Because that's what he does. People start shooting and bleeding and dying and stuff. Most people run in the opposite direction—he runs toward it." He shook his head. "It's crazy."

"He drove me up there," Robin said. "We were having dinner and—"

"Dinner?" Adam laughed. "Wow."

"What's that supposed to mean?"

"Nothing." Adam made eye contact again with the bartender. "No, I'm just . . . Dinner's a very big step for J. He must really like you, Robskie. I'm impressed. And isn't it cool watching him do the FBI agent thing? Very manly. It's a turn-on. And a turnoff at the same time, because, well . . . He show you his scars yet?"

Scars, plural? Jules had more than one? "During dinner?" Robin asked.

"Was it room service?"

"No."

"Okay, I'm slightly less impressed."

"I've seen one of them," Robin said. "His scars. On his back."

"Well, go J." Adam smiled at Robin, but it was tight. "And go Robbie, you devil, you. I'm proud of you, babe. Way to push the edge of your sexual envelope. Who got to be the wolf?" He wiggled his eyebrows.

Robin went to work on his new drink. "Very funny."

"I guess you got the story, then, huh? How he was shot?"

He sloshed it on the bar. "Jules was **shot**?"

"So you didn't get the story," Adam said. "It was just sex, huh? No talking? Why, J., you nasty beast."

"We didn't have sex," Robin growled. "He changed his shirt. I noticed his scar. That's all."

"Because you're saving yourself for me?" Adam said. "That's so sweet." He put his hand on Robin's leg.

Robin shifted away, but Hal kept him from shifting too far. "I can't believe he was shot."

"It was pretty bad," Adam said. "You know, he almost died."

Died as in dead? Shit. "When'd this happen?"

"Couple years ago," Adam told him, stopping to look closely at the fresh drink the bartender had just pushed his way. "What **is** this? Whatever it is, it's my new favorite drink."

"Long Island ice tea," Robin said. "Chadwick style," Hal added.

Adam smiled back at Hal. "Nice. I have a feeling I'd like a lot of things Chadwick style."

Robin scowled. "Who shot him?"

"Some terrorist," Adam said. "It happened right after I moved out here to L.A. I didn't even know about it until months after he was out of the hospital. No one bothered to call me. He was in some sort of shoot-out with some terrorist cell down in San Diego."

"San **Diego**?" California was not the first location that jumped to mind when a deadly shoot-out with a terrorist cell was mentioned.

Adam nodded, and suddenly the cat-and-mouse game that they'd been playing was over. He withdrew. Got very quiet. Vulnerable. Goddamn, he was so much like Jack, it took Hal's breath away.

"It was hard to live with," Adam said, "the not knowing if he's ever coming home again, every time he goes off to work. And he was all, like, **Why'd you** leave? What was I supposed to say? **Because I couldn't stand the thought of you dying and leaving me forever, so I thought I'd go first?**" He drained his glass, turned away from Robin. "And then it happened—my worst nightmare. And I wasn't there. When I found out, all I could think was, would someone have called me if he **had** died? Or would I just never have found out? I could spend my entire life thinking he's off saving the world, and in truth he's been cold and in the ground for years."

He touched Adam. Just a hand on his arm. "I'm sorry."

Adam nodded. "Thanks." He smiled, but it was rueful. "He, you know, makes it sound like I'm the bad guy. I know he does. And I don't really blame him for that. But there are two sides to every story. And he just . . . He never understood how fucking alone I felt every time he left town. And when he came back it was all, **Alyssa did this and Alyssa**—his FBI partner, you know—**did that and Alyssa saved the world again,** and how could I compete? One day I just stopped trying, and then when he came home, it was, **Whose boxers are these under our bed, you total fucking screwup?** And at least he noticed me, you know?"

Somehow they were holding hands. How the hell had that happened?

Robin had to get out of here, because Hal wanted to put his arms around Jack and hold him close. Very close.

He slid down off the bar stool. Okay. Walking—

not falling—walking. Although he was probably only walking in part because Jack was holding him up.

"Where're you going there, big guy?" Jack asked.

"I gotta get home." He fished for his car keys.

"Yeah, like you're driving." Jack took them out of his hand, put them in his own pocket.

"Hey . . ."

"I'll drive you," Jack told him with that sweet smile that Hal could not resist. "It's okay, baby. It's going to be okay. I'll take you where you want to go."

Cosmo awoke to find himself alone in Jane's bed.

He sat up fast, but then started breathing again when he saw the light under the door to her office.

It was a little after 0400—he'd pulled her into bed less than two hours ago.

She'd needed to rest and, like last night, he'd used sex to get her into a prone position. He'd also hoped it would provide the release she'd needed, but apparently he was the one who'd fallen fast asleep afterward.

He knocked softly on the door as he opened it, and she looked up at him from behind her desk.

"Sorry," she said. "Was I being too loud?"

He let his eyes get used to the light. "No, I just . . . noticed you weren't in bed, I guess."

"I couldn't sleep," she told him.

"What are you working on?"

"Just . . ." She shrugged. "An idea I had. It's too early to talk about it."

Cosmo nodded, crossing to sit in one of the

chairs parked in front of her desk. "You should have woken me."

"You looked so peaceful," she said. She smiled through her exhaustion and worry, her chin in her hand as she gazed at him. "Would you mind very much sitting there, just like that, forever?"

The heat in her eyes was unmistakable. He laughed, stretched, scratched his chin. She just sat there, looking at him.

Well, okay. They could go that way. Have sex all night. Her arm was healing nicely. Not quite up to chandelier-swinging or roof-walking, but pretty damn close.

And sex was a good stress buster. A solid outlet for emotions that were difficult to put into words.

Of course it couldn't beat talking, in terms of expressing complex feelings. But it was becoming more apparent that Jane didn't want to talk. Not to him, anyway. Not about things that mattered.

Like how she must've felt when she saw Murphy and Angelina lying there, so gravely wounded. Like how worried she must be that the shooter would target someone else. Like how she blamed herself. Like what she was going to do now—and she was definitely up to something.

It was actually ironic that she wouldn't talk to him, considering how much Jane loved words, communication, storytelling.

Sitting there, gazing into her eyes, he knew they were going to end up back in bed, which was not a problem for him. On the contrary. But he wasn't taking that route until after he gave talking a solid try. He started easy. "I ever tell you how much I liked your D-Day scene, the dream sequence from the movie?"

Jane smiled. "Thanks." She stood up. Started around her desk, toward him. Uh-oh.

"Jack's subconscious realization about Hal was, uh . . ."

It was hard to keep the conversation going when she was looking at him like that.

". . . nicely done."

"I'm glad you liked it. We're still scheduled to shoot that sequence in a few days."

"It must, um, be hard for you, you know, having to stay away from the set. . . ."

It was harder yet when she reached down, wrapped her fingers around him and . . . She gestured with her head toward the bedroom.

He went for point-blank. Jane style. "Talk to me."

Jane straddled his lap. Kissed him. Unfastened her robe. "I don't want to talk." She kissed him again, long and deep and loaded with promise. She pulled back to look down at him and smile. "And you don't want to, either."

Cosmo caught her hands before she . . . "Yeah, actually, I do." Although to be completely honest, he now wanted to talk later, because, holy God, she was unbelievably sexy with her robe open and her hair tumbled down around her shoulders and her smile . . .

That smile was just a mask she'd erected to hide all of her worry and fear.

"I want to talk about how we're not going to let this

guy have another chance to hurt anybody," Cosmo told her. "Not you, not me, not your brother, not anyone on the Troubleshooters team . . ."

"Good," she said, "that's good." But he could see from her eyes that she didn't believe it. She leaned forward to kiss him, pulling his hands to her breasts, which was a tad distracting.

"Jane," he started, but somehow she'd gotten her hands free and she slid off his lap and onto the floor in front of him and . . .

Distractions abounded. What were they talking about?

"We're not going to underestimate him again," Cosmo told her. At least he thought that was what he said.

She might've replied, he wasn't sure about that either. Well, actually, yes, he was quite sure that she said something, he just had no idea what the words were.

"This isn't what I meant when I said talk to me," he told her, "although, God damn, I love your creativity."

Jane laughed. Yeah, that was definitely laughter.

But when she lifted her head to look at him, her smile quickly faded. "Oh, Cos," she whispered, "what am I going to do if Murphy and Angelina die?"

Cosmo pulled her up onto his lap, holding her close. But before he could answer, before he could think of any words that might bring her comfort, she spoke again.

"Don't answer that. Don't validate it—the possibility that they might die—by saying anything at all, okay? Don't talk. Just kiss me, just . . . Please . . ."

Cosmo kissed her.

Sooner or later, she had to talk to **some**body.

But right now, she needed contact. She needed proof that she wasn't alone. She needed connection, comfort, release.

He could give her that. And more.

Cosmo picked her up and carried her into her bedroom, where, for the rest of the night, they didn't talk at all.

CHAPTER TWENTY-ONE

Jane looked up as Cosmo knocked on her office door.

"Got a minute?" he asked.

"Only if it's good news," she said. "Preferably about Murph and Angelina."

She was feeling better this morning for having slept—thanks to another of his miracle backrubs—despite the latest e-mail from Mr. Insane-o.

You think you're so smart, but I'm smarter. You'll be dead, and I'll be laughing. You'll be rotting, I'll still be free. I have a plan for you. . . .

"There's been no change," Cosmo told her now, coming to stand in front of the chair that he'd sat in last night. She'd preferred what he was wearing then, but hey. Having a hot, naked Navy SEAL in her office was probably something that could get old after a while. Or not. "They're both still in ICU."

That wasn't good news, but it wasn't bad news, either.

Other rather ambiguous news—or lack of news really—was the fact that the incessant phone calls from HeartBeat had stopped. Just like that. No more demands that Jane delete Jack from **American Hero.** She wasn't sure why, but she wasn't about to call to find out. **Hey, how come you've stopped bugging the crap out of me?**

"This is more of a question than news," Cosmo said. "At least I hope it is. Do you happen to know where your brother is?"

Jane flashed hot and then cold. Please, God, not Robin . . .

"Whoa," Cosmo said as the world tipped. "Whoa, Jane." He materialized on her side of the desk, pushing her head between her knees. "Breathe. Just breathe. And listen to me, all right?"

This was it. Her worst nightmare. One by one, her family and friends were going to get picked off by this lunatic. Everyone she knew was in danger. Including—especially—Cosmo.

He was talking to her. "Robin didn't come home last night, and he's not answering his cell. It doesn't—Jane. Listen to me."

She was. She was listening. Please God, please God . . .

"It doesn't mean anything," he told her. "You know your brother. You know he drinks. Way too much. He probably got tanked, lost his cell phone, crashed at a friend's. He's probably sleeping it off—you know this. Are you breathing? Keep breathing."

Jane lifted her head a little to see Cosmo kneeling in front of her, worry for her in his eyes. God, had she really almost fainted? Her stomach was rolling and she still felt light-headed and she didn't want him to leave her.

Not ever again.

Not until they caught the man who shot Murphy and Angelina. Or until the son of a bitch went back into whatever dank, disgusting cave he'd crawled out of.

She could not allow this madman to hurt anyone else. If they found Robin, she wanted him guarded 24/7, too. As well as Jack and Adam and the other principles in the movie.

If they found Robin? **When** they found him.

Cos was right. There were a lot of nights Robin didn't come home. It was his MO, and even if Mr. Insane-o weren't on the loose, Robin's drinking was getting out of hand. She had to talk to him about it, express her concern. See if he needed to talk about this "I might be gay" thing, as ridiculous as it seemed.

But right now she just wanted to hear her little brother's voice.

"You okay?" Cosmo asked.

"If Robbie's not dead," Jane said, "I'm going to kill him."

Cos laughed. "Well, all right. But he's not dead. And we **will** find him. Let's start by calling people he parties with. You got any sense who he might—"

"Gary, Harve, Guillermo," Jane listed as she pulled her personnel file up on her computer screen. "They're all crew. I have their numbers here." She dug her cell phone out from the papers on her desk. "I'll call Gary."

Cosmo looked over her shoulder at the monitor, his cell phone already out and open. "I've got Harve."

Jules stood outside of Adam's apartment door.

This was it. The moment of truth.

Show us, Carol Merrill, what's behind door number one!

Twenty minutes ago, Cosmo Richter had called to say that Robin was AWOL. No one had seen him since last night. "Do you know, by any chance," he asked, oh so delicately, "where he might be?"

Jules cut the crap. "If you're asking if he was with me last night, the answer's no."

Cosmo had reported that Robin was last seen at a dance club, a gay establishment—he'd actually used that word, **establishment**—in West Hollywood. He'd gone there with a member of the movie crew, who'd seen him leave shortly after midnight.

And oh, yeah. He'd left with Adam Wyndham.

Jules had had to pull off the road at that point. He'd sat in the parking lot of a Krispy Kreme, stared at the lit sign, and just didn't drive for a while.

Cosmo went on to say that he'd made a number of calls to Adam, but the actor wasn't answering his phone.

Jane was really worried about her brother and just wanted to touch base with him to be sure he was okay.

This wasn't about judgment or recrimination. Nobody was mad or even upset with Robin—Jules had to laugh when Cosmo said that. Nobody on **that** end of the phone was mad or upset. But the SEAL couldn't know what Jules was feeling. Why should he?

Cosmo couldn't run over to Adam's himself—he needed to stay with Jane. "I'd rather not send PJ," he told Jules, with the kind of sensitivity that no longer surprised him in his interactions with Navy SEALs. "But no one else is available."

"I'm available," Jules had said. It was a stupid, stupid, **stupid** thing to have said.

"Thanks. I was hoping you'd volunteer." Cosmo gave him the address, then continued to be tactful. "The other night, Robin mentioned an . . . attachment to you."

"He sure has a fucking funny way of showing it." Whoops. A little of that upset had inadvertently surfaced.

Cosmo was quiet for several long moments. "I hope I'm not asking too much."

Nah. Go to an ex-lover's to see if the first man he'd fallen for in years was there with the bastard, tangled together in bed, in a room that smelled like sex . . .

No problem.

"We don't even know if Robin's really there, right?" Jules said.

"Call when you arrive, please," Cosmo requested, which was his super-polite way of saying **Oh, yes, we do.** "Either way."

It had taken Jules twenty minutes to drive here.

Twenty minutes of hanging on to the steering wheel so tightly his knuckles had stood out in sharp relief.

Twenty minutes of should-haves and maybes.

He should have called Robin yesterday evening. To find out how that scene had gone, to make sure he was okay.

He'd meant to go out, to find him, to talk to him, but after way more than twenty-four hours on his feet, he'd fallen onto his bed in his hotel room and slept.

He should have set his alarm.

He should have called Robin anyway when he woke up at three a.m. and discovered it was too late to go out.

Maybe he could have stopped this.

God damn it, it should have been him.

And it should have happened weeks—months—from now, after Robin had time to think, after he was sure of who he was and what he wanted.

Jules locked his sidearm in the trunk of his car before he went up the steps to Adam's apartment.

It was upscale—one of those older buildings with Spanish architecture and a lovely center courtyard. No doubt Adam had moved in here just a few days ago after scoring the role of Jack. It was a big improvement from the hand-to-mouth squalor that Jules had imagined.

He took a deep breath and rang the bell.

"My mother hated both Robin and his mother."

Cosmo sat with Jane on his lap, waiting for Jules to call them back with the news that Robin was safe.

"Viciously," Jane continued. "So I hated them, too. It wasn't until I was older that I did the math—Robin was conceived back when my parents were still allegedly happily married. My mom must've been devastated, but still, it was hardly Robin's fault. But my mother never managed to get past that. And I . . ."

She paused and Cosmo just waited, running his fingers through the softness of her hair.

"I was awful to him, too," she finally admitted. "For years and years."

"You were just a kid." Both of their cell phones were out on Jane's desk, and Cosmo willed them to ring. Somewhere out there Robin was probably waking up. Surely he'd realize how worried his sister must be and then he'd call. "You can't beat yourself up for wanting to be loyal to your mother."

"But I knew it was wrong," Jane whispered. "God, the things I did to him. He had this set of ceramic kangaroos that Daddy brought back from Australia. When was that? It was right at the end of the southern belle's reign. Wife number three from Mississippi. She was a piece of work—she wanted us to call her Miss Ashley. I called her Miss Assface—which actually made her stomp her foot. I guess I was ten, so Robin was eight. Anyway, he loved these kangaroos, and I took them and put them on the floor, right where they'd get stepped on, and sure enough, Dad came home and the little one's head snapped right off. The bigger one lost its front paws. **And** Robin got into trouble for scratching Miss Assface's precious hardwood floor."

She laughed. "Not that that meant anything besides

a foot stomp and a four-second reprimand. We didn't have a whole lot of supervision at my father's house, even though we were there every other weekend, like clockwork. Most of the time it was just me and Robbie and the housekeeper, Mrs. E. She used to lecture us about how child care wasn't in her job description then lock herself into her rooms and let us run wild. So I'd torment Robin, and no one would stop me. And Robin, he'd just, you know, let me—like the attention I gave him was better than no attention at all. He was this fragile-looking, stinky little nerd of a kid." Janey shook her head. "I used to tell him that Daddy wasn't really his father. That he was the mutant spawn of some alien from outer space, and that was why he smelled so bad and didn't have any friends."

She was silent for a while, so Cosmo said, "He seems to have forgiven you."

"Yeah," Jane said. "I'm the one who can't forget. When he talks about our childhood, it's like all the bad stuff was erased. He only remembers the good."

"Like what?" Cos prompted.

"Like the way I glued his kangaroos back together." She laughed. "I did an awful job of it, too. It was really pathetic, all crooked, but he just looked at me with those big blue eyes like I was his hero." She sighed. "I don't know when it all turned around. There wasn't, like, one single incident. I just . . . I don't know. I started looking forward to those weekends. Maybe it was because Robin would do anything I asked. He was a perfect cohort. Like the day I wanted to see if syrup of ipecac really worked."

Cosmo smiled. Uh-oh.

She turned her head to look up at him. "Yeah, he was the guinea pig for that project—he actually volunteered. Of course, he'd volunteer for anything, and I took advantage of that. God, you must think I'm awful. And you're right. I'm a terrible person."

"I think you were a kid who didn't have the easiest childhood," he told her.

"Oh, and yours was all perfect and rosy?" she countered. "The kid with the funny-colored eyes, weird name, and gay father? You must've had barrels of fun growing up."

"Moving to California helped," he admitted as she settled back, her head against his shoulder again. "I went into a new school, just kind of kept to myself. Focused on my grades."

"Weren't you lonely?" she asked.

"Weren't you?" he countered.

"I had tons of friends," she told him.

"But Robin was probably the only one who really knew how you felt."

She sat up again. Looked at him. "I never thought of it that way, but . . . Yeah. Maybe."

Her gaze was scrutinizing, as if she wanted access inside his head, to see what else he was thinking. Which was that they had at least ten more minutes before Jules got to Adam's apartment. Cos was wondering if he had enough time to gently move the topic of their conversation away from Robin and over to Jane. How she was feeling today. How devastating and frightening it must be to know that someone wanted to kill her, how worried she was about Murphy and Angelina . . .

Of course, maybe he should just be happy that she was talking at all.

"So you and your brother became friends," he prompted her after the silence stretched on a little too long, even for him.

Jane nodded. "I realized he was seriously neglected. Like, he really did smell bad. No one was taking care of him, doing his laundry, making him take a bath. His mother was drinking—she was pretty much useless. Then one time, when his clothes were in the washer, I noticed he had all these bruises. And he admitted that these kids at school would drag him into the bathroom and call him names and pretty much stomp the shit out of him.

"I had this plan to go to his school and kick ass— I was thirteen and big for my age—only his mother went and died. DWI—she drove into a telephone pole. It was awful, Cos. Robin was so matter-of-fact about it, like he'd been expecting it. He had to move in with Dad, who'd just gotten divorced from the Australian bitch from hell, thank goodness for small favors. But new wife number five was the one we called the Space Cadet, and she didn't help at all. A year after they'd been living in the same house, she still called him Robert, and I was the one who made sure he brushed his teeth. I used to call him every night, and we'd run a checklist. I figured if he didn't smell so bad, maybe he wouldn't get picked on at school.

"We all kind of staggered through the next few

years, and then, when I was fifteen, my mother got engaged to this guy from Vermont and announced we
were moving east. But no way could I leave Robin, so
I asked if he could come, too." She laughed. "Well.
She let me know in no uncertain terms that that wasn't
an option. I believe the phrase **over my dead body**
was used at least twenty times. So I gave her an ultima-
tum. Either Robin came with us, or I'd stay in California with my father. Two days later, she packed up my
things and drove me to Dad's."

Cosmo winced. "That must've hurt."

"No," Jane said. "It was good, actually. Dad ended
up buying a house in my old neighborhood so I could
stay at my high school, and that meant Robin transferred into my old middle school. I gave him a
makeover, and he walked into the school as Jane Chadwick's cute little brother. It didn't hurt, either, that he
was getting taller every day. It really turned things
around for him."

"Except your mother was a continent away
from you."

Jane tried to make a joke. "That was just as good. I
mean, can you picture me in Vermont?" She stood up.
"Why won't Jules call?"

"You gave up a lot for Robin," Cosmo pointed out.
"No wonder he's forgotten the bad stuff."

Jane's intercom buzzed. "Excuse me, guys," PJ's
voice came through the speaker. "Patty's here, says she
needs to see Jane. I wasn't sure—is this an okay time?"

Jane went around her desk, pushed the button.
"Send her up." She shot Cos a look. "They think we're

getting naked up here. Gee, we had twenty minutes. Why didn't we think of that?"

Patty knocked on the door, and Cosmo opened it. "Hang on a sec," he told the intern, closed it in her face, and turned back to Jane. "I think your mother was wrong to give you up without a fight."

Her eyes filled with tears. "Oh, Cos, I really don't blame her. I was impossible. And she'd just found out that she was pregnant with the twins. . . ."

"She was wrong, Jane." He kissed her. "Some things are worth a little kicking and screaming." He went back to the door. Opened it. "I'll be downstairs. I'll let you know as soon as Jules calls."

"I have good news and bad news," Patty announced as she came into Jane's office.

"Bad first," Jane told her, bracing herself, wiping her eyes. These days she couldn't have so much as a conversation with Cosmo without misting up.

"You haven't been watching the dailies, have you?" Patty was brandishing a videotape.

"I haven't," Jane admitted. She'd been a little distracted. Murphy and Angelina in the hospital, Robin dropping off the map, Cosmo turning her life upside down . . .

"You may want to get Robin in here to explain **this.**" Patty marched over to the VCR.

"Um," Jane said.

"Don't tell me," Patty was scornful. "He hasn't come home yet. I hate to break it to you, Jane, but your brother's a snake."

Okay. Jane had been expecting this particular melt-down for days now, ever since Robin went into avoid mode. But Patty's timing was a little off. Jane would be far more in the mood for some solid Robin-bashing **after** Jules found him, safe and sound.

"Actually," Jane said, "he didn't come home and I'm very worried about him."

Patty snorted. "Did you try calling Charlene, from Costume?"

"We think we might've found him," Jane said, not wanting to make it worse by telling her exactly where. "I know you must be very upset, but please remember that I'm the one who told you, months ago, that he was a turd."

"Wait'll you see just how much of a turd." Patty savagely punched the TV's power button.

In the picture that appeared on the TV screen, Robin was gazing at Adam, his heart in his eyes. "I love you," Adam breathed.

"I know that, too," Robin whispered, and lowered his head to . . .

Okay. Yeah, Jane had written this scene. It was the farewell between Hal and Jack, but watching her brother kiss Adam like that was just a little too weird, considering.

Patty, however, was surprisingly unperturbed. "Wait a sec—I must've rewound it a little too far." She fast-forwarded through to the end of the scene. "Here."

The scene started again, with Jack opening the door to find Hal standing there. There were several lines of dialogue, but nothing that Jane could see warranted

Patty's crossed arms and "what do you think about that" attitude, other than the fact that this time around, her brother was playing Hal totally flat, as if they'd filmed a blocking rehearsal, his dialogue little more than marked.

Jane opened her mouth to speak, but Patty cut her off. "Watch your brother. Don't you see it?"

On the TV screen, Robin said, "They need someone who speaks fluent German." He was providing zero energy, considering this was a hugely emotional scene.

Patty spoke over Adam's line. "Wait for it. It's coming."

"I came to say I'm sorry," Robin said, sounding about as insincere as humanly possible. "And good-bye."

"Good-bye?" Adam repeated.

"See?" Patty said.

Yes, Jane did see. This was where Hal was supposed to give Jack an envelope containing a letter he'd written. **Open in the event of my death.**

"We're leaving tonight," Robin told Adam.

"No." Adam was playing it upset, but not heartbroken.

"I'm sorry. I'm already late. I have to go." Robin had either jumped several lines of dialogue, or yes, Patty, someone had indeed changed Jane's script.

On the TV screen, the two men clasped hands instead of embraced. "Godspeed," Adam said.

Patty triumphantly pushed the pause button. "Robin's been providing HeartBeat with rewrites of the Jack and Hal scenes. In this version they're friends, not lovers. They're shooting everything twice."

"Yeah, but look at what he's doing," Jane said. "He's phoning it in." She had to laugh. "He was keeping them off my back." She shut off the TV. "He had no authority to make those changes. And as long as I never saw the dailies and didn't know what was going on . . ." She sighed. "I know you didn't mean to make things worse, but now I'm going to have to call Heart-Beat and duke it out with them." And they were probably going to pull their funding. "Shit."

"No," Patty said. "They just called."

"HeartBeat?"

"Yeah. They said the D-Day sequence was definitely a go for day after tomorrow," she told Jane. "The beach and the helicopter have been secured, and the extras have been hired—they're taking care of all the arrangements for a four-day shoot, including catering and a special tent for the press. We just show up."

"HeartBeat?" Jane said again. They'd originally told her she'd have one day—at most—to get the location footage for that scene. She'd been planning to film the dialogue and close-ups inside, on the soundstage. "The studio previously known as Those HeartLess Bastards?"

"They've just released a statement saying that they're behind you two hundred percent," Patty told her. "That they absolutely are not trying to change a single word of **American Hero**—hah!—and that their thoughts and prayers are with Angelina and Vinh

Murphy and their families, and that they are doing everything in their power to ensure your safety."

Jane couldn't believe it. **"What?"**

"Jane, that was the good news." Patty had clearly expected Jane to be upset by the fact that Robin had "betrayed" her and thrilled by HeartBeat's sudden unexpected support.

"It's because of the attack—it's made national news, hasn't it?" Jane was practically foaming at the mouth. It had taken this, a brutal attack, to make HeartBeat offer their complete support. And the pathetic thing was, it could just as easily have gone the other way. She could picture the studio executives having a meeting to decide how to respond to this latest event. That's how they saw it—an event that would make their stock prices either rise or fall.

Meanwhile, Murphy and Angelina were lying in the hospital, fighting for their lives. And Robin was missing.

A knock on the door.

Jane leapt for it. It was Cosmo. "Got him," he said.

Oh, thank you, God! "Was he . . . where we thought he'd be?" At Adam's?

Cos nodded.

"Holy shit," Jane said. Robin had been serious, the other night in the car. **I might be gay.** Either that, or his role-playing game had gotten way, way out of hand.

"Where did you think Robin would be?" Patty asked, her voice tight, and Jane looked over and into her eyes. Eyes that were filled with far more hurt than anger.

Oops. Jane met Cosmo's eyes briefly before he shut the door behind him. "You're going to need to talk to him about this. I just don't think I—"

"If it's not Charlene, then who?" Patty asked. "Alana from makeup? Or what's-her-name—doughnut girl—from craft services? Or one of the Karens in accounting?"

"Does it really matter?" Jane asked as gently as she could.

"No," Patty answered. "You're right. It doesn't matter." She laughed the way women sometimes laughed when they were hurt but trying not to show it. "As long as it's not, you know, **Adam.**"

Jane didn't bat an eye. She didn't move a muscle. She absolutely didn't react.

But somehow Patty stopped cold. "Oh, my God," she breathed, staring at Jane. "Robin was with . . . **Adam?**"

"Maybe you better sit down," Jane said, but Patty turned and bolted from the room.

The expression of shock and dismay on Adam's face when he opened the door was all Jules had to see.

That, and Robin's backpack sitting right there by the front door.

Still, as his stomach twisted, as he dialed Cosmo's phone number, he requested verbal verification, looking up from his phone and into Adam's face. "Is Robin here?"

Amazingly, Adam considered lying. Jules could see it in his eyes. The same eyes that glanced over at that telltale backpack.

But even Adam knew when not to push it. So he nodded. Now the emotions on his face were a mix of guilt and remorse. "Yeah."

Cosmo picked up. "Richter."

"I've found him," Jules reported. "I'll see him safely home." And wasn't that going to be a treat. He snapped his phone shut over the SEAL's thanks, pocketing it.

As he came inside, shutting the door behind him, he let himself look at Adam.

His ex wore a pair of ratty sweats that he'd obviously pulled on to come to the door. He was leaning against the wall as if he were too tired to stand. His hair was a mess, his eyes were bloodshot, he needed a shave and a shower.

And a serious beating.

Jules worked to unclench his fists. "You look like shit."

"I feel like shit," Adam said. "Jesus, J., I don't know what to tell you. I was drunk and he was all over me, and—"

"Stop." **He was all over me.** How many times had Jules heard that? The next part of the speech was **I didn't mean for this to happen,** and if those words came out of Adam's mouth right now, in this situation where they both goddamn knew that Adam had meant for **exactly** this to happen, God only knew what Jules was going to do.

"Where is he?" As if he had to ask.

"In the master bathroom," Adam said. "He's been riding the porcelain bus all night. Ask me how much fun **that's** been."

Jules had never hit anyone that he wasn't on the verge of arresting, and as badly as he wanted to, he wasn't going to start now. He took off his jacket and hung it neatly on the coat tree near the door.

He could see into the living room from here. There was no furniture, just a few boxes. Beyond that, he could see a kitchen.

He went in, rolling up his sleeves.

It was spacious and beautiful with a tile floor, maple cabinets, and granite countertops. Stacks of more boxes that hadn't yet been unpacked sat in a corner. He opened the refrigerator, which was stocked—as he'd expected—with bottled water. Adam didn't drink from the tap.

"For the record," Adam said, following him into the kitchen, "for half the night, it was all about Jack. Jack this, Jack that. The rest of the time, he called me Jules. I think he's in love with you."

Jules managed not to throw the bottle he'd grabbed, but just barely. He closed his mouth over words that would only give Adam satisfaction. The bitch had to goddamn make it harder. He had to make it hurt worse than it already did.

How could it have come to this? Adam had loved him once—Jules knew that he had.

Adam opened his mouth to add some additional

pearl of wisdom, but Jules spoke right over him. "Make some coffee, and then sit here with your mouth shut. Do not leave the kitchen."

"You know, you can't just come in here and tell me what to—"

"Make. Coffee. Mother. Fucker."

Adam grabbed the coffee beans. "All right, all right. Chill. God . . ."

Jules carried the bottle of water into the living room and down the hall that led to the back of the apartment. He had to go through the bedroom to get to the bath, and he tried not to look at Adam's king-size bed. Tried and failed.

He failed so badly, he stopped walking. He just stood there, taking in the sheets and blankets that were twisted and askew, at the pillows that had been knocked onto the floor along with the color confetti of condom wrappers.

God damn it. So much for the hope that nothing had really happened.

"So, okay," he said.

Life was filled with tragedies of all sizes. And, frankly, compared to Murphy and Angelina lying in that hospital over at UCLA, this didn't even register.

And yeah, maybe if he repeated that to himself, over and over, this would hurt a little less.

But probably not.

I think he's in love with you.

Yeah, right, A. Thanks for taking advantage of Robin, for giving him yet another reason to loathe himself, for making everything that he was going through right now more difficult than it had to be.

Jules went to the bathroom door, took a deep breath, and pushed it open.

No surprises here.

The bathroom was as nice as the kitchen, with a shower stall big enough for two and an enormous jacuzzi tub. The most eye-catching feature, however, was the extremely well put together naked young man stretched out on the tile floor.

Robin was sleeping or unconscious—hard to tell which—with his head between the toilet and the wall.

Buck, stark, shiny-white-ass naked.

God, but it smelled bad in here. Jules stepped over Robin to flush the toilet, then stepped back to open the shower door and turn on the water, letting it heat.

He set the bottle of water on the sink counter and moved to get a closer look at the best way to extract Robin's head from— Ah, jeezus, he was sleeping with his cheek against the toilet bowl brush. Gross.

Someday this was going to be funny. Someday, years from now, he'd have lunch with Alyssa and they would laugh and laugh and laugh.

Robin stirred as Jules took his shoulders and dragged him away from the potential to bump his head on either the wall or the toilet. Or both. He groaned as Jules turned him over—hel-lo!—and helped him up into a sitting position. Jules grabbed the water bottle and helped him take a drink.

"Oh, fuck," Robin mumbled, closing his eyes, wincing against the brightness.

Jules crossed to the wall, turned off the lights. "Let's get you in the shower," he said.

Robin's eyes opened, and a certain amount of awareness dawned. "Oh, **fuck,**" he breathed.

"Actually," Jules said, working hard to keep his voice light, "where I'm from, the more traditional greeting is **Good morning.**"

He could see from the way Robin was looking around that he had no clue where he was. The hangover had already been noted. The fact that he was naked also registered pretty quickly. As well as the fact that he was . . .

Oh, to be twenty-four again and to wake up ready to take on the world, in spite of the other crippling side effects from a level-ten hangover.

Robin reached for a towel, but the sudden movement no doubt made his head explode. "Fuck!"

Jules had mercy and took the towel from the rack and . . . Hey, this was **his**—one of the many things that had gone missing when Adam moved out. Didn't it figure?

He tossed his towel to Robin, who modestly covered himself, and then stared at Jules, a curious mix of hope and fear in his eyes. "Did we . . . ?"

"Sadly, no." Jules had to turn away. He pretended to look through the bathroom closet to see if any others of his towels were there. Yes. Yes. No. Yes. "I'm just here for the cleanup. I promised Cosmo Richter

I'd shine you up and bring you home. Your sister was pretty worried about you—you picked a bad night to drop off the map, sweets."

Robin groaned and when Jules glanced back, he was looking decidedly greener. "Careful there, you're . . . Do you need to . . . ?"

Robin shook his head.

"Do you want me to help you into the shower," Jules asked, "or do you want to crawl—keep your center of gravity low for a while?"

He could tell from the expression on Robin's face that bits of last night were coming back to him. Still, he gingerly shook his head. "Where . . . Whose . . . ?"

"This is Adam's bathroom," Jules told him, no doubt filling in that final, important missing piece.

"Adam?" Never had a name been uttered with more horror and dismay. Robin turned a whole new shade of green.

Jules nodded.

And Robin lunged for the toilet.

Cosmo knew when he saw Tom Paoletti in Jane's conference room that the news wasn't going to be good.

"She upstairs?" Tommy asked.

"Yes, sir." Cos swallowed. He came farther into the room and saw that Decker was there, with PJ and Nash. Tess, too. She was crying. "Murph?"

Tommy shook his head, no.

Angelina.

Damn it to hell.

"You should probably come up with me, to tell Jane," Tom said.

Cosmo nodded. "Does Murphy know?" Jesus, help him.

"No." Decker answered for him. "He hasn't regained consciousness yet."

"Depending on his condition," PJ added, "his doctors may not want him to have this info right away."

"He loved her so much," Tess said through her tears. "What's he going to do without her?"

"They're just going to lie to him? Tell him she's not dead?" Nash asked. "Are we supposed to lie, too? Isn't he going to figure it out?"

His arms were around Tess, but it was probably more for his sake than hers. They were all feeling it—this strange feeling, this . . . fear.

Fear of death.

It was a new one for most of them, which might've seemed odd, considering their jobs involved facing danger and death at any given time.

Cosmo himself had made peace with his own death a long time ago. When his time was up, his time was up. So be it. Which was not to say that he'd die willingly. On the contrary. When the time came, he'd fight death to the, well, death. But it wouldn't be out of fear. His strength would come from his desire to live.

This, however, was different. The death of a loved one.

Christ.

For a group of control freaks—and, yeah, they nearly all fell into that category—this was terrifying.

Jane—dead. It was a horrible thought. Gone forever. Vanished. Erased. No more.

Just thinking about it nearly brought Cosmo to his
knees.

He could see it in all their faces, too. Especially
Tommy's. He'd come way too close to losing Kelly a
few years back. This must be hitting awfully close
to home.

"I think Murph already knows that she didn't have
much of a chance," Decker said quietly. "That's probably why he's not waking up."

"Hey, guys, what's going . . . on." Jane stopped just
inside the door. "Oh, God, no."

She looked from Tom to Decker and finally to
Cosmo, her eyes begging him to tell her it wasn't so.

"Angelina died a little while ago," Cos told her
quietly.

"Oh, God," she said, covering her mouth with her
hand. "Oh, no . . ." He moved toward her, but she
backed away. "I'm sorry. I'm so, so sorry."

She turned and ran out of the room.

Cosmo followed, even though he had no clue what
he could possibly say to her to make this be all right.
He caught her at the top of the stairs. "Janey."

She was crying. Sobbing. With enormous tears that
she could no longer hold back.

Cosmo tried to put his arms around her, but she
pushed him away.

"I'm going to Idaho," she told him. "I'm gonna go
to Idaho and I'm going to stand in front of the Free-

dom Network's compound gate, and I'm going to fucking tell them to come and get me! Just come and get me!" she shouted. "Just shoot me down, on national television!"

Now was not the time to try to reason with her. He reached for her again, offering only comfort. "Jane, I'm so sorry."

"I was glad," she told him between sobs, clinging to him at last. "When I saw all the blood and Murphy lying in the driveway, and I thought it might be you, but then I saw Angelina, and I was glad. I was glad. Thank God. That's what I thought. Thank God it's not Cosmo. **Thank God!**"

"Ah, Janey, it's only human to—"

"I can't stand this!" She pulled away from him again. "I want you all to leave. Tell Tom and Deck that they're fired. They're all fired. You're fired," she shouted down the stairs. "Go home! I'm shutting down production! It's over—I'm done!"

"Jane—"

"Who's next?" she asked, wiping furiously at her tears.

"God, please, just let yourself cry," Cos said as she asked, "Who's going to be next if it's not me?"

"We're going to find this guy," he told her, grabbing her and holding on this time. "Don't let him win."

"I don't want you to find him," she wept. "I want you to be safe. I want you to go back to San Diego and be safe."

"I'm not—"

"I'm breaking up with you," she told him.

"—going anywhere," he finished as she struggled to get free again.

"It's over," she cried, and he had to let go before she opened up her stitches. "Except, you know what? That's stupid, because we weren't really going out together. We never went anywhere—we just had sex. So, here. I'm telling you we're not going to have sex anymore, so you might as well just go home."

Cosmo made the mistake of laughing.

"You think this is funny?" she shouted.

God, of course he didn't. "You really think the only reason I'm here is for the sex?" he countered.

"I don't know. I don't know why anyone would want to risk dying for me!" She went into her office and slammed the door in his face, locking it behind her.

"Jane, come on," he said, his forehead against the door. "Let me in. Talk to me. Please?"

"Well, that was totally **Real World.**"

Cosmo turned to see Robin standing on the stairs, unable to keep from cracking a joke despite looking like shit warmed over. "Angelina's dead," he informed him.

Robin winced. "Oh, shit, I'm such an asshole. I'm so sorry. You must be . . . Were you very close?"

"I just met her," Cos said. "And I'm still in that surreal place, you know? It hasn't quite hit."

"If there's anything I can do . . ." Robin started, then rolled his eyes. "Yeah, like that's going to help."

He sighed and looked wistfully at Jane's door. "I guess she's too upset to talk to me."

Cosmo stepped aside. "You're welcome to try."

Robin shook his head and continued on up the stairs toward his rooms. "She doesn't need my crap right now, on top of everything."

"You okay?" Cosmo asked. "Get anything figured out?"

Robin looked back at him, horror in his eyes. "Does everyone know where I was?"

"I'm pretty sure it's just me and Jane," Cos reassured him. "I think she'd be okay with me speaking for her and saying that she loves you. Whatever you decide. Or don't decide. You don't have to decide anything." Christ, way to fuck **that** up. He was totally on a roll today.

Still, Robin seemed touched. "Thanks, but . . ." He turned his face away, hiding the sheen of tears in his eyes in what was apparently a time-honored Chadwick tradition. Never let 'em see you cry for anything less tragic than death.

Of course Cos should talk.

Robin didn't speak for several moments, but he didn't leave, either. So Cosmo just waited.

"Last night was . . . a mistake," Robin finally told him. "Things got completely out of control. I shouldn't have . . . It wasn't . . ."

Cos nodded, remembering that phone conversation with Jules Cassidy, who so clearly cared about Robin. "Made the wrong choice, huh?"

"No, I didn't choose anything," Robin said. "Not really. I was . . ." He shook his head. "Too drunk to—"

"Bull**shit,**" Cosmo said, and Robin took a step backward, startled at his volume and vehemence. "Take responsibility. You drank. You chose to make some very important decisions while fucked up. Deal with it. You did it. You think it was a mistake? Then do whatever you have to do to clean it up."

"I don't know if I can," Robin said.

"Do your best," Cosmo countered. "But start by taking responsibility. Be a man."

Robin stood there for several long moments. "Yeah," he finally said. "Yeah." He headed for his room. "Janey's a fool for locking you out."

The locked door wasn't the biggest problem here.

Cos had to figure out a way to get Jane to listen to him—or to Deck or Tom or PJ or any of them. He didn't care who delivered the message.

Forget the locked door. Even when it was wide open, he wasn't getting through to her.

She was too scared to hear what he was saying— that they weren't going to underestimate this guy again. The big danger that she was imagining was out there, sure, but the TS Inc. team and the FBI were taking precautions.

This guy—Mr. Insane-o—wasn't going to fire his weapon unless he was certain he could get away. He wanted to win, and winning meant he'd make sure they wouldn't catch him. Or kill him.

The profilers were certain he wasn't suicidal, and Cosmo had to agree.

With that information in their pocket, they could stay one step ahead of him and take care—all of them—not to go places where a sniper had both a position to shoot from and an escape route.

Like freaking Idaho. She couldn't have been serious.

The additional security cameras and sensors they were placing, with permission of neighbors, at all of the good sniping locations around Jane's house were going to help them feel more secure.

Robin stopped, turned back. "Do you know if Jane's really going to halt production, or, God, shut the movie down?"

"I don't know," Cosmo admitted. "I don't think she should, though. It gives the shooter power."

"It might make him go away," Robin pointed out.

"Not according to his latest e-mail to Jane," Cos told him.

"Which was?"

" 'This ends when you're dead.' "

"Shit."

"He's wrong," Cosmo vowed. "It's going to end when he's dead."

CHAPTER TWENTY-TWO

By the time this was over, Cosmo was going to be able to write a thesis on all the things people hide from each other.

So far he'd found some drugs, which he'd flushed, a couple of handguns that weren't locked up and that he'd made inoperable, and a shitload of porn. Alcohol, an entire collection of old Partridge Family albums, diaries, photos of former girlfriends, candy.

He wasn't expecting to find a shrine to Jane. Even though that wasn't just a device that played well in the movies—sociopathic individuals tended to display obsessive compulsive behaviors—he knew that their guy was smarter than that.

The killer surely knew they were looking for him. He'd be careful about what he left around for them to stumble across.

Because it was evening now—the time of day most people came home from work—Cos was doing drive-bys. Surveillance. Looking for the best way inside a house, noting which neighbors were nosy, what kind of cover fences and landscaping provided.

Checking the cars in the driveways at the addresses on the endless lists of suspects Jules Cassidy had given him.

Looking for that fucking elusive truck.

A dog barked, and a kid on a tricycle stared at him balefully from the driveway of the house he was checking out.

A black truck was in the driveway, too, a six in the license plate. But it wasn't the truck he'd seen that night. Different model. No dent in the bumper. And no honor student bumper sticker. Which of course didn't mean anything. Bumper stickers could be removed. As could dents.

Cosmo drove on.

The truth was, the man who killed Angelina Murphy, the man who wanted to snuff Jane, could be inside any one of these houses.

Cosmo's cell phone rang. He checked, and it was Jane's number. "Hey, I'm glad you called," he said into his phone. "I've been thinking—"

"Okay, stop before you say something we'll both regret," a very male voice said into his ear.

"Robin."

"Yeah, Chief," Jane's brother said. He sounded tired. "We've got a little problem here at Psycho Central. I had to lock Jane in the pantry. You better get over here."

Cosmo did a U-turn. "You had to **what**?"

"Jane wants to go to Idaho. She has this crazy idea and she's fired the entire security team, so— Shit! She's trying to kick down the door. If she gets out . . ."

Cosmo swore. "Sit on her if you have to. I'm on my way."

The finality of death affected people in different ways.

For some, Decker knew, it was a wake-up call.

Others pretended not to care, and they ran from it and hid from their overwhelming emotions, partying all the harder.

For yet others, it brought with it an overpowering sense of fear—so much so that they nearly stopped living.

For people like Jane, it pushed all of their "fight back" buttons, and they went to war.

Often without considering the consequences.

Decker could relate. He was part of that same subset. A seriously healthy chunk of himself was ready to march to Idaho, too. Except, unlike in Jane's plan, he'd blow past the Freedom Network compound's gate, kick in the front door of the main building, and tear out Tim Ebersole's throat with his bare hands.

Even though the FBI continued to find no evidence that connected Ebersole's group to their shooter—and they probably wouldn't—Decker knew as well as Jane did that the Freedom Network's hate-spewing doctrine had started the ball rolling.

Jane's plan had a little less throat-ripping. She was intending to surround herself with TV news crews and stand outside the Freedom Network's gate, demanding to speak to Tim Ebersole, to accuse him of the murder of Angelina Murphy, to serve him with a lawsuit. She was going to sue the entire Freedom Network on charges that were completely ridiculous. There was no chance she would win.

But that wasn't the point.

Accompanying the process server and standing there while the papers were slapped into Ebersole's hand was a great visual.

It made for a kick-ass news story. And it would link Angelina's murder to the Freedom Network, at least in the public's mind.

But there were just a few little glitches that Jane obviously hadn't quite worked out.

"You really think the fact that news cameras are there will stop this guy from shooting you?" Cosmo asked at a very high volume as he and Jane went toe-to-toe in the kitchen of her house.

Decker wasn't certain which subset the SEAL fit into—how Cosmo was affected by death. All Deck knew for sure was that the normally taciturn, allegedly emotionless chief had finally lost his cool.

"He'll be here in L.A.—how can he shoot me?" she argued.

"What, he's not capable of following you to the airport, hopping the next flight to Idaho Falls?"

It was clear from her expression that she hadn't considered that, but she was unwilling, or maybe unable, to back down. "If we timed it right—"

"But what if something goes wrong and—" Cosmo grabbed his head. "Christ, I can't believe I'm having this conversation!" He also looked a little shell-shocked at the fact that this argument was so public. He glanced at Deck and PJ and Robin, then stepped even closer to Jane, lowering his voice. "Jane, look, I'm happy to talk about this—I'm ecstatic that you want to talk—but let's—"

"I don't want to talk," she shot right back at him. "I want to go to Idaho! My flight leaves—"

"—go upstairs," he said, "and really discuss the—"

"—in less than two hours," she continued, shouting over him. "I'm packed, I'm ready, I can't just hide in here any longer! I can't!"

"Janey," Cosmo said, "God, I know what you're feeling, but please, **please** slow down and think about the danger—"

"Maybe it would be good if he did shoot me," Jane countered. "Think of the publicity that'll get for HeartBeat and **American Hero.** Film producer murdered in cold blood—film at ten."

Cosmo took a step back. "Jesus Christ, Jane!"

"Come on, Cos, you know she doesn't mean that," Jane's brother apparently felt compelled to interject.

"It ends when I'm dead. That's what he said. Maybe that's what we have to do to end this." She looked at Decker. "If I wore a bulletproof vest . . . We talked about setting me up as bait, but what if we went in there intending to make it **look** as if I were dead—"

"Over my dead body!"

"No," she shouted, her attention firmly back on Cosmo. "That's the point—not over your dead body or anyone else's! Angelina's was enough, God damn it!"

"Damn straight!" Cosmo shouted back at her. "Angelina's was enough! I will not let you put yourself at risk like this, so help me God—"

"Yeah?" she said, getting in his face. "What are you going to do? You gonna restrain me—you gonna lock me back in the pantry?"

"Yes," he said. "Yes, I will."

Jane appeared to be stunned.

Cosmo wasn't done. "I'm not letting you go to Idaho just to make yourself feel like you're doing something, just to fucking feel better—excuse me!—for something that is not your fault! You know how many people blame you for Angelina's death, Jane?" He didn't wait for her to answer. He was in full roar now. "One. You. So get over it. Putting your own life in danger isn't going to bring her back—nothing's going to do that. It's just goddamn selfish."

His words—**selfish**—had to have cut deeply, but Jane played her hurt as just more anger. "What right do you have to tell me what I can and cannot do?"

He said nothing. He just shook his head.

She went on the attack. "You take risks all the time. You go out there, doing God knows what—you could come face-to-face with this psycho and then what?"

And then I kill him. Cosmo didn't say it, but Decker knew full well that if any member of his team did a one-on-one with the man who killed Angelina, odds of the man living to stand trial were slim to none.

Jane pressed what she perceived to be her advantage. Little did she know . . . "If I can take a risk that could make this end—"

"What if he takes a head shot, like he did with Angelina?" Cosmo asked. "No Kevlar vest in the world can save you from a bullet to the brain."

"That's why it's called a risk—"

"No," he said. "Uh-uh. I'm not going to let you do that."

She widened her eyes. "Let?"

He crossed his arms. "That's what I said."

As Decker, PJ, and Robin continued to try to blend in with the kitchen wallpaper, Cosmo and Jane stood and glared at each other.

Cosmo broke the silence first. "You know, I can handle your anger. It's part of your grieving process, it's another side to fear—and I know what that feels like. And I understand why you're pushing me away, so I'm okay with that, too. I know you're scared that I'm going to get hurt, or that Robin is, or Deck or any of us . . . but this isn't the answer. Yes, I take risks—calculated risks—because that's my job. I've had training. I've had experience. We all have. When you say, 'I wanna go to Idaho,' and we say, 'Mmmm, bad idea,' you say, 'Maybe some other time, then,' not, 'Out of my way, assholes.' " He shook his head. "I wish you would talk to me about what you're feeling—I'm right here, I'm standing **right** here, Jane—but I know how hard that can be, too. You want to spend two weeks—two months—talking about Robin or your screenplay or your father's ex-wives, I'm ready to listen. I'm happy to listen. I'm also willing and ready to give you all the time and space that you need, with the understanding that even if I back away, I'm not going anywhere. What I'm not willing to put up with is this disregard for your own safety, your taking foolish chances with your life.

"You are not responsible for Angelina's death. But if you go to Idaho like this and get yourself killed—that one will be on you. And me—if I let you do it.

"And as far as what right I have to tell you what you can and cannot do—I have none. I have no right—other than the fact that I love you. And I goddamn will do whatever I have to do so that I don't end up in Murphy's shoes." His voice broke. "Don't do that to me, Janey."

Nobody moved. Nobody said a word. Not even Jane's idiot brother. Decker held his breath.

Jane started to cry, her anger morphing back into the heartsickening grief they all were feeling. She ran out of the room, but before she went, she threw her airline e-tickets onto the kitchen table.

Thank God.

Cosmo followed her. "Jane . . ."

"I broke up with you," Decker heard her say as she ran up the stairs, before she slammed her door shut.

Decker looked down the hallway to see the SEAL sitting on the stairs, exhausted, looking like he'd just run a marathon.

"Yeah," Cosmo said, rubbing his forehead, "but see, I didn't break up with you."

Patty blew two months' rent on a dress, a pair of shoes, and a haircut that made her look at least twenty-three.

Which was perfect because it was the age on her fake ID, handed down from her older sister.

She did her makeup in the car with her radio on and her cell phone turned off.

Her phone had started ringing almost immediately upon leaving Jane's.

She'd run out of the house—hadn't waited for her stupid escort home. She hadn't even gone home, though all cast and crew were being "strongly encouraged" to stay indoors with their shades pulled down.

Taking those kinds of precautions seemed ridiculous, considering her boyfriend had left her for a man.

Well, okay, so Robin Chadwick wasn't exactly her boyfriend.

But she'd gone right to the clinic, got tested for HIV.

The nurse had given her a solid scolding for having unprotected sex, telling her she was no more at risk than she would be if Robin had been completely straight. It was his multiple partners and careless lack of protection that created the high risk. Gay or straight, AIDS didn't discriminate.

Was that supposed to comfort her?

The test results wouldn't be back for several days. And even then, she'd need to be tested again in six months.

No way was she going to die without having lived first.

Patty got out of her car, teetering for a moment in her new heels. As she walked around the corner toward the restaurant, she'd let herself get used to them.

She was over an hour early, but that was okay. She'd sit at the bar and watch the door, practicing the perfect surprised smile. **Victor! What a coincidence! Are you**

having dinner here tonight? My date seems to have stood me up. Join you? Why, I'd love to!

Victor Strauss' personal assistant had told Patty that his boss was coming here for dinner tonight. It had been laughably easy to get the information out of him without being too obvious.

She imagined the warmth of Victor's hand at her waist as he escorted her to his table. Or—yes, her future was almost unbearably bright—as he escorted her into the Oscar ceremony next spring.

He'd touched her in the hospital, after Jane had been hurt by that falling light. It had been for the briefest moment, just to move her out of the way of an approaching gurney. But he **had** touched her.

She'd play hard to get—at least until the test results came in. Please, God, let her be negative.

Starting now, she'd be more careful. She'd already stocked both her purse and her car with condoms.

Drat, the restaurant was much farther away than she'd thought. She had to cross the street, walk another two blocks.

Patty waited at the corner for the light to change, aware of the looks she was getting from the late-afternoon crowd around her. Who was she, dressed up like that? She must be Someone.

Somebody jostled her, nearly toppling her from her shoes, somebody else grabbed her and— "Ow!"

Something sharp—a pin?—stuck her, right in the butt.

She turned around.

A man with a gym bag was standing behind her. "Sorry."

Yeah, right. If he'd been young and looked like Ashton or Orlando she might've smiled. Instead, she gave him a dirty look.

The walk signal finally lit up, and the crowd surged forward and . . .

It was farther from the curb to the street than she'd thought, and she staggered. The road felt almost rubbery and . . .

The man with the bag took her arm. "Let me help you, dear."

"No thank you," she said, but her mouth felt funny, her face almost numb. "I have a date with Victor Strauss."

"She's had a little too much to drink," the man said to an older woman who was looking at her. Concern, not admiration, was in her eyes. She was speaking, too, but was that Russian? Patty couldn't understand her.

"No," Patty tried to say. "I need a drink," but everything was really blurry.

The man slipped her arm over his shoulders, which was good, because her legs were useless and . . .

"Here's the car," the man said, only it wasn't her car at all. Still, she was just so glad to sit as the world faded and went gray.

Shortly after midnight Cosmo knocked on Jane's door.

"Go away," she called.

He said something, but it was muffled and she couldn't make out the words. He knocked again—that she couldn't miss.

She'd spent the evening crying. For Angelina, whom she'd never even met. For Murphy, who'd brought his love for his wife to everything he said and did, every breath he took.

For herself.

Jane just sat at her desk and waited for Cosmo to go away.

But this time he unlocked the door and came in.

Pocketing what looked like some kind of lock pick.

"Well, that's comforting," she said. "Lock, schmock."

He looked worn out. "I needed to . . . I don't know. Make sure you were okay, I guess," he said, sitting down across from her.

She wasn't okay, but she didn't say a word.

He was sitting forward, elbows on his knees, hands on the back of his neck, staring at the floor.

He was sitting in that same chair that . . . Damn it! Was she ever going to be able to look at him again without thinking that they were alive, and Angelina wasn't? Every time they laughed, she'd think about the fact that Angelina couldn't laugh. And Murphy **wouldn't** laugh, probably not ever again.

Every time Cos smiled at her and made her heart leap, it would immediately sink because she'd remember that Angelina's heart was never going to leap like that again. As for Murphy's . . . God.

Every time they made love, every time Cosmo told her that he loved her . . .

He loved her. He'd said that he **loved** her.

And all she could think was how come she got to have this gift, this beautiful, wonderful gift, when Angelina and Murphy's love had been stolen from them forever.

And try as he might, Jane knew that there was nothing Cosmo could do or say to convince her that the woman who was in the morgue tonight wasn't there because of her.

"You're not the only one who feels responsible," he said when he finally spoke, as if he could read her mind. As he lifted his head to look at her, she realized with a jolt of shock that he had tears in his eyes. He sat back in his seat, holding her gaze, as if daring her to comment. "Tommy and Decker are both devastated. We all are. There's not a man or woman among us who hasn't thought, 'If only . . .' If only we'd reminded Murph to check to make sure he wasn't followed when he left here that morning. It's standard procedure. Hell, it's so ingrained in me, I do it automatically. It never occurred to me to remind anyone, but maybe if I had, we wouldn't have had to go into that hospital room tonight and . . ."

He had to stop, folding his arms across his chest, the thumb of one hand against the bridge of his nose. He exhaled, a soft burst of pain. "We went in there, Janey, and told Murphy that . . ."

Jane couldn't move. She couldn't speak. Her heart was in her throat.

"We told him she was gone," Cosmo said brokenly. "We had to tell him. He was yelling and . . . He had to be strapped down. He woke up, and he kept asking about her, and the fucking doctors wouldn't tell him the truth, so he started demanding they let him see her. He was ready to stand up and start walking the halls, searching for her, so we went in. Me and Tommy and Decker."

Tears were sliding down her own face, too, as she sat there, her hand over her mouth.

"If I live to be five hundred," Cosmo whispered, "I will never forget the way . . . Jane, I've watched men pass away. Something changes in their eyes when they're gone. And I swear to God, today I watched Murphy die. He was still breathing when we left that room, but . . ." He shook his head.

"I'm sorry," Jane wept. "I'm so sorry."

Cosmo had come here, not because he thought she needed him. He'd come because he'd needed her.

And now Jane also cried because, if it had been up to her, she would have kept him locked out.

She stood up, went around the desk to reach for him, but he was already over by the door, wiping his eyes on the bottom edge of his T-shirt.

"Cos," she said, and he hugged her, but he held her close for far too short a time.

"We can all beat ourselves up about this, Janey," he told her quietly. "We can feel sorry for ourselves and try to wish it away with should haves and shouldn't haves, but there's one man who I know for goddamn sure is responsible for killing Angelina. He's out there and I'm going to find him."

"Cos . . ." Jane followed him out into the hallway but he didn't stop. "Be careful," she said, even though she knew he would be, as he clattered down the stairs, out the door, and into the night.

CHAPTER TWENTY-THREE

It was two days after that awful mistake of a night, before Robin ran into Jules again.

It was two days of being escorted onto the set and home. Two days of being grateful that the scenes he was shooting weren't with Adam and that the set was closed, due to the danger from the sniper.

This morning, Patty hadn't shown up at the studio. Apparently she wasn't answering her cell phone, and Janey was worried to death about her. Troubleshooters team members had gone scrambling to her apartment, where they'd found nothing. No dead body, no sign of a struggle, but also no clues as to her whereabouts.

Robin had been worried at first, too—until Jane had revealed that Patty had found out about his encounter with Adam, and everything fell into place.

She'd gone back to Kansas or wherever. In a few hours, they'd get a call from her mother, telling them she'd arrived safely home.

Which would be a relief of sorts. Running home was much better than running to the **National Voice** and publicly outing Robin.

Which would have been a real irony, especially since he now knew for a fact that he wasn't gay. He didn't remember much of that night at Adam's, but what he did remember was . . .

Hal.

Hal had loved every minute of it.

But that didn't mean that Robin was gay—just a damn good actor, consumed by the role.

He hoped to God he never got cast to play a serial killer.

As soon as **American Hero** was done filming, he'd exorcise Hal, and his life would return to normal. Until then, he just had to cope with Hal shoving Robin's own thoughts aside, and daydreaming about . . .

Not Adam. He didn't want to spend a lot of time reliving the frantic near-violence of . . . Shit. It had been sex ramped up to an intensity that overwhelmed him and filled him with guilt.

No, what haunted him was that kiss he'd shared with Jules. It stayed with him, the memory far clearer than anything he might have done with Adam.

Robin had also spent the past two days vowing not to drink, but then caving in and breaking into the private stash of Puerto Rican rum that he kept in his closet. The rum was there, allegedly because he'd never brought it downstairs to the liquor cabinet after he got back from last year's vacation cruise to Aruba, but really so that he'd have it close at hand during times of stress.

And talk about stress.

Janey was tied in a knot.

For the past two days Robin had watched Cosmo—who had the patience of a saint—give his sister space. He alternately sat at the computer in the conference room, or pored over street maps of the Los Angeles area with some kind of list, or went out—usually in the middle of the day, oddly enough—to find the man who'd murdered Angelina.

The question in Robin's mind wasn't **if** the SEAL would kill the bastard when he found him, but rather **how** he'd kill him.

Alana in makeup had told him that SEALs were capable of killing a man with their bare hands. Just grab and twist and bye-bye, Mr. Insane-o, we hardly knew ye.

Robin wished Cosmo would hurry up already.

He really liked Cos. A lot.

Not in **that** way. Go away, Hal.

In a potential brother-in-law way. Janey usually picked losers, but Cosmo was kind of a fabulous cross between Jesus and the Terminator. The friendly Terminator, from **Terminator 2.**

The man loved her—he'd said as much during yesterday's shouting match in the kitchen. That shit was better than reality TV.

Robin was actually looking for Cosmo upon his arrival home from the set, when he found Jules Cassidy instead.

Sitting at the conference room table, reading through some official-looking documents.

Robin stopped short, and Jules glanced up.

But went right back to reading.

Probably because he expected Robin to run away.

Jules had left a couple of messages on his voice mail. Messages Robin hadn't returned.

Yet.

He was intending to. When he'd figured out what to say.

Be a man.

Robin took a deep breath and went into the room. "Hi."

Jules looked up. An arctic breeze blew through the house, and Robin's heart sank.

"I'm waiting for Cosmo Richter," Jules said. "Do you know where he is?"

"Dumping seventy different Hefty trash bags filled with Mr. Insane-o's body parts in seventy different Dumpsters across the city?" Robin suggested.

Jules didn't smile. "That's not something you want to say to a federal agent."

"I was kidding."

"Not funny."

Okay. "I'm sorry I didn't call you back." Robin forced himself to sit down across from him.

"I was worried about you. Guess I shouldn't have been." Jules went back to his reading.

"I didn't know what to say to you." No apology on earth would make up for what had happened.

"There's nothing to say." Jules straightened his pile of papers, clipped them together, and put them back into his briefcase. "I'll wait in the kitchen." He pushed back his chair.

"I can't imagine what it must have been like for you

to walk in there." Robin's voice shook. "To know that I'd do . . . what I did, even though I knew how much you cared for Adam . . ."

Jules froze in the process of pushing himself out of his seat. "You honestly think . . . ?" He laughed, sat back down, applied pressure to the bridge of his nose, as if he had a killer headache. "You think I'm upset because of Adam."

"I know you still love him," Robin said. He knew that even though Jules had expressed very real interest in Robin, he hadn't yet let go of Adam. "I also know that Adam's . . . infidelity was one of the reasons you split up, which must have—"

"I once had this shrink," Jules told him, "who theorized that I kept taking Adam back, kept giving him a second, third, eighteenth, forty-seventh chance because I never had that opportunity with my father, you know, because he'd died? When Dad was gone, he was gone. Adam, though . . . He would cheat or maybe even leave, but then he'd reappear. It was hard—it has been hard—not to try again. I couldn't have my father's love, right? But I could have Adam's. The irony was that Adam couldn't—can't—give me what I needed, any more than my father could return from the dead." He laughed. "And in the end the man who loved me the most is the dead one."

Jules stood up.

Robin stood, too. What was he saying? That Adam didn't love him? Wasn't that kind of obvious? And didn't that make both his and Robin's transgression even worse?

"Are you and Adam—" Jules stopped. Started again. "Have you . . . been with Adam again?"

"No!" Robin said, startled. "God! I hate his fucking guts. It wasn't . . . I'm not . . . gay. I'm not. I know that now. Definitely. It was just that one, you know, time. No repeats. No thanks. Not interested."

Jules gazed at him. "Let me get this straight. You know that you're not gay because you don't want to have sex—again—with someone whose guts you fucking hate? That makes perfect sense." He gathered up his briefcase. "You, my friend, are in total denial."

Be a man. Robin blocked his route out of the room. "All that stuff between you and me, Jules, that was . . . I was just . . . acting. I told you that. I'm sorry if you took me too seriously. I should have been more clear and . . . Well, I shouldn't have messed around with you in the first place, because I like you, I really do. As a friend, you know."

Jules nodded. "Friend, comma, straight. Check."

"And what happened with Adam . . ." Robin took a deep breath. "That night . . . I was just exploring Hal's inner demons and it got out of hand. It wasn't real."

Jules nodded again. "It didn't mean anything," he said. "Right. Like I haven't ever heard that before. But this time it really didn't mean anything. It was just meaningless sex between a coupla guys, one of whom fucking hates the other. Thanks for clearing that up." He moved to step around Robin.

Who stepped to block him again.

"I don't want you to think it was entirely Adam's

fault," Robin said, "because it wasn't. I was . . ." He cleared his throat. "Curious."

"Yeah, I've always been curious, too." Sarcasm rang in Jules' voice. "I really hate Tim Ebersole, the leader of the Freedom Network, and I spend, oh, five, six hours a day wondering what it would be like to have sex with **him.**"

Jules' anger was palpable, but beneath it lay hurt, which was far harder to deal with.

Be a man. Robin didn't run away. He stood there. Met Jules' gaze. "I don't know what to say besides I'm sorry," he said quietly, "and that I hope you'll forgive me. I hope we can be friends again someday."

Jules just laughed. But then he put down his briefcase, stepped closer and . . .

Robin saw it coming.

Jules was going to kiss him.

He saw it coming, and he should have taken a step back, because this wasn't research, it wasn't necessary, it was . . .

Sweet. It was unbearably sweet, just as it had been up in Jules' hotel room.

And he not only not stepped back, but he stepped forward, toward Jules and . . .

And it wasn't Jack kissing Hal, it wasn't Adam kissing Hal, Hal wasn't involved at all, it was Jules kissing **him** and it felt so unbelievably . . .

Right.

Robin wanted to run away, he had to run away, but his legs were melting and his arms were wrapped around Jules, who just kept on kissing him. Harder, deeper, longer, hungrier, Jules sucked the very breath from him, then—God!—reached between them and . . .

Stopped kissing him.

And there Robin was. Breathing hard, stone sober, staring into the desire-filled eyes of this man who quite obviously wanted to be far more than his friend.

Staring into the eyes of this man who had the pretty obvious proof of Robin's own equally enormous desire in his hand.

God, God, God . . .

"You," Jules said, "are one hell of an actor."

Robin couldn't speak, couldn't move, couldn't pull away.

He didn't want to pull away. He wanted . . .

Oh, dear God, he actually knew **exactly** what he wanted.

Try as he might, he couldn't stop himself from leaning forward and kissing Jules again and . . .

"Whoops, sorry, guys." They leapt apart as Cosmo did a quick 180.

"Wait," Jules said. He was nearly as wigged out as Robin. "Wait! I apologize—that shouldn't have happened in such a . . . a public place. That was completely—"

"What, you mean, here in Robin's home?" Cosmo said, completely unperturbed. He glanced around the room. "Seems pretty nonpublic to me." He looked at Robin, who'd totally had to sit down. "We cleaning things up or making more of a mess?"

Jules answered for him, running his hands down his

face. "Mess," he said. "I think this qualifies as a mess. Although only a potential mess. Because we didn't quite get to the messy part and . . ." He laughed. "God, I didn't mean that the way it sounds. I think I better tell you what I came here to tell you, Chief, and then go." He glanced at Robin, and added, "Actually, if you could give me two minutes, I'll meet you in the kitchen."

Cosmo nodded. "No problem. Take your time."

Jules watched Cosmo close the door behind him, then turned to Robin. "I'm sorry, I took that much too far."

Robin still couldn't speak. He just shook his head.

Jules sat down beside him, real concern in his eyes. "You all right?"

He'd thought he'd had it all figured out. But now . . .

Hal was sitting back and letting Robin take the blame for that one all on his own.

And he was back in panic mode.

"Robin . . ." Jules touched his arm.

Robin rocketed up, out of his seat.

Jules sat there for a moment, his head down. "Okay," he said when he finally spoke. "This is a scenario I didn't consider. I had it all figured out—what I was going to say when you realized that you were gay and . . ." He looked up at Robin, who had to turn away, toward the curtained windows. "I'm not ready to forgive you. You know, for the other night. For Adam. I may never be, so even if my little fantasy moment there had kept going, it wouldn't have gone much further. I've said it before, I'll say it again—I'm not going to be your science project. Especially not experiment number two in an as of yet undetermined number. And even if you begged my forgiveness, even if you got down on your knees in front of me—and I do mean that in the crudest possible way—"

Robin's hands were shaking and he jammed them into his pockets.

"—that wouldn't change a thing. You know when I kissed you right then?" Jules continued. "That was partly because I wanted to show you what you can't have. That's what you threw away when you went home with Adam."

He was serious. As Robin turned back to watch, Jules picked up his briefcase.

"I'm not going to sell myself short again," Jules continued. "Not even for great sex. Well, okay, maybe for great sex, but not for great sex with you. Not when I know what we could have." He laughed. "But since you're not gay, it's all kind of moot, isn't it?"

He stood there, just looking at Robin, as if waiting for some kind of response.

Robin finally found his voice. "Shit, I need a drink."

Jules laughed and headed for the door. "Yeah, that'll help."

It was obvious that Jules Cassidy was tremendously embarrassed that Cos had walked in on him and Robin. The first thing he did when he came into the kitchen was apologize again.

Cosmo got out his wallet and pulled out his PFLAG card and tossed it onto the kitchen table.

Jules stopped stammering. "You have a . . . brother who's—?"

"Father," Cosmo said.

"Your **father.**" Jules laughed, but quickly stopped himself. "I'm sorry, I'm just so . . . surprised."

"My family was somewhat alternative," Cos explained.

"So, coming from that background, you decided to become a SEAL because . . . ?"

Cos shrugged. "I kind of fell into it."

"I'm sorry. No one **kind of falls** into **that** training program and walks out with a SEAL pin."

"I joined the Navy to go to college," Cosmo said. "Money was tight—my dad died from a car accident and the hospital bills were . . . I wanted to go to college, so I enlisted. Did two years at sea, hated it. Kept bumping my head, and the food on board sucked. But I needed to stay in to get my degree, so I applied for the SEAL program. I would've done anything to avoid another six-month cruise." He smiled. "Nothing like a little incentive to get through BUD/S."

Jules laughed. "That's unbelievable." He sat down across from Cosmo. "You always scared me," he admitted. "Out of all the SEALs in Team Sixteen . . . well, there are several of you who set off my homophobia red alert."

"It's the eyes," Cosmo said. "I thought it was the haircut for a while, but . . ." He shrugged. "Not much I can do about the eyes."

Jules laughed again as he opened his briefcase. "I have that list you called me for: cast members who own World War Two–era military uniforms, both German and American, cross-referenced with DMV records as to what kind of car or truck they own." He looked up at Cosmo. "What exactly are you thinking?"

Cosmo took the computer printout, flipped through it. There were about forty names on the list. Some of them he recognized from Jules' first list of cast members with Nazi uniforms—he'd already checked them out. Just a few of these actors owned trucks. Which didn't mean anything. Not only could his hunch be dead wrong, but if it wasn't, the truck he'd seen could be borrowed or stolen or simply not registered.

"I asked Jane about how extras get cast," he told Jules. "You know, why pick Bob Smith over Tim Jones, if all they're going to do is be part of the background. She said that age and physical description play into it—you don't want to have a four-hundred-pound, balding, sixty-something man if you're looking for seventeen- to twenty-one-year-olds for a boot camp scene, right?"

"Obviously," Jules said.

"So you weed out all the unsuitables not just from their headshots, but also from Polaroids you take during an extras casting session. See, the extras show up, the casting agent makes sure they're human, tries to eliminate the psychopaths and troublemakers, takes a quick photo of what they look like right now—headshots can be several years old and not accurate—and has them fill out an information sheet: Where do you live, do you own your own uniform or other period clothing, do you have an early 1940s model car or maybe a military vehicle like a jeep, and finally, what's your availability?

"Jane told me that anyone who owns a vehicle or costume gets put into a separate file," Cosmo continued. "Their car or uniform gets checked for historical accuracy—if the extras pass that test, they get placed in a high-priority pile. They're going to get used first because they come fully equipped—make sense?"

Jules nodded.

"From that list, it's a crapshoot, depending on the actors' availability. Jane told me that Patty takes that list and makes phone calls. Whoever's home to take the call and is available at the time of the scheduled shoot gets the job," Cosmo told him. "And when she needs crowds of extras—like for the big D-Day scene they're going to start filming tomorrow—she'll go to the general list."

"But the actors who own their own uniforms get called first," Jules clarified. "So if I'm Mr. Insane-o and I want to get a job working as an extra on a World War Two movie so I can terrorize the producer, I should get an authentic-looking uniform."

"Or a period car," Cosmo said. "If you have a car that can be used in a street scene, the production assistant is going to become your new best friend. You'll get a lot of extra work, maybe even a day-player role—you know, a coupla lines like "Look out!" or "Incoming!" as kind of a trade-off for them renting your cool car. But I've already got that list from Patty—it was very short. I've already, um, checked them all out."

"Yeah," Jules said. "That brings me to the other thing I wanted to ask you about. My good friends at the LAPD have reported a curious rash of break-ins in the Los Angeles area. Nothing's stolen, nothing's vandalized. Just a jimmied lock or an alarm system that's been compromised, and a sense from a bunch of homeowners that someone was inside their house while they were at work."

"Really?" Cosmo said.

"Yeah." Jules closed his briefcase. "Even more bizarre—all of the addresses come from our master list. You know—cast, crew, studio employees?"

"No kidding."

Jules shook his head. "Nope. I've spoken to Tom and Decker—they're as baffled as I am."

"Sounds pretty mystifying."

"Yeah," Jules said dryly. "I'm completely mystified." He stood up. "You find this guy, you call and you let us take it from there, you understand?"

"My priority right now is to keep Jane safe," Cosmo said.

"Yeah, right. Answer my question with a vaguely related statement that promises nothing." Jules laughed as he went out of the kitchen. "I won't notice that you were evasive. I'm only a federal agent."

———

Jules was on the verge of leaving the house, a process that involved coordination with the entire Trouble-shooters team—although with all of the video cameras and sensors, not to mention the watchful personnel, the Chadwicks' front yard was now probably the safest place in all of Los Angeles—when he heard Jane shouting.

"Cos! **Cosmo!**"

Jules had to leap out of the way as the SEAL came out of the kitchen like an express train. He went up the stairs by jumping and grabbing hold of the railing, flipping himself up and over it.

Jules followed the more conventional way as Jane came barreling out of her upstairs office, her cell phone in her hand, a stricken look on her face.

Cosmo nearly knocked her over, grabbing her shoulders, doing a quick visual. She looked okay, all in one piece.

"He's got Patty," she said, and burst into tears.

"Who's got Patty?" Cosmo demanded.

Robin had come into the entryway, drawn out of the conference room by the ruckus. Jules didn't let himself look down at him.

"He just called me!" Jane told him. "Mr. Insane-o. He called and said he was going to kill Patty if I didn't . . . if I . . . Oh, God, Cos, we have to call Jules!"

"Jules!" Cosmo called, holding tightly to Jane.

"He called on your cell phone?" Jules asked her. "Just now?"

Apparently Jane hadn't noticed him climbing the

stairs. She blinked at him in surprise. "Wow, you're good," she told Cosmo with a watery smile. But it faded as she answered Jules' question. "Yeah. He said if I didn't do exactly what he told me, he'd do to Patty"— her tears returned with a vengeance—"what he did to Angelina."

CHAPTER TWENTY-FOUR

Jane sat in her conference room as the FBI set up equipment that—according to Jules Cassidy's opinion—probably wouldn't help them trace much of anything, if and when the killer called back.

The killer who'd kidnapped Patty.

The tension in the room was thick. Cosmo was hovering nearby, as was Robin.

Of course, it was entirely possible that Robin was merely hovering near the liquor cabinet.

Jules came and sat down across from Jane. He looked tired, but he managed a smile. "Let's go over that phone call one more time."

"I'd rather talk about this woman who is going to pretend to be me," Jane told him.

"She's a trained FBI agent," Cosmo said.

"Which will do her a hell of a lot of good if, as you've pointed out, this guy takes a . . . what did you call it? A head shot," Jane said sharply. The phrase meant something very different in her business. "No one dies." She looked back at Jules. "I need you to promise me that—"

"I can't," he told her, his elegant lips set in a grim line. "I'm not going to lie to you. But you also need to know that forensics has determined that the bullet that struck Angelina in her head was most probably a lucky—or unlucky—hit. The shooter fired six rounds total, and the first round entered her right shoulder. It was only after she was down, on the ground, that a bullet entered the back of her head."

Oh, God. "How do you know?" Jane asked.

"Forensics is a science, Janey," Cosmo told her. "It's math and physics. When you know several of the variables, like where the shooter was positioned and the point and angle of where the projectile entered the victim's body, you can figure out how and where the victim was sitting or standing when she was shot."

"In Angelina's case," Jules added, "we also know that when that first shot was fired she was walking down the driveway to her car—facing the shooter. Our guy is good, but no way could he have hit her in the back of the head."

"If that's the case, then give **me** a bulletproof vest—" Jane started, but Cosmo cut her off.

"Not an option."

She didn't look at him. "I'm talking to Jules."

"It's **not** an option, Jane," Jules agreed. "In some ways, this is even worse news. It means that whoever this guy is, he's probably good enough to know not to take intentional shots to the head—it's a smaller target, easier to miss. He's also smart enough to know that even if you didn't come to us with the news that he's taken Patty, he's giving you enough time to scrounge up a vest or a flak jacket. He's got something else in mind, and we're not going to take a chance risking your life."

"But you'll risk someone else's," she pointed out.

"A professional agent," Cosmo said, "who is trained to handle this type of situation."

"What's her name?" Jane asked.

"Janey," Robin said, "why don't you just answer Jules' questions? What does her name have to do with—"

Jane was on the verge of losing it. "Because if she's going to die for me, I should at least know her name!"

Jules sat forward and took her hands in his. "Jane. I know what you're thinking. But you have to know that if you'd tried to deal with this on your own, both you **and** Patty would've ended up dead."

"So now just Patty's going to die." Jane hated this. "Patty and some woman I've never even met."

"When I find out the agent's name, I'll let you know," he told her. "I'll make sure you're in the loop—every step of the way."

Jules Cassidy had very nice eyes. They were a warm shade of dark brown, with long lashes. Nicer still was the kindness she could see in them, the sincerity in his almost too-handsome face.

What was wrong with her brother? What devil inside of him had made him go home with Adam instead of Jules?

Who, it was also very obvious, had been badly hurt by that.

Jane had seen it so many times before. Hurricane

Robin swept in, crashed around, and destroyed all potential for happiness.

Gay, straight, bi, she loved her brother, but God, he was a screwup.

"Right now we don't have a definite plan," Jules admitted. "We need to wait until this guy calls you again, see what his demands are, where exactly he wants you to go. Meanwhile, we'll be using every resource available to find Patty—everything from state-of-the-art satellite technology to Mr. Mysterious over there"—he gestured to Cosmo—"and his amazing ability to walk through locked doors."

Cosmo. Who loved her.

He was standing on the other side of the room, as if he didn't want to crowd her, or impose, or . . .

"See if you can't remember more of the exact conversation," Jules urged her. "When your phone rang and you saw it was Patty's cell number . . ." he prompted.

"I answered by saying, 'Thank God, you're safe,' " Jane told him. "And this man laughed and said, 'Oh, I'm keeping Patty nice and safe.' "

As her voice wobbled, Cosmo shifted slightly. **I'm right here.**

She cleared her throat. "I said, 'Who is this?' He said, 'Your worst nightmare,' and I said, 'Robin?' because I thought maybe he was, you know, messing around with me."

It was such clichéd dialogue from a B-grade thriller, she'd actually thought . . .

Over on the other sofa, Robin covered his eyes with his hand. Jules glanced at him. "And he said . . . ?"

This was where it got a little blurry. "He laughed," Jane said, closing her eyes to concentrate, "and said, 'I've got Patty and' something like, 'if you don't want me to do to her what I did to Angelina'—" She had to stop again. Take a breath. Look at Cosmo, who nodded encouragement. "—you'll do exactly what I say. You tell anyone that I called—' and that was where I interrupted him. I said something like, 'But the FBI's already been notified that she's missing.' Even though we hadn't called you yet," she told Jules. "I knew it was the next step."

"Do you think she's already dead?" Robin interrupted.

"No," Jules answered him. "His goal is probably to lure Jane to a place where he can kill her and escape. He's got to figure that in order to get Jane to play his game, he'll need to offer something we call proof of life—a chance to speak to Patty on the phone, for example. A real conversation, not just a recording of her voice."

"He said, 'If you tell anyone about this phone call, she's dead,' " Jane said. "And then he said something about calling back later tonight with instructions."

"He used that word? **Tonight?**" Jules asked.

"I don't know," Jane admitted. "He may have just said later."

Jules looked over toward the other FBI agents, who nodded. "Well, either way, we're ready for him to call.

When he does, we're going to want you to keep him talking. Whatever he asks, tell him you're going to have trouble getting away from your security team. He's probably going to give you a deadline. He'll try to push it so we have as little time as possible to prepare." Jules' cell phone rang. "Excuse me."

He stood up as he took the call, moving away from the sofa.

Robin stood, too, crossing to the bar, where he poured himself another drink. Just what he needed.

"You did the right thing." Cosmo sat down next to her on the sofa. Closer but not too close. "Asking for help with this, instead of doing something crazy. I wanted to . . ." He cleared his throat. "I want to make sure you know how much that means to me."

Jane couldn't hold his gaze. Please, God, don't let her start to cry again. It seemed as if all she'd done these past few days was cry.

Angelina, however, would never cry again.

Cosmo was silent for a good long time. When he finally spoke, his voice was quiet. "I lost a really good friend a few years ago," he told her. "Frank O'Leary, who was with me when . . ."

"You saved Yasmin's life," she finished for him.

He nodded. "He was killed a few years after that. In a terrorist attack—when a gunman opened fire in a hotel lobby in Kazbekistan."

"Oh, God."

"It won't always feel like this," he said. "So raw."

"It will for Murphy." She clenched her teeth to

hold back her tears. "Oh, Cos, all I keep thinking is I shouldn't have tried for so much advance publicity for **American Hero.** I should have just quietly made it and released it, and people like Tim Ebersole and the Freedom Network and the psycho who killed Angelina might not have even noticed it."

He thought about that for several moments. "But was that really what you wanted," he finally asked. "To make a movie that no one noticed?"

"No, but . . . then I keep thinking I should just give in. Quit. No movie is worth dying for," she told him.

"You're wrong." He spoke with such conviction, no hesitation at all. "I've been to countries where people aren't allowed to make movies, where free speech will get you thrown in jail or even killed. Every American should have a TDY—temporary duty—in one of those places. It's life-changing, Janey. Too many people take freedom for granted—you should see what it's like to live without it. You come home, and you think **Thank God,** because you live in a country where you have freedom from persecution, freedom from oppression and fear, freedom of religion. . . ." He ticked them off on his fingers. "Freedom of speech. Freedom to disagree. Have you ever heard that expression, **I will fight to the death to protect your right to disagree with me?**"

Jane nodded.

"Frank did. He fought to the death. Frank and Matt and Scott and Jeremy and—" Cosmo shook his head. "They made the ultimate sacrifice for our country, and there are others, just like them, making sacrifices every single day. You can't imagine what it's like to be out there, at risk, to have friends die, and then come home and see this"—he struggled to find the words—"to see people—Americans—trying to silence the voices of other Americans, just because they disagree. People calling other people unpatriotic because they don't share the same opinions. Frank didn't die for that, he died for democracy—for a country ruled by **all** the people, where all voices, even unpopular ones, have the right to be heard. Even the Freedom Network has the right to spout their Nazi bullshit as long as they don't threaten or take away someone else's rights when they do it. Because telling someone to shut up—**that's** un-American. That dishonors my fallen brothers.

"We're at war," Cosmo told her. "American servicemen and -women are out there, in the thick of it, fighting for freedom. We're counting on people like you to hold the line here at home. Oppression starts when we back down from a threat, when we let ourselves be bullied and frightened into silence."

He was quiet for several moments, then he said, "Frankie O'Leary's birthday was the day after mine. He was born in this little town in Louisiana. He had this really thick accent—Cajun, I think. And even though he could tone it down when he wanted to, there was this one officer—regular Navy—who really chaffed his . . . Well, Frank didn't think too highly of him, and whenever Admiral Tucker was around, he always cranked the accent to eleven. Drove Tucker nuts." Cosmo laughed softly, remembering. "Frankie really loved Elvis Presley—his gospel years—and he liked to water-ski. He was something out there, you should have seen him. His girlfriend's name was Rosie, and his last words, his last thoughts were of her—of how much he loved her."

It took him a moment, but Cosmo finally cleared his throat and went on. "I call her a couple times a year and we talk about him. On his birthday, on Memorial Day, and later in the summer, in August, too. He was really into astronomy, and he loved this one meteor shower, you know, in early August—Perseid, I think it's called. I think it might've been around the anniversary of the first time he asked Rosie out. He was really into romancing her, you know? He treated her really nicely."

Jane gave in to her tears.

"We honor his memory the other 362 days of the year by doing him proud," Cosmo continued after another of his long pauses. "By fighting on. By holding the line. By living large and remembering that freedom doesn't come for free. That's what you're going to have to do for Angelina, Janey. I know she didn't sign on to fight this war, but the man who killed her is as much of a terrorist as the man who killed Frank, and we cannot let the terrorists win."

"What about Patty?" Jane had to ask. "And this FBI agent, this woman?"

"Trust Jules and his team to do their jobs," Cosmo told her. "Do what they say, Jane. Will you promise me that you'll do exactly what they say? No foolish risks, no craziness, no heroics?"

Fear made her heart beat harder. "Where are you going?" Talk about no craziness, no heroics . . .

"I'm going to go find this guy before he hurts anyone else." He kissed her so sweetly, his mouth so gentle, his hand warm against her cheek. But he only held it there briefly. "I'm sorry I was so public when I said . . . what I said."

I love you.

Oh, God.

"Cos," Jane said. "About that . . . We need to talk."

We need to talk were not the four little words Cosmo had been hoping to hear Jane say.

At least not right now, in response to his declaration of love.

But okay. He glanced over at Robin and Jules. They were on the other side of the room—Jules still on the phone, and Robin getting yet another drink. Cosmo would have preferred complete privacy, but . . . Here they were. Needing to talk.

Jane had tears in her eyes, which made his chest hurt.

"I know I'm not very good at this," he said quietly. "I've made mistakes in the past by not saying anything at all, and now I guess I've gone and said too much, too soon."

"No," she said. "It's not you, it's me."

Oh, and weren't those the most damning words in a state-of-the-relationship conversation?

"Maybe," Cosmo said, "we shouldn't be talking about this right now. Maybe, when this is over, when we have Patty back, and this guy is—" He exhaled hard. "Maybe, if we have time to take things slowly, maybe then . . ."

Maybe he could make her fall in love with him, too.

"I just . . . hate the thought of disappointing you," she told him. "And I know that's all I've been doing."

What? Cosmo struggled to understand. "Janey, I'm not . . . Well, yeah, I've been a little disappointed that you won't talk to me about . . ." He leaned forward, took her hands. "Listen, you wouldn't be human if dealing with any of this came easily. I wish you trusted me enough to share your fears." He paused again, wanting desperately to get this right. "I know you feel responsible for everything that's happened, and I wish you'd talk to me about that. But that's okay. Because, you know, it works both ways. And if we stay together long enough, well, it's just a matter of time before I disappoint you, too. No one's perfect. I'm not looking for perfect. Yeah, you drive me crazy sometimes. But I've never been so happy as I am when I'm with you— even when you're driving me crazy."

Her tears fell on their clasped hands. Christ, he didn't mean to make her cry. Hurting her was the last thing he wanted to do. This was where, in the past, he would have simply surrendered.

But not this time. This time he was going to stay and fight.

"After we catch this guy," he told her, "and things get back to normal—"

She lifted her head. "I cry too much. I try not to

but . . . And I have an awful temper. I get angry and I say things, terrible things, that I don't mean. I'm awful that way, like an overgrown four-year-old. I'm not at all funny or fun to be with—that's just an act. I'm . . . I'm . . . grim and . . . I'm a giant balloon of self-doubt and I've fooled **every**one into thinking I'm someone else—"

"Jane," he said. "I see you. The real you. Very clearly."

"Really?" There was hope in her eyes as she gazed back at him. Hope and all those tears that she was no longer trying to hide from him. "Are you sure? Because I've gotten so good at being Mercedes that sometimes the line starts to blur. Sometimes I even fool myself."

Cosmo nodded. "She can be a little . . . intimidating. But you know what I've noticed about her?"

Jane shook her head.

Cos touched her cheek, catching a tear with his thumb. "She's really nice. Sweet nice," he clarified. "As opposed to nun nice."

She laughed at that. It was soggy and more like a gulp or a sob than a real laugh, but it was a good sign.

"I'm hard to live with," she said.

"Yeah, and who told you that?" he asked. "Your mother? She's been wrong before. But, okay, maybe this time she's right. So what? I'm hard to live with, too. Next issue?"

She laughed again. "It's not that simple."

"Yes, it is."

"No, it's—"

"Do you love me?" He went for it. Point-blank.

Tears welled again in Jane's eyes. She wasn't kidding about that crying thing. "Yes," she whispered.

He misted up, too, as he kissed her. God, what a pair. "Then it is that simple," he said, his forehead against hers. "I'm crazy in love with you, Janey. I'm in love with both of you, with all of you—however you want to define it. And if you love me, too . . . Tell me—with that on our side, what can't we handle?"

"I'm not sure I deserve you," she said.

"Yeah, well, get over it," he told her. "Because I deserve you." He kissed her again. "I have to go. Promise me you'll do what Jules says. No foolish risks."

She wiped her cheeks with both hands. "I'll be careful."

He looked at her.

"I promise," she said.

"Call me if you need me," he told her, and started for the door.

"Cosmo."

He turned to look at her.

"It **does** go both ways," Jane said. She wasn't trying to hide her worry from him anymore, thank God. "I don't want to get a call from Tom Paoletti and Decker every Memorial Day."

He came back to the sofa, his heart in his throat. Jesus. "I don't want that for you, either."

He could tell from her eyes that she was very aware that he hadn't promised her that that would never happen. As a SEAL, it was a promise he couldn't make, a promise he might not be able to keep.

He just kissed her again, then went out the door.

The sound of an incoming fax didn't wake Robin, so Jules kicked the leg of his chair as he went past. "Go to bed."

Robin opened his eyes. "Did he call?" He pushed his hair back from his face as he straightened up in his seat.

"Not yet," Jules said. "Aren't you in that D-Day scene that's being filmed tomorrow? I thought Jane said you had a predawn call." He glanced at his watch. "Which is in, like, an hour. Okay, forget about bed. You better go take a shower."

Robin shook his head gingerly, grimacing at the pain from his hangover. "No way is Janey going to continue production—"

"She has to," Jules said, dialing his cell phone, calling Cosmo. "Business as usual. We've got to assume the killer's watching. Seriously, Robin, you better get going."

"Why hasn't he called?" Robin asked.

"I don't know," Jules admitted. "Maybe he's just screwing with us."

He got bumped right over to voice mail. "Richter, it's Cassidy. I just received a list of names from the IRS, believe it or not. It's standard procedure to check any list of suspects with them, see if any names stand out. I think it dates from the days when nearly all FBI agents were accountants. Anyway, I cross-referenced this list with the extras who own uniforms, and four names were flagged." He consulted the fax. "One's for tax evasion—Christopher Martins. Two had errors in their social security numbers, which could be intentional or not—Paul Ramirez and William Hart. The fourth's a little odd. A Carl Linderman is marked for **paying** taxes last year, apparently after a few years of reporting zero income. I'm not sure what that's about—why that's a problem. I mean, he could be a student, right? Anyway, there it is. Call back so I'll know you got this message—actually, why don't you call Jane? I think she'd probably like to hear your voice. The past few hours have been pretty tense over here. Thanks."

He made another call to Tom Paoletti with that same information, then flipped his phone shut and glanced back at Robin, who was watching him.

"What?" Jules said.

"Adam's going to be on set," Robin told him. "I haven't seen him since . . ."

That night.

Jules was too tired to do more than close his eyes in an attempt to hide his very emotional reaction to that news. What was he supposed to say? Congratulations?

"Cos just got your message," Jane called out from the other side of the room, her cell phone to her ear. "He just missed your call. He says he'll put those four at the top of his list."

"Thanks, sweetie," Jules answered her, then turned back to Robin. "Good luck with that."

"Today's the day I die." Robin must've realized that

that probably wasn't the best thing to say to the FBI agent in charge of tracking the psycho who wanted to kill his sister. "In the movie," he quickly added. "It's a dream sequence, a nightmare, and I actually die—Hal dies—a whole bunch of different ways."

Jesus, Jules needed a vacation. "Have fun," he told Robin, and walked away.

CHAPTER TWENTY-FIVE

"I wasn't anywhere near Omaha Beach in Normandy on the sixth of June 1944," Jack Shelton told Robin in his reedy old voice. "By the time the Twenty-third arrived, the fighting had moved quite a ways into France. But I stood on that beach and imagined what it had been like for those boys who'd leapt from the Higgins boats and rushed onto the shore. I marveled at the lack of cover—it was a beach. There was nowhere to hide from what must've been a rain of bullets from the German machine-gun nests in their concrete bunkers on the cliffs."

Robin stood with Jack now on the beach in California, where they would spend the next four days filming the battle sequence.

"Aside from the copious amounts of water and sand, this doesn't look all too much like Normandy," Jack informed him.

Instead of cliffs, there was a steep, brush-covered hillside on the south end of the beach. A jumble of giant rocks was at the bottom, forming some kind of breakwater that extended out into the ocean. The rocks looked slippery and dangerous where the waves broke over them, and just plain dangerous farther ashore.

The set designers had scattered bits and pieces of Hitler's famous Atlantic Wall on the sand—giant bars of twisted steel, chunks of concrete to keep tanks at bay, rolls of barbed wire to make life more difficult for the foot soldiers. Although only the barbed wire was real. The steel and concrete were foam and plastic.

Digital effects would be added via computer—more of that wall, a more realistic-looking cliff, the massive Allied armada dotting the "channel," aircraft overhead.

Jack had told Robin that some of his peers—aging set designers from Hollywood's golden era—looked down their noses at filmmakers who used digital effects. They called it cheating.

Jack believed that digital effects were just another cost-cutting item in a filmmaker's toolbox.

Which was true. Without it, Janey wouldn't even have attempted to include this D-Day sequence in **American Hero.** It saved a bundle on casting, too.

Additional Marines would be added digitally, although hundreds of the real deal—well, real stuntmen and extras anyway—had already arrived, parking in the big lot and reporting for costume and makeup in a circus-size tent nearby.

There were three other tents set up right on the beach. One was to provide shade for the actors. Another was for the production team, as well as for the special effects explosives and for special makeup and latex body parts for those doomed to "die" in particularly gruesome ways.

The third tent was for props—battle gear as well as authentic-looking weaponry.

Normally such items would've been handed out in the costume tent in the parking lot. But because of the heightened security—a chain-link fence had been hastily constructed around this part of the beach, and a metal detector was set up at the gate, through which everyone had to pass—none of the actors or stuntmen were being given a prop gun until after they were on the enclosed set.

As Robin strolled down the beach with Jack, he saw Adam, in uniform, deep in discussion with the director and the stunt supervisor, choreographing a rush up the beach and a dive to cover behind a small ridge of sand. The ridge was rigged to explode, as if deflecting an artillery hit.

The special effects team had also set up lines of smaller explosions designed to look like machine-gun bullets hitting the sand. Adam had to be close to them, but not too close, in order for the danger to look realistic.

The AD was farther down the beach, talking to a large group of extras, pointing out the areas that were restricted to the stuntmen only.

Harve was with those stuntmen, giving them a refresher course on using the squibs and blood packs that they wore hidden in their uniforms.

Another group was already in place even farther down the beach, near the "cliff." One of the extras was hard at work, digging a foxhole.

"He's a little odd," Jack said, following Robin's gaze. "I was talking to him earlier—he was quite keen on trying out that entrenching tool."

He certainly was energetic. "Some of these guys are part of a group of Civil War reenactors," Robin told the old man. "They can be a little intense. They like to live the part—it's kind of like having a hundred Robert De Niros as extras."

Jack nodded. "Speaking of living the part," he said. "You're looking a little worn around the edges. You really must take better care of yourself, Robin. While it's true Harold had an unearthly quality to him, it was more angelic than dead and buried."

"Yeah, well, Harold never had to worry about—" Robin stopped himself. "I'll work on getting to bed earlier. In the meantime, I better get into makeup, see if they can do anything to help."

"Oh, and Adam was looking for you," Jack called after him. "He was hoping to get a chance to speak to you before filming starts. I told him I'd tell you to keep your eyes open, to watch for him."

"Thanks," Robin called back. He'd watch for Adam, all right. In order to avoid him like the plague.

The sound of the sirens in the distance was the first clue Cosmo had that his unauthorized presence in

William Hart's little stucco three-bedroom ranch had been noted.

The second clue was a female voice coming from the shade-darkened gloom at the bedroom-end of the hall. "Drop whatever you think you was stealing, hands up, and turn around slow. I got a gun, and I'm not afraid to use it."

How had she heard him? He'd been silent. And invisible. Cos was tempted to ask her if she wanted a job and hand her Tom Paoletti's business card, but instead, he kept his hands where she could see them as he turned.

True to her word, the very young, very short woman standing there was holding a Colt .380 handgun.

"Police are on their way," she informed him.

She may not have been afraid to use the weapon, but her stance was ridiculous. It was extremely likely that she didn't know **how** to use the damn thing. And it sure as hell looked to Cosmo as if the Colt's safety was on.

With Patty's life in danger, and Janey climbing the walls, Cosmo didn't have time for lengthy explanations to either Charlie's littlest angel or the nice policemen speeding their way here. Yes, the kitchen door had been unlocked when he'd let himself in, but that only meant that—if they refused to listen—he'd be facing felony home invasion charges instead of a B&E. The booking process and bail hearing would be just as time-consuming.

But he also knew—and he had absolutely no doubt

about this—that Jane would be very unhappy if he got himself shot and killed this morning.

The sirens were getting louder as Cosmo tried to get a better look at that weapon.

"Is that real or a toy?" he finally asked, and she slapped on the hall light.

"It's very real, and I **will** shoot you if you move."

Not with the safety on like that, honey.

Cosmo dove for the dining room. He went out the ancient sliding glass door feetfirst, right through the already cracked glass—which freaking hurt, but not half as much as it would have if he'd given gun-girl the time to push that safety down.

Bleeding from God knows where, he leapt from the back deck and raced across the backyard, staying low and zigzagging in case she decided to shoot him.

The fact that she didn't fire that weapon was good.

The bleeding, however, was not so good. Although as far as he could tell, the worst of it was a couple of superficial gashes to his forearms.

Cosmo used the bottom of his T-shirt to keep from leaving a telltale trail behind him as he circled around, heading back to his truck. As he crossed into a neighbor's yard, he could see that there were three police cruisers parked haphazardly in front of William Hart's little house, lights still spinning.

He'd gotten out just in time.

And he could probably cross William Hart off his list of suspects. At least they could be sure Patty wasn't being held at Hart's home. Kidnappers generally didn't call the police for assistance.

Cosmo moved swiftly, keeping to the neighborhood shrubbery. His left arm was bleeding a little too conspicuously, and . . . **Damn it.**

Down the street, another police cruiser was stopped right behind his truck.

Cos had parked on the main thoroughfare, some distance away, but apparently not far enough. This cop was just hanging there, keeping his eyes open, no doubt watching for someone who looked as if he'd just run through a sliding glass door.

Someone, say, with blood dripping down his arms . . .

Cursing, Cosmo turned and swiftly headed south.

He needed to get out of this neighborhood before he went into a store to buy a new shirt, making a lot of noise about how he'd fallen off his bike on the way to a breakfast date with his new girlfriend and her father.

Until he got that new shirt—preferably one with long sleeves—he had to keep a low profile, but he might as well head toward Carl Linderman's apartment. Linderman was suspect number four on the IRS list, flagged for . . . wait for it—it was a good one . . . paying his taxes.

This was probably a waste of time. Chances were pretty slim that the killer was a) one of the extras who owned his own uniform, or b) one of the four that the IRS had flagged, and especially c) Carl Linderman, whose apartment Cosmo had already checked out.

Still, the fact that Linderman's name kept showing up on so many lists made it worth another look.

Cos would have to come back this way later for his truck.

And—fuck!—for his cell phone, which he'd left in the slot in the dash, right above the radio.

From somewhere down the street, a police siren whooped, and Cosmo moved through the early morning fog, cutting through backyards, as swiftly as he possibly could.

"Holy shit!"

Jane looked over at Jules Cassidy, who was talking to someone on his cell phone. Was that a good "Holy shit!" or a bad one?

"Holy **shit,**" he said again, and this time he sounded angry. "Four **hours** ago? And you didn't think your Jane Doe might be someone we'd want to know about?"

Jane Doe.

"No," Jules said into his phone. "No, she was kidnapped. Yes, a federal case—"

Jane Doe was the name the police, the hospital, or the morgue gave to an unidentified dead body. Jane stood up.

"You do have a computer, don't you? With—" Jules glanced over at her. "Hold on," he ordered whoever was on the other end of his phone as he correctly interpreted the expression on her face. "Patty's alive," he told Jane. "She's over at Century City Hospital. She's safe."

"What?" she breathed.

"Yeah, she was found four hours ago. From what they can tell, she got hold of her kidnapper's rifle and blew him away—in self-defense. It's already been run through ballistics. It's the exact same weapon that killed Angelina and Ben Chertok."

"Holy shit," Jane said. "Are you telling me . . . ?"

"We're pretty sure your Mr. Insane-o is dead."

Decker pulled up to the crime scene just a few seconds after Jules Cassidy arrived.

Someone had already draped both the building and the car parked in the driveway with yellow tape.

The car in the driveway was an ancient Pontiac Catalina. White, with a peeling black top.

Hot damn.

Cassidy was on the verge of being led inside, but he saw Deck coming and waited for him to catch up.

"Our guy's name was Mark Avery," Jules said, no greeting. Deck knew the FBI agent had been up all night, too, but he didn't look even slightly rumpled. He was clearly a disciple of his boss, Max Bhagat, who was an impeccable dresser. Beneath Jules' suit, his shirt looked clean. Deck would've bet big money that Jules kept an electric razor in his glove compartment and used it at red lights on his way over.

"Twenty-four years old, he had an arrest record, but nothing too serious," Jules continued as he led the way inside and down the hall toward the kitchen. "Disturbing the peace, public intoxication, starting brawls by spouting white supremacist sentiment in black and Latino neighborhoods. He was earmarked as someone to look at for hate crimes in this part of town. You know—anti-Semitic graffiti shows up on the synagogue? Go talk to Avery. Always suspected, never convicted. It'll be interesting to see if that kind of thing disappears now that he's dead. Phew, it smells bad in here."

It did. It smelled awful. Not just from the faintly metallic scent of the blood that had been sprayed against the far wall and now pooled on the linoleum floor. It was as if someone hadn't taken out the kitchen garbage for two or three weeks.

Jules must've been thinking the same thing because he used a pen to lift the lid of the plastic kitchen garbage container. It had a brand-new white bag inside, as if Mark Avery had said to Patty, "Hang on a sec before you shoot me. I have to take out the trash."

"The rifle was on the floor over here," Jules said, moving to the opposite side of the kitchen, "near where Patty was lying. She's apparently still really out of it—no official statement from her yet. She was given Rohypnol—aka the date rape drug." He paused. "You know anything about Rohypnol?"

Decker shrugged. "Isn't it supposed to make you really docile? Easy to manage and manipulate? It's a horse tranquilizer, right?"

Jules nodded. "Walking unconscious." He ran his hand across the lower half of his face. "As far as what the detectives who arrived first on the scene could tell, she somehow got both the weapon and the opportunity, and . . ." He shrugged. "Maybe Avery thought the drug had kicked in, but it hadn't yet." He looked at the forensics evidence decorating the far wall. "No wonder he didn't call Jane last night."

There appeared to have been a slight struggle, or maybe someone had had a temper tantrum. The remains of a meal had been swept from the kitchen table and onto the floor. And one of chairs had been knocked on its side. Jules carefully stepped over a broken glass as he made his way to the refrigerator.

"We've taken a computer from one of the bedrooms," he continued. "Apparently it contains an entire unpublished blog—you know, weblog or journal— where Avery recounts exactly what he did. How he followed Murphy up to Malibu and . . ." He shook his head. "There's a ton of evidence. Internet addresses match the ones used to send those e-mails to Mercedes Chadwick. Shit, we've apparently even got a Quicken program that keeps track of expenses for his trip to Idaho, when he killed Chertok."

He opened the refrigerator, frowning at the contents.

Deck moved to look over his shoulder.

It was empty.

Well, nearly empty. A jar of mayonnaise sat forlornly on the center shelf.

The two men stared at it.

"Sometimes," Jules said, "when a case ends unexpectedly, in a way that you don't really anticipate, like without a lot of unnecessary violence, it can feel kind of weird. Not that I'm not extremely grateful that the violence was contained to this little kitchen, because I am."

"Yeah," Decker said as Jules shut the refrigerator door.

Jules looked around the room, frowning slightly. "Where's Jane?" he asked. "When I left the house, she wanted to go to the hospital—to see Patty. Did she?"

Decker nodded. "PJ, Nash, and Tess are with her. They took her garage to garage."

Jules nodded, too. "Good."

"Want to go look out back, see what's in the trash?" Deck asked.

Jules led the way. "Yes, I most certainly do."

"They're gone."

This time, Cosmo didn't even try to go in covertly. He just walked right up the middle of the driveway that led to Carl Linderman's apartment, and sure enough, the elderly neighbor lady poked her head out of her kitchen door.

"Your friends," she informed him. "They moved out. Couple of nights ago."

"Really," he said, his pulse quickening. Carl Linderman, who had been hired as an extra for the next four days, had moved out? After—no doubt—being told by his nosy neighbor that a "friend" had been in his apartment, looking for him.

"They loaded everything up into his truck—which

is black, by the way. It's the plumber living in the apartment upstairs whose truck is red. But they loaded the truck at three o'clock in the morning. Was I glad when they left. Do you know how hard it is to sleep when people are whispering?"

Black truck, not red. "Maybe Carl was helping his roommate move out," Cosmo suggested.

"I don't think so," she told him. "I haven't seen either of them around since then."

"I hope you're mistaken," he lied to her with a smile. "I was supposed to meet Carl here this morning. I still have his key."

What he had was his lock pick, but he blocked her view of the door as he made short work of the lock and . . .

Whoa.

The apartment was empty.

Not only was it empty, it was spotless. Someone had cleaned the hell out of it. The place gleamed.

Cosmo walked through. Not a beer can remained. Not a pizza box. Not even a dust bunny.

And, he suspected, nary a fingerprint.

Carl Linderman. Who owned both Nazi and American army uniforms. Who'd been on set over at HeartBeat a number of times, according to their records. Who owned a truck that wasn't red, but black—a truck that wasn't registered with the DMV. At least not under his name.

But Carl Linderman and his **roommate . . .** ?

Okay, so that part didn't work. The FBI profilers

had been shouting since day one that their guy was a loner.

And yet . . .

Cos let himself back out the door.

Neighbor Lady had a told-you-so smirk on her face.

He gave her the victory. "You were absolutely right. Do you know, did they have help cleaning the place?" he asked her. "I mean, I know these guys, they're total pigs, but that place shines."

"Marilyn, she owns the house," the woman told him, "she told me they cleaned it themselves. Even took their garbage with them when they left. There's nothing in the cans out back. Can you believe that?"

Oh, yes. Yes, he could. It was called sanitizing. He did it all the time in covert situations, when he wanted to erase his presence in any given area. "Any idea where they went?"

She shook her head. "Nope." Her eyes narrowed. "You a cop or something?"

"Or something," Cosmo said. "I need to call the FBI. May I use your phone?"

He could see a great big no in her eyes at the thought of letting someone who looked like him into her house, even to call the authorities. But her curiosity kept her from slamming the door in his face. "They in trouble?"

There was time for keeping secrets and a time for speed. Cosmo went for speed. "I'm pretty sure they're connected to those death threats made to Mercedes Chadwick—you know, the movie producer?"

She was nodding—she knew Mercedes' name.

"They may have helped kill the wife of one of her security guards," he said. "We think they've kidnapped her personal assistant."

"Yeah, I heard about that," she said.

In her eyes, Cosmo could see the fear of inviting him into her kitchen rassling with the possibility of appearing on **Larry King Live** as the woman who saved the day.

Larry King won. She stepped back and let him in.

As Robin stood on the beach, an extra dressed in a Nazi SS uniform limped past, another man's arm around his shoulders. The second man's head was lolled back—his uniform was covered with fake blood that looked amazingly realistic.

"He all right?" Robin asked. The last thing this movie needed was extras with sunstroke, needing hospitalization.

"Just rehearsing," the conscious man told him.

Rehearsing extras. Good grief. Some of these guys were unbelievably intense. Or maybe they were aware that he was one of the producers, and they were auditioning for a day-player role. God save him from that.

"It's looking good," Robin said, giving a thumbs-up as he backed away. Although, hey there. The limp-necked man was wearing an American army uniform. Chances were not too many Nazis would be carrying injured Americans to safety on Omaha Beach on D-Day.

Don't call us, boys, we'll call you.

He escaped toward the tent, his head pounding. Maybe he could find someone in craft services who could refill his prop canteen with something stronger than water.

"Robin Chadwick!"

Robin turned to see another one of the extras marching toward him. This one had war in his eyes.

And okay, yes, he'd definitely seen the guy's face before, but where? What had Robin done to offend him, while in some drunken fog?

Of course the possibilities were even more limitless now, after . . .

Adam.

Who chose that moment to appear at Robin's shoulder. Freaking perfect timing.

"Hey," Adam said quietly enough so no one could overhear. "You don't call, you don't write, you don't send flowers. What's a nice boy like me to think?"

Oh, good.

This was going to be so much fun. Robin's headache, courtesy of last night's worry, lack of sleep, and relentless drinking, drew itself into an ice-pick point of pain directly behind his left eye.

"Are you happy now?" the angry extra asked as if Robin would know what the fuck he was talking about.

"Um," Robin said.

"Alana in makeup told me," the angry extra started, and it all became crystal clear.

"Okay, hang on there." Robin cut him off. "Alana told **me** she didn't have a boyfriend. I asked, I swear, and she said . . ."

Okay, maybe that wasn't where this was going, because now the extra was confused. But after his confusion passed, he got even angrier.

Adam's eyebrows, however, were raised in amusement.

"You're a total asshole," the extra said. "You slept with both Patty **and** Alana?"

And Charlene and Margery and Susan and . . .

Adam. Robin didn't dare look in his direction. Holy Jesus, just standing next to him like this was awful. He didn't remember much of that night, but he remembered enough.

Don't think about that, don't think about that. . . .

"Alana told me there are rumors going around that Patty is missing," the extra said. Wayne—that was his name. That's right. Robin had seen him sniffing around Patty's office. "That this guy who's after your sister grabbed her."

Ol' Wayne was really upset. Shit, if he knew the truth . . .

But Robin couldn't let on that anything was wrong. Mr. Insane-o had warned Jane not to tell anyone. So he fell on the grenade.

"She went home," he told Wayne, playing the part of said total asshole, letting him see what he wanted to see. "And yeah, yeah, it was my fault. I got too drunk one night and . . . That shit just always happens to me, you know?" His tone was pure "it's not my fault," and he even managed a disdainful laugh. "But she was really upset that I wouldn't, like, **marry** her, so . . . she went home to her mommy."

But Wayne was shaking his head. "I know for a fact that she had no intention of going home. She was completely over you, asswipe. She was already seeing someone else."

"Dude." Robin shrugged expansively. "Believe what you want. What can I say? It was a mistake. I apologized. What else can I do? As much as I'd like to, I can't go back in time and un-fuck her."

He could see that Wayne wanted to hit him at that. If someone had said that about someone Robin cared about, he wouldn't have been able to let it go. But Wayne was a better man than he was. He turned and walked away.

He was a nice guy, and he really liked Patty. And when he found out that she was kidnapped, or dead, he was going to be devastated.

Robin's hands were shaking, his head was throbbing, and he had to sit down. But there was nowhere to sit except right in the sand, and when he turned, Adam was still there, watching him.

"So is there anyone on set you haven't slept with?" Adam asked. But then he looked closer, stepped closer, concern in his voice. "Are you all right?"

"I need you not to touch me," Robin said through clenched teeth.

Adam backed up. Nodded. "Okay," he said quietly.

"That's where I thought we were, so it's not . . . too disappointing." He forced a laugh. "Unlike Patty, I didn't rush out and order wedding invitations."

Robin closed his eyes. He couldn't even look at Adam. How did he get here? To this place where his life was so completely screwed up? Where it hurt just to breathe?

Adam lowered his voice even more and spoke quickly. "I know you wish you could go back in time and un-fuck me, too. But you can't. I'm not going to pull a Patty and run crying to my friends. I'm not going to tell anyone, Robin. What happened between us is between us. So you don't have to worry about me outing you. I'm also not going to dog you, so you can cross that fear off your list, too. But just so you know, that doesn't mean I don't want a replay, because, well . . . just my luck, I do. If you ever decide you want to, you know where to find me."

Robin just stood there for a long, long time. And when he opened his eyes, Adam was gone.

Patty was still unconscious, sleeping off the last of the drug she'd been given, so Jane wasn't quite sure how all of the reporters who were down in the hospital lobby had gotten the word that she'd be here.

But of course it made sense—the story of Patty's kidnapping had broken in a very major way. All of the TV affiliates wanted a shot of a reporter in front of the hospital for their noon news segment.

The evidence in the apartment where they'd found

Patty was incredible. Apparently, Mr. Insane-o, who had a name now—Mark Avery—had planned to use Patty to lure Jane away from her twenty-four-hour protection. Apparently, that plan—the LAPD detective she'd spoken to had told her Avery went into graphic detail in some kind of computer journal—had also been to kill Patty after letting Jane speak to her on the phone.

But Patty had saved both Jane's life and her own.

It was kind of funny, actually, to think that even though Jane had been surrounded by Navy SEALs and former Marines and FBI agents, her twenty-year-old powder puff of a college intern from Oklahoma had been the hero of the hour.

Jane had been checking her cell phone when she came out of the elevator. Cosmo still hadn't called her back. Where **was** he?

"Mercedes, what are you going to do first, now that the threat is over?" one of the reporters called out, taking her by surprise.

God, she was a mess. She froze for a second as all those cameras swung in her direction. Jeans and a T-shirt, no makeup on her face, her eyes red from the tears of relief she'd cried upon seeing for herself that Patty was safe and in one piece.

PJ Prescott's grip on her arm tightened. "Want me to get you out of here?" he murmured.

She shook her head. Smiled her best Mercedes Chadwick smile. And, holding Angelina in her heart, she grabbed hold of what most definitely was a killer promo moment for a movie that deserved to be seen, made in a country where freedom most definitely did not come for free.

"Hang on tight," she murmured back to PJ. "We're going to hold the line."

CHAPTER TWENTY-SIX

"They found him, you know," the neighbor lady said as she let Cosmo into her kitchen, pointing to the wall phone that was between the door and the refrigerator, next to a key rack and a photo of what had to be her two grandchildren.

"Found who?" he asked as he dialed Jane's number.

"It's been on the news all morning," she told him, watching him like a hawk in case he tried to steal one of her refrigerator magnets.

Damn it, Jane didn't pick up. Of course she wouldn't—an unknown number coming into her cell?

He tried calling Jules and got bumped to voice mail. Same with Decker. He didn't take the time to leave a message.

"How many calls are you making?" the woman asked.

There was a little TV on the kitchen counter, its volume muted and— Christ!

That was Jane on that screen, being interviewed, half a dozen microphones jammed in her face. Cosmo lunged for the volume.

"Hey!" the neighbor squeaked in alarm, moving to the other end of the kitchen.

"Shhh," he ordered as Jane's voice came through the set's cheap speakers.

". . . past few weeks **have** been frightening." She was wearing the same jeans and T-shirt she'd had on when he'd left the house hours ago. "It's still a little hard to believe it's really over. I'm going to celebrate by going on location, where the cast and crew of **American Hero** are reenacting D-Day—the Normandy invasion. It seems only fitting that my first step out into the sunshine, into freedom, should be onto our version of Omaha Beach."

Over? What the fuck was going on? Why did she think this was over? Unless . . . He turned to the woman as, on the TV, Jane continued to talk about freedom of speech. "You said they found him? Found who?"

"The man who was trying to kill Mercedes Chadwick," she told him. "Someone named Mark Avery. He's dead. That girl he kidnapped killed him with his own gun."

"Mark Avery," he repeated, forcing his voice past the fear that threatened to clog his throat. "Not Carl Linderman?" It could be an alias—the two could be one and the same. "Did they say that he was an extra in Jane's—Mercedes'—movie?"

"Nope. They had lots of information about him, lots of evidence that proved he was the stalker, but I've haven't heard anything about him being an actor." Her eyes narrowed. "If you're with the FBI, how come you don't know all this?"

"I need to borrow your car," he said as he dialed Jane's phone number again. He'd seen an old station wagon out in the driveway as he'd come inside.

"If you think I'm just going to hand you my keys—"

She didn't have to—they were right in front of him, hanging on that key rack. Cosmo pocketed them. "You're welcome to come along, but I won't be able to guarantee your safety when the shooting starts."

She gasped, then said, "I'm calling the police!"

"Good. Tell them to send backup and a SWAT team to the **American Hero** set." Again, Jane didn't pick up, but this time, he left a message. "Jane. It's Cos. Don't go onto that beach. I'm pretty sure that the killer wasn't working alone, that there're at least two of them, and one's still at large. You are not safe. I repeat, do **not** go onto that beach."

"Too late," the woman said, and he turned to see on the television—a little caption saying "Live" in the corner of the screen—Jane going through some kind of gate, and toward a crowd of applauding extras in what looked like bloodied uniforms.

She was there. On the beach. In the freakin' open.

Dear, sweet Jesus . . .

"Do you have a cell phone?" he asked.

"Do I look like someone who has a cell phone?" she came back at him.

Cosmo dialed Jules' number on the kitchen phone, then tossed it to the woman. "Hit redial until this number is answered," he ordered her. "Tell the FBI agent who picks up that you have a message from

Chief Richter—that Mercedes Chadwick is still in danger, that I have reason to believe that the shooter wasn't working alone, that we need to get her off that beach now!"

As Janey made a speech for the news cameras, Robin stood with the elder Jack in a small patch of shade cast by the hillside, trying, unsuccessfully so far, to exorcise his headache.

He focused on the day's good news. Patty was safe. Mr. Insane-o was dead, and the danger was over and done.

Because of that, Jane was able to be on set for this D-Day sequence. Robin knew how badly his sister had wanted to be here today. But he also knew she'd trade it all in a heartbeat to have Angelina back.

The helicopter had arrived early for this afternoon's aerial shots. That was good news, too. Although, they still had two rather lengthy ground segments to get on film before the light got too harsh.

Out on the beach, the extras were starting to get restless.

But Jane was finally done. The news cameras were pulling back, packing up, most of them ready to move onto the next news story, despite her invitation to stay and watch some of the filming.

Some of the cameras had already taken footage of the extras waiting on the beach. It made for a good visual—Nazi storm troopers lounging alongside American Marines. And it was always a little freaky to see guys who'd been made up to look dead or dying, as they popped open cans of Pepsi, as they laughed and talked.

"Hey, Nazi, you've got the wrong kind of gun," Jack suddenly called. "He didn't hear me," he told Robin. He pointed out an extra who had his back to them as he walked away. "He's a German officer, but he's carrying an American rifle—a Springfield. It's completely inappropriate. Is there **anyone** in the prop tent who isn't an idiot?"

"Most of the action's going to be down at the other end of the beach," Robin pointed out, because the last thing he wanted to do was chase after some extra who'd been given the wrong prop.

"Hey, Nazi!" Jack called again, but the extra, who was starting to climb up the hill, still didn't hear.

Robin was saved by the assistant director's call for places.

"He won't be visible up there," he reassured Jack, all but pushing the old man toward the spectators' tent.

Jules was in Mark Avery's kitchen when his cell phone rang.

He didn't recognize the number, which meant that it could be Adam calling from a pay phone, so he let it get bumped to his voice mail.

The back door opened and Decker came in. "I just spoke to Tess. She, Nash, and PJ are still with Jane. They're on the beach, on location with the movie crew."

"She couldn't wait?" Jules asked. "Even just a day or two, until we . . . ?"

Until they what?

Found even more evidence against Mark Avery? How much did they need?

Jules didn't know why he was so on edge. But as he looked around the room again, at the broken glass on the floor, the knocked-over chair, the blood-sprayed wall, he realized what had been bugging him. "It's like we're on a movie set. Everything is so carefully laid out."

Decker nodded. "Yeah, it's very **Crime Scene Detecting for Dummies** isn't it? Here's the murder weapon, here's the evidence. Except for the mystery of the kitchen garbage . . ."

Jules laughed. "Yeah." Without a doubt, that was the biggest mystery in here. Something had made this room stink like this, yet the pails out back were as empty as the refrigerator. Neither the police detectives nor the FBI team had removed the trash as evidence. And he'd called and found out that garbage pickup was on Tuesdays. Those cans should have been full.

"I'm going over there," Decker said, heading out the door. "To the beach. See if I can talk Jane into being more cautious."

Good idea. He'd do the same. "Where's Cosmo?" Jules asked, following him into the bright morning sunshine. It had been quite a while since the SEAL had called in. "He can talk her into just about anything."

His phone rang again. Same number. Goddamn it. This had got to stop. He answered it. "Cassidy."

"About time you answered," a cranky old voice berated him. "I have a message from someone named

Richter, who better not be lying because if he is, he just stole my car."

Robin was supposed to run up the beach in a zigzag pattern, with Adam beside him, which just shouldn't have been that hard to do. The camera shot started as a close-up, then did a slow zoom out to reveal the enormity of the battle that raged around them.

When he reached his mark—about a hundred feet away from where they started—he was to fall as if hit by German machine-gun fire.

He was rigged with squibs, and blood would spray as each "bullet" struck. It would look totally realistic, especially in such a wide shot.

"We ready?" the director asked over his megaphone, and Robin closed his eyes, letting Hal take control.

"And . . . action!" A starter pistol was fired—the cue for the extras to go to war.

Most of them were just pretending to fire their prop weapons, but the stuntmen all had guns that shot blanks. It was noisy as hell, and in order to signal a cut, a flare would be fired.

It wasn't easy to run through the soft sand in his boots. His legs pumped, and he kept his head down, weapon cradled in his arms and—

Shit! His foot caught on something and he went down early—too early—and—

Mother of God! The stock of his gun smacked him right in the balls, and Robin let out a stream of very un-Hal-like curses.

"We're still rolling," the director said through the megaphone. "Keep going—Hal and Jack back it up."

"He wants us to start over again," Adam shouted over the din.

No shit, Sherlock. But Robin had all he could handle just to stay curled in a ball, trying not to puke.

Well, so much for the trying not to puke part. He managed, however, to turn his head so the few remaining TV news cameras Janey had brought onto the set didn't get the full Technicolor yuckatation.

"Aw, Jesus," Robin heard Adam say as the director shouted, "Cut," and a flare was shot into the sky.

"Why aren't you wearing a jock?" Jane asked her brother, who had been helped up into the shade of the tent. He lay there in the sand, still looking a little green.

Men were such delicate creatures, and Robin was particularly fragile. She'd learned that back when they were teenagers, and even used it to her advantage a time or two.

He shook his head. "I didn't think I'd need one."

"Do you want me to see if Charlene can dig one up?" she asked, then shrieked, because she was being lifted into the air. PJ had grabbed her by one arm and Nash by the other, and together they were carrying her backward, away from the edge of the production tent.

"Decker just called," PJ informed her. "He wants you out of here."

Jane was exasperated. She straightened her shirt as they put her down in the center of the tent. "What's his deal? He didn't strike me as being such a worry-wart."

"Yeah, well, Jules Cassidy and Cosmo are both worried, too," PJ said. "And that's enough to get **me** worried."

"We now think that the shooter may not have been working alone." Jane turned to see Tess, who was carrying what looked like an umpire's vest and a heavy jacket, coming from the direction of the parking lot. She now spoke to PJ. "These are the ones you meant, right?"

He nodded. Took them from her. Held them out for Jane. "Put these on."

"Okay, wait." She looked at Tess. "All along it's been, 'The profilers say he's an outcast, a misfit, a single male suspect, he's working alone. . . .' And suddenly he's not? What's the deal with that? And . . ." She looked from the vest and jacket to PJ. "News flash: It's neither December nor the Antarctic."

"Profilers occasionally are wrong," Tess explained.

"This is a Kevlar vest, and this is a flak jacket," PJ told her. "If someone shoots you while you're wearing these, you might live."

Damn it. "This was supposed to be over," Jane said as PJ strapped the vest onto her and stuffed her arm into one of the jacket's sleeves.

"Decker and Jules are both on their way," he told her.

"Jane, they're going to want you to leave," Tess said. "Once we have backup, we'll bring a car right into the tent for you." She noticed Jane's eye roll. "It's possible they're just being overly cautious, but . . ."

"If Deck told me he thought there might be two feet of snow on a sunny day in June," PJ said, "I'd go out and buy rock salt and a snowblower."

Damn it. "Where's Cosmo?" Jane asked, the first flicker of real fear slipping out from beneath her annoyance. If Mr. Insane-o wasn't working alone, then she wasn't the only one who was still in danger.

Tess and PJ exchanged a look, then both shook their heads. "Maybe Deck'll know," Tess said.

It wasn't as easy for PJ to force her other arm into the jacket, and Jane shook him off, stabbing it into the sleeve herself.

Robin was back on the beach. The director was getting ready to call action again.

"Can I at least watch the video monitor?" Jane asked.

PJ kept her from moving closer to the edge of the tent. "I'll drag it over to you."

Cosmo owed Carl's elderly neighbor four new tires for her 1989 Taurus wagon.

He took off yet another patch of rubber as he cut across three lanes of oncoming traffic to pull into the beach parking lot.

The rent-a-cops at the gate, hired by HeartBeat as additional security for this on-location shoot, all leapt to their feet in alarm as the car bottomed out.

Make that four new tires and a muffler.

But Cosmo hit the brakes and threw the car into reverse because, oh my holy God, there it was.

The truck he'd spent the past week looking for. With a six in its plate number and that little dent on the back right of the bumper.

Parked in full view, right here in the lot with all of the other extras' cars.

The bumper sticker that boasted of an honor student from Somewhereville had been scraped off, leaving telltale scratch marks behind.

Cos had no doubt. This was definitely the truck he'd seen all those nights ago, in front of Jane's house. And he would bet every penny in his savings account that it belonged to Carl Linderman.

It was chilling that it was here like this—apparently Carl was confident that no one would be looking for him.

On the other hand, the fact that his truck was here was mildly reassuring. Surely Carl would have set up some kind of escape route if he was intending to target Jane here and now.

Either that, or this time he wasn't intending to escape.

No way. This guy was not suicidal. He was a game player. He got off on outsmarting his opponents.

And it was hard to be smarter than the police and the FBI if you were dead.

Of course, searching the truck might provide a hint or two as to Carl's intentions.

But first things first, and making sure Jane was safe was at the very top of Cos' priority list.

He was just about to gun the station wagon and head for the gate, when a car pulled alongside him, the driver leaning on his horn.

It was Jules Cassidy.

Cosmo rolled down the passenger-side window.

"Got your message," the FBI agent called to him. "Jane's here. She's safe. The rest of the team's with her; Decker, too. He was a few minutes ahead of me—he's probably already inside."

"This is the truck I've been looking for." Cos gestured with his thumb over his shoulder.

"You're sure?" Jules asked.

"Positive."

He nodded. "I'll run the plates and call for a warrant."

Yeah, like Cosmo was going to sit around and wait for that. "Do we need to wait for a warrant if the truck's unlocked?" he asked. "What's the rule? Unlocked and open? Or the evidence needs to be in full view, right?"

Jules had worked with Navy SEALs before, and he knew that they didn't always follow the rules.

He should have been able to resist the temptation, but when Cosmo had said, "Why don't you go down and tell those clowns to open the gate so we can drive right in, while I check to see if the truck's open," Jules had said, "Okay."

The gate, however, was—as his Navy SEAL friends would say—a goatfuck of a different dimension. It was locked shut, with a chain and a big padlock. None of the guards seemed to know where someone named Steve was, and apparently Steve had the only key.

Jules was welcome to walk in, passing through the metal detector, but if he wanted to bring the car, he'd have to wait for Steve.

From the other end of the parking lot came the sound of shattering glass.

"Truck's open," Cosmo shouted.

Yeah, right.

"Find Steve," Jules told the guards, a portly gent named Clarence and a clueless soul named Joe, "fast. Because in about thirty seconds, a Navy SEAL with an agenda is going to be in your face, ready to chew through this fence with his teeth."

The difference between these guards and the personnel who worked for Troubleshooters Incorporated was like night and day. These boys didn't have the training necessary to handle something big like this. The best of them probably only had experience catching shoplifters at the local Wal-Mart.

Clarence ran to see if Steve was in one of the Porta Potties.

About time.

Cosmo trotted up. "Check out what Carl Linderman had in his truck."

An MP-5 assault weapon.

"Along with a fuckload of ammo," he continued. "It was under the backseat, kind of sticking out. In full view of the unlocked, open door."

"Is that a prop?" Clueless Joe asked nervously. "Because they told us that all the prop guns would be handed out once the actors were inside the gate—"

"Hope he doesn't mind if I use it," Cosmo added. "Look, I want to drive right in so you can get Jane the hell out of here. Can we take your car? I left mine blocking in the truck." He looked at the gate, focusing on the padlock for the first time. "What the fuck?"

Decker was here. Jane saw him arrive, saw him deep in discussion with the other Troubleshooters, no doubt figuring the best way to get her home as quickly as possible.

So much for her triumphant return to the set of her movie.

"And . . . action!"

As Jane watched the video monitor, Robin launched himself forward.

The camera shot slowly widened to include Adam as Jack, who held on to his helmet with one hand and, looking totally and quite appropriately out of his element, raced after Robin for dear life.

This was a long, single shot that had been intricately choreographed, with soldiers falling and dying all around the two lead players as they crisscrossed up the beach.

But then it happened again. Just over halfway to the point where Robin was supposed to fall, he slipped.

Adam didn't notice for quite a number of steps because his head was down, but then he looked over, realized he was alone, and skidded to a stop. He turned, saw Robin back on the sand, raised his face to the heavens as if seeking deliverance, then trotted back to him.

But Robin didn't get up.

And Adam dropped to his knees next to him, his body language suddenly urgent. He jumped to his feet almost immediately, shouting something back at the cameraman, something they couldn't possibly hear in the din.

"Sweet Jesus, did your little brother whack himself in the family jewels again?" Harve shouted over the sounds of war. "Tick, tock! Clock's running, children!"

The extras fought on—only those closest to Robin and Adam had an inkling that anything was wrong.

But then Harve stared up at the tent, where little bits of sunlight were suddenly appearing in the fabric overhead. "What in heaven's name . . . ?"

"Jane! **Jane!**" Jack—the real Jack—came running.

She'd had no idea the elderly man could move that fast.

"The helicopter pilot," he wheezed. "We were talking, and . . ." He gasped for air. "He's been shot!"

Those were bullet holes in the tent. Someone out there was shooting real bullets.

CHAPTER
TWENTY-SEVEN

Robin was bleeding.

And that was the understatement of the century. He'd bled before—from a punch in the nose, from a paper cut, from the time he'd put his fist through that window when he'd first gotten drunk at thirteen years old, from his run-in with Eliza Tetrinini's older brother just last year.

He knew what bleeding was.

This was something else entirely.

Blood was pouring from his leg. His thigh. Which freaking hurt like a bitch.

One minute he'd been running and the next—

"You're way too early," Adam admonished him, but then was sympathetic. "Oh, shit, you had a blood pack malfunction? God, what a mess. Damn, that looks . . . real." His voice went up an octave. "Jesus, Robin, what did you do to yourself?"

"I don't know," Robin gasped. Oh, fuck, it hurt.

"Jesus!" Adam leapt to his feet, waving his arms at the director, trying to get them to stop.

And right where he'd been kneeling, a puff of sand went into the air as if . . .

What the fuck had happened? Had they somehow accidentally crossed into an area where explosives were set to go off, imitating the impact of bullets into the sand?

The stunt director and Harve both had assured him that these miniature explosions weren't dangerous.

But accidents obviously happened and—

"Motherfucker!" Something hot and piercing slapped him in the arm, pushing him back onto the sand. His hand came away covered with even more blood, and he suddenly knew. "Someone's shooting real bullets," he shouted to Adam, who turned tail and ran—the coward—leaving him to bleed to death on their make-believe version of Omaha Beach.

Jules knew that the sound of automatic gunfire from the mock battle scene was driving Cosmo crazy.

Steve with the key still hadn't appeared, and the time for playing nice was drawing to an end.

Fortunately, Jules had learned from past experiences and had gotten complete insurance on the rental car, which, he could tell from the grim line of Cosmo's mouth, was about to be used as a very expensive set of wire cutters.

But then his cell phone rang.

It was Tess Bailey. "Jules! Code red! Shots have been fired. At least two men are down, including Robin Chadwick—"

No.

"Get in the car!" Jules shouted at Cosmo as he slid behind the wheel. "Code red!"

Please, God, don't let Robin be fatally wounded. Not while they were standing out here, stopped by a nine-dollar padlock and chain . . .

Tossing the phone to Cosmo, who climbed into the passenger side, Jules jammed the rental car into reverse. The tires squealed as he backed it up enough to get the distance for the speed he'd need.

"Keep Jane covered! We'll be right there," Cosmo told Tess, bracing himself on the dash as Jules gunned the car directly for the gate.

Her brother had been shot.

Someone—Jack maybe—fired the flare that called for a cut in action, and the sudden silence was eerie.

But it wasn't completely silent—it just seemed that way compared to the sounds of battle.

Without the rattle of gunfire to cover them, Jane could hear voices crying out in pain, calling for help.

And, just like in the real aftermath of a battle, there were sudden frantic calls for the medic.

A military company usually had a handful.

They had only one.

Jane had been pushed onto the ground, behind a stack of boxes even though no one knew where the gunman was. He could be anywhere, couldn't he? Any one of those guns carried by the extras could be real, capable of delivering death.

And, obviously, she was not the only target.

She could hear Adam, still shouting, "He's bleeding, God damn it! Someone help me—I can't carry him by myself!"

"I'm staying down," Jane told PJ, Tess, and Nash, who were all but sitting on her, weapons drawn. There was no way she could fight her way past them to her brother's side. Obedience was her best bet in terms of helping him. "See? I'm very safe, I'm being very good—now go help Robin and the others!"

God, how many of the extras had been hurt? How could this have happened?

"An ambulance is on its way," Tess told her.

Decker had appropriated the director's megaphone. "Drop all weapons! I repeat, all extras drop all prop weaponry immediately!"

There was a huge crash—the sound of metal against metal—as a car blasted through the main gate.

And then she heard a familiar voice: "Jane! Where's Jane?"

Cosmo had arrived.

Adam came back.

He hit the ground as he reached Robin, as if he were sliding into home plate.

He'd also brought Wayne with him. Wayne, whose day job was in a hospital.

Wayne, who hated Robin's guts.

"Get out of here—get to cover," Robin gasped.

They were out in the open, completely vulnerable. All of the other extras had stayed back, afraid that this was some kind of improvisation, some additional scene that they hadn't been warned about. Some of them actually thought that the cameras were still rolling.

"It's okay, Robin, everyone's put down their guns. Whoever was shooting has stopped. We're gonna move you up the beach," Adam told him, "to the tent. An ambulance is on its way."

There was a crack—a gunshot—and Adam and Wayne both covered Robin with their own bodies.

"Well, aren't I the big liar," Adam said when he lifted his head. He looked at Wayne. "Let's get him out of here, Doc."

Wayne was looking at the tourniquet Robin had tried to tie around his leg—which had been freaking hard to do with a bullet in his left arm. "That needs to be tighter. This is going to hurt," he told Robin, "and I'm glad for that. I hate you for what you did to Patty, you asshole, but I'm not going to let you die."

"Just do it," Robin said through gritted teeth.

And then there was only pain.

Pain, and Adam hanging on to his hand despite some lunatic shooting at them.

"It's gonna be okay, babe, you're going to be okay," Adam said over and over as Robin heard himself scream.

Mercifully, the world went black.

Cosmo held tightly to Jane behind the barrier of those crates. What the fuck had she been thinking, leaving the house like that before checking with him?

Of course, he hadn't exactly been easy to reach, with his cell phone back in his truck.

"It was over," she told him, her face buried against his chest. Had he spoken aloud? She answered as if he had. "Patty's safe, and it was over—"

"We have to get you into the car," he told her. Into the car and then out of here, as quickly as possible.

She lifted her head, and from the look in her eyes he knew this wasn't going to be easy. Why should it be? Nothing else had been up to this point.

"My brother's out there," she said. "I'm not leaving him!"

"Yeah," Cos said. "You are. If I have to throw you in the car and drag you out of here."

She bristled. "You wouldn't dare."

"Just watch me," he fired back at her.

But another rifle shot echoed, and Cos pulled her down instead, even closer to the ground.

"Oh, my God," she said, "Oh, my God. He's just shooting innocent people! We have to make him stop! Cos, I can make him stop!"

"Oh, no, you can't," Cosmo told her. "Your job right now is to keep your head down and do what we tell you to do."

"It's me he wants!" she told him.

"Yeah, well, I want you, too, Jane," he said. "I need you to hold on just a little bit longer. We have him cornered now."

"What?" She was incredulous. "He's the one with the gun!"

"Yeah, but we're the ones with the helicopter," he pointed out. "Stay here, do you hear me? I need to take a look at that beach. Tess!" he shouted, and the woman came closer, ready to jump on top of Jane if she moved an inch. It wasn't so much that he didn't trust Jane. He just knew that she found the growing body count unbearable.

"Do we have a visual on the shooter?" Cos shouted as he hustled to a pile of boxes over at the far edge of the tent. Christ, were those bullet holes above them in the red-and-white circus pattern? **Crack!** They were— a new one appeared as he watched. There had to be some kind of raised terrain in this area—that's where the shooter would be positioned.

"Negative on the visual," Decker shouted back as he crossed the tent, too. He lowered his voice to normal conversation level as they met behind that barrier. "But five men are injured, all across the beach. My guess is he's somewhere on that hillside."

Hillside. Jackpot. And there it was. Covered with brush. Cosmo's eyes were good, but he would've given his left nut for infrared binoculars right about now.

Jack appeared. The old man was one of the few people besides the Troubleshooters team who wasn't on the verge of losing his cool. "I saw a Nazi—an actor in a brown uniform—climbing up that way with a Springfield rifle," he reported. "Range on that thing is huge. There's nowhere on this beach that's safe. Most of the extras still don't know what's going on. They think it's some kind of stunt we've set up for the news cameras. But as soon as they figure out that it's not, there'll be a stampede, probably for this tent. With your permission, I'd like to start leading them into the parking lot."

"Do it," Decker ordered. "But keep your head down." He raised his voice. "PJ, Nash, keep your eyes on that hillside, watch for a muzzle flash."

When Robin opened his eyes, Wayne had been replaced by an angel who looked a lot like Jules Cassidy.

Didn't it figure?

"Am I dead?" Robin asked, reaching up to touch the angel's face. His fingers left a streak of blood.

"Now!" the angel said and Robin felt himself being lifted.

The pain came smashing back—this definitely wasn't his ascension to heaven—as he was half carried, half dragged up the beach.

Holy God! He was so cold his teeth were chattering, so this probably wasn't hell, either.

But it was damn close.

Crack! Crack!

They stopped moving, dropped back to the sand.

"Shit!" Adam said. "That was too close!"

"Wayne, are you hit?" Jules asked.

"No, sir. Are you?"

"No," Jules said. "But it sure seems that this guy doesn't want us going anywhere, does he?"

"Me," Robin managed to gasp. "He doesn't want **me . . .**"

Wayne, gutsy bastard, experimented, crawling several steps toward the tent.

"Keep going," Robin begged him. He looked at Adam, who'd run to safety, but then come back for him, and Jules, who should've been up in that tent, taking care of Janey. "All of you. Please . . . I don't want you to die, too."

"If he wanted to kill us," Jules said, remarkably calmly, "he'd have done it already. I have a feeling he's got a different agenda."

Jules' rental car had been moved right in under the tent, but Cosmo quickly realized that the sand was too soft to use it to get Jane to safety. It would take too long for the car to get up any kind of speed—and that was provided it didn't just sit there, tires spinning.

Meanwhile, the shooter would Swiss-cheese it.

It served a better use here as an additional barricade.

Jane—having been admonished repeatedly not to move—was hunkered down behind it on the far side of the tent, along with Harve and Gary and other members of the production crew and quite a few extras who'd figured out that those bullets were real and had run for cover.

Decker had moved the crates, positioning them to be used as protective barriers, so the Troubleshooters team could move from one side of the tent to the other.

The shooter took random potshots at them, no doubt hoping to hit Jane through sheer luck.

This was like some kind of unreal freak show, with old Jack Shelton manning the megaphone like an ancient master of ceremony, instructing the extras to move slowly and calmly off the beach and into the parking lot, where they'd be safe.

There was a bottleneck at the gate, which meant there were quite a few sitting ducks still on the beach, not to mention a crowd heading for the fence at the far end.

There was another fairly large group huddled at the base of the hillside, protected by an outcropping of rocks.

Crack! Crack!

"He's on that hill," Nash announced. "About three-quarters of the way up."

"PJ!" Cos grabbed several coils of heavy-duty extension cords from a pile of equipment. "Can you fly that helo?"

"That toy?" PJ laughed. "With one hand tied behind my back, baby."

Cosmo shouldered the weapon he'd taken from Carl Linderman's truck. "Let's go end this game."

Robin needed a hospital.

He'd gone into serious shock, and Jules tucked his jacket around him, wishing he could do more.

"I'm sorry," Robin whispered.

"You're not quitting on me, are you?" Jules asked.

"Go," Robin begged. "Please. I don't want you to die, too."

"I'm not going to let you die." But Jules could hear distant sirens. Ambulances and police approaching.

This was the moment of truth. If the shooter was intending to get away, he was going to have to make his final move now, before the SWAT teams arrived.

And whatever it was he had in mind, Jules was certain it involved using Robin as a bargaining chip. The shooter obviously had him sighted in his rifle scope, and Jules knew that the man had Jane's cell phone number. He'd called her before—he'd call again.

"Adam," he said, "act! Wayne! Make it look like Robin's dying."

They both sat up, not quite understanding.

"We're losing him!" Jules said loudly, leaning over Robin, pretending to give him CPR.

Wayne leaned in, touching Robin's neck. "I don't have a pulse!"

Adam hovered, looking distressed.

"He might be watching through a scope." Jules turned his face away from the hillside where the shooter had to be positioned. "Let him read your lips. Robin, listen to me—only pretend to die, sweetie, all right?"

When he leaned in for one last round of fake mouth-to-mouth, Robin kissed him.

He opened his eyes, and they were filled with pain and remorse. "I'm so sorry," he whispered again. "I was too much of a coward."

"You're going to be okay," Jules told him. He didn't have to fake the rush of tears to his eyes. "Save the deathbed speech for another day."

Adam took over. "He's gone," he said, facing the hillside. Anyone watching could surely read his lips. "He's dead." He reached down and pulled Jules' jacket up over Robin's head.

"Get ready to lift him," Jules ordered. "Robin, don't scream this time. Remember, you're dead."

Robin was dead.

As Jane hid behind Jules Cassidy's battered rental car, she watched the video monitor. Adam had just pulled something—a jacket—up over her brother's motionless face.

"No," she said. "No . . ."

Tess was beside her. "Jane, you've got to keep your head down." But then she saw the screen. "Oh, God . . ."

Jane was going to be sick.

On the screen Jules and Adam and another man picked up her brother's body.

Her brother's body.

Jane couldn't breathe.

"Keep your head down," Tess ordered her. "I'm going to go help them bring him inside. We'll bring him to you, Jane—do you understand? I know you want to see him, but do not move from behind this car."

Jane managed a nod and Tess disappeared.

Her cell phone rang, cutting through the babble of voices, through the sound of the helicopter thrumming to life out on the beach.

And Jane knew, with a certainty that was chilling, exactly who was on the other end. Sure enough, the number showing was that of Patty's cell phone.

"You are so dead," she said instead of hello.

The man laughed. "Today's a good day to die, don't you think?"

It was the man who'd called to say Patty had been kidnapped. Whoever had been found dead in that apartment this morning, it wasn't this man—the same man she'd spoken to last night. Patty—completely drugged—probably hadn't pulled the trigger of that gun, either. It was all an elaborate setup, a ruse to bring them all to right here and right now.

A right now in which her baby brother had just been killed.

"You're not going to get away with this," she told him, her voice shaking.

"I'm not looking to get away," he said. "Like I said, it's a good day to die. You have twenty seconds to step out from that tent, or I'll start shooting. I was going to say that I would start with your brother, but gee, it looks like he's already dead. I'll have to change my plan. Oh, but look, isn't that your boyfriend, the Navy SEAL, getting into that helicopter? I think, instead, I'll start by shooting him. He'll make such an easy target when he gets into the air. Or maybe I'll shoot the pilot and he'll die in the crash. Two for one. Wait, three for one. Someone else is getting on board, too."

"No!" Jane said.

"You have the power to stop me," he said. "Nineteen. Eighteen . . ." The connection was cut.

"Harve!" Jane shouted for her makeup man. "I need you! Now!"

Decker slid open the helicopter's starboard-side door as Cosmo ditched the coils of extension cord he'd taken from the production tent. They didn't need it because there was a length of mountain-climbing rope right on the helo's deck. As Deck watched, Cos quickly tied it to a built-in anchor.

It would be easier on their hands than the plastic extension cord, in case they had to fast-rope to the ground. Although without gloves, the trip down was pretty much going to hurt, even with the rope.

But it wouldn't hurt until later. In the moment, Decker knew he'd feel no pain. He'd be focusing on the here and now.

And here and now that pitted two poorly armed SEALs against one psycho with a sniper rifle.

Deck had only his handgun. And the room broom that Cosmo had conjured up from God knows where didn't have much range, either. They'd have to get close.

Whereas psycho-sniper could start shooting at them before they even left the ground.

Decker hoped PJ really knew how to fly this thing. They were going to need to do some fancy maneuvers to keep from getting drilled.

"Go!" Cosmo shouted.

PJ revved the engine and . . .

It sputtered and coughed.

"Shit!"

"PJ!" Cos didn't sound happy.

"I'm trying! Come on, baby. . . ."

The helicopter was having trouble getting off the ground, which was more of an assist from God than an actual heavenly sign.

Jane was certain that no matter how many seconds Mr. Insane-o had given her to get out from underneath the tent, he wasn't going to shoot until the chopper was in the air.

Still, she knew if Tess or Nash saw her, they'd tackle her and toss her back behind the car. But they were both dealing with Robin's body, carrying him behind the wall of crates, helping him sit up so they could see—

Helping him **sit** up?

Her brother was alive. His face was pale but his eyes were open, and he was talking.

If Jane **had** needed a sign from God, that would have been it. But she didn't need one. She knew what she was doing. She had total faith that this was her only choice. She also knew that Cosmo would think otherwise, but he was wrong. This was not a foolish risk.

Moving to the edge of the tent so she'd be in position when PJ finally got that chopper off the ground, Jane used her cell phone to call Decker.

"Shoot to kill," Decker shouted. "Jane just called. The shooter called her. She said he was suicidal—said it was a good day to die. He's not likely to surrender."

No way. Suicidal? Cosmo didn't believe it. But there was no time to argue.

He was glad for the MP-5's shoulder strap. Because when PJ finally jerked the helo up and into the air, he had to hold on with both hands to keep from falling out the door.

"Sorry," PJ yelled.

There was no time to exchange a "Navy pilots are better" look with Decker, because even though they'd gone straight up first, PJ was now blasting toward that hillside.

Then again, maybe Navy pilots weren't better, because Cos had never seen a toy like this—a nonmilitary helo—move at quite this speed.

As far as suicidal shooters went . . . Even though he didn't buy it, he had no problem with a shoot-to-kill order.

None at all.

"Shit, is that Jane?" Decker shouted over the roar of the blades. "What is she doing?"

Words to chill his heart.

Cosmo hung out the door, looking down and back and—

It was.

Jane.

Running down the beach.

Toward the hillside.

Moving in a zigzag pattern.

Her long hair flying behind her.

She looked up at the helo, at him, her face a pale oval, already too far away for him to see clearly. Cosmo heard the **crack** of the rifle shot, saw her jerk and fall, blood spraying behind her.

Jesus Christ! She was wearing both a vest and a flak jacket—the shooter must've hit her in the head.

And with that knowledge, Cosmo became the man everyone thought him to be.

A robot.

"Shooter at ten o'clock!" Decker shouted.

Cos went out the door, searching the brush below him and slightly to the left for any sign of movement. As he slid down the rope, it tore at his hand, but he didn't feel a fucking thing. He held the MP-5, ready to fire as soon as he got within range. . . .

But the gunman didn't fire again and time slowed down the way it often did when his finger tightened on a trigger.

As an instant became an eternity, Cosmo caught the glint of sunlight on a rifle barrel. The blue of the sky was such a pretty color, it almost hurt to look at it. Cirrus clouds were wispy overhead. He saw the spidery veins of the leaves of the brush. . . .

He saw the green of a uniform hidden there behind those leaves and he slid closer and closer and . . .

Nazi.

Jack had seen a Nazi in a brown uniform, he'd said, climbing this hillside.

Brown, not green.

Jack might've been wrong. He was old—his eyesight might've been failing him. His memory might've been rusty.

Still, Cosmo hesitated for a lifetime and then another lifetime, enough for the shooter to raise that rifle and blow this helo right out of the perfect blue sky.

But the barrel didn't move. And the barrel didn't move.

Their man wasn't suicidal. He was a game player. How did a game player win a no-win scenario?

The sunlight on that barrel sparkled and jumped, but the movement was all Cos'. The rifle didn't move and it didn't move and it didn't move as his finger tightened on that trigger.

And down the hillside, away from that still-life portrait that could have been titled **Green Uniform with Rifle,** in that moment that lasted an eternity, something did move.

Cosmo caught a flash of brown out of the corner of his eye a fraction of a second before he finished squeezing that trigger. A fraction of a second before he released a deadly hail of lead into the wrong man.

Jack wasn't wrong about that uniform.

In that eternity that lasted that fraction of a second, Cosmo saw—as clearly and as cleanly as the veins on those leaves—Murphy's eyes as he learned Angelina was dead. Cosmo saw Jane, too, hair flying, blood spraying as she jerked and fell.

And he turned, finger tight against the trigger as he swept the MP-5 in the direction of that movement of brown, letting go of the rope and dropping the last dozen feet or so onto the rocky hillside.

He sensed more than saw Decker sliding down the rope after him as he skidded and scrambled for footing, as he dashed through the waist-high brush, as he came face-to-face with a man in a Nazi uniform, bleeding from three different entry wounds, none of them fatal.

The man was fumbling to get a sidearm free from a waist holster, but he froze when he saw Cosmo.

And Cosmo froze, too.

Jane was bleeding. Profusely.

Jules could see the blood from here.

He'd watched as she'd bolted from the tent, as she'd run across the beach, as that rifle had cracked and she'd been violently pushed back, as she'd hit the sand with a sickening crunch.

And, as he held Robin down to keep him from trying to run after her, Jules had heard the ragged firing of an automatic weapon. It paused and then fired again.

Jules told Adam to stay with Robin. He made sure Tess was there to greet the ambulances and police, whose sirens were getting louder and louder as they finally approached.

Then he ran out onto the beach.

Wayne, the extra who'd helped Jules and Adam carry Robin back to the tent, was right on his heels.

The kid had no fear.

The helicopter thrummed overhead, Cosmo catching a quick ride back to Jane by clinging to a rope. He leapt off and ran the rest of the way while the chopper made a rough-looking landing farther down the beach.

Cosmo reached Jane right about when Jules did, his pace picking up when he saw that she was covered—**covered**—with blood.

But then she sat up.

It was like something out of a horror movie. She just opened her eyes and sat up.

Cosmo dropped his weapon and stared at her. He was breathing hard, much harder than he should have been from that short run.

Jane met his gaze. Neither one of them spoke.

Jules caught Wayne's arm. Pulled him back.

Jane opened her flak jacket to reveal the empty bladders that had held all that blood. Fake blood. "He didn't even hit me. I just fell when I heard the sound of the gunshot."

Cosmo nodded. Looked at Jules. "We'll need a body bag on that hillside." His voice was raspy, and he had to stop and clear his throat. "Decker's still up there. He's got the weapon and some kid our guy took hostage. Kid's really out of it. Doped up or something. He was parked behind the sniper rifle. I'm pretty sure we were supposed to kill him, thinking he was the shooter, while our guy snuck down the hill and walked out of here with the rest of the extras." He turned and looked at Jane again, and his voice shook. "I thought I told you to stay behind that car, in the tent."

"I couldn't," she said.

He nodded, and then he walked away. Not far. Just about four yards. He sat down in the sand. Arms around his knees, he stared out at the ocean.

PJ dashed up, first aid kit from the helicopter in his hands, like that would've helped at all had Jane really been shot.

"You have medical training, right?" Jules asked him.

PJ nodded.

"We could use you up in the tents," Jules continued. "We've got a bunch of extras who've been wounded. None fatally—Robin's probably the worst off. He's first in line for an ambulance."

Jane looked up sharply at that, and Jules went to help her to her feet. "He's been asking for you," he told her.

She hesitated, looking over at Cosmo.

"Cos, you coming?" Jules called.

Cosmo turned slightly, just enough to acknowledge him, not quite looking back over his shoulder. "In a minute," he said. "Just give me a minute."

CHAPTER
TWENTY-EIGHT

Adam was in the lobby, sitting next to Jack Shelton, when Jules came into the hospital. Jane Chadwick was there, too—down at the end of the room near the gift shop, giving an on-camera interview.

Which had to mean that her brother was okay, didn't it? He'd tried calling on the way over, but couldn't get through. He'd spent the entire ride imagining the worst.

"Robin's out of surgery. He's going to be all right," Adam told him, and the relief was so intense Jules had to sit down. "The doctor came out to report that a bullet nicked his artery, but they worked their magic, and now he's **resting comfortably,** which is a really stupid thing to say. I mean, the man was shot. What's comfortable about that? You okay, J.?"

Jules looked up. "Yeah. Just . . ." He shook his head. Thank God.

"Not used to being on the other side of it, huh?" Adam said, standing up and feeding coins into a nearby soda machine. "Welcome to my world."

As Jules rubbed the back of his neck, he could hear Jane talking to the reporter.

"The story we're telling in **American Hero** has nothing to do with Judge Lord—except for the fact that because Hal grew up in a world with zero tolerance, he was forced to hide who he really was. His entire life was a lie—except for a few days in Paris, in 1945."

Adam shoved a bottle of Coke, cold and slick with condensation, into his hands. "This was just another regular day for you, wasn't it?" he asked.

Jules laughed at that. "No," he said. He shook his head as he opened the soda and took a long drink. Sugar and caffeine—the two essential food groups. "Thanks."

Adam shrugged as he sat down next to him.

"No, this was . . . a big day," Jules said. "A long day." He looked at Adam, who was still wearing his costume. Dirt—makeup along with the real thing—streaked his face. "Robin probably would've bled to death if you hadn't helped him."

"I didn't help him." Adam shrugged it off. "It was all Wayne."

"Well, you found Wayne, and you went back out there. You did good. I'm . . . proud of you." Jules held out his hand to Adam.

"So . . . what?" Adam said. "I save Robin's life and all I get is a handshake?"

Jules laughed.

Adam did, too, and moved to embrace him.

But Jules put his hand up. "Yes, all you get is a handshake," he said. "And my eternal thanks."

Adam wasn't laughing anymore. He took Jules'

hand. Looked searchingly into Jules' eyes. "We're really done this time, aren't we?"

"We're done," Jules agreed, and for the first time, it felt true. It didn't feel good, but it didn't feel devastating, either. It just . . . was. He gently pulled his hand free.

Adam got to his feet. Took a few steps away. Turned back. "You sure?"

"Very," Jules said.

"If you think Robin's going to—"

"I don't," Jules said. "Good-bye, Adam." He'd never said those words before. He'd always used a variation on "See you soon." **Au revoir. Ta. Later, dude.** "Good luck with the movie."

He wouldn't go to see it, but Adam probably already knew that.

Adam turned to Jack, who was sitting nearby, obviously trying hard not to listen in. "Do you need a ride?" he asked the old man.

Jack shook his head. "Thank you, but no. Scotty's on his way."

Adam nodded and forced a smile. "See you on set, Jack." He didn't even glance at Jules again as he walked away.

Which was a pretty typical Adam thing to do. As Jules watched, Adam put on his sunglasses as he approached the automatic doors and went out into the morning sunshine without looking back.

From the row of chairs on the other side of the soda machine, Jack spoke. "It's very odd," the old man said, "to see one's life re-created for a film."

Jules looked around, uncertain at first whether Jack was talking to him. But he was the only one in the immediate area, so he smiled politely. "It must be."

"Hearing words that I spoke over sixty years ago, seeing mistakes that I made repeated by actors . . . But I have to be honest, young man. Watching you with Robin Chadwick . . ." Jack shook his head. "More than anything else, it's the way you look at him that makes me remember, most vividly, how painful it all was."

Jules ran one hand down his face as he laughed. "It's that obvious, huh?"

"Only to me."

"I don't know what it is about him."

"He's got that magic," Jack agreed. "But he drinks too much." He made a tsking sound. "The question one needs to ask oneself is whether or not the fabulous cheekbones are worth the price of the heartache and pain."

"Do you think if he went into rehab—" Jules stopped himself with a laugh. "Listen to me. What am I saying? I'm so not doing that to myself. Not again. There's got to be someone out there who won't make me bleed."

"I'm certain there is," Jack said.

"Said the man whose life is being made into a movie—that ends unhappily."

"It only ended unhappily for Hal," Jack pointed out.

Jules scoffed. "You weren't devastated? Come on, I've read the script. I read that letter Hal wrote to you. God . . ."

"Please do not write. I will not answer you," Jack quoted. **"Do not come to see me. I will not know you."** He shook his head. "It took a while—years— but I came to realize that he wasn't being needlessly cruel. He was, in fact, sparing me. Hal knew he couldn't give me what I truly wanted—a love that could live and bloom in the sunlight. Oh, we could be together, sure—in secret, in the darkness, hiding and sneaking around, sharing a few short days every few months or so. If he hadn't written that letter, Hal could have had it all. His family, his career, his wife, his life. And me, as well. Instead, he set me free."

"Jack!" A distinguished-looking white-haired man in a Mister Rogers sweater was coming through the hospital doors. "Thank God you're all right!" He stopped short in front of Jack, taking in the dusty remains of what had once been a very nice pair of pants and an Armani shirt. His voice wavered. "**Are** you all right?"

And then it was Jules' turn to pretend not to listen. "I'm fine," Jack said reassuringly as the two men embraced. "Jane insisted the doctors check me out."

"And?"

"A few bruises," Jack said. "My hip's a little sore. Nothing a good soak in the Jacuzzi won't cure."

"They said on the news that you helped save hundreds of lives."

"The key word there is **helped,**" Jack said modestly.

"Cosmo Richter told me you're the one who saw the extra in the Nazi uniform climbing that hill with a rifle," Jules couldn't help but chime in, and both Jack and his partner turned to look at him. "Without that information, Cos probably would've killed the wrong man."

"Jules Cassidy, Scott Cardaro." Jack introduced them. "Jules is an FBI agent. Scotty's my current twinkie."

Scott laughed as he held out his hand for Jules to shake. His eyes sparkled in a face that was handsome and youthful despite the wrinkles. "Will you listen to him? I'll be seventy-one next week. I haven't qualified as a **twinkie** in decades. And when he uses the word **current,** people tend to think I moved in last week." The look he gave Jack was exasperated but affectionate. "We'll have been together forty-nine years this December."

Jules sat back in his seat. "Forty-nine . . . ? Wow." Forty-nine years was pretty damn close to forever. "Congratulations."

"Thank you," Jack said. He turned to Scott. "We were just discussing the movie. Jules here is under the impression it ends unhappily."

"Only for Hal." Scott echoed Jack's earlier words. "I, for one, intend to cheer and applaud wildly when Hal rides off into the sunset." He grinned. "Not a day goes by that I don't send up a little thank-you message to Harold Lord. You know that old saying? When God closes a door, he opens a window." He winked at Jules. "Someday we'll invite you over for dinner and tell you the story of how I climbed in Jack's window. But right now, the Jacuzzi calls."

Jack winked at Jules, too. "Sometimes you get lucky and the cheekbones come for free."

As Jules watched, bemused, Scott carefully helped Jack out of his seat. He tucked the older man's hand into the crook of his arm and together they headed for their home. The home that they'd shared for forty-nine years. In the sunlight.

Cosmo had vanished.

Jules Cassidy, however, was sitting in the hospital lobby, waiting for her.

Jane could see him as she shook the reporter's hand, finishing up the TV interview.

No one had died today—for that she'd be forever grateful.

Well, no one except for the man who'd killed Angelina, and try as she might, she couldn't feel sorry that he was gone.

Cosmo had shot him. And of course the speculation that was already going around was that he'd done it in cold blood. That the man had been injured and at his mercy and—

"Mr. Insane-o's real name was John Bordette," Jules told her as he rose to his feet to greet her. "You knew him as Carl Linderman, but he also went by Barry Parks and John Weaver. He may have had other aliases, too, but we haven't found them yet. He actually paid taxes for all four of these identities. That's how he screwed up—how we found him. Because he paid taxes." He shook his head. "The real Carl Linderman—I'm sure he's buried in his basement. But he was in his late seventies, on complete disability. He'd stopped filing tax returns about four years ago. Then, just last year, he's suddenly filing again, reporting income from stock dividends. Not huge amounts—sixteen, seventeen thousand dollars a year. But it was just kind of weird that out of the blue he's dotting all his I's and crossing all his T's. So he was put on the IRS's 'that's kind of weird' list. When we cross-referenced your list of extras and stage crew, his name got flagged. Cosmo went to check him out and—"

"Have you seen Cosmo?" Jane asked.

"I'm right here."

Jules jumped, too, as Cosmo came out from where he'd been lurking alongside a candy machine. His pants were filthy, and the shirt he had on was a hideous plaid. Had he been wearing that early this morning, when he'd left the house? As he approached, Jane's heart was in her throat.

Promise me no foolish risks.

The way he'd looked at her on the beach was beyond angry, beyond upset, beyond any emotion she'd ever seen before on his face, even when he'd told her about Murphy.

"Sorry it took me so long to catch up to you," Cosmo told her. "When you went to the hospital with Robin, I was giving my statement to the local police and the FBI and the state troopers and . . ." He looked at Jules. "I think at one point, the coast guard was even there."

Jules laughed. "I think you're right. And then someone from JAG showed up."

"It took a while," Cosmo told Jane. "By the time I got a ride out here, you were giving a TV interview." He turned back to Jules. "Any luck connecting our guy—what was his real name?"

"John Bordette," Jules said.

"He tied to the Freedom Network?"

"Only his Barry Parks persona is on their membership roster. But that's not enough of a connection. He's also a member of the Springfield Friends of the Public Library. That doesn't make them responsible for his actions, either." Jules shook his head. "We think it's more likely that Bordette was planning to put Mercedes' murder on his résumé in an attempt to gain entry to the Freedom Network's inner sanctum. We did place Bordette in Idaho Falls just prior to the Ben Chertok murder. We also think we may have cleared up the mystery surrounding what was thought to be an unrelated suicide from about that same time. This kid shot himself, and his family insisted it couldn't be self-inflicted. Turns out the kid worked in the same grocery store as Bordette. He was the same kind of trouble-maker and loner as Mark Avery—their similarities are kind of eerie, actually."

"Mark Avery was the man Patty allegedly killed?" Cosmo was trying to get it straight.

"Here's what we think happened," Jules said. "John Bordette, a borderline psychopath, has aspirations of being one of Tim Ebersole's lieutenants in the Freedom Network. He has this dream—it's kind of like a twisted buddy movie. John and his new best friend,

Timmy, attempt to 'make America safe for real Americans,' and zany high jinks ensue. Anyway, Tim won't take John's calls—gee, I wonder why not—so John figures he'll show the Freedom Network what he's made of. He decides to get rid of their 'arch enemy,' ADA Ben Chertok, and does so, fatally shooting him. The kid from the grocery store either knows too much or was part of a backup plan that John didn't need. Whatever the case, John wastes the kid on his way out of town, making it look like a suicide.

"He hides for a while, makes sure he's not a murder suspect, then calls up Timbo. Except, whoopsie, Tim **still** won't take his calls. Nobody in the Freedom Network gives a flying fig about Ben Chertok's execution. Johnny's back to square one. He sits and stews, and probably wastes Carl Linderman to cheer himself up and add a new identity to his list. But then, hey, what should appear on the Freedom Network website?" Jules looked at Jane. "Your face in the center of a bull's-eye. But this time John's not just going to kill you quickly and easily. He's going to make sure that people know he's going to kill you. And he's going to kill you despite your 24/7 protection from a team of professional bodyguards.

"He meets Mark Avery, sets him up from the start—because the way John's going to kill you is to make all this noise and create all this danger, but then make you think that the threat is gone. It starts with that rifle shot at the house, while Mark's car is driving past.

"He probably told Mark to do some kind of surveil-lance run on his own, and then got in place some-where back behind the house, waited for Mark to show up, and fired the shot.

"John waited for the uproar to die down, then drove home in his truck. He smeared mud on his li-cense plate just in case, but he probably didn't figure Cosmo would be out there, hiding in the dark, watch-ing the street, all those hours later." Jules paused. "Any questions, class?"

"You don't know all of this for sure, right?" Jane asked. "This is just your theory?"

"Some of it's fact," Jules told her. "And we tend to be pretty accurate when it comes to theories like this."

"Kind of like your profilers, who kept insisting Mr. Insane-o worked alone?" Jane asked.

"There's a big difference between working with a partner or in a team, and forming a temporary alliance with someone you see as disposable," Cosmo told her. "The profilers were saying our guy was not a team player—which was true."

"So, okay," Jules said. "Johnny scrounges up some uniforms from World War Two—probably with Mark's help—and, in his Carl Linderman persona, gets cast as an extra. He has access to the set, where he sends that e-mail, creating the lockdown. The accident with the light happens—and we're virtually certain it was just an accident—and lucky for John it brings the stalker story even closer to the top of the news. He likes that, but there are still people who aren't taking him seriously—possibly even Tim Ebersole.

"So John shoots Angelina to make sure he's caught everyone's attention. Then he grabs Patty and sets it up to look as if she killed him. Only it's his disposable friend, Mark Avery, who's dead. John's still out there and you're still very much in danger. But you're supposed to emerge from hiding and we're all supposed to be high-fiving each other for a job well done, and John, he still can't settle for gunning you down in your driveway—thank God. He's got to prove that he's so much smarter than we are, and he's got to have the high drama, to catch Tim's eye.

"So he plans to take you out while you're shooting the battlefield sequence—that'll surely make the news in a major way. After you show up on location—and you make it so easy for him by coming onto the set on the very first day of a four-day shoot—he sticks some hapless extra with the same kind of horse trank that he used to drug Patty—and that's something we know for sure."

"But how'd he get that rifle onto the beach?" Jane asked.

"The rifle **and** a sidearm," Cosmo interjected. "All he needed was a little advance notice, and since he had a Nazi uniform, he was probably one of the first people called."

"That's probably right," Jane agreed. "HeartBeat took care of the extras casting, but they worked off of our lists."

"They called him, gave him the dates and times and location," Cosmo speculated. "He probably asked if there would be additional security. You know, 'Wasn't someone connected to the movie just killed?' They probably told him about the metal detectors and the fence, reassuring him he'd be safe. I bet he came out here that same night—before the fence went up. Buried both of those weapons in the sand."

Jules nodded. "A number of extras and crew reported seeing someone digging right over by the hill. They didn't think much of it at the time, but . . . So there you have it." He sighed. "Look, if you don't need anything else, I'm going to head out. If anything new comes in . . . Well, I'll certainly keep you posted."

"How much longer will you be in town?" Jane asked.

"Probably only a few more days," Jules told her.

"Will you stop in and see Robin before you go?" she asked. "I mean, he's sleeping now, but . . . Maybe tomorrow?" Her brother had been asking for Jules in the ambulance.

"I'm not sure I'll have time," Jules told her, and her heart sank. It was clearly his polite way of saying no.

"Please give him a second chance," Jane said. "Everyone deserves a second chance, don't you think? God, you'd be so good for him."

She couldn't believe she was saying this, couldn't believe how badly she wanted her brother to be in a relationship with another man.

A man he so obviously adored, and who so clearly cared for him, too.

Jules laughed quietly. "I'm not sure he'd agree. He's not exactly . . ." He shook his head. "You know what would be really good for Robin? A thirty-day, locked-door rehab program, and some serious, in-depth psychoanalysis." He picked up his briefcase. "I'll give you a call tomorrow. We're still looking for Bordette's stuff—he moved it all somewhere, probably into self-storage. We're hoping to find a computer. Who knows? He wrote a fictional blog for Avery. Maybe he had a real one of his own." He shook Jane's hand, then Cosmo's. "Good work out there today, kids."

And then there she was. Alone with Cosmo—well, except for the lady at the hospital information desk. And except for Deck and Tom and the other members of the Troubleshooters team who were waiting for her in the parking lot, ready to escort her home.

"What are you so afraid of?" Cosmo asked her. "I'm the one who needs to apologize."

Was he kidding? He'd told her to stay under the tent.

"I lost it back on the beach," Cosmo said. He was serious. "I . . . I just . . ." He shook his head. "Me flipping out like that was the last thing you needed, with Robin shot, and . . . I'm sorry I wasn't there for you."

Jane stared at him. "I'm the one who's sorry—for scaring you. But, Cos, God, I had to. He called me and he said he was going to kill you. I thought if I could distract him, if I could make him think that he'd shot me . . . I couldn't just sit there and let him kill you. I couldn't."

"I know." Cosmo sat down on one of the hard plastic chairs. He looked utterly exhausted. And was that drying blood on the sleeves of his ugly plaid shirt?

"You're not . . . mad?" she asked, sitting down next to him.

He shook his head, no. "Janey, I know you. You thought it would help. And I can't be mad at you for doing exactly what I would've done in your shoes. Although, you know, **training**? As in, I've had a lot, you've had none?"

"But . . . I fooled him—Bordette—didn't I?" she asked.

Cos looked at her, the muscle in his jaw jumping. He didn't say anything for a long time, but she just waited.

"You fooled me, too—made my heart stop," he finally told her. "I almost let him shoot me."

"What?"

"Bordette was pulling a gun. His sidearm. It caught in his holster. He was a half second from firing it anyway, right through the damn thing, right into my head."

"Oh, my God . . ."

"I actually thought about it. About just letting him do it."

He was serious. Jane reached for him. "Cosmo . . ."

He held her tightly, too. "God, I stood there, and I thought how hard it was going to be to live the rest of my life without you. I thought about Yasmin losing her husband and children and cursing me for saving her life. And I thought about Murphy's eyes . . ."

"Oh, Cos . . ." This day had come closer than she'd ever imagined to being a terrible tragedy. She could barely breathe.

"It was just for a second. Less. It passed. I'm not afraid to die, but . . . It's not going to happen that way. And then . . . on the beach, when you were okay and . . ."

"I **am** okay," Jane told him. "I'm okay, and you're . . ." She looked at his arms, pushing his sleeves back. "You're hurt."

"I had this plan," he said, as if he didn't hear her, as if he didn't even notice the gashes and drying blood on his arms, "that after this was all over, and you were safe, I was going to take you to dinner at my mother's. And if you survived, if you didn't run screaming out of the house, I was going to ask you to marry me."

Dear God . . .

"That came out wrong," he said, pushing her hair back from her face, brushing some smudge of dirt or something from her cheek with his thumb. "It sounds like I'm saying . . ." He paused again. "What I **meant** is, if I thought that living with me was going to be torture for you, I wasn't going to ask. See, my mom's a pretty big part of my life, and . . . I want you, Janey, but I don't want you to be miserable."

She couldn't believe what he was saying. "You were really going to ask me . . . ?" Past tense. He **had** a plan.

"I'm a SEAL," he told her. "Our country's at war, and I could die. God knows it's happened to better men than me. But it could be me next time—leaving you forever." He held her gaze. "I never realized before exactly what that meant, what that might feel like. Today was . . . eye-opening."

"So that's it?" Jane said. "You have this epiphany, and I don't even get to meet your mother?"

There were tears in his eyes and the smile he gave her was so sad. "I love you too much."

"Too much?" she said. "I didn't think that was possible with something like love."

"I don't want you to feel the way I felt today." He shook his head. "It was just a few minutes, and it was enough for a lifetime."

"Do you really think it never occurred to me that you do something extremely dangerous for a living?" she asked him. "You really think that's like some big headline news flash? 'Cosmo Could Die . . .'? You say you know me, but you don't know me at all if you think that's going to scare me away. You love me. Too much—whatever that means," she told him, her voice shaking. "I love you ferociously. With that going for us, what can't we handle?"

Cosmo kissed her, and she knew it was going to be all right. "Say that again," he demanded.

"I love you ferociously," she told him, and kind of ruined the impact of a word as strong as **ferociously** by starting to cry. Although he didn't seem to mind. He actually seemed to like it, maybe because his own eyes were suspiciously moist, too. "Enough to endure whatever comes our way."

Jane wrapped her arms around him and—

"Excuse me, we're looking for a Cosmo Richter?"

Cos pulled back and Jane looked up to see two police officers standing in the hospital lobby.

"Oh, shit," Cosmo said. "Excuse me." He met Jane's questioning gaze. "I think I'm about to be arrested for stealing a car."

"What?" Jane started to laugh. "Are you serious?"

But Tom Paoletti and Decker were suddenly both there. They intercepted the police officers, pulling them out of the lobby, far from Cosmo and Jane.

"Officers, I'm sorry, I can't go with you," Cos said as he gazed into Jane's eyes. "I've got other plans for tonight."

CHAPTER TWENTY-NINE

Robin had had a slew of visitors to his hospital room over the past few days.

Adam came twice, which was awkward and weird.

Janey and Cosmo came every morning and every night.

Harve and Guillermo and Gary all smuggled in bottles of whiskey, bless their hearts.

His dad even flew in with what's-her-name, his latest wife, although they didn't stay long.

There had been no sign, however, of Jules.

Robin would've at least liked to thank the guy for saving his life.

And then, on day three, the least likely visitor in the entire known universe walked into his room.

Patty Lashane.

Robin had just been silently bemoaning the fact that there was nothing good on TV at two o'clock in the afternoon. ESPN had women's college lacrosse, which was even less interesting than **Rugrats,** and why wasn't there a channel that showed all **SpongeBob,** all the time?

"How are you, Robin?" Patty asked.

And suddenly scary women carrying big sticks and wearing little plaid skirts seemed fascinating. He somehow managed to smile at her as he reluctantly turned off the TV. "Pretty good," he said, "considering I was shot. Twice."

"I know," she said.

"You, uh, had a pretty harrowing experience there yourself," Robin said.

"I don't remember any of it," Patty told him.

She was wearing a suit. Wide-legged pants with a matching jacket. Nice shoes. She'd gotten her hair cut, too. "You look good," he said as she sat down in the chair across the room.

"Thank you," she said. "I have a lunch date."

"With Wayne?" he asked.

She blinked at him. "No. With Victor Strauss."

"The director?"

She bristled. "Is that so hard to believe?"

"No, of course not. You're like, what? Twenty? And he's ninety. This is Hollywood. Go for it."

"He's not that old," Patty said.

"What about Wayne?" Robin asked.

"Wayne Ickes?" She laughed as if he'd made a big joke. "He and I are just friends."

"He helped save my life," Robin told her. "You should have seen him—total hero material. Everyone's ducking for cover and he's right there. . . . Adam, too."

Which really was the surprise of the century. But he didn't want to talk about Adam. Not with Patty, who knew that he and Adam had . . . God. "Wayne's brave, he's nice, and he's obviously hung up on you."

She fiddled with her handbag, and he knew the nonchalance was an act. "He's dating Debbie, the new craft services girl," she admitted, and when she looked up at him, there was misery in her eyes.

"Ouch," Robin said.

"He thinks I'm with Victor—you know, **with** Victor—because he saw the flowers that Victor sent me when I was in the hospital and . . ." She shook her head. "I'm pretty sure Victor only wants what you wanted."

No shit, Sherlock.

"Except Victor's not faking it," Patty said. "He's definitely not gay."

"I'm not gay," Robin protested. "I just . . . happened to have sex once with . . . you know, another man."

"Is that why you slept with me?" she asked. "So people would think you were straight?"

"I'm not gay," he said again, unable to keep desperation from his voice. "I was really trashed when I . . . I got a little too into character, and . . . I'm not even sure what happened that night with Adam. I don't remember too much about it."

"I got tested for AIDS," she told him. "I'm negative."

AIDS. Jesus. "That's good," he managed to say. "Look, Patty, I know you're still mad at me, but—"

"I won't tell," she said. "But you owe me. You take my phone calls. You remember my name. I'm going to be a producer myself one of these days, so you'll read the scripts I send you and—"

"Are you blackmailing me?"

She smiled at him sweetly. "Absolutely." She stood up. "I have to go. I really came by because I wanted to let you know that I'm not pregnant. You know, so you could stop worrying about it?"

Pregnant? "Whew," he said.

"You jerk. You didn't even remember, did you?"

"I've been thinking about other things," Robin admitted. He tried to change the subject. "I wish you'd call Wayne and tell him the truth about you and Victor."

"It's too late," she said.

"It's never too late," he told her. "You want me to call him? I'm going to call him, okay?"

Patty shook her head. "Do you remember **any**thing about that night with me?" she asked.

Robin didn't answer right away. It was funny, actually. He could barely remember the nights he'd spent with Patty and Adam. And yet he remembered every kiss he'd shared with Jules. In great detail.

"Yeah," he lied now, because he'd already done enough damage. "I remember that it was really great."

"It was over in about ten seconds," she informed him. "I didn't even get to . . . you know. And then you barfed all over my bathroom. On a scale from one to ten, you're, like, less than zero."

"Well, wow, thanks so much for dropping by," he said. "You really cheered me up."

She lingered by the door. "I'm glad you didn't die."

"I'm glad you didn't, too," Robin told her. "And thanks for . . . you know." Not rushing right out to give an interview with the **National Voice.**

"Your calling Wayne doesn't make us even. You're still less than a zero," she said, as she went out the door.

"So that went well." Jules came into Robin's room, surprising the hell out of him. He must have been waiting right outside in the hall. He had on his FBI agent clothes—dark suit, white shirt, red tie.

"Ah," Robin said, managing a smile. How much of that had Jules overheard? "It's unexpected-visitor day. Lucky me."

"It's warm in here." Jules took off his jacket before he sat down in the chair Patty had recently vacated.

"I was cold. The extra blanket was too heavy on my leg, so . . ."

Jules started rolling up his sleeves. "I came to say good-bye."

Robin gave up trying to smile. "Are you going back . . . ?"

"To D.C.," Jules told him. "My work here is done."

There wasn't much Robin could say in response to that. At least not with that lump in his throat.

"Did your sister tell you that we found John Bordette's computer?" Jules asked.

"Yeah." Robin took a sip from his water cup. "Dude was looney tunes. His keeping a ghoulish journal like that was . . . Yeesh. She said he wrote this really creepy poetry, too."

"Some of it was pretty good," Jules said. "Very dark, though."

And there they sat, just looking at each other.

"Have the doctors talked to you about a therapy program?" Jules finally asked, and Robin nodded. "You've got to start slow. Don't expect to get out of the hospital and then go for a five-mile run the next day."

Robin nodded. "Adam told me you were shot a few years ago."

He wasn't sure what made Jules look so startled for a moment—the fact that he'd brought up Adam, or the fact that he and Adam had obviously discussed him.

But Jules quickly composed himself, even laughed softly. "Gee, I was under the impression that you guys didn't spend all that much time talking."

"We talked a lot," Robin told him. "Mostly about you."

"Oh, well, that makes everything all right, then." He blew out a quick burst of air. "Sorry." He stood up. "I think it's probably time to go."

Robin moved wrong, or too fast, or maybe God was just giving him a giant noogie, but he yelped and cursed from the sudden flare of pain.

Jules was instantly at his side. "Are you okay? You need me to get the nurse?"

Robin shook his head. **Don't go.** He didn't say it. He couldn't say it. He pretended the tears in his eyes were the involuntary kind, the kind that came with intense pain. It was just a side effect, along with the sweat he could feel on his forehead and upper lip. He took a drink from his cup, which helped.

"How are you managing the pain?" Jules asked.

"The head nurse likes me," Robin said. "I'm doing fine."

Jules leaned closer. "You smell like whiskey."

"Yeah," Robin said. At this proximity, he could smell Jules' cologne. He always smelled so good. And his eyes were so brown. "And then there are my very considerate friends."

"So much for my hope of you coming out of the hospital sober." Jules was really upset. "God damn it, Robin—"

"Hey, come on . . ." Robin moved wrong and ended up zinging himself again. "Fuck, fuck, fuck . . ."

When he opened his eyes, Jules was taking the lid off his water cup. He sniffed it, then took it into the bathroom and poured the contents down the sink.

"I realize how futile this is," he said as he brought the cup back into the room. "You'll just refill when I'm gone."

"So don't go," Robin said, making it a joke.

Jules took it seriously. "And wait around for the next time you get so drunk that you want to experiment again? No, thank you. I'm going home." He poured a new cup of water from the pitcher on the counter, and reaffixed the top. "Did you know that Jack and his partner, Scotty, have been together for almost fifty years?"

Whoa. "You mean, like, exclusively?"

"I mean, like, committed to each other. Completely. Which includes fidelity. That's not a purely hetero concept, you know—and they lived faithfully and very happily ever after."

"Man," Robin said. "Sex with just one person, for the rest of your life? It sounds a little too limiting."

"Said the straight man to the gay man." Jules came back to his bedside. "Your roots are showing."

"What is this? Bash the invalid day?"

"Your hair's much darker than I thought." Jules reached out and touched Robin's hair, parting it so he could get a better look. "So you're really, what? Black Irish? Black hair, blue eyes?"

Robin nodded. Dear God, that felt too good. "Robin O'Reilly Chadwick," he said in his best Irish brogue, praying that Jules would stop. Or that he would never stop. He wasn't quite sure which. "Top o' the mornin' ta ya, Jules Cassidy."

Jules smiled. "It's afternoon."

"Not to a hard-drinkin' Irishman, it's not."

That did the trick. Jules stepped back. "I gotta go. My plane leaves in just a few hours."

Robin tried to memorize him, standing there with his tie slightly loosened, his sleeves rolled up. As he took his jacket from the back of the chair, Robin didn't really check out his backside. He was just admiring the fact that the man was in such good shape.

Liar.

Jules slung his jacket over his shoulder, turned for one last look. . . .

"Keep in touch," Robin said.

"I don't think that's such a good idea."

"So this is **good-bye** good-bye? Have a nice life?"

"Yeah," Jules said. "I think that's best."

"I thought we were friends."

"We're not," Jules said. "I can't be your friend because you're not in a place right now where you can really be **my** friend, so . . ."

"Why, because I don't want to suck your—"

"No." Jules cut him off. "Because you do."

"Okay," Robin singsonged, to hide how rattled he was. "If believing that floats your boat . . ." He could do only a half shrug without making his eyes roll back in his head from the pain.

"I'm sorry," Jules said. "I deserve better than that. I deserve someone who really wants me." His voice shook. "God damn it—I deserve sunlight."

"I'm sorry, too," Robin whispered.

"Take care of yourself," Jules said, and swiftly went out the door.

"Wait!" Wasn't Jules even going to kiss him? One last lingering breathless taste of what Robin claimed he didn't want? One last sweet touch of lips, a gentle rasp of tongues to remind him of what he was too scared to let himself have?

Pretty boy. Homo. Little faggot.

Jules stuck his head back in the door, so obviously hoping to hear the words that Robin couldn't say, wouldn't say.

"Steer clear of that mean Peggy Ryan," Robin told him instead.

Jules nodded. "Yeah," he said. "Thanks."

And then he was really gone.

Robin shifted his weight, got slammed with the pain, and let tears rush to his eyes.

"What are you doing?" Jane asked as she came out the conference room doors and into the backyard.

Cosmo was standing at the edge of the property, staring at the back of the house. Still looking for that freaking bullet. He didn't bother to tell her. She knew.

"Your mom called," she told him. "She's running a little late, so if we can delay picking her up by about forty minutes . . ."

"Sorry about that," he said.

"No," she said, "I think she's really considerate. Calling ahead so we don't have to sit in her living room, waiting for her? Listening to the soundtrack from **Jekyll and Hyde.** Again."

He laughed. "All you have to do is ask her to play something else." His mother quite possibly loved Jane more than she loved him.

"I didn't want to tell you this," Jane said. "But I secretly love that musical. Your mom's going to let me borrow it, along with **Les Mis** and **Phantom**—my other big faves—so I can put them onto my iPod and create a continuous loop—just keep it playing all the time."

Cosmo cracked up. Thank God she wasn't serious.

But then she hummed a few bars from the duet from the second act. God, he **hoped** she wasn't serious.

"So what's the hardest part about being a SEAL?" she asked him.

"Having to spend time away from you," he told her. Not only was it true, but his answer got him a seriously intense kiss. What was it both Jane and Robin always said?

Score.

"I was kidding," Jane told him, her arms up around his neck, her fingers in his hair, her body soft against him. "About the iPod."

"You're hair looks great," he told her. She was wearing it up, intricately piled on top of her head. "But is it really going to last?"

"This is just a trial run. Wait'll you see me tomorrow in my dress." She wiggled her eyebrows. "Wait'll you see me **out** of my dress. The crew bought me special-occasion underwear."

Words failed him so he kissed her again.

Forty minutes. For. Tee. Minutes. Before he could suggest, oh, say, a preview of that underwear, Jane spoke.

"This'll be a really good house for kids, don't you think?" she asked.

Kids? Shit. Cosmo didn't answer that one for a long time.

They were driving to Las Vegas—with his mother, no less—to get married, because his leave was almost up, and Jane didn't want to wait.

He was surely going OUTCONUS with SEAL Team Sixteen. Probably to Afghanistan. Maybe Iraq. For God knew how long.

He suspected they were one of a very small number of people who brought along the mother of the groom when they eloped. But Jane had insisted on that, too.

Demanding woman. Now she wanted kids, too.

"Are you ever going to speak again?" Jane asked him. "Or have I just silenced you for good?"

"Yes," Cosmo managed to tell her. "A very good house for kids."

"That's what I thought, too. I mean, you know, in a few years, after we get it fixed up." She was silent for, oh, maybe a tenth of a second before she asked, "What's the second hardest part? Of being a SEAL? Not counting BUD/S training."

Over the past few weeks they'd talked, pretty much endlessly, about all the types of training he'd gone through, that he continued to go through, as part of the U.S. Navy's Special Operations. He knew Jane needed to hear as much about it as he could tell her. Knowing he had the ability to take care of himself while he was off on a dangerous mission would help her sleep at night.

So he'd damn near talked himself hoarse. He'd loved jump school. He'd loved the diving and under-water demolition, too, and he'd told her all about it. He loved the nonstop learning about what the Teams referred to as their toys—the high-tech equipment that they used while out in the "real world." Survival training was always interesting to say the least, and PT was PT. Some of the guys suffered through; others merely endured it. Cosmo's relationship with the endless physical training was slightly more friendly. He appreciated it. It kept him in top shape.

He'd talked at length about that, too.

Now he didn't hesitate. "Report writing."

Jane laughed, which was his intention. There were sides to his job that he disliked far more than writing a report, but today was a special day, and he wanted to keep things light.

"That's right," she said. "You mentioned something about that. You know, other people—normal people— are afraid of heights or close spaces or snakes. . . ."

"It's not a fear," he said. "It's more of a dread. It's just . . . not something I particularly enjoy doing."

She got serious. "Aren't you going to have to do a lot of it if you go to work for Tom Paoletti?"

"When," he reminded her. He wasn't ready to leave SEAL Team Sixteen, not for a few years at least. But when he did retire—and being a SEAL was a very young man's game, so that wasn't too far in the future, old man that he was at thirty-two—he had an open invitation to join Tommy's Troubleshooters. Just a few days ago, they'd talked a bit about Cosmo opening a Los Angeles office. "It's no different from what I have to do as a chief in the Navy."

"I can help you, you know," Jane told him.

"No," Cosmo said. "Thank you. Very much. I know what I'm supposed to do. List the facts, give my version of what happened. I just . . . I don't know, always have trouble getting started."

"I was thinking more along the lines of helping by

providing incentive to finish quickly, so you can come home to me." She kissed him again.

Yeah, he could definitely see that there would be some serious motivation to get his reports handed in quickly in his future.

They'd decided to keep his apartment in San Diego, and Jane, whose schedule was more flexible, would bounce between there and Hollywood. And, she had pointed out, during those months when she was making a movie, they could always meet halfway, at Cosmo's mother's place in Laguna Beach.

That was not his ideal location for a romantic rendezvous, but he loved the fact that his fiancée honestly liked his mother.

Fiancée for only a few more hours. By this time tomorrow, she was going to be his wife.

She smiled up at him. "So. Forty minutes—well, thirty-something now. We could either look for imaginary bullets, or . . . I don't suppose you want to see my new underwear?"

Jane laughed as Cosmo threw her over his shoulder and carried her inside.

PARTNERS—AND LOVERS—
SAM STARRETT AND ALYSSA LOCKE
ARE BACK IN ACTION IN
AN EXCLUSIVE SHORT STORY!

S am Starrett's daughter had finally surrendered and
fallen asleep when the telephone rang.

He closed her bedroom door as silently as possible and raced down the hall toward the living room,
where he'd last seen the cordless phone.

Yesterday, three-and-a-half-year-old Haley had
missed her nap and their dinner had been loud and far
more tearful than dinosaur-shaped mac and cheese
warranted. Apparently, without an afternoon rest, having to choose between green beans or peas as a side
dish was a tragic dilemma of astronomical propor-
tions.

Sam, always good at creative solutions, thought
he'd solved the problem by heating up both vegetables.

At which point Haley wept inconsolably because
the spoon she wanted to use was in the dishwasher.

It was then that Sam understood. As a former Navy
SEAL and one of the top counterterrorism experts currently working in the private sector, he recognized that
he was caught in a dread no-win scenario. He realized
that even if he hand-washed the spoon, there would be

something wrong with the fork, or the color of the napkin, or maybe even the brand of parmesan cheese he and his wife, Alyssa, kept in their fridge.

It was obvious that the real problem wasn't with the peas or the spoon or the cheese. Haley missed her mother—Sam's ex-wife, Mary Lou—and that, plus lack of a nap, had locked them into orbit around the Planet of Inconsolable Unhappiness.

Sam could totally relate. He, himself, was struggling hard to keep from joining his daughter there because Mary Lou wasn't the only one out of town. Just over a week ago, Alyssa had gone OUTCONUS.

A diplomat on a peace-keeping mission to Kazbekistan—a third-world terrorist hotbed nicknamed "the Pit"—had contacted Troubleshooters Incorporated, the private security company where Sam and Alyssa both worked. Former Senator Eugene Ryan was adamant about not showing up in the battle-weary country surrounded by heavily armed, dangerous-looking "bruisers" as guards. At the same time, he wisely didn't want to go in without adequate protection.

And so he'd requested Alyssa join his security team.

In a country that wasn't exactly known for its equal rights, no one would expect a woman to be an expert sharpshooter and total kick-ass bodyguard despite her lack of height and bulk.

Sam had desperately wanted to go along—but his goal was not to keep Ryan safe. No, he wanted to watch his wife's six. But he was the exact physical type that the former senator didn't want along for the ride.

Not to mention the fact that he'd promised his ex-wife that he'd watch Haley this week. . . .

And so he'd driven Lys to the airport and kissed her good-bye, working overtime to keep her from noticing his tightly gritted teeth.

It had to happen sooner or later, but as he'd watched her walk into the terminal, he had to admit that he'd been hoping for much, much later. But here it was. For the first time since they were married, Alyssa was off on a dangerous assignment without him. And it would be another week, at least, before she came safely home.

So last night, as the green beans and peas were both heating in the microwave, Sam had sat down with Haley on the floor of the kitchen and told her it was obvious there was nothing to do but go on and have a good ol' cry.

"Why are you crying?" she'd asked.

"Wah," he'd said. "The Dallas Cowboys lost the football game last week."

His pretend sobs had made her giggle, at least for a little while.

Still, the entire rest of the evening had been filled with the potential for an all-out meltdown.

The first few days had been fun. An entire week at Daddy's was a novelty for Haley, who'd never spent more than a weekend away from her mother. Sam knew it had been exciting for her, too, to look at the pictures from the brochure and imagine Momma and her new husband having a romantic vacation aboard a cruise ship.

As for Sam, he'd appreciated the distraction—what was Alyssa doing right now? Was she in danger? Was he going to have to wait another five days before she had a chance to call him again?—as he took his tiny blond daughter to the zoo and over to Old Town San Diego.

But today, over their Cap'n Crunch and orange juice, Sam and Haley had started counting the days on the calendar—four—until Mary Lou came back home.

Four days was definitely doable, provided they didn't miss any more of those very important naps.

If he could convince her to fall asleep. He'd just sat with her for over an hour, holding her hand.

The phone shrilled again as Sam searched for it among the pile of toy cars and dolls on the living-room rug. He loved his little daughter dearly, but please, sweet Jesus, don't let her wake up yet.

He managed to find and grab the cordless phone before it completed that second ring. "Sam Starrett." Shoot, he must be tired. This was his home phone, and here the correct greeting was "Hello."

The woman on the other end didn't seem to mind. "Please hold for Mr. Cassidy," she said.

Well, la di dah. Lookie who got himself a secretary.

Sam had left a message for Jules Cassidy just yesterday, asking for an update in the FBI's search for a serial killer known as "the Dentist." He and Lys had handled a missing person case last year which hadn't ended happily. They'd found the young woman they were searching for—or rather, they'd found what was left of her after the Dentist worked her over.

They'd also discovered that the Dentist had been posing as a ski instructor in New Hampshire, using the alias "Steve Hathaway."

Alyssa—normally tough as nails—had been unusually upset when they'd found the body, even though the murder had occurred six months earlier. She'd taken it personally—so Sam had started getting regular updates on the case from Jules, her friend and former partner from her FBI days.

It was obvious to Sam that, after seeing that dead girl, Lys wanted to kick the Dentist's ass straight to hell where he belonged. She was afraid—and rightly so—that it was just a matter of time before the killer targeted his next victim.

After months of no progress, a man had recently surfaced in a resort town in Colorado who fit Hathaway's description. Sam was hoping the FBI agents working the case would locate the Dentist's grisly souvenirs from his victims and have enough evidence to take him into custody before Alyssa returned.

Giving her that news would be a wonderful welcome-home present—a thought that made him smile. Forget about flowers and chocolate. His wife wanted a psycho-killer behind bars.

She was different from most other women, no doubt about that. Which was not to say she didn't love chocolate . . .

Ah yes, Sam missed her very much.

There was a click, and Jules finally came on the line. "Sam."

"Hey," Sam greeted him, genuinely glad to hear Jules' voice. Five years ago, if someone had told him that he'd be happily married to his old nemesis Alyssa Locke, and best friends with **her** best friend—an openly gay man—Sam would've laughed his ass off. But obviously a lot could happen in five years. "Thanks for calling me back, **Mister** Cassidy."

There was the briefest pause, then Jules said, "I guess you're not watching TV."

"What? No. I've got Haley for the week and anything besides **Sesame Street** is too intense for her," Sam said, as he now began searching for the remote control beneath the Spider-Man and Powerpuff Girls coloring books that covered his coffee table. Haley got nightmares. It was Big Bird or a Disney DVD or the TV stayed off. Although it was possible that too much Big Bird was now giving Sam nightmares.

When he actually slept, that is.

"Sam, hang on a sec." Jules put his hand over the receiver as he spoke to someone else on his end. Usually irreverent and upbeat, he sounded serious. Hell, he was calling Sam **Sam** instead of SpongeBob or Pollyanna or one of those other humiliating nicknames that he usually used.

"What happened?" Sam asked as Jules came back on the phone. He answered his own question. "Another dead woman without teeth in Colorado."

"This isn't about the Dentist," Jules told him, as

Sam found the remote and aimed it at the TV. "Listen, do yourself a favor and don't turn on the news."

Too late. Sam had already flipped to CNN where . . .

"Oh, shit," he breathed, sitting down heavily on the sofa.

Peacekeeper Attacked was the headline that hung over the anchor's right shoulder, along with a picture of Eugene Ryan. ". . . in northern Kazbekistan, where the former senator's helicopter was believed to have been shot down."

Oh, God, no . . .

"We just received confirmation," Jules told him, "that one of Eugene Ryan's helicopters was hit by a shoulder-fired missile, just north of Ikrimah, which is a city in the northern province of—"

"I know where Ikrimah is," Sam interrupted him. "**One** of . . . ?" How many helos were transporting Ryan's delegation? Jesus, he couldn't breathe.

On the TV, the news anchor was now delivering a fluff piece on a pie-eating contest, a big smile on his face.

"One of two," Jules delivered the grim news as Sam hit the mute. Which meant there was a fifty-fifty chance Lys was on the helicopter that went down.

In flames.

"Before we lost radio contact," Jules continued, "the second chopper reported that there were definitely casualties, but we don't know how many and we don't know who."

"Before," Sam repeated. "You lost . . . **radio contact**?"

"I am **so** sorry," Jules started, but Sam cut him off.

"Fuck sorry!" Sam winced, looking toward the room where Haley was sleeping. He lowered his voice, but it came out no less intense. "I don't want sorry. I want the information that you've—"

"We don't **have** any information." Jules raised his voice to talk over him. "All we have is speculation. Rumors. You know as well as I do what good that—"

"What are the rumors?" Sam asked.

"Sam," Jules said. "You **know** rumors are just—"

"Did the second helo go down, too?" Sam had to know.

"No," Jules said, but then added, "Not exactly. What we think happened, and, sweetie, breathe. This is mostly guesswork. Even though we have a few people who claim to be eyewitnesses, we have only their word that they were actually there. So yeah, they reported that after the first chopper crashed, the second swung back around to assist the survivors. According to these unreliable sources, it apparently landed, going out of view, behind several buildings. Then, allegedly, there was a second big explosion."

"And?" Sam asked tightly.

"And nothing," Jules said. "It's all speculation. You know as well as I do that this could be nothing more than one of the local warlords planting disinformation—"

"There was an **and** in your voice," Sam insisted. "God damn it, Jules, tell me all of it."

Jules exhaled hard. "The attack happened shortly before sunset. There've been unconfirmed reports of a fierce firefight in that area pretty much all night."

Sam was going to be sick. "So, best-case scenario is that my wife is on the ground in a hostile part of Kaz-fucking-bekistan, engaged in a gun battle with people who don't just want to kill her for being American, but who want to kill her slowly, on camera, broadcast over the Internet."

Worst case was that Alyssa was already dead—that she had been dead for hours.

"Who's going in after them?" Sam demanded.

"I don't know," Jules said. "Look, I'm going to make some phone calls, see what I can find out, okay? It may take me a while."

"Jules," Sam started, but he didn't have to say it. Jules said it for him.

"I'll call you back as soon as I hear anything. Good news **or** bad."

"Thanks." As Sam hung up the phone, the news anchor made a joke about a pop star who was getting married. It was absolutely surreal.

How could anyone laugh when Alyssa might be dead?

He turned off the TV, but then turned it back on, flipping to the other news stations and then back, hoping for something, anything that would let him see just what Alyssa was up against.

If there were any way to survive this, Lys would find it. Of that Sam had absolutely no doubt. She was strong, she was skilled, and she had the heart of a warrior.

But if her team was badly outnumbered by their attackers, if it was a handful against several hundred, they would soon be overpowered. And all of the skill, strength, and heart in the world wouldn't keep her alive.

Sam splashed water on his face, then dried it with his towel. It was one of the blue ones that he and Alyssa had picked out when they'd moved into this little house together, a few weeks before their wedding.

"Blue is all about serenity and tranquillity," she'd told him as they stood in the department store, when he'd suggested they get brown because it would hide the dirt and stains.

But she was serious, which had surprised him. For someone so down-to-earth and practical, as they'd decorated their house she'd paid a lot of attention to the mood created by color, as well as something called Feng Shui. Which was all about furniture placement and good vibes and all kinds of touchy-feely New Age voodoo.

Of course, maybe there was something to that Feng Shui crap, because Sam had never been happier and more at peace in his entire life than he had this past year, living here.

Then again, he'd be beyond ecstatic living in a cardboard box, as long as Alyssa was with him.

Please, God, keep her safe.

Sam took a deep breath, then opened the bathroom door.

The phone rang again, and Joan DaCosta, the wife of SEAL Team Sixteen's Lieutenant Mike Muldoon, picked it up out in the living room.

As the news of the downed choppers spread, friends and relatives were calling him to find out details and offer their support. But it had quickly gotten overwhelming. "I'm sure Alyssa's all right. I'm sure she's fine . . . ," they reassured him. But they wanted him to say it back to them, too.

And the truth was, as optimistic as he usually was, in this case, he wasn't sure about anything. And no one **really** wanted to hear how he was scared shitless, and that this sitting still and waiting for news was driving him freaking nuts.

No one, that is, except for Joan and Savannah and Meg, the long-suffering wives of his three best friends from his days as a Navy SEAL.

Meg Nilsson—Johnny's wife—had been the first to arrive. She'd just opened his front door and walked inside his house, God bless her, announcing, "Hey, it's only me. I didn't ring the bell—I didn't want you to think I was someone bringing you bad news."

She'd brought her two daughters—Amy, a teenager from her first marriage, and four-year-old Robin, who had Johnny's eyes.

Amy possessed a maturity and sensitivity far beyond her years. She'd ushered both Robin and Haley outside, where she kept them occupied and entertained. Even now, hours later, Sam could hear their laughter from the backyard.

Shortly after Meg arrived, Chief Ken "WildCard" Karmody's wife, Savannah, pulled into the driveway. Mikey's Joan was right behind her.

They'd each given him a hug and told him they weren't going to let him go through this alone.

"Joan'll let me know if it's Jules on the phone, right?" Sam asked now, as he went back into the kitchen, where Meg and Savannah were sitting together at the table. At first glance they seemed to be unlikely friends.

Savannah was a high-powered attorney who had just made partner and opened a law office in San Diego, after years of a bicoastal marriage. She came from money and worked not because she had to, but because she wanted to. Sam suspected though, if and when the time came to start a family with Kenny, she would throw herself into it with the same wholehearted devotion.

Kind of the way Meg did. A brunette to Savannah's elf-princess blonde, Meg Nilsson worked part-time from a home office. Her standard uniform was very different from Van's lawyer clothes—T-shirts and shorts, sneakers on her feet—better for chasing after Robin.

Sam knew for a fact that it wasn't easy for Meg and John to make ends meet on John's salary.

And yet Savannah and Meg were friends. They both loved their husbands—who willingly traveled to war zones and other places that were hazardous to one's health.

They both knew that their husbands might be injured or even killed in the line of duty at any given moment.

They knew what it felt like to carry around that anxiety, to live for those overseas phone calls that usually came in the middle of the night. "I'm sorry it's so late, but I finally have cell service—it's weak, but it's there—and I'm not sure when I'll get it again . . ."

Four days ago, before the helo crash, he got a call like that from Alyssa. And for five minutes while he spoke to her, he could breathe again. She had been safe, and he knew it.

For those five minutes.

It ended far too quickly, and as soon as he hung up the phone the anxiety came screaming back.

Alyssa had been scheduled to be away for just a short time. SEALs, however, often went out for months. Sam absolutely couldn't imagine living like this for more than a few weeks.

"Jules said it would be a while before he called again," Meg gently reminded him.

"Have you tried cleaning the refrigerator?" Savannah suggested. "I've found it helps a little if you just keep moving."

Sam sat down, wearily rubbing his forehead. Jesus, his head ached. "I did the fridge the night Alyssa's flight left," he said on an exhale. "Then, in the morning, I took an axe, went out in the yard and removed this old stump we'd been talking about getting rid of." He'd chopped the crap out of it in about four hours.

"I usually stick to cleaning out closets." Savannah was impressed. "I've never tried anything that involves an axe."

"I have," Meg said dryly. "Don't bother. It doesn't help."

Nothing helped.

"If you want," Savannah suggested, "we could help you organize your closets. It'll keep you busy. And you'll also win big bonus points when Alyssa comes back."

When Alyssa comes back. They were sitting there, all three of them, pretending that **if Alyssa came back** wasn't what she really meant.

God, he hated this. But the alternative was sitting in his kitchen by himself. Or trying to fool Haley into thinking everything was all right, and sneaking into the bedroom every ten minutes to turn on CNN, to see if there was any new information that made it to the cable news station first.

So he told Savannah, "I did the closets on the second night. It took a while, but I wasn't going to sleep, so . . ."

"It's amazing, isn't it?" Meg asked, clearly working to keep the conversation going. "Just how much junk two people can accumulate in a short amount of time?"

"Yeah," he agreed. "I found this old hat—a baseball cap—that I thought I lost years ago and—" He broke off. "I can't do this. I'm sorry, I can't stand it. I'm just sitting here, so freaking helpless—I can't do a thing to help her. Even if I got on a plane . . ." It would take him at least forty-eight hours to get to Ikrimah. He closed his eyes. "Right now, she could be dying. Right now. Right **now.** And I can't help her."

Meg took his hand. "I know," she said quietly. "It's hard, isn't it?"

Sam looked at her, and he knew that **she** knew exactly what he was feeling. "How many times have you done this?" he asked.

"Thought John might not be coming home?" she clarified. She didn't wait for him to respond. "There've been, oh, I guess three or four times somewhat similar to this situation. But, you know, every time he's out there and there's some news report about a helicopter crash or a suicide bomber or . . ." She laughed as she shook her head. "Believe me, there's a lot of prayer involved when you're married to a SEAL."

"And a lot of really clean refrigerators," Savannah added.

"Pristine closets."

"Well-gardened yards . . ."

"You see, John knows where he is when he's on an op," Meg told Sam. "He knows when he's safe and when he's at risk. But all I know is he's somewhere dangerous and . . ." She shrugged. "It sucks."

No kidding. "I had no idea," Sam admitted. "Before this, I just . . ." He shook his head. When he'd gone wheels-up with the team he'd understood that it was no picnic for the wives, girlfriends, and significant others they left behind. But he'd had no clue just how awful it could be.

Joan appeared in the doorway, cordless phone in

her hands. "That was Mike," she told them. "The Team's training exercise'll be over in an hour. He and John and Ken'll bring dinner when they come."

The phone rang again, and Joan retreated toward the living room. "Starrett and Locke residence," Sam heard her say. But then she gasped. "Oh, my God!"

Sam was up and out of his chair, and he nearly collided with her as she came racing back into the kitchen, thrusting the phone at him.

"Jules," he said as he clasped it to his ear. Please God, let this be good news. "What's the word?"

"It's not Jules," Joan said, but he waved for her to be quiet, because all he could hear was static, and then . . .

"Sam, it's me—I'm all right," Alyssa said—beautiful, wonderful, vibrant, and so-very-alive Alyssa—her voice suddenly clear as day.

"It's Lys," Joan announced, which was good because try as he might, Sam couldn't get the words out.

"Ah, Jesus, thank you, God," was all he could manage, and even that was little more than a whisper.

Meg and Savannah both leapt to their feet. Meg pulled one of the kitchen chairs behind him, and Savannah tugged him back into it, Joan pushing his head down between his knees—as if they thought he might actually faint.

"Hey!" But, shit, he **was** dizzy and on the verge of falling out of the chair, so maybe they were onto something there. But before he could thank them, they all left, hurrying out into the backyard to give him privacy.

"The SAS came in and . . . Gordon MacKenzie, remember him?" Alyssa asked him. "His team pulled us out. He remembers you—he wants to know what you think of his SAS boys now."

Gordon MacKenzie . . . ?

"Gordie told me his SAS team did some training exercises with SEAL Team Sixteen, back a few years," Alyssa continued as Sam desperately tried to regain his equilibrium. "He said they learned a lot from you— that you used to rate them on a scale from one to ten. But you never gave them anything higher than an eight."

Yeah, he remembered that. MacKenzie had gotten in his face and accused him of being a hard-nosed asshole. Actually **arsehole** was what he'd said in his quaint Scottish accent. Sam had countered by standing his ground and saying he'd give them a ten when they fucking deserved a ten. And no sooner. Maybe they'd earn it next year, he'd told MacKenzie when the exercise had ended.

"Sam, are you still there? Can you hear me?" Alyssa was saying through the phone.

"Yeah," he said. "Yes. Lys, are you really all right?" Frickin' Gordie MacKenzie's team had helped save Alyssa's life. Next time he saw the dour bastard, he'd kiss him on the mouth. "Where are you?"

"The helo just landed on an aircraft carrier," she said. "We're safe." She sounded exhausted, and she exhaled hard. "Those of us who made it out alive."

"Are you hurt?" he asked, heart in his throat.

"Just a little tired," she told him—she always had

been the queen of understatement. "Well, yeah, okay, I could use a few stitches—just a few, don't get upset, I'm fine. We're pretty dehydrated, though. They've got us all on IV drips."

"I am so freaking glad to hear your voice," he told her, and she laughed. "You have no idea . . ."

"Yeah," she said. "Actually, I do. Although, don't be jealous. I have to admit, as glad as I am to talk to you, I was even more glad to hear Gordie MacKenzie's voice this morning."

No kidding. "Tell Gordie that I love him," Sam said.

Alyssa laughed again. "Those aren't the three little words he's longing to hear from you, Sam. Seriously, what they did was . . . It was remarkably courageous. We were trapped and . . . I honestly didn't think any-one was coming for us—that anyone would be able to . . . I thought . . . It was bad," she said quietly.

Sam had to put his head back down between his knees. Alyssa, who never gave up, who wouldn't dream of quitting, had honestly thought she wasn't going to survive.

"He doesn't need me to give him a ten," Sam told her. "He knows."

"Still . . ." There was a storm of static. ". . . ignals fading—I have to go. Sam—"

"I love you," Sam told her. **Thank God, thank God, thank God . . .**

"I know." Alyssa's voice was fading in and out, but he could still make out her words. "There was a point where it would have been easier to, you know, just . . . have it over and done, but . . ."

"Thank you," he said, hoping she could still hear him. "For not giving up."

"How could I?" She sounded as if she were a million miles away. "You were with me, you know. Every minute. I could feel you by my side." Sam could just barely hear her laughter over the static. "Ready to give me shit if I so much as faltered. Gordie told me you have a permanent spot on his shoulder, too—whispering into his ear. And here you thought you were taking it easy, sitting around the kitchen with your feet up."

Taking it easy. She had no idea.

"I love you," he heard her say right before his phone beeped.

He looked at it and, yeah, the signal was gone.

Sitting around the kitchen . . . He'd been on dozens of dangerous missions. He'd risked his life more times than he could count.

None of it had been as hard as the past few hours.

Sam dialed Jules Cassidy's phone number, left a brief message. "Alyssa called. She's all right."

Through the kitchen window he could see Meg and Joan and Savannah out in the backyard with Haley and the other girls.

Sam punched Johnny Nilsson's cell number into his phone. The SEAL lieutenant was still out on a training exercise, so he left a voice mail. "Alyssa's safe—I just got off the phone with her. But that's not the only reason I'm calling. I think it would be smart if you brought your wife an armload of flowers when you came home," he told his friend. "Tell Mike and Kenny, too. Not just tonight, but every night for the rest of your lives."

It was already a half hour past Haley's bedtime when Sam sat on the edge of her bed. He'd promised she could watch a little bit of the football game with him, only it had started later than he'd thought.

"You want Duck or Hippo in there with you tonight?" His daughter frowned, and he quickly added, "Or both, on account of it being a special occasion."

"Because Alyssa's okay?" Haley asked.

"Yeah," he said, smiling into her anxious blue eyes. "And because she'll be home the same day as your mama."

Haley nodded, taking that in. "Amy said we had to stay outside in case you wanted to cry and say bad words," she told him. "Did you?"

"I think I said a few," Sam admitted. "And, yeah, I might've cried a little."

Haley nodded, so seriously. "If you want, I could put my fingers in my ears, like when the fire truck goes by."

Sam struggled to understand. "You mean . . . so you won't have to hear me cry? Haley, I'm not going to—"

"In case you say more bad words," she explained.

"I won't," he told her, struggling now not to laugh.

"How about giving me a hug and kiss good night, Cookie Monster?"

"Sometimes there's nothing to do but have a good ol' cry," she said, repeating his words from the night before. "If you want, I could cry, too."

"No." Sam smoothed back her hair and kissed her on the cheek. "Thank you, but no." He tucked both Duck and Hippo in with her.

"If you want," Haley suggested, clinging to his fingers, "I could hold your hand. Keep you company until you fall asleep. I'm not very tired."

But her eyes were all but rolling back in her head. Amy had done quite a job, running Haley back and forth across the yard playing Tag and Red Light Green Light and Follow the Leader and other games Sam didn't even know the names of.

He'd keep that in mind tomorrow. Maybe they'd take a ride over to Coronado, buy a kite, and run up and down the beach a few thousand times.

"I love you, Haley," he whispered, but she was already asleep.

Sam left her door open a crack and went into the living room, where he turned on the TV and watched the football game right to the bitter end.

He then watched the news, where the anchors solemnly reported that five members of Eugene Ryan's delegation to Kazbekistan had died when their helo was shot down.

Five families had gotten the kind of phone call he'd been dreading. They had been given the message Meg and Savannah and all of the other wives of the SEALs in Team Sixteen prayed they'd never receive.

Their husband, wife, son, or daughter was never coming home.

It was entirely possible that any tears that Sam may have shed were the result of the Cowboys losing the game.

But probably not.

ABOUT THE AUTHOR

Since her explosion onto the publishing scene more than ten years ago, SUZANNE BROCKMANN has written more than forty books, and is now widely recognized as one of the leading voices in romantic suspense. Her work has earned her repeated appearances on the **USA Today** and **New York Times** bestseller lists, as well as numerous awards, including Romance Writers of America's #1 Favorite Book of the Year—three years running in 2000, 2001, and 2002; two RITA awards; and many **Romantic Times** Reviewer's Choice Awards. Suzanne lives west of Boston with her husband and two children. Visit her website at www.suzannebrockmann.com.

LIKE WHAT YOU'VE SEEN?

If you enjoyed this large print edition of **Hot Target**, look for **Flashpoint** which is also available in Random House Large Print from Suzanne Brockmann.

Flashpoint (hardcover)
0-375-43304-X ($23.95/$35.95C)

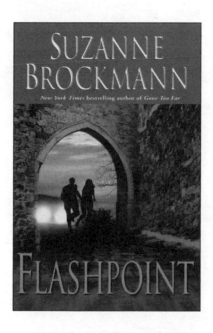

Large print books are available
wherever books are sold and at many local libraries.

All prices are subject to change. Check with your local retailer for current pricing and availability. For more information on these and other large print titles, visit www.randomlargeprint.com.